Praise for *A Wolff in the Family*

"*A Wolff in The Family* is an absolute page-turner! Immediately immersive, readers will be drawn into the hardships and small joys of the Wolff family as they attempt to make a living in rural Utah. Falk-Allen paints a realistic picture of the West during the early part of the twentieth century with her vivid prose and realistic characters. An intriguing story about social norms, gender roles, and, ultimately, love. This is a fast, absorbing story that will keep you up long into the night. Couldn't put it down!"

—Michelle Cox, author of *The Fallen Woman's Daughter*

"An empathetic lesson in resilience and forgiveness, *A Wolff in the Family* takes an unflinching look at complex familial ties, gender roles, and the hardships of women in the early 20th century through one family's story across the United States. With the kind of drama that builds, this captivating book is a multifaceted tale with flawed and human characters and the complicated decisions that make a life."

—Joanne Howard, author of *Sleeping in the Sun*

"*A Wolff in the Family*, historical fiction with a touch of memoir, belongs among the great multi-generational family sagas, such as *The Forsyte Saga*, *East of Eden*, and *The Thorn Birds*. Falk-Allen weaves a complex story of light and dark, of human failings compounded by the oppressive gender roles in traditional families. The characters come alive on the page, drawing you into a vivid world of yesterday."

—Jude Berman, author of *The Die* and *The Vow*

"Heartbreaking at its core, *A Wolff in the Family* takes the bones of a long-hidden family secret and fleshes it out to include a large cast of characters who come alive on the page. Readers will despair with Naomi and her children as they navigate separate, but equal, hardships apart, with hope as their only beacon. Readers cannot help ask the questions: What skeletons are buried in my family lore? Do I dare uncover them? Kudos to Falk-Allen for taking this project on, making it both compelling and relatable, and shedding light into dark corners of family history. A bold and important read."

—Ashley E. Sweeney, author of *Eliza Waite*

"Writing a novel based on a family story requires an author to choreograph what is known and what must be surmised into a compelling narrative. Francine Falk-Allen has skillfully accomplished this saga-to-novel rebirth in A Wolff in the Family. The hard-scrabble life, children and marriage of Naomi Wolff vividly recall a world of societal rules, privation, race and class restrictions, and the human spirit that can prevail over all of them. Another great read from this author!"

—Barbara Stark-Nemon, author of *Even in Darkness* and *Hard Cider*

"A moving and evocative family saga, consummately constructed, and beautifully narrated. Francine Falk-Allen delivers a novel that is emotionally engaging and powerful—but at the same time relentless in its probing of gender inequality, and how its consequences have manifested across generations in America."

—Robert Steven Goldstein, author of the novels *Will's Surreal Period*, *Enemy Queen*, *Cat's Whisker*, and *The Swami Deheftner*

"Women have always wanted agency over their own lives, and in this fascinating fictionalized account of her family history, Falk-Allen reminds us that such agency has not always come easily. With its universal themes of love, sacrifice, and freedom, *A Wolff in the Family* shows us how far we've come, even as we recognize and find resonance with the characters' deepest longings."

—Ginny Kubitz Moyer, author of *The Seeing Garden*

"*A Wolff in the Family* lives up to its name, following the Wolff family through the early years of the 20th century. But it's more than that—it's a saga of life in the West, complete with vivid descriptions of injustices toward women and children, interrupted educations, love, and loss, all told in the vernacular of the era. This well-crafted novel will break your heart, bring you joy, and make you grateful to be living in the 21st century."

—**Susen Edwards, author of *What a Trip* and *Lookin' for Love***

"*A Wolff in the Family* absolutely made me feel curiosity, apprehension, relief, outrage, hope, compassion, and more. The book's cinematic storytelling, with vivid details about the characters, their habits, and their personalities, as well as the energetic pacing of events captivated me from the start. I could not put it down! The immersive descriptions of domestic life put me in the shoes of the Wolff women and girls, who, along with all the other family members, became real to me because of Falk-Allen's excellent character development."

—**Ilze Duarte, PhD, writer and literary translator, recipient of the 2024 Sundial House Literary Translation Award**

"I was intrigued by the fascinating, well-drawn characters and plot twists in *A Wolff in the Family*. The author brings us into a time and a world she has researched well and portrays with historical accuracy. No spoilers here, but a surprise near the book's conclusion grabbed me. I recommend this novel for an enjoyable read that will likely keep you wondering what will happen next."

—**Marcia Naomi Berger, author of *The Bipolar Therapist: A Journey from Madness to Love and Meaning***

A Wolff in the Family

A Wolff in the Family

A Novel

Francine Falk-Allen

Published 2024

Printed in the United States of America

Print ISBN: 978-1-64742-802-0

E-ISBN: 978-1-64742-803-7

Library of Congress Control Number: 2024910035

For information, address:

She Writes Press

1569 Solano Ave #546

Berkeley, CA 94707

Illustrations by Hannah Orth

Interior Design by Kiran Spees

She Writes Press is a division of SparkPoint Studio, LLC.

This work of historical fiction has been researched for speech that was commonly used and accepted in its era. To remain faithful to early 1900's American usage, the term "Negro" is used instead of "Black," and "Indian" is used to refer to people indigenous to North America.

For my maternal grandmother,
the real "Naomi," may you rest in peace.
I hope I told your story faithfully.

Characters

The Wolff Family

Frank J. Wolff b.1887
Naomi Sims Wolff b. 1890
  Their children:
  Frances b. 1908
  Anita b. 1910
  Carl b. 1912
  Hermann b. 1913, twin
  Henry b. 1913, twin
  Frank Jr. b. 1916
  Marie b. 1917
  George b. 1918, twin
  Grant b. 1918, twin
  Willie b. 1920
  Dorothy b. 1922
  Clarence b. 1923

Frank's Parents:
Frank J. Wolff 1853-1911
  (b. Switzerland)
Caroline Laschevski Wolff
  b. 1859 (Prussia)
Their children (8 living, 1918):
  Frank b. 1887
  Louise b. 1896
  Otto b. 1903

Mary Ellen, Frances's friend in Kansas
Deborah Abbott, The Wolffs's neighbor
Lucille Klumack and Lucille's brother, Ronald Klumack, Frances's
  friends in Ogden
Mrs. Birch, Frances's boardinghouse employer

Mrs. Hancock, Anita's boardinghouse employer

Caleb, Anita's beau

Frank Sims (no relation to the Sims family below) b. 1906, Frances's beau and husband

    Their children: LaVon and Gene, b. 1929 and 1931

Robert "Bob" Allen b. 1914, Frances's second husband

    Their daughter: Francine b. 1947

The Sims Family

Naomi's parents:

Joseph Sims b. 1846

Nancy Beeman Chalmers Sims b. 1846

    Their children (5 living, 1918):

    Julia b. 1882

    Jessie b. 1883

    Naomi b. 1890

Lucy, Julia's sister-in-law

Nancy had 3 children by William Chalmers (1832-1879):

    Alice b. 1872

    Fred b. 1877

Nancy's parents had 12 children; 10 living, 1918

The Woods Family

Edward Woods 1885-1918

Minnie Dawson Woods b. 1888

    Their children:

    Lawrence b. 1911

    Beatrice b. 1913

    Martin b. 1915

    Nina b. 1917

    Ellen b. 1919

Minnie's mother:

Irene Dawson b. 1861

The Foreland Family

Isabelle Chalmers Foreland b. 1853 (cousin of William Chalmers,
    Nancy Beeman Sims's first husband)

    Isabelle and James Foreland's children (4 living in 1918):

    Charles "Charley" b. 1880

        Charles' daughter: Connie b. 1931

    Bill b. 1882

The Palmen Family

Marie Emilie Uhlrich Palmen, b. 1895 (Germany), married to
    Walter Palmen b. 1902

    Richard, b. 1938, Marie's son

Marie's associates:

Herr and Frau Schafer, on the ship *Deutschland*

Mrs. Muller, rooming house matron in NYC

Scipione Guidi Family, violinist employer in NYC

Sarah Gerhardt, Mormon friend in Ogden

Mrs. Schneider, Lutheran friend in Ogden

Rhoda, Walter's friend

The Lutheran Children's Home Personnel

Susanna and Mr. Weinrich, managers and guardians,
   b. 1876 and 1874
   Their daughter: Ruth b. 1909
Margaret b. 1910, their assistant
Edna and Thomas Miller, potential adoptive parents

Note:

When characters do not appear in the story, they are not named as children above. For example, Joseph and Nancy Sims had five children, but only three have roles in the story, so the rest are not named in this list.

Chapter 1

Ogden, Utah
January 1930

Frank Wolff stepped off the train into the cold night fog and onto the even colder concrete platform at Ogden station. He shivered involuntarily; steeling himself against the damp air, he stifled a second shudder. One more trip on the Union Pacific line, home again. But this time was unlike any before, and he didn't intend to make the trip to Winfield, Kansas, again unless the railroad sent him through that area.

He ran his hand over his sandy-colored, pomaded hair. Minnie hated it when his hair was out of place, and he liked that about her. A tidy woman, as it should be. They were so well matched. If only she'd been available more than twenty years earlier. He was amused that she wanted him to refer to her as "Mrs. Woods" around others. They never used first names in public. Well, only in the boardinghouse kitchen, in front of her kids. And his children, when they'd been there. Oh, it would be good to get back to her next month.

He was tired. Beyond tired—exhausted. He had not expected this sadness to fatigue him. He had not expected, even, to feel sad. Every step felt heavy. Well, it was done. *What I've done, I've done for the benefit of all concerned*, he told himself. And the children would be better off, in the long run. He'd been surprised by the elegance of the old house acquired by the Lutheran Children's Home; it was much swankier than their modest home in Ogden had been. The children would likely go to good homes . . . at least they'd probably be Lutheran. And maybe to families who were well-off—sometimes when people adopted it was because they had no children and had more money to spend on the ones they took in as a result. And . . . he knew that sometimes people adopted children because they needed more farm labor. Well, it wouldn't hurt the children to do some hard work, if that came to pass. Mein Gott, *I did farmwork myself as a teenager.* It was tough, and would be tougher for younger kids. He put those thoughts out of his mind for now. Best not to dwell on what he had no control over.

He paused inside the tall, airy lobby. This was one of the loveliest terminals on his route. He never tired of the architecture. He sat down on one of the polished wooden benches, his worn leather overnight satchel beside him, and glanced around to see if anyone had left a newspaper. He just needed a moment to himself, a moment of stillness. He picked up an *Ogden Times* left by a traveler; *ach, gut,* today's edition. A man needs his daily paper. He found the advertisement for the sale of the house. Good, the agent had done his work. Hopefully Anita had gone by there and cleaned the place up to show it. He wished Frances were still around; she was a pro at housecleaning. Naomi would have missed her home, her domain, her better kitchen, the whole place, but he sure didn't want it. Too many memories.

Minnie Woods would never leave her house, he knew. Women got so attached to location. Besides, the Woods house was, well, quite a house. Almost new. He loved being on the railroad and all the stops in between—the freedom of being gone for weeks, months at a time—but he also liked being anchored in one place and the stature he gained through his steady home life.

Well, there's nothing for it but to go home for the moment. A beer would taste good right now and help him sleep . . . but oh well, he'd have to do without. How long could Prohibition go on?

Maybe he would call Mother in Missouri tomorrow to let her know he'd arrived, and check on Carl and Henry. Or he could just write a letter. That would cost less.

Chapter 2

Ogden, Utah

Eleven Years Earlier: Early 1918

Frances Wolff had expected, as friends and adults had told her, that the Mormons in Utah would have horns on their heads. But though she'd kept her eyes peeled ever since they first arrived, she hadn't seen a single person with horns. She realized that either she'd been duped—which didn't sit well with her, as the eldest daughter of seven children and already a responsible babysitter much of the time—or maybe the people she'd known in her first nine years as a little girl in Kansas had all bought into a tall tale. Even though her family attended a Lutheran church, as Daddy wished, she figured she'd probably meet some Mormons in school and see if they had other strange features, even if they didn't have horns.

School was always a good distraction from her tasks as a little second mother, even though it presented her with more work that had to be done. She made embarrassing judgment errors sometimes, she thought, despite the other children's expectations that she was the knowledgeable one, the one with the most education. She recalled the pump incident from the previous winter . . .

They'd gone out to the pump in the backyard in Ellis, before their move to Utah. She'd been with three of her brothers and Mary Ellen from next door.

"Frances, lick the pump handle. It's fun to lick the frost off. I dare you!" her little brother Carl had encouraged.

So she had, never one to back away from a dare. Besides, she was older and knew what was what.

Her tongue promptly stuck to the metal handle. "Ow! Ay canth ge ma tonn aahff! Helf!"

"Haaaa-ha-ha ha!" Carl cried. "Frances licked the handle! Thought you were supposed to be the smart one!"

"Help her!" Mary Ellen cried out, while the boys stood there almost paralyzed, realizing this was not really as funny as they thought it would be. "I'll run and get some warm water."

She ran into the house, where there was often a kettle on the stove, and came back out with a cup of warm water.

Pouring it on her friend's tongue, she said, "Oh, Frances, I'm so sorry. I didn't know this would happen."

Frances's tongue disengaged from the cold metal. "You boys are in for it!" she warned. "Wait'll I tell Daddy when he gets home!"

Then, more quietly to Mary Ellen, she said, "Ow. Now my tongue's sore."

"Ah, raspberries," said Carl, all of six years old and pretty smart himself. "He might not be home for days, and then you'll prob'ly forget anyway."

"Well, don't be sure he won't give you a different kind of licking," Frances shot back.

They laughed with the abandon of small boys as they ran off to play stickball in the street.

"Don't you just hate your brothers sometimes?" Mary Ellen asked.

"Oh . . . no," Frances said thoughtfully. "I don't hate them. They're good little guys. And really it *was* kind of funny. But I don't like tricks played on me. It's enough that I'm the last one in the tub on Saturday nights; first the baby, then Frank, then Henry and Hermann, then Carl, then Anita, and then me! Always last. The water is as dirty as dishwater, plus not hot anymore, especially after the boys have been in it. I asked Mother to let me go first sometimes, since usually I'm not as dirty as the littler kids, but she says the littlest ones go first, and I was the first baby. So they're just getting their turn. But someday I am not gonna live here anymore."

"Where would you go?"

"I don't know. But it won't be someplace where I have to take a bath in other people's bathwater."

"Frances?" Naomi called out from the kitchen. "Do you know where your brothers are?" She was only now getting used to the layout of the new place in Ogden. So many things to rearrange, especially in the kitchen, on top of keeping track of seven kids. She did love that they had indoor plumbing, and that the house was a little bit bigger and close to downtown. And not too far from the station, making it easy for Frank to walk to and from work when he was in town. When the family took the train, they could carry their suitcases fairly easily.

"Last time I saw Carl, he was walking home from school," Frances called back. "And the twins are in the backyard. Little Frank's with them, I think."

"Well get out there and make sure they aren't in any trouble, and then I want you and your sister to help me make dinner."

"Sis?" Naomi's voice began to have a touch of desperation as she called for Anita. "Time to help me make dinner." She shook her head, muttering, "Where are these girls when I need them?"

"If I have to go out and watch the boys, can't Sis help you?" Frances asked from the living room, where she was reading.

Naomi's tone sharpened. "Frances, come in here."

After a moment, Frances appeared at the kitchen door, looking sullen. "What?"

Naomi picked up the yardstick from its usual convenient corner and gave Frances three swift swats on her backside and the backs of her legs. "Don't talk back to me. When I tell you to do something, you do it."

Her legs still stinging, Frances pressed her lips together with resentment and took advantage of the more desirable task, away from her mother's oversight, of checking on her little brothers outside.

Finding them playing with sticks in the dirt, one of which Frank, who was three, was attempting to put in his mouth, Frances felt some relief that she'd come out when she did. She took the stick away from Frank and told Hermann and Henry to pay better attention to their little brother, even though they were only five, and "Be careful with those sticks or you'll poke somebody's eye out." She hoped she hadn't just put an idea into the twins' heads.

"And you boys, you're gonna have to clean up anyway for dinner, so try not to get too dirty or Mother will have a fit, and we'll all get in trouble."

Especially me, she thought, *for not keeping an eye on you.*

Just as Anita walked into the room, her mother announced, "Your father called the Abbotts next door. He's not coming home tonight." Naomi bit her cuticle and paused a moment in thought. "He has to stay in Lyman, Wyoming for a couple days; they have him managing the maintenance crew again. Seems like they have him staying in Wyoming overnight more and more." She pursed her lips. "Well, that's a few hours away and he can't just hijack the train; he'll be home tomorrow or the next day. You kids wash up and we'll have dinner without him. Frances, put Marie in the high chair as soon as your hands are washed and get the potatoes out of the oven."

The family gathered at the table.

"Okay now, who wants to say grace?" Naomi asked. "Nobody? Frances, you say it so we can get started."

Frances cleared her throat and began: "God is great, God is good, and we thank him for our food. Amen."

"Before we start," said Naomi, "I just want you kids to remember that we are luckier than some folks. We got food on the table every night. Your daddy works hard to make sure of that. And I'm not penny-wise and pound-foolish. I can stretch fifty cents to make sure we eat something, even if it's nothing fancy. But tonight we got chicken, so let's all remember God takes care of people who live right. Okay, dig in."

Anita saw the boys eyeing their father's share of Sunday chicken, even though they knew Mother would save some for Frank Sr., just in case he came home on Monday. Daddy got a big breast piece, or a whole chicken leg. Then Mother chose her piece, and then Carl, the oldest boy, got the next best, then Frances, and on down. Little Frank got a wing or a back.

Anita, now eight and old enough to contemplate things, thought, *What will happen when Mother has her next baby? Will they ever buy more than one chicken? Mother looks like she's going to pop.*

"Mother . . . ?" she began tentatively.

"Yes, what?"

"Well . . . I just wanted to ask . . . when is the baby due? It seems like . . . well, it seems like maybe you are getting pretty big."

"Ha!" Naomi snorted. "Big—I'm the size of a truck, or maybe I'm carrying a couple of watermelons. This baby is not just one. Too many kicks in there. It may be a while yet, but soon. Two months, maybe."

"More twins?!" Anita exclaimed. She looked at Frances, knowing what this could mean for them as the two oldest children—the extra little mothers. *At least Mother favors me*, she thought, *since Daddy favors Frances, so Frances gets more chores. But . . . seven, eight . . . nine children in this house? Good thing we moved.*

"Yes. I'm sure it's twins again. Sorry, girls. It'll be good practice for you when you grow up. You will know all about taking care of babies!"

Anita glanced at Frances, who returned the look and rolled her eyes when her mother couldn't see.

"Frances, hurry up and finish your dinner and you can give Marie those mashed peas and some bread soaked in milk. I'll nurse her when I put her to sleep, but she needs more than I can provide her now."

Frances sighed but didn't talk back.

In Lyman, Wyoming, Frank briskly walked from the station to the Woodses' house. What a find this had been. Not only did a few railroad men stay there off and on, but the woman of the house, that Minnie Woods—oh, boy. Now there was a gal who knew how to raise kids and still take charge of renting out a room. And nice white skin. Full hips too. Not that Naomi wasn't a beautiful girl, but she got so tanned being out in the sun, tending her garden. She thought it was natural, from being a farm girl in Turner, Kansas. All those kids were taking their toll on her tiny frame, though. He hoped Mrs. Woods's husband would be gone again, down to Utah to visit his family, and they could have a little time to be alone after her kids were in bed.

Woods was sickly . . . He was only a couple of years older than Frank, but with this flu going around, Frank wouldn't be surprised if it got the man.

Chapter 3

Ogden, Utah
Early Summer 1919

Scarlet fever had run through the house for a month after the second set of twins were born the previous fall. Frances had been sick in bed but was starting to feel better; the fever was subsiding, and she wanted an apple from the tree outside her window. But with nine kids in the house now and her father being gone out on the rails so much, her mother had her hands full; Frances knew better than to ask her for much of anything, especially to go out and pick her an apple.

The mustard plaster on her chest burned, and she was tired of it. She took it off, climbed out the window, and ate a couple of the green, unripe apples. She liked the tart crunchiness.

This turned out to have been a bad idea. She did manage to get back into the house before her mother knew about her escapade, but on top of already having the raging sore throat and vomiting, she got a horrible stomachache. Good thing they now had an indoor toilet; it would have been awful to have to run to the outhouse both for the scarlet fever's effects at the top end of her body and this new problem at the other end.

"How'd you manage to get sick on top of sick?" Naomi asked her that afternoon, perplexed.

"I don't know," Frances said evasively. "I had an apple, that's all."

"Well, I sure didn't give you an apple," Naomi said, her head cocked to the side. "Did the other kids?"

"No, they didn't."

"Did you get it from the tree?"

"Yes."

"So, you climbed out the window and got it?"

"Yes, I did."

"It must have been pretty green to make you sick. You have to wait till they get ripe or that's what happens, they'll give you a belly-ache." She shook her head. "Well, just be glad you're sick, because you would have gotten a switch for sneaking out that window otherwise. And I bet you ate more than one, to get sick like that. Frances, you're the oldest; you have to learn not to be foolish anymore. I have enough to take care of without worrying about you getting in trouble too."

"Okay." Frances lifted a shoulder. "But I just wanted an apple. And I wanted to go outside. I'm tired of being sick."

"Promise me you won't climb out the window anymore," her mother implored. "You could break your arm or something."

"Okay, I promise," Frances said reluctantly. She had been so tired of lying in bed, especially after helping take care of the other kids when they'd had the fever too. Being the oldest just wasn't very much fun.

"Frank, if it's all right with you," Naomi started tentatively, "I'd like to go see my mother and dad in Turner, and take the kids on the train. Mother and Daddy haven't seen George and Grant yet, and only got to see Marie once right after she was born, when we still lived near them in Kansas. We could all go." Naomi chewed on a fingernail as she waited for his response.

Frank put down his newspaper, cleared his throat, and waited a moment before he spoke. He was in a good mood: he'd had a good night's sleep, had already gone for his walk around town, and had eaten with a pal at Harvey's Lunch Room. When he considered her request, he knew it was fair, given he got to see his own mother in Prairie, Missouri, whenever his train run went through Kansas City. It was lucky there was a station there.

But . . .

"All these kids? All nine of 'em? On that long train ride? It's more than a day!" Frank thought about the Overland Route: Ogden to Evanston and across Wyoming through Cheyenne, across Nebraska, change trains, and on down into Kansas. With nine kids. But the Wyoming leg would be really pretty, and Naomi would probably love that.

"'All these kids?' I'm here with them all day every day, usually by myself! None of them are old enough to stay home alone. You know that. Little Carl is only seven. Frances is responsible, but she's still only ten. And there's no one here in Ogden I feel like I could leave 'em all with. It would be like . . . a vacation. The kids can play on the farm; Frances and Sis can watch the babies . . ." Naomi seemed to realize she was starting to prattle on; she paused, then went on hurriedly before Frank had a chance to protest, "It'll be good for the kids to run someplace where there's no sidewalks and climb trees and all. We could see your mother and both of us see our brothers and sisters. Everybody could come out to the farm, and the kids could get to know their aunts and uncles and cousins a little bit."

Oh, yes, the more the merrier, thought Frank. *My idea of a vacation is different than yours. But I know you're right, my pretty little wife.*

"And how are we going to get from the station to the farm?" He already knew the likely answer to this but wanted Naomi to think ahead and do the planning.

"Mother'll come get us . . . or one of the farmhands. I can write to them and let them know when we're coming. I hope you'll say yes." Naomi's big green eyes searched her husband's face and she smiled coyly, despite another growing belly.

Frank realized there was little to support what he really wanted, which was to either stay home or go out on the rails alone again. Everyone in his family rode for free, anywhere he wanted to take them, and Naomi had long known this. It just had been easier when there were fewer children.

He cleared his throat again. "Okay, we'll go. But man, oh man, these kids better be good, and I don't want to hear any complaining. Children should be seen and not heard."

"Yes, they've heard you say that often enough. But I'll give 'em a good swat if they act up. Or you will. You can't expect them to be silent as the grave on a long train ride, though."

Frank sighed. "Well, I don't want to be needing to swat anybody. Last thing I need is for one of the engineers to say Frank Wolff and his wife can't control their children. I want to get that promotion to engineer. But I can see I don't have much say-so in this affair." He gave Naomi a quick side-eye and half smile. "I have two weeks off next month; we'll go then."

He glanced at Naomi before opening the paper again; she looked almost giddy. Satisfied that he'd made her happy, he got back to the news.

᥉ᕗ

Two days later, Frances cautiously approached her father, still home on a short break, during his daily newspaper perusal. He was on his second homemade beer. Frances knew that he was careful about when he took his home brew so that most people wouldn't know about it.

She leaned against his overstuffed chair by the front window and read a few of the headlines over his shoulder, where she rested her hand.

"Daddy? Is that really the first time a Utah Indian rode in an airplane?"

"Hmm? Oh, that photo . . . Yes, I suppose it is. They're gonna get too big for their britches, probably," responded Frank, momentarily distracted from the article he was reading—something, Frances saw, about Europe trying the warlords of Germany, the "Huns," for their roles in the World War. With his German Swiss ancestry, her dad always followed the news over in Europe. His father had come to the United States in 1879, and his mother a year later. They had always spoken German at home, making him fluent in their native tongue, even though he'd been born in Missouri.

Frances leaned closer. "Daddy . . . can I sit in your lap?"

"Ha!" guffawed Frank. "My gosh, no, you can't! You're too big for that anymore." He looked at her affectionately, though.

"Umm . . . can I talk to you?"

"For a minute or two, yes." He lowered the *Ogden Times*. "What is it?"

"Well . . . when we go to Kansas, Mother said I have to help with the babies. And be the main babysitter."

"Yes, of course you have to help. Your mother can't do all the work by herself."

Her heart sank. "But when will I get to play, like the other kids?"

"You'll have some time for that. But now you're growing up, and you have to assume more responsibility. You got plenty of time to play when you were little."

"But ten is still a little girl. I will still get to take my doll with me, right?"

"Well, ten is really a big girl. But yes, I imagine you can take a doll if there's room in one of the suitcases. Ask your mother." He raised his paper back up. "Now go on and play, and leave me be to read my paper and drink the rest of my soda here."

"Soda," uh-huh, Frances thought, but she did as she was told. Before her mother could ask her for help, especially with all those socks that needed darning, she left the house and walked up Grant Avenue to see if her friend Lucille was home; maybe they'd be able to play with Lucille's dolls.

On her way, she pondered her father saying, "Ten is really a big girl."

Frances was not at all sure she wanted to grow up.

Chapter 4

Ogden, Utah,
to Wyandotte County, Kansas
Summer 1919

When they packed, the older children decided to take a few dolls, books, stuffed animals, cars and trucks for all the kids.

"For heaven's sake," muttered Naomi. "You're expecting us to take half a toy chest of junk."

"Mother," Frances reasoned, "toys and books will keep the kids quiet on the train. And Grandma Sims may not have any toys or books there."

"Well, that's true about the train, but on the farm you don't need toys; you can play outside and pretend with things you find around. The barn is a great place to play."

If I even get to play, Frances thought.

"But can we still take these?" Anita pleaded.

"Oh, I guess. But you girls need to spend some time deciding on the clothes you're taking. And then we'll see if we can get all of it into a couple of suitcases. If everybody will just be good, we're going to have a really nice time!"

❧

Frances and Anita helped Naomi make sandwiches and wrap them in waxed paper the evening before the trip. They also brought some cheese, and more bread—none of that was going to keep in the icebox—and some (ripe) apples, a box of saltines, and a bottle of water with a couple of tin cups.

"Oh," Naomi said, mostly to herself, "I forgot to tell the iceman not to come." She looked at the girls. "That should do us. Your dad doesn't want to feed the whole family with train food. Our tickets are free, but not the food. In any case, we can't carry much more than this!" She gestured toward the door. "Sister, run next door and ask Mrs. Abbott would she please tell the iceman we don't need any ice next week; he can skip us for two weeks. Frances, did you do the ironing I asked you to do yesterday?"

Frances nodded. "Yes . . . yes, I did; that was partly stuff we needed to pack, remember?"

"Oh, of course. I've got so many things to do, I'm runnin' around like a chicken with its head cut off."

Ick, thought Frances. It was enough that she had to help pluck the darn things, she didn't want to think about how they came to their end.

They really did get up and run sometimes; she'd seen that on the farm. Grandma Sims said it was because of the chicken's nerves. That got on Frances's nerves, all right. At least in town they bought their chickens at the store and didn't have to watch the slaughter.

She made a mental note to not be around when they caught the chickens this time.

The next day, the family took the early-morning Union Pacific train toward Evanston, Wyoming. Frank had briefed Naomi on the route, and the three oldest kids wanted to see it on a map. They'd sat round the kitchen table the week before and circled all the places they'd go through. Frances and Anita had swallowed hard when they saw how far it was, knowing that just to Evanston was more than two hours.

"Okay, you kids," Naomi warned while Frank counted the tickets to make sure there were eight there, two for the parents and six for the children. (No tickets were needed for the three youngest. Hopefully there'd be room on the benches for Marie and she wouldn't be squirming on someone's lap the whole time.) "You need to stick together, all hold hands, and stay close to me and your dad at all times. Frances and Sis, you're in charge of counting every time we get on or off the train to make sure everybody is with us, wherever in heaven's name we are. You two make sure you've got somebody's hand and they've got somebody else's, all the time. We'll have the baby buggy so the babies can sleep in it. You understand?" She looked into her two eldest daughters' green and blue eyes, which were wide with both anticipation and new responsibility. They knew there was no room for error.

"And you boys? You obey your sisters, and no yelling or roughhousing on the train or in the stations. No running either. And all of you, no crying or your dad or me will give you something to cry about!"

Frank put in his two cents: "You kids, you have to be a good example for other children on the train. You are the children of a rail fireman, maybe an engineer soon, and a good Swiss and English family, and you will show everyone what good manners you have. If everyone is real good, horehound candy or a peppermint or a cookie maybe. Just maybe. We'll see."

They all knew their father—and their mother—meant business. Naomi knew that Frank already had candies in his pockets, and Frances, Anita, and Carl suspected this.

What a parade they made, the eleven of them—eight on foot and three in the wicker buggy—on the five-block walk to Ogden Union Station, down Grant Street and on over to Twenty-Fifth Street, with Frank and Naomi carrying the suitcases and the older children carrying bags of toys and lunches.

At the station, so far, so good, with everyone on good behavior and holding on to the now-sweaty hand of a sibling. It looked like the Union Pacific would be on time—as were they. Their father wouldn't have tolerated their being tardy. No excuse for that.

The train was a noisy proposition, clacking along with the soot and ash from the engine sometimes making its way into the passenger cars, if people kept their windows open—which many did, due to the outdoor heat. When the dusty breeze got to be too much, folks closed them . . . and later opened them back up again. Everyone just put up with their fellow travelers' choices.

Naomi remembered what her mother, Nancy, had told her about the trains in the late 1800s—that they were all disturbingly dirty, with the engine debris blowing back into the passenger coaches. But it was the fastest way to get anywhere, so people just took the trains and expected to get dirty. After her first husband died, Nancy had married Naomi's father, Joe Sims. In the mid-1880s, they'd taken her two children from the first marriage, Fred and Alice, and moved from Illinois to Missouri. They'd ridden the Union Pacific for that long trip, and Nancy had declared it was much cleaner than other train lines; workers had come through the coaches to sweep, wipe the seats, and clean the windows from time to time. Naomi was glad that her husband was a Union Pacific employee.

The news butchers would climb on the train at many stops, young boys selling apples, candy, newspapers. Frank bought a paper in Green River, and eleven pieces of candied fruit to pass around. The kids' eyes were wide with wonder to see boys about the ages of Frances and Anita working, and they were especially happy to get a sweetmeat from their father.

Between Rawlins and Laramie, the brakeman came around and let everyone know they'd be stopping at Cheyenne for the station house, where they could get dinner. Frank instructed everybody to get themselves as presentable as possible.

They arrived at Cheyenne at dusk, with Naomi pushing the buggy with Marie, George, and Grant, and everyone else carrying suitcases and bags. Frank grumbled about the fact that they couldn't stow them on the train, since he knew they'd likely board the same car for the next segment of the journey. Not to mention that they'd ordered one sleeping berth to share in shifts, and they could've taken advantage of it while the train was stopped.

Naomi knew his reasoning for letting it go: Who was he to buck the rules? He didn't want to bother the brakeman with the inquiry.

"Everybody stay together," she whispered to the children. "Hold on to somebody's hand and follow Daddy and me, no matter what." Before leaving the train, she had re-pinned her hair and wiped a little dust from her face with one of the dish towels she'd brought along in her bag. Frank had used his handkerchief and run a comb through his hair.

The family managed to stay orderly with just a little complaining and shushing. They found two large tables they commandeered, and while Naomi and Frank decided what to order, Frances, Anita, and Carl took the younger children, except for the two babies, to line up for the washroom.

It looked like trout was the best thing on the menu that everyone would be happy to eat. They ordered three plates plus some potatoes, green beans, and bread. That accomplished, Frank went off to wash up while Naomi tried to keep George and Grant from fussing.

A young waiter approached the table with a tray of water glasses. Naomi noticed his clean and well-groomed appearance (and handsome face), and felt a bit self-conscious about being disheveled.

"Pardon me, ma'am, but I was told to bring all these waters to this table. Are you watching the babies while you wait for your folks to come back?"

Naomi laughed, flustered at the implied compliment. "Why, yes, yes, those glasses are for this table, and the one next, there. But these are my own babies, as are the rest who'll be joining us. They're just washing up . . . along with my husband."

The fellow blushed. "Oh, well, gosh, I wouldn't have taken you for old enough to have these young'uns. I beg your pardon. But if you don't mind me sayin', you're a very pretty gal and havin' babies hasn't hurt you a bit. If you don't mind me sayin'."

"No, no, that's kind of you." Naomi blushed as well. "Now, do you work here all the time, or just in the evenings?" she asked, tucking a stray hair with a hairpin, emboldened by the flattery and enjoying the attention.

The waiter drew a breath and leaned in a little closer to answer just as Frank returned. "I work here evenings and Saturdays, and trying to finish high school in the days, right now, don't you know." Glancing at Frank, he backed up a step. "I'll leave you to settle in now," he said, and turned away toward the kitchen.

"What was that all about?" Frank inquired.

"Oh, just a little conversation," Naomi replied, looking down and smoothing the bodice of her blouse.

"Maybe you shouldn't be starting up a conversation with strangers," Frank commented stiffly.

"It was harmless, Frank. He was just being nice, so I asked him if he worked here all the time, just to be friendly."

"Well . . . you don't want to seem too friendly. Man, oh man," he said, turning his head from side to side to show his disapproval, "you just never know. I see things on the railroad, you know. And I know men sometimes take liberties with unsuspecting women." He curtly nodded his head once for emphasis.

Naomi smiled to herself, a little pleased at Frank's protectiveness but even more that a young man had paid her a compliment. It was nice to know that someone other than her husband took an interest. "Well, Frank, he's likely ten or more years younger than me, and I think he was just being polite to a tired traveler. Maybe people order more if the waiters are friendly, I don't know. But I take your point," she said, not wanting to argue; he'd start to get angry if he thought she was talking back to him. It was just . . . well, she felt like she was not a bad judge of character.

Anita returned then, Hermann and Henry in tow. "Everybody's washed up, finally!" she announced.

"Anita, you keep an eye on George and Grant while I get my turn in the washroom, and I'd like you and Frances to change their diapers as soon as you eat—or sooner, if the food doesn't come right away," Naomi told the girls, looking at Frances as well.

She didn't miss the look the girls exchanged at this, but she chose to ignore it.

At the mirror, Naomi surveyed her youthful face of twenty-nine years. *Well, I hope that young man is right. Maybe I do look younger. Maybe I even look like a sixteen-year-old girl, some days. Even with a rumpled blouse on me.* She pinched her cheeks, rouged her lips anew, and smiled a little at her reflection, holding her head up straight like in her wedding photo, bracing herself for a dinner with nine children and her possibly jealous, sometimes demanding husband. *Maybe that young waiter's attention will help keep Frank on his toes.* She shook her head and scoffed at her own big ideas. But a smile always makes you look younger; she knew that much.

On the next leg of the trip, a half hour past Topeka, the brakeman went round waking people up and letting them know they'd soon be at Kansas City, just before noon. The children were cranky. Naomi heard the three eldest children tell the others to try and be quiet and maybe there'd be a treat when they got to the station. The reward horehound candies Frank had pocketed in Ogden had been passed around at nine the night before, since the kids had been so good at dinner. Because Marie was too little to have a hard candy yet, Naomi had given her a cracker with a little sugar sprinkled on top as her treat.

While Frank, Frances, and Anita accounted for all the children, bags, and suitcases and made sure they didn't leave any stray toys on the train, Naomi found a beverage vendor and ordered six soda pops: Coca-Cola, Dr. Pepper, Bubble Up, ginger ale, and root beer. The kids could choose their favorites. She had noticed that the Coca-Cola made the kids a little too energetic; she saved those two for Frances and Anita. Thirty cents for the six bottles. Frank might not like that, but the kids deserved a treat after being as good as could be expected for all those hours. She bought a bottle of milk for the twins and Marie, seven cents, and she got cups of pretty good coffee in cardboard cups for herself and Frank, with cream and sugar, for the same five cents each that the sodas cost. That would probably smooth things over with him. Besides, he wouldn't argue in public—and it was all less than a half-dollar, she reasoned.

"We're about on time; I'm hoping Mother or someone will be along to fetch us real soon," Naomi told the children, occupied with the sweet taste of fizzy beverages. "Until then, we'll sit here in the station *nicely* and wait patiently." *Prob'ly I'm the one who needs to be patient the most*, she told herself.

Frank made his way to the newsstand to pick up the morning edition of the *Kansas City Sun*. Naomi walked over to deliver his coffee, and he gestured to a paper in front of him.

"Well, I'll be," he murmured to her. "'*The Kansas City Call: News for African Americans*.' Darned if the Negroes didn't go and print themselves their own paper. Huh. Well, probably a good idea for the ones who can read and write. Wonder what they've got to write about?"

Naomi responded, "Prob'ly the same as other folks," and handed him his coffee.

Nancy Sims hurried into the station, looking this way and that for her daughter and her brood. "There you are!" She embraced Naomi briefly. "So these two handsome boys are George and Grant! Hello there, give your grandma a kiss!"

The babies eyed this new woman and blinked when she smooched them.

"And look how big Marie is now!" she said. "She's walking?"

"Oh yes," answered Naomi. "One less to carry, at least part of the time." She beckoned to the children. "Say hello to Grandma Sims, kids," Naomi directed. "You didn't come alone, did you?"

"Oh, no, I drove the truck and a hired hand we've got working for us for the summer drove the horse and buggy," her mother said. "The older kids can ride in the back of the truck, and you and Frank up front with me. Frances, Anita, and the babies can ride in the buggy with Charles—or Mr. Foreland, I guess you better call him, even though he's kind of a cousin. You know your dad is working out in California, right?"

"No, no, I didn't remember that, but now that you mention it, I think you said that in your last letter. San Dego, or Dee-yago, or someplace?"

Her mother nodded.

Naomi sighed. "Well, he's always off somewheres. Mama, do you think you should be driving that old truck at seventy-three?"

"Oh, pishposh. Of course. With Joe away so much, I've gotta do what two people might be doin'. Good thing he's my second husband! I'm used to somebody bein' gone. If your dad can work on a farm down in the sun in California, I can work on a farm in Kansas, that's for sure. Come on, let's get your gear and head home. You could all prob'ly use a good lunch about now."

"Kids, take your bottles over to the counter and get our penny deposits back," Naomi instructed. Frances, Anita, and Carl collected the bottles and recovered the deposit before helping their parents and grandmother with the bags and suitcases.

"Charles, could you please help Frances and Anita and the babies up into the buggy?" Nancy asked the muscular, dark-haired, tanned fellow waiting for them outside the station.

"Oh, yes, ma'am, I'd be happy to," he replied, already hoisting some bags into the back of the buggy and patting the horse to calm her.

Frances tried not to stare. Her grandmother's hired hand looked like he was an Indian. There were a few Indian kids at school in Ogden, but she didn't play with them and hadn't ever met any of their parents, so she'd never been with an Indian up close.

He held out his hand to support her getting into the buggy seat and she suppressed a desire to recoil, having never held the hand of a person who wasn't white before. But it felt like the hand of her father or one of her uncles, same as them.

Anita handed her the twins and then got up into the seat; Frances slid over so that she'd be on the far side and Anita in the middle. She stared straight ahead, trying not to glance over at Mr. Foreland too much.

Nancy called out from the truck, "We'll see you girls out there. We'll go on and get lunch started. It'll only take us forty minutes to get there, and you'll be along a little later."

Frances groaned inside. She knew it was only nine or ten miles, but in the buggy it was going to take them at least an hour; this man wasn't going to send the horse into a trot with two young girls and two babies aboard.

Anita began a friendly conversation with the fellow.

"Mr. Foreland, do you live around here?" she asked. "I hope you won't think I'm nosy to ask."

"Oh, no, that's fine," he said. "No, my family has a farm over in Missouri, about seventy miles from here. Over in Dover. Ha ha. That rhymes." He gave Anita a courteous smile.

"So, then, you moved to Grandma Sims's farm?"

"Well, not exactly. Your grandma mentioned to her older daughter up our way that she needed help, and my mother's kin are cousins to your grandma's older kids. So I came down to work, and I'll just be here until after harvest in the fall, and then go on back to my folks' place."

The ride went on like that—small talk, with Frances keeping her mouth shut and listening to all the mundane, superficial details discussed by Mr. Charles Foreland and her sister: were there any new foals, did Grandma Sims still have a lot of chickens, who else was working at the farm, and so on.

Frances wanted to ask lots of other questions—like, was he born in a tepee? Did he live on one of those reservations? Did he have a wife? Did he call her a squaw? Maybe he wasn't even an Indian, but he sure looked like one. And what kind of name was Foreland? Maybe English, like her mother's people.

It seemed like the man was polite, and not much different from any other man she'd known who'd worked at her grandma's farm. Well, she'd just wait and see.

Chapter 5

Wyandotte County, Kansas
Summer 1919

All the kids had a good time exploring in the barn and around the farm. Lots of places to hide when they played hide-and-go-seek.

On this festive day, the four older boys got in trouble for breaking some canning jars when they were climbing around in the storage shed. Naomi found a piece of lath and paddled all of them good, not waiting for excuses or whose idea it had been to climb up on the shelves. Frank had taken the truck and gone up to Prairie to help bring his mother and siblings and their families down, so Naomi was responsible for disciplining the kids, to her annoyance. It was supposed to be a fun day for everyone.

"Frances and Sis!" Naomi shouted out the back door. "You girls, come here!"

The two sisters were taking a break from tending the infant twins and Marie, fiddling around aimlessly, talking about nothing of consequence, speculating on which of their Wolff, Sims, and Chalmers cousins might be coming to visit. When they heard their mother call for them, they looked at each other. Frances rolled her eyes, Anita chuckled, and they trudged back toward the house.

"Yes, Mother?" Anita said as pleasantly as she could.

"The minute I let you girls do what you want, there go the boys, getting in trouble. They broke some canning jars out in the shed; you must have heard the ruckus. I expect you to keep an eye on them when I can't. I'm in here trying to help your Grandma Sims put a meal together, which I should've made you help with, so now you're gonna do that."

"Mother," Frances tentatively asked, "what about 'I am not my brother's keeper'? Like it says in the Bible."

"Ha! Don't try using that on me. That doesn't apply to you girls. That was I think Cain and Abel, and you sure aren't them."

The girls followed their mother into their grandmother's kitchen, where food preparation was in full swing.

"Frances, you can roll out the pie crust; you're good at that. Sister, peel and cut up those boiled potatoes for the salad, and then wash up the rest of these pans. Later on you can set the tables. We'll eat outside, since there's so many of us."

Anita eyed the pile of potatoes and sighed. Through the doorway to the dining room and on past that into the living room, she could see Carl and Hermann, each sitting on small wooden stools facing a corner, contrite and quiet, and she surmised that Frank Jr. and Henry were in the other corners. She knew the humiliation of this punishment but thought it probably wasn't of much use for Frank, who wasn't quite four yet. She was still young enough to remember how hard it had been just six or seven years ago to figure out what was right and what was wrong. She widened her eyes at Frances, who shrugged back when their mother and grandmother weren't looking.

The girls went about their tasks, asking which bowl to use or if the pie crust was big enough and thin enough, but otherwise trying not to bother their beleaguered mother.

"I swear, these kids," Naomi said to Nancy. "I can't have my eyes goin' nine ways at once. But if they don't get a lickin' when they misbehave, they won't learn right from wrong."

"I know what you mean," Nancy said. "You kids were all the same. And my folks paddled me too. Prob'ly been like this since Adam and Eve. But you know . . ." she ventured. "You *do* know what's causing you to have so many kids, now?" She chuckled and poked her daughter in the ribs, then put her pipe down on its holder on the table, sat down, and with a wink at Naomi, started in slicing up the hard-boiled eggs.

Naomi bit off a cuticle and turned to lightly "*phth*" the tiny fragment to the floor. Frances saw this, pursed her lips, and quietly tch'd. She found her mother's nail-chewing habit disgusting, regardless of where Naomi deposited the bits, and once again internally vowed never to bite her nails.

"Oh, *Mother*," Naomi said. "Well, yes, of course, but you know . . . Frank's an amorous man."

"Yes, and I see you have a bun in the oven again," Nancy said.

"Seems like almost every time he comes home from a railroad run, here comes another Wolff nine months later."

"Well, the children are useful to us; it's not like they're a burden. They help out around the house, especially Frances and Sis, and Carl is startin' to do some boys' work too—mostly in the yard and such. But you're right. And I think I've got myself another set of twins coming up."

"Three sets! My Lord. Well, they say it skips a generation, but I don't think your grandma or Frank's grandma had themselves any twins. I'll have to ask Caroline Wolff. But you might want to think about bein' a little less friendly when Frank comes home."

"Oh, I guess I can be unfriendly enough sometimes . . . but I do get awful tired of being alone every day with a passel of kids. So I'm as glad to see him as he is to see me when he's home!" Naomi paused a moment, then went on, "I did let him know that I thought it was my turn to come out here for a vacation, such as it is. It's awful good to see you, Mama. I missed you after you moved back out of our house when we were first married, and it's been too few times since then, since we moved so far away."

"Well, you know those days when I stayed with you and Frank was just because your dad was away working, until we moved again. I'm tired of movin', I'll tell ya. A woman needs her own home if she can manage it."

The sound of the truck and two more cars coming up the long drive from the main road interrupted their conversation. Nancy stretched her neck to see out the window and said, "Oh, darn. They're early. I should have known; it can't be more than twenty miles, and your husband is not one to fool around once he gets somewhere."

As Frances looked on, her grandmother picked up her pipe and its stand and stashed it under her apron on her lap.

❧

Soon Caroline Wolff was through the door, making her greetings to the family. "What have we here? *Mein Gott!*" she commented upon discovering the boys in their corners.

"Hi, Grandma Wolff," said the three older boys in a quiet, disjointed chorus.

"We got in trouble," offered Carl.

"*Ja*, I can see that!" she said. "I hope you weren't talking back. *Kinder* . . . I mean, *children* should be seen and not heard. Whatever was done, are you going to be good now, and give your Grandma Wolff a hug?"

Carl answered, "No, not talking back, we broke something, but yes, we're trying to be good now," as the three older boys jumped up, thankful for the reprieve, and little Frank hesitantly got up from his spot, waiting to see what was next.

"Little Frank," she insisted, "you come over here, too, and give Grandma Wolff a hug like a good boy. I bet you don't remember me!"

He complied, warily.

"Now, you can't be breaking things," she told the boys. "You must learn to be careful. Things cost money, and your papa has to work hard for everything you have."

"It wasn't Daddy's things," offered Henry. "It was Grandma Sims's jars."

"Oh, canning jars? Well, those are very important. They are for food for the winter. If you were my boys, I'd make you work to pay for them!"

"We're too little!" said Hermann with alarm.

"Carl is not too little. How old are you, Carl?"

"I'm seven, Grandma Wolff."

"I'll talk to your Grandma Sims about what you can do to make it up."

"But we didn't do it on purpose! We were climbing up to see what was on the top shelf, and . . . it just happened."

"And next time you won't let that happen, *ja*? On purpose or not doesn't matter once the damage is done. Okay, well, I say you better play while you can, and we'll see what's what later."

All the boys quickly sneaked outside to find their cousins.

Frances and Anita dutifully greeted their paternal grandmother when she strolled into the kitchen. After quickly hugging them, she said, "Hello, there, Nancy! I see you are busy as usual. Now, what can I do to help?"

"Oh, you just go and wash up at the pump, Caroline, and I'll find something for you to do, for sure," Nancy said with a smile.

Caroline smiled back and nodded. Frances didn't miss the wink she gave Naomi while pointing with her eyes to the wisp of smoke escaping from under Nancy's apron. As she went out the back door, she said over her shoulder, "I told Carl he needs to work off the cost of the jars the boys broke. I don't think he liked that a bit!"

Nancy said under her breath to Naomi, "Well, yes, and he prob'ly won't appreciate that the other boys are too little to do much. We'll have to think of something they all can do. Maybe sweep the shed. Caroline's idea is a good one, have to admit."

Listening to the conversation, Frances thought, *And I'm the one who will have to teach them how to sweep.*

Nancy went upstairs—to hide her pipe, Frances knew. Her grandmother believed that no one except her immediate family knew she smoked a pipe. Her poor eyesight and age-diminished olfactory sense added to her illusion.

When she returned to the kitchen, Nancy asked the room in

general, "Now where did I put my glasses? I've been looking all over for them; that's why I had to leave the kitchen."

"Grandma Sims," said Frances quietly, "they're on top of your head." *Right where they most always are. And we all know why you went upstairs.*

"Oh, for heaven's sake, so they are. I never think to look there for them."

Frances and her mother exchanged a look of quiet amusement.

The late lunch was a lively affair, with the huge extended family in attendance at long wooden tables at the back of the house, under a few large old oak and sycamore trees. The men, especially the Missouri branch of the family, missed having a beer, with Prohibition having been passed in Missouri just a month or two before. But Kansas had had Prohibition long before, partly just because of the German beer drinkers in the area and their penchant for overdoing it at local saloons.

Spirits were high naturally on this warm afternoon, and all agreed that cool root beer, sarsaparilla, and lemonade went down well, especially with fried chicken and potato salad. And some of the men discussed the possibility of home brewing. The women pretended not to hear, some of them missing a beer as much as their menfolk.

Naomi wandered from one brother, sister, aunt, uncle, or cousin to another, usually with either George or Grant on one hip, catching up on family news and gossip. Because Nancy had been married twice, and most everybody had a lot of children, if you could get everybody together at once there was a *lot* of everybody.

Frank's family was a little easier to wrangle, given the lack of remarriages, although on both sides they'd born a lot of children since many died young and family hands were important in farm communities. Frank's siblings had been able to come as well. The children's favorite uncle was Frank's brother Otto, who was only sixteen; it felt a bit strange to Frances and Anita to call someone who was only about six years older "Uncle Otto," but that was tradition.

After lunch, Naomi told Frances and Anita they were in charge of the young kids for a while, then took a break and walked her pregnant self around the farm. Frank was sitting with his family, paying her no mind.

The old horse, Josie, that they kept to pull the buggy and the plow nickered at her from the other side of the corral fence. Naomi had half an apple in the pocket of her dress; she offered it to the mare, who gobbled it appreciatively, then nosed her to see if she had any more treats.

Naomi rested her foot on the kickboard and leaned her arm against the top rail. She wasn't that far along, just maybe six months, but it was nice to get a little weight off her feet anyway.

"Hello, there . . ." Mr. Foreland approached with a polite nod of his head. "You know this ol' gal?" He stroked Josie's nose and scratched behind her ears. She whinnied and tossed her head, and then gave him a nuzzle.

"Oh, yes," Naomi replied. "My folks got her when I was young. A teenager, at least. She's aging, but not old enough for the glue factory yet!"

Foreland laughed and looked at the ground, smiling.

"You like horses?" Naomi asked. "Seems like Josie likes you, anyways."

"Oh, of course. You got to when you work a farm. Sometimes they're the best friends you got too. My mother says all animals have spirits just like humans. She calls them 'the four-footeds' and says we should respect them."

"Well, there's more truth than poetry in that," Naomi said. "Your mother sounds pretty smart. My daughter Anita—we call her Sister— told me you live over in Dover, Missouri. Over in Dover. That's funny. I'm a poet, I guess!"

Foreland smiled a half smile at this but kept his eyes on the horse. Naomi thought he was amused at her rhyme.

"Yeah, my folks own a farm over there," he said. "We moved up there from where we used to live in Oklahoma, few years back. Before that, we lived up in Missouri, where I was born. We was in Missouri for maybe twenty years. Back and forth, I guess, goin' where the gettin' was good."

"Yes, you gotta go where there's a living to be made, that's for sure." Naomi nodded. "We just come about a thousand miles from Ogden to visit over here. Talk about your long train ride! But I really wanted to see my mother and my family, and Frank's got family over this way too, as you can see. You don't have to work your own farm this time of year?"

"Well, we hired extra help and 'stead of letting 'em go, I said I'd go get work somewhere else for the summer. Kind of had the itch to do something different anyway. You know, a little travel, even if it's only for work. I always think I'll take a train someplace else someday. Maybe I'll even go all the way to Ogden!"

He glanced at her to see if she got the joke. She smiled but thought that Ogden might not be all that exciting to a fellow alone.

"I'll go back and help for the end of fall harvest, though. Hoping your mama—I mean, Mrs. Sims—won't need me anymore by then."

"I was born over in Turner . . . not too far from here. An' it's okay you call her my mother—that's what she is." Naomi shot him a playful look.

"I don't like to seem too forward, especially with a married lady," he said carefully. "An' I think I know where Turner is. I've seen the turnoff to the south on the way out here to the farm."

"Yes, I'm really a Kansas girl," she told him. "We've only lived in Utah for a couple years now. You know, once you work on a small farm like this, you're practically family. I mean, not exactly, but first names I think are all right, especially since you're a cousin. My husband might not agree, of course!"

She started to put a finger to her mouth to chew a nail—but caught herself and lowered her hand. She wasn't sure why she felt a little self-conscious, but, like her mother's concern about people seeing her smoking a pipe, she wasn't comfortable having Mr. Foreland see her nervous habit.

"So it's okay by me if you call me Naomi," she rushed on, "but my husband will probably want you to call me Mrs. Wolff! He likes things a certain way."

"You can call me Charles if you like too. But 'Mr. Foreland' if your husband prefers it. An' I reckon everybody likes things just the way they like 'em."

They both chuckled a little. Naomi was a bit embarrassed by the familiarity and thought he might be too.

"Well," she said, "I'd best get back inside before one o' my kids starts acting up. And I'm sure you got work to do."

"I do, I do, all the time. But it was nice talkin' with you."

Back in the house, Frank had seen Naomi out the window, having a conversation over by the corral.

When she came to his side, he asked her, "What were you talking about with that Indian?"

"Now, Frank, I'm not sure he's an Indian," she said. "He might be, I can see that he does look kinda like one, but he talks just like anybody else. Like any farmhand. His name's Foreland; that sounds like a white name to me. Maybe English like Sims, even. Plus, he's related to the Chalmerses. We were just talkin' about the horse . . . you know, that Josie's been on our farms since I was young. Sis told me he was from Dover. He said his family's got a farm there, but they didn't need him for the summer, so he came down to help Mama. That's all we talked about. It's okay for me to have a conversation with my mother's farmhand, isn't it?"

Frank was thinking the guy was a little too good-looking, even for an Indian. Rough around the edges, not a city fellow, but still, something about him. And there had been that waiter at the station house. "Man, oh man, I told you before, you need to be careful talking to strangers. They might . . . they might think things."

"Oh, for heaven's sake, Frank. I'm home with the kids twenty-four hours a day while you're gone talkin' to who knows who every day when you're on the railroad. Here I am—pregnant again, surely not of interest to any man—and I took a little walk over to the corral to see the horse for a few minutes. A body never gets time to herself! I just like a little adult conversation once in a while, other than the iceman at home and my mother here and women at the church. No harm in that. You know it doesn't mean anything!"

She bit a fingernail, searching her fingers for one that wasn't down to the quick.

"Listen, believe you me, I don't like some Indian or half-breed or whatever he is thinking he can just talk to my wife any time he likes, especially alone." Frank knit his brows. "He's not family; he's a hired hand. You should only be talking to him if you need to ask him to do a chore, and he's your mother's worker, anyhow. You bet she can tell him what to do. And you know I don't like it when you talk back to me. Don't be getting uppity."

She shook her head, smiling, put one arm around his waist, and gave him a squeeze. "Actually, he's Mother's distant cousin by marriage."

Then how'd they get that Indian blood in there? Frank thought. He didn't approve.

Frank stood up straight and looked away, but he put his arm around her as well and gave her a pat on her hip, enjoying his wife's affection and comely little body, even with its swell of pregnancy.

Chapter 6

Ogden, Utah
Autumn 1919

Frances noticed that her mother had changed since she lost the twins in August, the new babies who had been due in September. Following the previous home births, there had been the sound of one or two tiny infants crying their little wail, and the adults—her mother, sometimes Daddy, the doctor, and sometimes a nurse—cooing and exclaiming over the new life, counting toes, making claims about who the baby looked like.

This time there had been only her mother's deep sobbing from behind her bedroom door, and later the hurried arrival of a man, and then his departure with two small bundles. Since that time, Naomi had been morose, and was biting her fingernails even more than usual, whenever she didn't have her hands busy cooking, cleaning, or sewing.

Anita had been upset as well to hear her mother's anguish and not be allowed in the bedroom. She'd cried copious tears for two days, until Frances finally admonished, "You've got to stop crying. You are going to make Mother feel worse."

Anita hiccupped her sobs and sniffled while Frances handed her a handkerchief. "I've been sad too," Frances told her sister, "but we're the oldest, and we have to set an example for the boys and Marie. Or they'll be scared."

Frances had cried her own tears but had gone up to her and Anita's bedroom and shut the door to do it, and even then had sobbed as quietly as she could. She knew she had to take over part of the household duties her mother might not feel like performing, and part of her sadness was her own self-pity, which she didn't want on display. But she was also sorry the two little souls had not made it into their family, even though it would have meant more children for her to babysit, with the twins, George and Grant, only a year old themselves. And she was scared. Scared about her mother's sadness, scared about what this meant for the family, for herself, for her mother, and scared that something terrible could happen when you had babies.

A month after the death, there was still a pall on the house. Naomi sat and stared out the window for long periods of time. Anita would ask her if she was all right, and she would always say, "Yes, I'm fine."

Frances approached Frank on a Saturday, while he was reading the morning paper and she was using the carpet sweeper in the living room. Naomi had gone for a walk to Skaggs Cash Store, six blocks away, to buy some groceries.

"Daddy?"

"Yes, what?" he answered.

"Daddy . . . what exactly happened . . . last month? Did the babies die quickly after they were born? Could they not breathe? What happened?"

Frank lowered the *Ogden Times*, took off his glasses and rubbed his eyes, and then replaced the spectacles, hooking the wires back around his ears, buying time. He looked down and then looked into

Frances's eyes while she stood with her hands on the handle of the carpet sweeper.

Man, oh man, he thought. "I'm not sure . . . I'm not sure you are old enough to understand these things, Frances. When you are older, you can ask your mother about this."

"Daddy, I'll be twelve next year. And sometimes . . . sometimes I'm like a mother in this family too."

"You shouldn't say that," he scolded her gently. "You don't do nearly what your mother does, and you don't know how it is to worry about your own children—whether they know right from wrong, whether they get hurt, where are they and why are they late. 'Honor thy father and thy mother.'" He glanced at his paper, hoping that was the end of this topic.

Frances didn't look satisfied. She sat down on the couch, an expectant look on her face.

After a few seconds, Frank let out a sigh and continued, "The babies were what they call 'stillborn.' This happens sometimes, that a baby will die inside the mother. We don't know why it happened. That was why the doctor came and took them a little early. Maybe going on the train last summer was too much for her. Maybe not. Sometimes things happen and we will never know the reason. We hope maybe God wanted them back in heaven and didn't want them to suffer this life. But the babies were not alive inside her. You remember she said she couldn't feel them kicking anymore? Well, that was why."

Frank was agitated. *My God, couldn't Naomi have explained this to her oldest daughters? This is not a man's job, to do this. Even if it is Frances, my best little girl.*

"How long, then, will Mother wear black?" Frances pressed. "I mean, she only has two black dresses, and we wash them all the time . . . and she's so sad every day. Will she be sad forever now?"

"Oh, those are more of the kinds of questions no one knows the answers to," said Frank. "But your mother said she's going to stop wearing black when we get ready for Christmas, maybe sooner. She knows it's hard for you kids too. So, then you will know she is trying not to be sad, but she might just not be showing it. So, you do your best to keep helping her. That is probably the only thing you can do to help her feel better—to not worry her that you aren't keeping up your end of things."

"Okay . . ." said Frances doubtfully.

But Frank was finished talking. He picked up his newspaper, signaling that the conversation was over.

In November, for Thanksgiving, Naomi wore her prettiest fall dress, a brown print with little flowers. Frances noticed the color in her cheeks, and the fact that she sang "You Made Me Love You" while she stuffed the turkey with bread from the previous weekend's baking.

She had Anita slice the bread and lay it out on cookie pans to dry out, and then Frances had cut up the celery and the onions, her eyes watering the whole time, for Naomi to cook in bacon grease while Frances cut the dried bread into cubes.

Anita brought Hermann into the kitchen, after she'd finished her share of the duties, with him dressed in one of her old dresses and a bow pinned in his hair.

"Look at Hermann!" she said, laughing. "Or maybe I should say Hermoine."

Frances smiled, tch'd, and shook her head.

"Oh, my goodness, what have you done with the boy?" Naomi asked with alarm.

"He wanted to!" Anita insisted. "He likes to dress up in girls' clothes."

Everyone in the kitchen laughed, amused by the little boy's behavior.

"Well put 'im back in his own clothes for dinner. Sakes alive." Naomi shook her head, but she was smiling.

When all the adults and older children were seated at the dining room table, set with Naomi's best tablecloth and the best of her dishes, and the little kids were gathered around some wooden boxes with a tablecloth on them, Frank cleared his throat.

"Now, first I have to mention that I miss my Manischewitz," he said. "But I'll be damned if the Prohi are going to get me, so I'll drink the grape juice."

You've said that every holiday for the last two years since Utah got Prohibition, Frances thought. *How many times do we have to hear this? Fine with me if nobody has any alcohol.*

Naomi raised her little glass of grape juice and said, "Well I'll drink to that!" and everyone chuckled.

Grandma Sims had come out for the holiday; she was getting ready to move to Oklahoma, where Joe had found some property. While he was handling the particulars, she'd taken advantage of the lull in farm activity to come visit her daughter. Frances and Anita had given up their bed for her, and were sleeping on the living room floor for a few nights.

After dinner, when everyone was full of pumpkin and apple pie and Frank was settled in his chair with the *Ogden Standard*, the two women shooed the kids out of the kitchen so they could talk while they did the dishes and put the leftovers in the icebox.

"Naomi, you're looking good," Nancy said. "I was worried that after this last August you'd be peak-ed and skinny and down in the dumps."

Naomi's letter about the stillbirth of the twins had come a week or two after the fact. Nancy had thought perhaps it was a blessing in disguise. Frank and Naomi didn't have a farm; they didn't need a large family.

"Oh, Mama, things are pretty much back to normal," Naomi said. "I'm feeling good. It was a sad thing, but you can't dwell in the past. I'm all healed up."

"So . . . back to normal . . . you mean you and Frank are also 'back to normal'?" Nancy kept her gaze on her daughter.

"Mother!" Naomi exclaimed in mock embarrassment, then looked at Nancy and smiled. "Yes, we are—as of last month, if you really want to know; of course we are."

"Already. Well, I'm not surprised, I have to say." Nancy took a dish towel from the rack. "Oh, you know that hired hand . . . Charles Foreland? The distant cousin? He turned out to be a really good worker. I'm hoping he'll come on down to Oklahoma next spring and help us plant. If his family can spare him."

"Oh, yes, I remember him." Naomi smiled. "Well, he seemed like a nice enough fellow. You sure can use the help when Daddy is away so much. But that's a lot longer ways for him to go."

"Well, his family used to live in Oklahoma, has kin there, and so he knows that area and the land down there."

"I think he mentioned that when I talked to him for a few minutes." Naomi paused. "When did you say you're goin' down there to the new farm?"

"January. I wanted to have one more Christmas at the farm in Wyandotte County, and then we'll pack up and go. Did you know there's a town called Wyandotte in Oklahoma too?"

"I think Sis told me that when she was looking at maps for school."

"Small world, isn't it?"

"Well Kansas and Oklahoma are a small world, that's for sure," Naomi said wryly. "I've seen a lot and learned some, living here in Ogden. I sure like having running water inside, for one thing. And once in a while, if I'm careful with how much I spend, I can go buy something in a store instead of making it myself. Plus, the grocery store is not too far to walk. I can get oranges for the kids' Christmas stockings without having to sell my hair. You know what I mean, I wouldn't do that, but you can get things, food and supplies, when you want them. I made them some real cute stockings to hang up; I'll show you later."

"Oh, my farm girl's a city girl now!" Nancy laughed.

"Mama, I don't think I'll ever be a real city girl. But it's easier in many ways."

They sat down at the table and enjoyed a longer chat after Naomi made coffee.

Chapter 7

Ogden, Utah
1920

Anita, Frances, and Carl all noticed that their mother's spirits had picked up this year. And that she seemed to be pregnant again.

August brought another brother, Willie, to lighten the mood of the house—and at the same time, Frances thought, spread the income a little more sparsely.

Now there were ten: seven boys and three girls. Two sets of twins. Two older sisters watching over the brood in late afternoons, evenings, and weekends. One infant, two toddlers, and one still too little to go to school. Six in school, five there for six hours a day, one, little Frank, for a half day only. Frances knew her mother blessed the day when they each started school. For five mornings a week, she only had four at home in the morning. Sometimes they all slept at once, and she got to also.

Frances turned twelve in late November. There was a cake— Frances's favorite, yellow vanilla with frosting and little flowers on top. Naomi showed her how to add an extra yolk to the batter to get the yellow cake color and more custardy flavor, and then how to add more powdered sugar to stiffen part of the frosting to make flowers. Plus, she added just a few drops of berry juice—from fruit she'd canned in the summer—to part of the frosting to make a separate little bowl of pink for the flowers. Frances was allowed to invite Lucille over to the family party the Saturday before Frances's actual birthday. Everyone sang "Happy Birthday."

On her birthday card, Naomi wrote, *Dear Frances, You have been good this past year, and it really helps me when you do all your chores without being told. Thank you! You're a big girl now! Love, Mother.* Her dad signed it, *Ditto, Love, Daddy.*

Frances felt a little guilty for feeling resentful sometimes, but she was happy to have the cake and the little party. The present from her parents, handed to her in a large, heavy box wrapped in pretty paper, turned out to be a nice dark blue wool winter coat—store-bought, a little too big, size 13 years. Frances was small for her age. But this meant it was more like a teenage girl's coat style, which pleased her. She knew she would grow into it probably before she got into high school, and she could wear it to South Junior High next fall in 1921. She knew her mother had picked it out, but her dad had probably gone to Last and Thomas clothing store with her to pay for it. So this was a very special present.

"Thank you, Mother . . . thank you, Daddy. I really like it! You remembered blue is my favorite color."

Naomi had asked Frances, the week before, to also help make the fruitcakes for Christmas so they could be wrapped in cheesecloth and put away to age for a month. She'd let Frances nibble on a few pieces of candied fruit as they worked, and to lick the bowl and spoon afterward, savoring the meager amount remaining of the spicy batter with its cinnamon, nutmeg, mace, and brown sugar flavorings.

Lucille commented after the birthday party, "I like your coat.

You'll look pretty in it at school. I think it's okay that it's a little big. Lots of kids wear clothes that don't fit perfect."

Frances thought Lucille was real nice. It seemed like Mormon kids were mostly pretty kind; she couldn't see they were much different from Lutheran kids, except Lucille had told her that at church they didn't have wine for the sacrament, they had water to symbolize the blood of Christ. (Of course, no churches had wines during Prohibition anyway, but they had grape juice.) And the Mormons thought Joseph Smith, who started their church, was a prophet. She'd have to think about that part.

Chapter 8

Evanston, Wyoming
Late Autumn 1920

Minnie Woods was not bereft. It had been two years since Edward had passed from that damnable flu in 1918. He had not been well the last few years, but it was a shame that he had died so young, only thirty-two. Ellen was born just after that; she would never know her father. If, in fact, Edward actually was her father. Minnie hadn't always been chaste when Edward was away for long stretches, down in Utah seeing his family or working from state to state on farms, although mostly he'd farmed their own land in Lyman. She got lonely and was not immune to the flirtation of a boarder or the dry goods clerk. Why not enjoy a man's company if he offered it? She was mostly careful.

Edward's family had even wanted him buried in Ogden, not near her and her children in Wyoming! That was the least of her worries, and she'd not had the emotional strength to argue with his parents, Phyllis and Richard Woods. They had status there in Ogden; Richard's brother had been mayor at the turn of the century.

She'd mourned the abrupt end of her nine-year marriage and the companionship of her husband, of course, but some of her grief had been due to the stunning realization that she was going to be raising five children alone. Good lord, how was she going to manage? The sewing she'd been taking in was not going to support six people.

Two years later, the children now ranged in age from one and a half to nine years. At least they were well-behaved.

She had sold the place in Lyman, and the farm as well, and moved the forty miles into Evanston to be near her mother, Irene Dawson. It was a bigger town with more opportunities. She'd rented a house on Ninth Street, close to stores and schools and only three blocks from the train depot on Front Street, and once again begun renting out rooms with nightly or weekly arrangements, to the railroad men who passed through Evanston on their way to Ogden, San Francisco, Cheyenne, Kansas City, St. Louis, and even Chicago, back and forth along the lines. There was far more call for rooms to board in Evanston than in Lyman, fortunately.

Sometimes the men paid for a whole month to have the room reserved, even though they weren't there more than ten nights during the month. Her mother had started working in hotels when she was in her forties, after Minnie's father had died. At least Ernest Dawson had lived a bit longer life than Edward. Before that Irene had operated the machines at picture houses on Saturday afternoons, fearless about learning new ways to earn money. And Irene had sat down with Minnie when the Woodses still lived in Lyman and told her just how to figure what she should charge a boarder, and how to make sure the boarders kept their agreements. Minnie had learned to charge a fifty-cent deposit that they couldn't get back until they gave back their room key, towels, and sheets. She also insisted they left the room and front door keys at the house whenever they left town. Changing the locks was too expensive.

The children all slept in one bedroom some nights, or in the parlor on the davenport or the floor, as they'd done in Lyman, when necessary.

She could rent out a room for two dollars a night, including breakfast and dinner. Along with the funds from the sale of the properties, plus what Edward had left her and the tiny amount she'd saved from her pittance inheritance from her father, plus working as a dressmaker, she could definitely make do. In fact, she had her mother's head for business and was looking ahead. She knew just how long it would take her to save up enough to buy a bigger house, which she would run like a small hotel. She was keeping her eyes peeled for real estate opportunities in the neighborhood, and could count on her mother to help her learn about loans. It would not be long before she'd be all set. She was determined that her children would graduate high school and not have to go to work as teenagers to support themselves.

She had let Frank Wolff and her other regular boarders know that she'd be moving to Evanston, and felt they'd be likely to rent from her again. She'd given Frank in particular her mother's address, enabling him to inquire there about her whereabouts. She knew that the railroad men stayed over in Evanston frequently, since there was often additional work to be done at the main depot. Even if handsome, blond Frank didn't have to stay over—Ogden to Evanston wasn't a very long trip, after all—he'd have an excuse if he wanted one. Which she hoped he did.

Frank had a layover in Evanston in early December. He could have taken a late train back to Ogden, but he told himself he'd get home so late that it would hardly be worth it.

He called the Abbotts next door.

"Hello, is this Deborah Abbott?" he asked when she answered the phone. He was a little uncomfortable using a telephone.

"Yes, this is Mrs. Abbott. Is that you, Mr. Wolff . . . Frank?"

"Why, yes, it is. You recognize my voice."

"Of course. We're neighbors, after all. Is everything all right?"

"Oh yes, everything's fine. I am just calling to ask if you could send one of your kids over to Naomi and tell her I'll be in Evanston for a couple of nights. There's work to be done here, and then I'll head on home in a couple of days. If it's not too much trouble. I know it's around dinnertime and all."

"No trouble, Frank. I'll send Amelia or Bobby over right away."

"Thanks. Thanks a lot. Well, good evening to you."

"Good evening to you as well."

He checked the address on the slip of paper Minnie Woods had given him one more time. The paper was getting worn at the folds, he'd taken it out of his wallet and looked at her neat handwriting so many times.

He walked the short block from the depot to The Hotel Evanston on Front Street, where Minnie's mother worked, and tentatively approached the clerk at the front desk.

"May I help?" asked the well-groomed fellow.

"Yes, I am looking for someone who's an employee here, I believe—Mrs. Irene Dawson?"

"Oh, yes. May I ask what this is regarding?"

"Her daughter told me to ask for her here. Regarding something other than hotel business. I didn't want to bother her at home since I haven't actually met her before." Frank realized he was jabbering; he hadn't meant to give out that much information.

"I'll see if she's still in the back; she handles our bookkeeping on some days, and I don't know if she's left yet."

Frank was beginning to perspire. *What the heck*, he thought. *I've got nothing to be nervous about. Minnie told me to check with her mother.*

A minute or two later, a tidy, plump woman who looked to be around sixty appeared at the desk. "You were asking for Irene Dawson? That's me . . . What is this about?"

"Oh, Mrs. Dawson, I'm Frank Wolff. I'm an engineer with Union Pacific who rented a room from time to time from your daughter, Mrs. Woods, in Lyman. She told me she might be boarding out rooms here in Evanston and that you could give me her location." He pulled out the slip of paper with Mrs. Dawson's name and address on it and hoped she would recognize her daughter's handwriting.

She peered at the note and nodded. "Oh yes, yes of course. She's at 160 Ninth Street, just a few blocks from here. Here, I'll write it down for you."

He put the two notes into his wallet, thanked her, and gave her a polite nod before heading back out to the street. *Well, that wasn't too bad. All business. Nothing to indicate to her that I'm fond of her daughter.*

Frank collected his bag from the depot office and said good night to the night clerk. All his ducks in a row, he made his way to 160 Ninth Street, where he found a modest clapboard house with a good-sized porch and attractive front garden. Nicer than the Wolff home in Ogden, in fact. Well, Minnie had done all right, hadn't she?

Chapter 9

Evanston, Wyoming
Late Autumn 1920

Frank knocked at Minnie Woods's paneled front door with its little square glass windows across the top. One of her sons—the oldest one, around ten as Frank recalled—opened the door and looked at Frank, apparently expecting him, as an adult, to speak first.

Frank expected the boy to say hello first, and they stood there awkwardly for a moment. *What the devil is his name? Would be useful to remember it now . . .*

Minnie called out from another room, "Lawrence, who is it?"

Lawrence, that's it.

"It's a man, Mother. I don't know his name. You know him from staying in Lyman, though," the boy said, not taking his eyes away from Frank's face.

"Please tell her it's Frank Wolff." Frank paused a second before he said, "Lawrence," wanting to reinforce the boy's name in his memory and trying to look reassuring.

"It's Frank Wolff!" Lawrence shouted, turning to see if his mother was on her way.

Frank heard her rapid footsteps and soon saw Minnie's calm, confident, round face smiling at him in the doorway.

"Lawrence, you remember Mr. Wolff, our boarder," she said cheerfully. "Come in, Mr. Wolff."

She held eye contact with Frank and he managed a careful smile, not wanting to divulge to her son the feelings he had for his mother. He was not sure himself what these feelings meant, but he was very clear that he felt amorous toward Minnie Woods, and always had.

Minnie tucked a tendril of hair behind her ear. "Will you be looking to board with us again here in Evanston? I do have a room available if you are interested."

Frank almost laughed at her formality.

"Why yes, Mrs. Woods," he answered, equally formally. "Yes, I am . . . interested. I may be here for a couple of nights before I head on back to Ogden."

"Well, here, Lawrence, take Mr. Wolff's bag to the available room and move the things you'll need out of there, please. Tell your brothers they won't be sleeping in there tonight."

"Mr. Wolff, make yourself comfortable in the parlor here. I'm clearing away our dinner, but I can make a plate for you. Pot roast and vegetables—I'll heat them back up in the oven. It won't take me but a few minutes."

"Oh, thank you, that would be . . . nice, Mrs. Woods. I am a bit hungry; I didn't eat at the depot."

Minnie smiled at him again for a long moment. "Well, their food is a sight less tasty than mine, anyway!"

She bustled into the kitchen and he settled himself in the parlor, pleased that Minnie seemed so glad to see him. And pot roast? An unexpected bonus. He'd have been happy with a sandwich.

One of Minnie's daughters was in the parlor too, reading. Though Frank never took much of an interest in children, especially other people's, he thought he ought to at least be cordial to the little girl, who looked at him guardedly.

"Are you doing your homework?" he asked.

"Not exactly," she answered, not offering more.

"What's that book you're reading?"

"*Doctor Doolittle.*"

"Oh, I think one of my children got that book from the library."

"This is a library book too. Where are your children?"

"They live in Ogden, with me and their mother."

"Oh. That's in Utah." The child cast her eyes back to a page of the book, although Frank didn't think that she actually continued reading.

Frank was hoping Minnie would have that dinner ready soon. He appreciated, though, that the girl didn't speak unless spoken to.

"Beatrice?" Minnie called from the kitchen. "Would you please go check on Ellen and see that her bottle hasn't fallen on the floor?"

"Yes, Mother," the little girl called out, and quickly took advantage to escape down the hall, where Frank supposed the bedrooms were.

He looked around for a newspaper and found one tucked neatly into a magazine rack. Minnie always kept a tidy house, even with five children about the place. Well, there was quite a difference between five and ten, after all, and she had to keep it neat for boarders.

Minnie appeared in the doorway. "I'll sit down here with you for a minute or two while the food heats, unless you'd like your privacy."

"Oh, no, please, sit down." Frank was gratified.

"Where did you come in from this trip?"

"Oh, the usual, St. Louis. I stopped for half a day in Prairie to see my mother, but just another run."

"Weather okay over there?"

"Well, it's snowing off and on everyplace, you know. So sometimes the tracks have to be cleared, especially coming through the passes. Cold, of course, but they've got heat on the trains now."

"Oh, yes, I know; that was real good coming over from Lyman when we moved. We had to make a couple of trips in order to bring the car and all our goods and furniture. Thank goodness it's a short trip."

"I'd have been happy to come and help," Frank blurted out.

Minnie's eyes widened a little, then she smiled and shook her head almost imperceptibly at him. "Oh, that would have been too much to ask . . . Mr. Wolff," she said, aware that the children could probably hear their conversation. She tilted her head, widened her eyes again, smiling, and gave him a look of incredulity.

Frank chuckled. He had a pretty good idea what she was thinking—*How would that have looked?* "Well, it would have been okay with me if you asked," he said. *Probably not with Naomi, though, if she knew.*

They gazed at one another.

"I'll see if your dinner's heated up," Minnie said after a long moment. "Why don't you come into the kitchen, if you don't mind the informality. It's warmer in there than in the dining room."

At the kitchen table with its eight chairs, Frank's dinner was set at the end, and Minnie sat in the closest chair.

"After the children are sound asleep, we can talk more freely for a while," she said quietly.

He laid his hand on top of hers on the table.

"Careful." She pulled her hand away, but slowly, smiling at him.

Chapter 10

Ogden, Utah
Summer 1921

Frances really wanted new school clothes. She was starting South Junior High in September. She was over all those ideas about not wanting to be a big girl, and her new coat last fall had made her realize that she'd love to look nice all the time. She'd be a teenager in a few months.

She was pinning a clean diaper on Willie when Anita brought in a basket of diapers from the clothesline, sat down on one of the beds in the nursery, and began folding.

"At least we only have one in diapers right now!" Anita commented, shaking her head.

"No kidding," Frances responded. "I wouldn't care if I never changed another diaper."

"Oh, well, when you're a mother someday you'll be doing it again. Just like Mother did for all of us all these years."

"We'll see. I don't think I'm going to have ten children."

"Ten if she's *done* having kids." Anita rolled her eyes.

"Oh, my gosh, don't even say that!"

The girls giggled, enjoying a little commiserating.

Anita added, "And you prob'ly won't have a choice how many kids you have, anyway."

If I've got anything to say about it, I'll have a choice, Frances thought. *There must be a way to keep from having a big family.*

"Mother told me they're not going to buy me any new clothes for school this year," Frances told her sister. "So that probably means you too. She said I haven't grown that much and can wear the clothes I've got. She said I could go to rummage sales at the churches or she'd buy me the material for one dress. But I don't think I can sew something really nice, only a real simple dress. I don't want to look like I came out of the poor house going to my new school!"

"Well, we aren't exactly poor . . . but we aren't exactly rich," Anita said. "What are you going to do, get the material, then?"

"I am thinking about getting some kind of work," Frances confided.

"Work?! There's enough work around here to do. What would you do?"

"I don't know. Maybe babysit somebody else's children? But that might make Mother mad. Maybe sweep up at a store or something. I know how to sweep, that's for sure."

"I bet Mother won't let you go work someplace else." Anita shook her head.

Frances sighed. "I know, I'm a little afraid to ask her."

"I dare you!"

"Oh, you think I won't do it?"

"I double dare you!" Anita smiled and gave Frances a wide-eyed look.

Frances began bouncing and then rocking Willie in her arms, singing,

Rock-a-bye baby, in the treetop,
When the wind blows, the cradle will rock.
When the bough breaks, the cradle will fall,
And down will come baby, cradle and all.

"That is such a strange song!" exclaimed Anita. "I have never understood how anyone could sing that to a baby."

That put Frances's nose out of joint.

"Well . . . it's just a song," she said defensively. "It's a lullaby, and it makes babies be quiet." She'd never really thought about the words. Everyone always said what a nice voice she had, and she just sang whatever song came to mind.

"Ha! A lullaby about a baby falling from a tree." Anita stood, her folding done. "I'd like to know who wrote that song."

With that, she left the room, leaving Frances cooing to little Willie as he fell asleep.

Frances and Lucille talked about fashions and even boys sometimes, especially at Lucille's house if Frances could get out of babysitting and chores. School was out for three months, and they were enjoying lazing on Lucille's bed.

"I have to figure out a way to get some money," Frances lamented. "I want new clothes for school, and this time I really want something store-bought. And Mother and Daddy said there was no money to buy me new clothes. They just don't understand. I don't want to look like I'm poor, especially when there will be older kids. That's okay for Anita at the grammar school, but not for me." She knitted her brow in thought and stared out Lucille's bedroom window.

"My brother," Lucille mused, "worked picking beans last summer and made some money. I bet he can tell you how to get work doing that."

"Picking beans?! I don't know . . . I mean, I picked our beans the last two summers, but that's probably not the same as doing it on a big farm. I did do it at my Grandma Sims's farm in Kansas, though." But Frances did like the idea of getting advice from Lucille's big brother. She was beginning to like boys, and she had a lot of respect for boys and men. They always seemed to know so much. And Ronald was one of those genial Mormon boys.

"Would you ask him for me?" she asked timidly.

"We'll do it together tomorrow," Lucille suggested.

The following afternoon, Lucille and Frances went to Ronald and asked how to go about getting work picking beans.

"First of all," said Ronald with authority beyond his fifteen years, "you got to go down to Farr's feed store on Washington and see if there's any ads up on the board there saying, 'Help wanted: farm labor.' Then you see where they are; for instance, if the ads are from a farm that's close to town, and if they will pick people up at Farr's or somewhere else on such and such a day and so on. And they usually bring a truck to get workers, early in the morning, and bring you home late in the day. If there's more than one ad, you can see if they are saying how much they are paying and what crop and what month and all that."

Frances cocked her head to the side, thinking this over, trying not to stare at Ronald and hoping she had a nice look on her face. She felt a little self-conscious about her decaying teeth. Her family never went to the dentist, and she knew other families did. She didn't know if Lucille's brother would notice, so she kept her mouth shut while he spoke.

She knew where Washington Avenue was and remembered going to the feed store with her mother to buy seed for the garden. "That's kind of a long way from here, isn't it?" she asked.

"Well, it's two or three miles, I guess," Ronald answered. "You could walk it. Be a long walk. Or you could take the streetcar—that's what I'd do. Only about a nickel, round trip. Oh, and you're gonna need a hat. You got a straw hat?"

She didn't have one, but she could tie a bandana on her head. Or she'd use some of her pay to buy a hat. She was going to have to do something to get those nickels for the streetcar too. Maybe babysit for someone. Things cost so much money.

"I don't," she told Ronald, "but maybe I can borrow one or buy my own after I make a little money. How much do you get paid?"

"I made $2.75 a day, working eight hours with a half-hour lunch break. And I'll tell you what, it was hard. But you're small, and not as strong, so probably they would pay you less. Maybe $1.50 a day, or maybe twenty or twenty-five cents an hour."

Frances was pretty good with numbers for a twelve-year-old; she multiplied these numbers in her head. She wasn't sure she could work eight hours a day like adults could. But if she worked even four hours a day for five days, she'd have enough to buy a dress and a straw hat and go to the picture show too. If her mother would let her.

And if she could get a ride home midday.

It was one thing to talk about earning money and quite another thing to do it. First of all, you had to get up at five, get your breakfast, and walk the three miles to the feed store—or get the streetcar, if you had three cents for the one-way trip—in order to be at the bean field by seven.

At less than five feet tall, Frances was one of the smallest workers in the bean field. But there were other children there too, some of them with their families, come from other parts of Utah or Wyoming, and a nice girl reminded her how to snap the green beans at the end of the stem so that they'd be ready for market. When you got tired, it was easy to forget what you were supposed to do and not supposed to do. And some of the workers were not very nice; they acted like her being there was taking money out of their wallets. Well, she guessed, in a way, it was. They weren't all helpful like the girl across the row from her.

She learned this thing about the stems when she'd gotten in a little trouble. At home and on Grandma Sims's farm, they didn't care about stems, maybe because those weren't going to be sold. These were the things you thought about when you picked beans for several hours a day.

That first day, she had dumped her beans from the cotton shoulder bag into the basket in her row and the foreman had stopped her, putting his big hand on her arm, which alarmed her. He said gruffly, "You cain't put them beans with stems on 'em in the basket, girl. You take those out and snap off the stems, best you can. But you don't get paid for the time to take the stems off, you hear?"

She nodded obediently, embarrassed to have been reprimanded, but she hadn't known. She thought she'd paid attention when they told her what to do and she was tempted to say, "Nobody told me that," but she knew it was not smart to talk back, and she tried always to be respectful of men and ask the right questions of them. She also wasn't sure if she was out of the "Children should be seen and not heard, and only speak when spoken to" part of her life yet. So, she dutifully lifted and picked out the beans with stems on them, made a sling in her lap with her apron, and sat down on the dirt out of the way of the other workers and snapped off the stems.

The task only took her about fifteen minutes, and when she approached the foreman timidly and showed him the corrected work in her bag, she said, "See, I took the stems off like you said. I'll work an extra quarter hour today."

"Okay, that's good. I hope you learned a lesson. Now you can go ahead and put them in the basket."

Each afternoon, Frances pocketed her eighty cents, sometimes a little more. She'd been right that she wasn't going to be able to work eight hours a day, especially when she was expected to help with dinner and the children when she got home. Mother was happy, though, that she'd gotten herself a job and was intending to buy herself a dress. It meant she wouldn't even have to buy material for Frances to sew.

There was another family that left early, after lunch. Frances rode back to Ogden in their truck most days, and they usually dropped her off closer to home. If she couldn't get a ride, she'd try to work at least six hours. She noticed that the foreman was nicer to the people who stayed all day.

Then of course she came home all sweaty, and bath night wasn't until Saturday, so then she'd do what Mother called a "spits" bath, where you used so little water to wash parts other than your hands that it was like spitting in a basin.

Frances worked for four weeks. That was what she'd figured out she needed to do to buy the straw hat (Ronald had been right; she really did need one, the bandana was not sufficient) and maybe three good dresses, since a cheap one for a girl was $2.50 and an extra good or warmer one was about $5.00. She'd still have a dollar or two left over to spend as she wished—maybe to go see *The Last of the Mohicans* picture show at the Ogden Theatre, unless there was a romance playing at the Orpheum. Most of the bean crop was in, anyway, and she didn't think she wanted to go on to picking tomatoes or melons or any of the more difficult crops.

She was excited about getting some new clothes—real, store-bought dresses. She and Lucille were going to take the streetcar (Lucille had a little spending money her parents had given her) down to The Leader clothing store on Washington to shop. It was only about a block from Farr's feed store, and Frances had seen the signs in the windows at The Leader saying they had a sale.

Naomi cautioned Frances before she left the house that morning, "Now, don't you go down to the train station area. That street is full of places girls shouldn't go without their parents. I don't want to hear later that someone saw you down there. Just because it's close to home doesn't mean you can spend time there."

She'd given Frances her most serious look, her green eyes staring into eyes the exact same shade but twenty years younger.

Frances had heard that there were places where people went dancing, but she knew she wasn't old enough to go into them yet anyway. She enjoyed watching other friends' sisters practice dancing at home, and she was learning the foxtrot with Lucille, trading off doing the girls' and the boys' steps, so they'd be ready for high school dances. That seemed like a long way into their future right now, but it was never too early to learn things older girls knew.

"I *know*, Mother. Everybody knows that."

"Please don't take that tone with me, young lady!" Naomi shot back. "You're lucky I let you work, and go off to spend money like this. I could be asking you to put it into the house account. Don't you forget that."

"All right," Frances said, looking at the carpet. She fidgeted a bit with her purse and hoped this didn't mean she was going to have to listen to a lecture and be late meeting up with Lucille.

"You go on and have a good time," Naomi said. "Pick out something real pretty for yourself. You worked hard. And be home by mid-afternoon so you can help with the mending or take Marie or one of your brothers out for a walk."

"All right, Mother," Frances said, trying to contain her excitement. "We're going to maybe go for a soda after we're done shopping, and then stop at Lucille's to show her mother what we got. I'll come home right after that!"

"What color do you think you'll get?" Lucille asked as they gazed out the streetcar window at the houses, the park, and the stores they passed. Frances was thinking how satisfying it was to have her own money to even be able to take the streetcar. Maybe they'd get a root beer float on the way home, or at least a soda, like she'd told Mother, at Farr Better Ice Cream on Twenty-First Street. She wondered if the feed store was owned by the same man.

She realized at that moment that she was lost in her thoughts, which was how she often was, and should respond to Lucille's question, which she thought was about what color dress she wanted.

"Oh, blue, for one of them. Blue's my favorite. Not brown, I don't like brown very much."

"I just want a print with flowers in it," Lucille said absently.

"I'd like that too, except I have to think about dresses for fall and winter. I won't be buying anything like that today," Frances replied, ever the practical oldest sister.

"Oh. Yes, I didn't think about that. Maybe I'll get something more for fall too," Lucille said without much conviction.

Entering the clothing store felt like walking into a wonderland to Frances. She knew that Lucille, with her smaller family of siblings, had bought dresses before, but Frances had often worn either dresses made by her mother or hand-me-downs from cousins. She knew she'd had more store-bought dresses when she was very small, but not once their family grew.

Frances voiced some of her thoughts to Lucille, since she was her best friend. "When Daddy gets promoted to engineer, I won't have to work in the summer anymore. Mother and Daddy will be able to buy my clothes. I am learning to sew, though; then when I want something nice, to go to a dance or something when I'm in high school, I can make things that might be more expensive."

"Oh, I remember you said your father was getting a better job—I don't mean better someplace else," Lucille hurried to clarify, "I mean, well, maybe a higher-up position. And I guess they'd pay him more, then."

Lucille's father was an insurance salesman and wore a suit to work every day. Railroad men did something more like physical labor, unless they worked in the depot office. Frances appreciated that her friend was always careful not to emphasize the difference between their fathers' jobs.

The girls leisurely looked through the racks of dresses in their size range, age twelve or thirteen. Most were drop-waisted; styles had changed quite a bit the previous year, and it was popular for women to look more flat-chested and thin instead of voluptuous. This was of benefit to Frances and Lucille, who, at their age, fit that body style without even having to try.

Frances found a dress in royal blue, with green piping along the collar and the cuffs on its sleeves. She approached a sales lady and asked if she could try it on.

The pretty clerk—neatly dressed in a white summer polka dot dress, and made up with red lipstick—smiled, tickled that these two girls were on a shopping spree alone. "There are dressing rooms in the back of the store; come with me and I'll show you."

Frances, appreciative of how encouraging the woman was being, fell in behind her. Lucille followed, though she hadn't picked anything for herself yet.

The clerk led them into a hall with curtained doors all along it. The walls stopped at the top of the doors; you could see there were lights inside each dressing room. She slid one of the curtains aside and showed Frances where to hang the dress; at her diminutive height, she could barely reach the hook.

The clerk hung the blue dress on the hook for her and said, "You can hang your own dress here too, on one of these extra hangers, while you try on your selection. I'll leave you two girls. Just call out if you need any help." She smiled again before walking away.

Lucille was taller, so she took the dress off the hanger and handed it to Frances, who had turned aside modestly to take off her own dress. She was just beginning to develop, and even Lucille had not seen her in her undershirt lately. Frances turned slightly to hand her dress to Lucille and take the new dress. She lifted it over her head; it even smelled like a new dress!

It fit well—a little bit long, but Frances knew how to take up the hem and then let it down again if she grew in the next year or two. She hoped she'd get a little taller; at four feet, ten inches, she didn't want to be called a midget, like some of the boys at school had teased her. Lucille said they did it because they liked her, but Frances wasn't sure.

Frances looked at herself in the dressing room mirror and couldn't suppress her smile.

"Oh!" said Lucille. "That looks just fine on you! Do you like it? You do, don't you?! Is this your *selection*, miss?"

The girls both giggled.

"Yes, I do like it," Frances said, looking at the price tag. "This is $3.98. I can afford that, and still get two more."

The girls tried on several other dresses, finding some unflattering, some that didn't fit, some that were too expensive, and some just right, like Goldilocks and the porridge. They couldn't remember ever having had so much fun. Frances found two more dresses she liked, and Lucille, knowing that her mother would buy her at least one fall or winter dress for school in a month or two, did at last get a summery flowered dress.

Finding that she had been economical enough in her dress shopping that she had a little money left, besides the two dollars she was putting aside "just in case," Frances bought some new underthings in addition to her dresses. She was tired of darning everything all the time, and some of her unmentionables were getting a little tight.

She was happy to have three new frocks, even though her fingers were raw from all the field work, and happy to have a friend like Lucille, even if she wasn't a Lutheran.

Chapter 11

Ogden, Utah
Midsummer 1921

A couple of days after Frances's shopping trip, Naomi and Frank sat in the kitchen after dinner, drinking coffee, while Naomi held Willie. She eventually put him on the floor to crawl after his two brothers, George and Grant, who were rolling two wooden cars around. Naomi had learned early on with Hermann and Henry that with twins you had to give each of them the same thing, or the one without would make you regret it.

"You know, Frances got those three pretty dresses with the money she earned picking beans," she said to her husband.

"Yes, that was quite something!" he said, feeling a swell of pride for his eldest child. "I'm happy she learned that she can earn money and buy the things she wants. She's got a good head for money, seems like."

"Yes, that's true . . . and I'm glad as well. But . . . Sis feels bad now. She sees Frances has new clothes in the closet, and she's got nothing new. I told her the same thing I told Frances—she can have some material and make herself a dress—but she's not as skilled a sewer yet as Frances is. And even Frances said she can't make the nicer things she'd like to be wearing. The girls are only twelve and eleven, after all."

"Well, Frances will be thirteen in a few months. Shouldn't she be learning to do things older girls can do, like sew the more complicated clothes?" He didn't see what the problem was.

"I suppose, yes. But I was thinking . . . maybe we should make Frances give one of the dresses to Sis."

"What?" Frank shook his head. "That doesn't seem fair. The girl worked hard for her money, and she spent it on something useful. And I wonder if maybe you just favor Anita."

"Well, I don't know that I favor Sis any more than you favor Frances, but Sis had to do some extra chores around here while Frances wasn't around. And how's it going to look when we go to church and one of our older daughters is all dressed up in something new and her sister, only a year younger, is in something old, hmm?" She stooped to grab a bug out of Willie's hand, flicked it into the garbage, and sat back in her chair.

People will talk, no doubt about that, Frank thought. "Huh. I hadn't thought of that. People will think we bought Frances a dress and not her sister."

"I think we have to agree on this," Naomi said. "I don't want it to look like it was just my idea. So, we have to tell her soon, and together; it can't be when you've gone again."

Damn it, Frank thought, but he said, "You're right. She's not gonna like this, but it has to be done."

Frances wondered why on earth her mother said that she and her father wanted to have a talk with her alone after Sunday lunch when the other children were all outside. She hadn't done anything wrong that she could think of. She hadn't even talked back lately, though she'd felt like it once or twice. Maybe it was something good—a reward for going out and working and buying her own clothes. But she knew that one less pair of hands around the house had made things harder on her mother and Sis. She thought back and realized that she hadn't helped as much with the canning this year. It seemed like a "damned if you do, damned if you don't" situation . . . though she'd never say "damn" out loud.

"Frances . . ." began her father.

She felt more concerned, now, with her father starting the conversation.

"You know, we are glad you had the gumption to go out and find some work, and earn some money, and then go buy the dresses you wanted. That showed you are growing up."

"Yes," chimed in her mother. "That was a really good thing."

Frances wondered where this was heading.

Frank cleared his throat and looked at the living room floor, then steadied his gaze on her. "You know, Sister had to do a lot of your chores while you were gone those weeks."

"But I did as much as I could!" Frances protested. "And it was summer, we don't have things like ironing school clothes and making bag lunches and doing homework . . . I think I did as many chores as I usually do! Maybe not as much canning for those weeks, but mostly—"

"Yes, all that is true," Naomi interrupted, "but now Sis feels bad that she doesn't have a new dress too, and we think it's just a little unfair."

"I can't help that. She could get a babysitting job or something. And Sis . . . she's only a year younger than me! She could have picked beans too!"

"She would have had a hard time getting other work while she was doing your chores," said her father. "So, we want you to give one of your dresses to Sister."

"What?!" Frances felt the blood rise in her cheeks. "That's really not fair! I worked so hard! My fingers hurt every day. I had to work for days just to buy even one dress!"

"Yes, we know that. That is what people have to do as they get older, as children get bigger," Frank said with conviction. "They have to work to get the things they want."

Frances looked from her father to her mother and back. She couldn't believe they were asking this of her. And Sis had actually *dared* her to get a job. She couldn't hold back the tears. "But talk about not fair! It's not fair for me to have to give away what I worked for. I'm still not a grown-up!" she blurted out, sobbing and turning her face away as she wiped tears from her cheeks.

"You're almost grown, though," said Frank. "You are going to be a teenager. My gosh, you get to go to junior high. I didn't go to school after eighth grade. I started working on my parents' farm and then got jobs in grocery stores and driving a horse and buggy, and then as a newsboy on the railroad. You are lucky you can stay in school. That is better than your mother and I got. Do you see that?"

Frances tried to compose herself. She didn't want the other kids to come in and see her crying. They would think she was in trouble for doing something bad, to have a talk with her parents alone and then be crying.

"Yes . . . I guess. I still think it's not right, though. Sister's just as big as I am. And just as smart. Maybe smarter. Mother, you just want to do this because Anita is your favorite. You love Anita more."

"Hey, hey there, now," said Frank, his voice becoming void of tenderness. "You are not to speak to your mother this way. You stop your crying, or we'll give you something to cry about."

Frances didn't say anything more, but she was having a lot of angry thoughts.

Naomi put her hand on Frances's arm. "I love all you kids the same. And you can choose which one you want to give Sister. Then you'll be keeping the ones you like the best."

"I like all of them the same," Frances said.

"I think you need to go to your room and make your decision," Frank said sternly.

Frances set her jaw hard, got up slowly, and went to the kitchen to get a rag to wipe her face before the other kids saw her. Then she went to the girls' bedroom and shut the door quietly, though she felt like slamming it.

Frances decided to give Sis the blue dress with the green piping. One of the other dresses was blue too, and she did like it just a little better. She took the garment she'd chosen out of the closet and gazed at it. Now every time Anita wore it she'd have that pushed in her face, remembering how hard she had worked to buy it.

Life was just not fair, especially for girls. She made an inner vow not to speak to her parents unless she had to. That was what her dad did when he got mad; he'd walk around the house in a snit for a week, if he was home. So, she'd do the same.

Now she really was getting interested in growing up, whatever that meant and whatever it took. But not so she could buy more dresses for her sister.

Chapter 12

Ogden, Utah
February 14, 1922

Almost everyone in the house had had the influenza. The older kids were glad to all be back in school. Frances missed the tradition of exchanging valentines with her schoolmates, as they'd done in the early years of elementary school, but Lucille had given her one, as had one of her other friends at South Junior High. And her mother always gave each of the children a homemade valentine and made heart-shaped cookies or cupcakes with pink frosting. The children made valentines for their mother and father and sometimes their siblings.

Frances always arrived home later than the other children, who got out of grammar school earlier. She anticipated the surprise would be on her bed that afternoon . . . but no valentine. She was disappointed, but assumed her mother just hadn't had time with so many sick kids recently. George and Grant were still coughing a lot.

She pulled her homework out of her book bag and took it in to the kitchen table to get started on her algebra. There was nobody in the kitchen. Out the kitchen window, she could see Carl with Hermann, Henry, Frank, Marie, and George in the backyard. Why wasn't Grant with them?

She checked the nursery, and there found not only her mother, Sis, and Grant but also a doctor, with his stethoscope placed gently on little Grant's chest.

"Mrs. Wolff, he doesn't sound good," he said as Frances entered the room. "This influenza seems to have moved into his bronchioles, and I'm afraid it's sounding like pneumonia. We can take the child to the hospital, or you can continue to care for him here at home. I'd suggest you keep him in your room, away from the other boys."

Naomi hated to sound like the money made a difference, but she had to ask: "How much does it cost at the hospital, Dr. Emmett?"

"It's about ten dollars a day," the doctor said. "That's for a shared room or a room in a ward with others. He'd have nursing care but not a dedicated nurse. That's extra."

"I don't know . . . I need to ask my husband and he's away." *Frank will be skeptical. That's a lot of money, especially if Grant has to be in the hospital for days.*

"Can you reach him?"

"I can try sending a telegram, but he's out on the rails and I'm not sure where to send it."

Naomi wrung her hands and bit a fingernail absentmindedly. *Oh, why do I have to always be the one to make these decisions?* "If we keep him home, what should I do to care for him?"

"He needs to breathe steam, but if this gets worse . . . I fear he is too small for us to give him mercury to try to kill the bacteria," Dr. Emmett said grimly.

"Why didn't the other kids get this sick?" Naomi asked, her brows knitted.

"He probably just doesn't have as strong a constitution as the other children," the doctor said. "We see this in twins sometimes—that one will be strong and the other one weaker. Besides the steam, you can also give him a menthol rub on his chest and have him sleep sitting up, or at least at an incline, with several pillows. He'll breathe easier if he's upright."

"Oh, my lord, my lord," moaned Naomi.

"Mama!" whispered Grant, which set off his croupy coughing again.

"Honey, try to be calm," Naomi told him tenderly, kissing him on the head and stroking his arm. She looked up at her daughters. Anita, holding Willie and standing near the doorway with Frances, looked almost panicked. Frances's brow was furrowed with worry.

"Girls," said Dr. Emmett, "you should keep your baby brother out of this room until Grant is set up in your mother's room. Make sure he doesn't sleep in the same room. How old is the baby now, Mrs. Wolff?"

"He's a year and a half," Naomi said distractedly. "Yes . . . we'll get Grant set up in our bedroom on the folding cot, and move Willie's crib into the hall for the night."

"Well, the baby's not in extreme danger at his age, but we don't want him to get this," the doctor said. "It's doubtful he could fight it off. But Mrs. Wolff, did I understand that you are pregnant?"

"I am. Again."

"How many months?"

"I'm not sure, but maybe three months."

He pursed his lips in thought. "You'll need to be very careful that you also don't get the infection. Perhaps tie a mask over your nose and mouth when you are close to little Grant."

"A mask?"

"Yes, I'll have my nurse bring you a couple. They can be washed regularly."

One more chore, Naomi thought wearily. Her gaze landed on Frances. Judging by her oldest daughter's expression, she was almost certainly having the same thought as her mother.

When Frank came home two days later, Grant was no better; in fact, maybe a little worse. Frank and Naomi sat at the kitchen table.

"What did the doctor say to do?" Frank asked his wife with concern, wondering if she was caring for these kids as well as she ought to be.

"He said . . . well, he said that maybe Grant should be in the hospital. But it costs ten dollars a day." Naomi related the rest of what the doctor had said, all the instructions, and finished with, "And then we'd just have to wait and see. But he's not getting better."

Frank had listened somewhat impatiently for the end of this information. "Weren't you watching him to see if he got sicker?"

"Yes, I was watching him! For God sakes, Frank. You know everybody in this house had the flu. His just turned into pneumonia, in his bronchial tubes I guess. I'm not a doctor. You can go talk to the doctor if you think I did something wrong!"

Surprised by her outburst, he softened his tone. "You don't need to swear. I just wondered what else you could have done. I mean, George seems to have gotten over the influenza."

"Don't you think I've done everything I could? Dr. Emmett said sometimes one twin is weaker than the other, so maybe that's the case with them."

"Well, Hermann and Henry, they're both strong."

"*Oh-h-h!*" Naomi growled. "I don't know *what* to tell you. If you are bound to blame me, well there's nothing I can do about that. I take care of all our children the same way. I haven't neglected Grant.

Frances, Sis, and Carl and I have all been taking care of him; he's hardly ever alone. It's not easy to watch over ten children more or less alone, Frank. And I've got morning sickness. I have to care for myself too; sometimes I am in there fixing ten breakfasts when I've just been sick in the water closet. Can't you see this is hard for me, to have our little boy so sick the doctor says he should be in the hospital?!" Tears filled Naomi's eyes. She put her forehead in her hand and rested her elbow on the table while she quietly sobbed.

Frank looked away. He was not sure if she was to blame; he just wondered. He wasn't here to see what she did or didn't do a lot of the time. *None of the kids ever say they are neglected. They never go hungry . . . well, that's thanks to me, mostly . . . and they're always clothed; they aren't running in the street barefooted except in the summer . . . they don't get hurt very much . . .*

"Okay, okay," he said, trying to use a conciliatory tone. Of course, this had to be upsetting for a mother. "Let's wait a few more days, and if he doesn't get better maybe we'll take him to the hospital."

If he has to be in there a week, that could be more than ten days' pay. The railroad pays if I get hurt, but I don't think they'll pay anything for my family to be in the hospital. What a kettle of fish. The poor little guy.

Some days it seemed like Grant was almost holding his own, but most days he was clearly getting worse. Some days his breathing was more labored and he slept more, though fitfully. His fever was the same. Naomi and the older children kept cool washcloths on his forehead and brought him water continually, although sometimes just swallowing made him cough. They got him to eat soup if they could. The girls kept a pot of water on the stove on low, then they could turn it up every hour or two and hold him standing on a chair over the pot, a towel over his head. At first he was strong enough to stand on a chair on his own over the pot, then he was weaker and someone had to hold him to keep him upright, and finally they were holding him in their arms, his upper body mostly dangling over the pot—no small thing with a boy who weighed almost thirty pounds.

Naomi had taken to staring out the window, cuddling Willie, when he was willing to sit still long enough. She cried sometimes when she was alone but didn't have much time to indulge in that.

Dear God, please let my little boy get better. Please show me what you want me to do. If I have done something displeasing in your sight, don't take it out on him. In the name of Jesus Christ, Amen.

This was her prayer, several times a day. She had had sick children before, and she knew other mothers who seemed to be good women had sick children too.

Chapter 13

Ogden, Utah
February 24, 1922

Dr. Emmett pulled the sheet up over Grant's small form. There was no need to close his eyelids; he'd been sleeping when he went.

"I'm so very sorry, Mrs. Wolff. So very sorry. You did all you could. He is with God now."

Naomi did not think she could live through this sorrow.

A wail escaped her, seeming to come not just from her heart and voice but from the center of her being, her gut, her soul. She dropped to her knees—her hands atop her son's body, her forehead resting on the mattress of the cot—while her body shook with grief.

"Oh, my God, my God. My boy. My darling boy." Her sobs permeated the house.

Anita put her hand on her mother's back.

"Mama? Mama!" cried George as he ran into his parents' bedroom.

Frances grabbed her little brother by the arm, turned with him back into the hallway, and quietly shut the bedroom door.

"My brudder! My brudder Gwant! Mama!" George cried, kicking and attempting to pull away from Frances.

She picked him up—a challenge, given her diminutive size and the weight of the three-and-a-half-year-old boy—and held him close.

"There, there, shh. Grant is with the angels now; he's with Jesus. Shh . . ."

She carried George into the living room, where her father had dozed off on the davenport, his head resting on the doily pinned on the back, a wedding gift Grandma Sims had made to protect the upholstery from men's hair oil. He opened his eyes, sat more upright, and looked at Frances with the squirming George in her arms. The tears in her eyes seemed to tell him what he needed to know.

"Oh, no. It's happened, hasn't it?"

"Yes, Daddy, Grant . . . he's . . ." She couldn't finish her sentence. She sat down with George at the other end of the davenport and tried to calm him while his sobbing subsided, and tears slid down her face quietly.

Frank reached over and put his hand on Frances's arm. "Where's Sis?"

"She's with Mother, and the doctor."

"And where is Carl?"

"I think he's making lunches for all the kids in the kitchen."

"Carl?" Frank called out. "Carl? Come in here . . ."

Carl answered from the kitchen, "I'm making sandwiches."

"Just come in here! Now!"

Carl appeared in the doorway, and upon seeing Frances and George in tears, his shoulders slumped. "Oh . . . oh, no . . ."

"Your little brother is gone, Carl," Frank said with a catch in his voice. He cleared his throat. "You have to go down to the church and tell Reverend Kaiswer or Reverend Schlicting that he's died. They will need to make funeral arrangements."

"But . . ." Carl hesitated. "Umm . . . I have a test today. And the church . . . it's a forty-five-minute walk. Can I go to one of the pastors' houses if they're home?"

"Damn it, son, your test can wait," Frank snapped. "Your mother will give your teacher a note or something. And yes, that's fine, go to the Reverend's house. Or find somebody who will send the pastor here. Maybe Mrs. Abbott will take you if her car is there. Check with her first. Just do as I say."

Frances volunteered, "I'll finish the sandwiches when I can get George calmed down. Or Sis can. Anyway, I don't know who's going to school today and who's not. Hermann, Henry, Frank, and Marie are all dressed and ready . . ."

As she spoke, Marie and Frank Jr. appeared in the hall, hanging back a little from the doorway, their faces full of concern.

"Kids, you go back in the bedroom for a few minutes." Frances called out, "Hermann? Henry? Keep Frank and Marie with you for a while. I'll be in there in a few minutes. Did you hear me?"

"Yes," the twins called out in unison, and each came to take a hand of their siblings.

Frank sighed in weariness. "The younger kids should all go. It will be easier around here if there are less children underfoot. Frances, you or Sis need to go get a neighbor to be here with your mother, or one of her friends from the church. You need to tell Mrs. Abbott, anyway, unless Carl does it."

"But aren't you going to be here?" Frances asked.

"Yes, yes, for heaven's sake, but your mother will need another woman here," he said with irritation. "You kids are just going to have to do what I say when I say it. I am not going to explain every darn thing I ask you to do! Now, do you understand me?!"

Frances and Carl nodded obediently. Carl got his jacket and left on his sad errand; Frances heard him sniffle as he went out the front door. He had just turned ten—too big to cry, but too young to shoulder the full responsibilities of a man. Still, he was the oldest boy, and he was expected to act like he knew what that meant.

Anita came out of the bedroom, her eyes red from crying. "Daddy . . . I think Mother needs you."

"Yes . . . I know. Frances, tell your sister what needs to be done." Frank stood slowly, stretching his back. He hung his head a moment, took off his glasses, ran a hand over his eyes, and, with heavy steps, made the sad walk to the bedroom.

Frances thought the day her brother died had been the most mournful day imaginable, but the funeral was even worse. First they sat through the regular Sunday sermon and then there was the memorial part, with Grant's casket at the front of the church. She could hear the sniffles and muffled crying of many women in the congregation, some of whom knew what it was to lose a child. Then the family piled back into several cars, provided by the kind Lutherans for the day's journeys, and made their way out to the cemetery.

They called it Mountain View because you could see the mountains, but you could see the Wasatch Mountains from anyplace in Ogden. And Frances had heard they were going to change the name anyway. These and other random thoughts had flitted around in her head while she helped dress the children in the darkest colors each had in the closet. Since she had a brown dress, Anita was wearing that and had let Frances wear the infamous blue dress, although it was perhaps a little too cheery for the occasion. Naomi was of course in black; Frank Sr. and Carl both had black jackets.

The grave seemed such a big hole with the mound of earth piled next to it, but Frances had heard a couple of women mention how sad it was to see such a tiny casket, so she knew that adult deaths must require an immense grave to be dug. What an awful job that must be. The casket was a simple one; Frances knew her parents wished they could have afforded something better to honor Grant, but they had gotten the maple with a white satin lining. Partly because that was what was available on short notice. She wished she could stop all these thoughts, but after all, her mother always said she was the practical one.

Frances and Anita had both lost their composure when they filed past his body in the church. Grant looked peaceful and still, but even more pale than when he'd been sick. Frances had choked back a sob and then taken infant Willie from Naomi's arms in order to get herself outside of the church as quickly as possible, and Anita had led George out by the hand as well. He'd been pretty hard to handle in the two days since his twin had died, and there had been a moment when they thought they might need to take him to a neighbor rather than bring him to the church and the cemetery. But Naomi and Frank had felt that the whole family should be together for Grant's service and burial.

Frances had cleared the kitchen and dining room tables before they left the house, in preparation for the people her parents said would be stopping by the house with hot dishes, bread, canned fruits, vegetables, and pies. Things that guests would eat, which would also provide leftovers that would keep a few days. Mrs. Abbott had said she'd come over to heat food up, set things out, and pour coffee for people. Bring over extra dishes. She was very kind to offer that.

Naomi and Deborah Abbott were not close friends, but they helped each other out from time to time.

Frances was glad to get home and not have much in the way of chores that day. She and her siblings mostly stayed in their rooms, or went outside, despite the cold, or hung around the living room and dining room out of the way, quietly listening to the adults talk.

"Such a shame."

"So sad. Just a little tyke."

"Poor Naomi, she's already home alone so much with all these young'uns . . . and now to have this on her heart."

"That ground must have been very hard to dig in this cold. Only blessing in this, such a small grave."

"Naomi, you let me know if there's anything I can do."

Frances knew she wouldn't. It wasn't her mother's way to ask outside the family for help unless she knew she could soon return the favor.

The men talked about the railroad or their other work, and whether the next snow would be heavy. Anything to avoid the sadness.

Chapter 14

Ogden, Utah, & Evanston, Wyoming
Summer and Autumn 1922

"Mother, this year can you buy me something new for school?" Frances asked her mother while they rolled out pie crust.

"No . . . no, we can't," her mother said wearily. "You know we had to pay a lot for Grant's doctor and his funeral and burial, and now I have another baby coming soon and we'll have to pay a doctor again. Plus, it's costing us more and more to live with all the mouths to feed around here. Your dad can't work any harder than he's already working. You worked last summer to buy your school clothes . . . and you can always get a little work doing something, ironing or babysitting or helping clean house . . . or cleaning one of the stores downtown. Besides, you need another dress like you need another hole in your head. What've you got, six or seven dresses now? Your dad and I . . ." Her eyes darted to Frances's, then back down at the pastry. "We won't be buying you any more clothing now that you're able to work and buy your own."

"But . . . I'm still your child!" Frances protested. "You still buy clothes for Sis and the others! I go to school, I do chores here, I take care of the kids . . . Other girls my age are just having a summer!"

"Well, you're not other girls, you're Frances Wolff, and she is a grown-up girl going on fourteen who can buy or make her own clothes. And I'll bet some of those girls are working; you just haven't talked to them to find out. If I were you, I'd get some work this summer, buy material, and get on that sewing machine. As for Sis—she ends up with your or somebody else's hand-me-downs, usually. It's not like she's the fashion plate of Ogden. Now, you just have to grow up, Frances." Naomi bit a fingernail.

Frances knew not to argue. But her face was hot with humiliation. She had thought the need to go out and work for her clothing was a one-time thing. It had never crossed her mind that that would be the end of her parents' providing clothing for her. That winter coat when she turned twelve was the last of it? She could hardly believe it.

What else will they take away? Shoes? Those cost even more than dresses. Good thing she didn't grow very fast.

Frances gritted her teeth—her bad teeth, which ached sometimes—and pushed the rolling pin hard.

Frank was thankful to get back to Evanston. After the winter, with its sickness and death, and then Naomi's moroseness despite her ripening belly, he was happy to be out on the rails again and happier still to stay at Minnie Woods's place. There was that woman in Chicago, but she was only a passing fancy. Every time he passed through, of course, but what he felt for her was nothing like the feelings he had for Minnie.

"Oh, Frank, good to see you again," Minnie said when he arrived, and she gave him a wink and a sly smile when her children were not looking. "Yes, as it happens, I do have a room free. We have another boarder right now, but the kids can sleep in the parlor."

He knew they might not get much, if any, time alone, but here was a woman with fewer problems and fewer children, and being in this house was like a vacation after being in his own. He hoped she'd arrange for the children to be elsewhere at some point in the two days he'd be there, if only for an hour.

Naomi thought this must be the hottest August she could remember. Shouldn't it be cooling by now? This pregnancy was really getting to her. She hoped she'd have another girl; the boys were helpful, of course, but what she really needed was more help around the house.

Her labor on September 3 was uneventful, other than that Frank didn't make it home in time to greet his eleventh child. Well, thirteenth if you counted those little ones in 1919. And she *was* a girl, thank God; Naomi decided to name her Dorothy.

For late summer and into the fall, Frances and Anita, when they were home from school, had most of the care responsibility for Willie, who was two and beginning, in the form of words and demands, to make his mark on the world—usually in an endearing way. Rarely still for a minute unless he was in his crib, though, just like all the rest of the Wolff kids. And getting used to a slap on his bottom if he caused any two-year-old trouble. George was pretty much back to being his normally cheerful self, and Marie had enjoyed kindergarten this year. Frank was six and a half and had a mischievous streak that bordered on devilish. Anita thought he hadn't had enough attention as a baby and toddler; Marie had come along only a year later, and everyone had been so happy to have a little girl that Frank had more or less become the extra boy.

Hermann and Henry were nine and a half now, and very helpful around the yard and for running errands and doing some of the heavier tasks—gardening, shoveling snow in the winter. And Carl, going on eleven, now had a paper delivery route and a bicycle and sometimes disciplined the younger boys with a cuff on the ear or by wrestling them to the floor if they didn't follow his lead. Carl was quieter than the other boys but firm in his mind, like his father.

Nicer, though, thought Anita.

Frank came home from Evanston in a foul mood. This time, he and Minnie had had no time alone together and she'd chastised him for expecting too much; after all, she had five children to raise and boarders to manage. At least she had kept a room open for him—but she had only half as many children as Naomi, and Naomi always made time for him . . . Of course, Naomi was his wife.

Maybe the next time he went through Evanston he'd just keep going and not spend the night. Maybe show Minnie what it was like to miss him. She had a pretty good idea of his schedule and usually knew the next time he'd pass through.

That was it. He'd stay longer in Chicago next time, even if Esther wasn't available there, and skip the Evanston overnight. Half the time Union Pacific didn't need him overnight, anyhow; he stayed by choice, in order to see Minnie.

He'd never have the feelings for Esther that he had for Minnie, or for Naomi, but she was fun for a night when he was out that way, especially after such a long run. He was glad he didn't usually have to pay for sex like many of the railroad men did; somehow being tall and blond and, let's face it, good-looking—he knew that from the mirror—and doing some sweet-talking was almost always enough. Sometimes it was hard to gauge, though, what it was women wanted; he knew that taking them out for a nice dinner and maybe a walk through a park seemed to be sufficient to woo them, since he was clearly not offering marriage and financial support to the women he had on the side. Thank God he didn't have to go through these gyrations with Naomi anymore—or with Minnie either, mostly. After all, he paid rent to stay at her place (or the railroad paid his rent there, when they actually did need him to stay), and the rest was her own free will. Sometimes he bought her a little gift—some flowers, a souvenir from a station, or maybe a simple brooch or a locket for her birthday—but he was careful about not spending too much on her. He couldn't afford it, for one. Their arrangement worked okay.

He arrived home to Grant Avenue on an autumn afternoon, when the younger children had all come home from school and were running in and out the doors, letting off their post–school day steam and being noisy as heck. Plus, the baby was crying in his bedroom while Naomi tried to calm her and nurse. Willie was running on his short legs from room to room, trying to catch any brother he could, his diaper about to fall off, and stumbling now and then when his chubby bare toes caught on a rug.

After a quick hello to Naomi, Frank shouted, "Okay, you kids! Everybody quiet down and stop running through the house! Children should be seen and not heard, for crying out loud!" He could never understand how Naomi could tolerate the chaos. When Frank was home, she usually rode herd on them, but she'd been a little less strict since the boy had died. The boy.

Grant, our son.

His admonition had only a moderate effect; the boys just laughed and speed-walked instead of running on their way from the back door out the front. They had a game of tag going and didn't intend to stop it. Little Frank called out, on his way down the steps, "Daddy can't stop us!" and laughed, which set the other boys to laughing too.

Frank stepped out on the porch and said—quietly, so that the neighbors wouldn't hear—"WHAT did you say, son?"

Little Frank stopped before rounding the house and repeated what he'd said, not realizing his father was not going to consider this a game. The twins and George snickered and tried to contain their mirth. Carl, oldest and fastest, had already made it to the back of the house. Besides, he definitely knew better than to tease his father.

Marie stood in the living room, her eyes wide.

Frank glared at his sons. "All of you boys back in the house, now. Marie, you get into the kitchen."

The four boys meekly came back into the house, but Henry tripped on the door sill on his way in and knocked over a vase, which crashed to the floor, breaking into several shards.

"Okay, that's it. That's enough."

Frank took off his belt and told the boys to bend over, one at a time, while he whipped them each several times.

Little Frank began crying.

"Stop that crying or you'll get it again!" Frank told his namesake through clenched teeth. "Now, I want each of you facing a corner. And you'll stay there until dinner."

Then he went into his bedroom and flopped down on the bed.

"Don't you dare let them leave the corners," he warned Naomi. "I can't stand all the noise around here. I come home tired and I want some peace and quiet."

Naomi waited a minute before she spoke. She had just gotten Dorothy to quiet down when the music of four boys being beaten and crying out had started up, which had set Dorothy to fussing again.

"I'm sure they deserved it, and I know it's the only way to get them to straighten up," Naomi said carefully. "But . . . as far as the noise goes, I live with it all the time. They're kids, and there are a lot of them. When they get home from school, after they've been sitting in a classroom all day, they need to run around."

"But not through the house, and not when their father has just come home from days of being out working. It is my house, and they need to respect that. And I won't have them talking back or laughing at me."

"Yes, well . . . I understand that. Better than anyone else in this house."

"Let's drop this. I just want to take a nap on my bed."

Naomi carried baby Dorothy into the kitchen, where Marie was playing with a doll. Willie toddled after his mother and grabbed her skirt, hoping for attention.

"Mama?" Marie asked her mother uneasily. "Am I in trouble too?"

"No, you're not, but all you kids have to learn not to make a lot of commotion when your father comes home. He likes peace and quiet and needs a nap." Naomi hoped for a little peace and quiet herself before she started dinner; Anita and then Frances would be home in a while. Sometimes the older girls went to the library after school, or stopped at a friend's house to visit.

She put the coffeepot on the stove to heat it up. She'd make a fresh pot for Frank after dinner. Only three children to watch, and only one of them a toddler on the move, and a cup of coffee. This was about as close as it got to solitude in her life.

When Anita came home two hours later, the living room was close to dark and four of her brothers were either standing or sitting facing a corner.

"What did you guys do?" she asked quietly.

"Frank talked back," Henry whispered, "and I broke a vase. And Hermann and George laughed when Frank talked back."

"Well, that would do it," Anita said, knowing her father and his expectations of his children. She gave her brothers a sympathetic look and went to her room.

Chapter 15

Stone Township, Oklahoma, & Ogden, Utah

Early October 1922

"Well, my girl, I'm surprised you could get away. But I'm glad to see you."

Naomi hugged her mother, who had taken Dorothy from her arms while Naomi pushed Willie in the stroller out of the station in Enid, Oklahoma. They piled her scant belongings and luggage into the back of the truck along with the stroller, and the four of them climbed into the cab.

"Mother, should you still be driving? You're seventy-six . . ."

"Seventy-six and healthy as a horse!" Nancy Sims replied. "And

I been drivin' this truck for years. I go slow; I don't let nobody push me."

"I just thought maybe one of your hired hands would come."

"Oh, like Charles Foreland?" Nancy laughed and gave Naomi a teasing look.

"Oh, is he working for you down here too?"

"Yup. I think I told you in my last letter. He'll be down here until harvest is in. Our wheat was real good this year, so I can pay 'im well."

"I wasn't thinking of Mr. Foreland. I just thought it was a long drive for you."

"Well, it's a nice drive on a nice day. So . . . I guess Frances and Anita are watching the rest of the children? They'll be cooking for Frank too, I suppose."

"Well, they're both old enough to be in charge at home, but of course they're in school too . . . and they can make fried-egg sandwiches for dinner, if nothing else. I taught 'em that a couple years ago so they'd be able to make something easy when I'm too tired or they have to make a meal on their own. You probably remember Frances is in high school; she'll be fourteen in a month. She sometimes works cleaning a boardinghouse, but she doesn't have much time to work, between school and helping at home."

"My gosh," Nancy said wonderingly. "She's a young woman already."

"I keep telling her that. I think she's halfway woman and halfway little girl yet. She hasn't gotten her period."

"Oh. I would have thought she would be in her courses by now. Well, she always seemed young in so many ways, but I thought it was just 'cause Frank coddled her when she was little, being the first girl and all. Daddy's girl. Do you pay Mrs. Abbott to take care of George, then?"

"No, no, I really can't pay her. But I give her fruit and vegetables I've canned, and I have the boys run errands for her. She doesn't have children at home anymore. But she works too; she's a nurse at the hospital. She's home in the morning, and Sis watches George in the afternoon. I'm lucky to have Mrs. Abbott. She's been real nice since I lost . . . since I lost Grant." Naomi looked out the window over the fields, wishing she hadn't brought up Grant.

"Oh, honey, I know—I know," her mother said soothingly. "Don't think about it. We're just going to have a nice time while you're here. It's only a week; you don't have to do much, unless you want to."

"I just had to get away," Naomi agreed. "I've not had barely a minute to myself; first the awful first part of the year, then the kids were all home from school all summer, and then Dorothy was born. Just one thing after the other. And seems like Frank spends over-nights in Evanston more than he used to. I guess they need him for maintenance and other things since now he's an engineer, not a fire-man. But his absence is stretching us apart some."

"Oh, I know all about that," her mother said with a slight shake of her head. "Your father has been gone away from me almost as much as he's been with me all these years. Women like us learn to survive on our own."

Charles Foreland greeted the two women with a wave from his perch on the tractor as they drove up the gravel drive. Nancy thought he looked unusually glad to see them; not a particularly demonstrative man, he had that reserve like many of the Cherokees around here. She glanced back and noticed his eyes still following the truck—maybe following Naomi's face, actually.

"Well, he looks cheerful today," Naomi noted.

"Yes, more than usual. Huh. Wonder what that's about." Then, with mischief in her voice, Nancy added, "Seems like he might be happy to see you!"

"Oh, nuts. That can't be true. I've barely ever talked to him."

"Well, you're a pretty woman, Naomi, and he's a single man, and you're here without your husband. Maybe he's at least looking forward to having you around to look at and maybe talk to."

"Oh, I'm a pretty woman? After bearing thirteen children and raising ten and working till my hands are raw? Yes, I'm just a regular Gloria Swanson, all the men falling at my feet!"

Nancy laughed. "Oh, girl, you're still pretty, don't you forget it. Don't you let Frank forget it either. Besides, you've got spunk. That goes a long way with men."

"Last thing on my mind is men right now, and that's the truth." Naomi sighed. "Just gimme some peace and quiet. Sittin' under a tree with a glass of lemonade sounds like enough to me. Maybe even reading a paper, like Frank does. Oh, Mama, I'm so glad to be here."

Back in Ogden, Frances was actually a little excited about fixing dinner. Fried-egg sandwiches were all well and good; she liked them a lot with butter, oleomargarine, or mayonnaise spread on the bread. But Carl had fixed them one night and Sis had made them another night, and that was about as much as Frances felt they could all stand in one week. Plus, they were almost out of eggs.

Wednesday night they'd eaten the pot roast their mother had made before she left. It was Saturday now, and with Mother out of town, Frances wanted to fix something a little different for Daddy. She'd had dinner at Lucille's recently and they'd had a casserole, something Mother didn't make very often, but it didn't seem that difficult. She'd asked Lucille's mother to write a recipe out for her, and found it to be pretty simple. She'd cook up some ground beef and boil some macaroni, cook some chopped onions, mix it up, grease a pan, spread it around, and bake it. With a lot of salt and pepper and cheese on top, she thought, Daddy would probably like it. And with green beans from the garden on the side—the kids could sit and trim them for her—it would be a pretty good meal, and would even cover most of the food groups she'd heard about in school.

She didn't have time to make a pie, but the kids would all have bread and butter with sugar on it and Daddy could have the few berries that were left in the icebox for dessert. Mother had said to save the oatmeal cookies she'd made on the prior weekend for Daddy if he wanted them.

The meal was a partial success.

All the children loved the satisfying casserole, but their father ate somewhat quietly.

Finally, Frances couldn't stand his silence any longer. "Daddy, do you like the casserole I made? We all worked on the green beans, but I made the casserole; it's Lucille's mother's recipe."

"Oh, yes, Frances, you did the cooking tonight; of course." Frank nodded. "That's your job as the oldest girl when your mother is away. And I like it well enough. It's not your mother's cooking, of course. But you're on your way to being a pretty good cook, and you will make a good wife to someone someday. I was hoping you'd make one of your berry pies. But you did a pretty good job for organizing this on your own. Next time I'm sure it will be better."

Frank was already pushing his chair away from the table when he noticed Frances's disappointed look. "Tell you what. Next time I'm here on a Saturday morning, I'll take Carl and the twins fishing uptown in the Ogden River; we'll hope to get some trout or bass, and your mother can teach you to fry up fish and potatoes. That will be a good meal. Don't worry, Frances, you'll make a good wife one day."

Frances felt deflated. The last thing she was worried about was being a good wife, not yet. And she'd made this meal especially for Daddy, although she also had wanted the practice in cooking something different. She'd thought he'd appreciate her experimenting and learning something new. It was true that Daddy was not very much interested in anything new—but still.

"I'm sorry, Daddy, I made this especially for you and thought you would like it," she said with a dash of resentment, her lips pursed. She made her signature bobblehead, ear-toward-shoulder movement that she couldn't help making when she felt like she was right.

"Oh, no, Frances, it wasn't *bad*," he said. "But like I said, you'll do better next time. You're a lot like me—you have to do things by trial and error. You look in the mirror and you'll see we've got the same nose!" He chuckled and gave Frances a wink. "Now, I'm going to read my paper in the living room, and I don't want any running around or noise. If you kids have to make noise, go run outside until it gets dark."

The younger boys silently passed a wide-eyed look back and forth between them. Little Frank suppressed a smile and a giggle. Frances frowned. Her mother absolutely would never let them play outside until dark. At night, there were more cars than horse carriages on Grant Avenue, and sometimes they drove too fast and the chance of them not seeing a child was higher.

Frank got up after most of the kids had murmured, "Yes, Daddy."

After he'd left the room, Anita, Carl, and Frances started clearing the table.

"I thought it was really good, Frances," Carl offered.

"Yes, I thought it was good too, Frances," added Anita in a somewhat rare showing of sisterly affection.

"Well, at least somebody liked it," Frances said, with little conviction.

"You know how Daddy is," Anita said quietly. "And you know all he really cares about right now is reading the paper and falling asleep in his chair."

"Well, that's the truth," Frances answered. "And you kids, you're not staying out until dark. You've got about an hour if you go outside, and then I want you all back in the house."

"But Daddy said!" Henry countered.

"Uh-uh, you know the rules," Frances said firmly. "It's not a free-for-all just because Mother's away."

"You're not Mother!" Little Frank piped up. "And . . . I want to go fishing too! It's not damn fair if I don't get to go."

"Well, like it or not, Sis and I are the mothers in the house until Mother gets home. It wasn't our idea to have to play Mama, and Grant Avenue isn't safe when it gets dark. And watch your tongue. If you get too smart, Daddy will wash your mouth out with soap."

"Aw, raspberries," complained Frank.

Carl put his hand on little Frank's shoulder. "We'll see, Frank. Daddy was just thinking about us older boys, but when we dig up worms in the backyard, if you help, he'll prob'ly let you come fishing too."

Frank Sr. was missing Naomi. He wasn't going to tell anyone that, and he might not even tell Naomi when she came home with the babies; he was still miffed that she'd gone to Oklahoma at all, but he understood that the last couple of years had been hard for her, losing the third set of twins and then losing Grant. And he liked that he didn't have to try to make her happy for a week—though he realized that was true most of the time anyhow; when he was gone on the rails, he was almost free as a bird, other than the hard work.

He started his shift Sunday afternoon, taking the train to Evanston. He wasn't even going to call at Minnie's house; he had arranged to transfer to a night train headed for St. Louis. Let her just wonder what happened. She couldn't reach him; he was in control. What was the name of that girl who worked in the boardinghouse in St. Louis? Maybe she'd be interested in a dinner out.

On his way back to Wyoming and Utah, he'd stop and see his mother in Prairie. She'd make him a perfect dinner: sauerkraut and bratwurst and potato pancakes. Now that was something to look forward to.

Frances had plans of her own for Sunday night. She'd been thinking about this for a month and thought that when her parents were both away overnight would be the best time to do it. She had been looking in the mirror more than usual lately and was all too aware of her nose being like her father's. Being in high school had made her more aware of her looks, and especially of her bad upper teeth, even though everyone seemed to agree that aside from the nose and teeth, she did resemble her pretty mother.

She took Naomi's hand mirror from her dresser into the bathroom and looked at herself again from the side, taking a good long look at her nose—the bane of her existence, as far as her looks went. Daddy had once told her to be proud of it; it was a Roman nose, with a bump just under the bridge, but otherwise long and straight and a little pointed. What did Roman women do about this, if they all had it?

Before she went to bed, Frances found a piece of flannel in her mother's sewing cupboard. The old piece they'd used for a baby sheet would do. She made a tiny cut on one end and ripped a piece about three inches wide and three feet long. Then she pulled the scrap as tightly as she could over the bump on her nose and tied it at the back of her head. It was uncomfortable, but she thought this would probably diminish that bump if she wore it overnight. And if it worked, she'd wear it every night until her nose was perfectly straight. It might be long and pointy, but she was determined for it to at least be straight.

Climbing into bed, Anita scoffed, "What in the world do you have tied on your head?!" and laughed aloud.

Frances answered defensively, "It's to make my nose bump flat. Don't laugh, you'll see."

Anita shook her head. "Now I've seen everything."

The girls both knew they'd hardly seen anything, except what you see in a big family every day: too many people with too many ideas and wants, and too many spankings.

Monday morning dawned a nice enough day, and Frances began readying herself for school. After she and Sis made breakfast for the family—simple cornflakes and milk, with a large serving of laughs from the children at the large, odd tie around Frances's head—she commandeered the bathroom and started to wash her face. She fiddled with the tie at the back of her head, but it was tightly secure. She washed around the flannel and felt a little panicky that she couldn't get it off. Anita had already left for school, and Carl was getting the younger kids out the door.

꙳ꙮ

Lucille had agreed to come by the house so she and Frances could walk to school together, and she was also curious about the success of the nose tie, having heard about her friend's plan. She appeared at the door just as most of the household was leaving and Hermann was taking George over to the Abbotts.

"Is Frances still here; is she ready for school?" she asked Carl.

"Oh, she's here, all right . . . but I don't think she's quite ready for school," he said with a smirk. In reply to her quizzical look, he said, "I think she's either in the girls' room or the bathroom." He shook his head, smiled, and continued on his way down the front steps.

Lucille found Frances on the verge of tears in the bathroom.

"Lucille! I can't get this thing off!"

"Oh, my gosh, Frances. Oh, my gosh. Here, let me help you." She struggled with the knot. "Boy, you really tied this thing on good. Do you have a crochet hook? I think I could loosen the knot with that if it was a strong metal one."

Frances found one in Naomi's sewing basket and handed it to Lucille, who worked the short, fat steel stick into the edge of the knot and gradually loosened it enough that she could untie it.

"There! Boy, that would have been a riot if you'd had to go to school that way!" Lucille said, hoping to make light of Frances's situation.

"Ha. I wouldn't have gone to school at all." Frances looked in the mirror and touched her nose.

It looked to Lucille like the bump was swollen.

Frances picked up the hand mirror, surveyed her profile, and groaned. "I think it's worse," she murmured, and her eyes began to tear up.

"Listen," Lucille said quickly, "you just took it off. You don't know how it's going to look by tonight. If anyone at school asks, just say you bumped your nose."

Frances stared at her nose from different angles and sighed. "Well, we're going to be late for school if I look at myself any longer."

The girls set off for South Junior High.

By the time evening came, Frances was pretty sure the bump on her nose was a little bigger than before. So much for her facial alteration technique.

Resigned to her genetic heritage, she wondered if anyone would ever find her attractive.

Chapter 16

Stone Township, Oklahoma
Early October 1922

Naomi sat under the shade tree out back of her parents' farm-house in the twig chair with a cushion in it, a pitcher of lemonade within her reach on the outdoor table, where the farmhands and the family often gathered for lunch. She'd brought along *The Age of Innocence*, by Edith Wharton, which she'd gotten at the Ogden library; she figured they'd never know she took it to Oklahoma, since it wasn't due back for weeks.

It was kind of entertaining reading about those people in New York City, with their strange ideas and ways. Who ever knew a countess, for heaven's sake? But it was supposed to be a little scandalous, and she thought it a good escape from her domestic—and, lately, too difficult—lower-middle-class life. She really didn't think about classes in society much; she didn't have time to think about that sort of thing. Her life was consumed by doing whatever was in front of her. She didn't understand all of the book, but it was something to do while she relaxed for this week, and sometimes it carried her right into a welcome nap.

Dorothy was asleep in the baby carriage next to her, and Willie played quietly with a stuffed animal and some blocks in the playpen her dad had made for visiting babies. With any luck, he'd fall asleep as well. She absentmindedly hummed "Toot, Toot Tootsie." They'd been playing that on the radio both at home and here almost every night.

It felt real good to do nothing, and Mama had been helping watch the babies so she could amble around the farm and nap now and then.

As Joe Sims approached his daughter, he saw that she was awake and looking more peaceful than when she'd first arrived.

"Oh, hi, Daddy," she said, smiling. "How did it go today?"

"Oh, my girl, you know, farmwork is farmwork. But we got a good harvest coming in. No rotten wheat this year. I'm tired, but I don't resent it today."

"How much longer you going to farm, Daddy? You and Mama gettin' on in years as you are . . . You are both seventy-six now. I worry about you."

"Well, darlin', you may's well keep on worryin' for a while cuz we'll be workin' for a while. But we get a lot of help from the hands, and that Charley will prob'ly be our foreman by next year, though he still goes up to Missouri to work his folks' land too. You'd know as well as anyone that the railroad makes it so's we can get help that don't live around here if we need to."

"Well, it's good you're home. You won't be going away again soon, will you?"

"Naomi, I have to go. I can make a lot more money in California, down in San Diego, when they harvest the oranges. That's part of why we can afford to pay the hands."

"But will you be with Mama for Christmas?"

"Yes, I'll go back down there first of the year. They harvest mostly in January."

"But don't you have to climb ladders? That just seems . . . risky."

"Oh, they have me managing crews, mostly. Inspecting the fruit. Making sure they fill the crates and there's nothing in there gonna cause the other oranges to go bad before they're shipped. Besides . . . the weather is way better down there than it is here. My rheumatism and arthritis get bad here in the cold, and not as much down there. It's kind of like a desert area, but with palm and orange trees."

"Don't you miss Mama, though?"

"'Course I do. But I'm so busy I don't get much time to think on what I wish is different. 'Sides, your mother and me . . . you know, we're mostly old friends by now. And you know that men have to go where the money is to take care of their families. You'd know that more than most women, married to a railroad man."

Naomi sighed. "I suppose I do know. When you get married, you have all these ideas. I mean, as a young girl, I did. I just knew I loved Frank and he seemed like he loved me and he had a good job and was a nice-looking man . . . and we'd be able to have a family . . . but then actually *having* a family—a big one—and having to manage on my own so much . . . it's not a fairy tale. At least on a farm, the husband is usually home."

"I guess that's mostly true," Joe said. "But when two people are workin' hard all the time on a farm . . . you know, you get so's you look at each other as these tired people you see day after day after long day. At least when Frank comes home, it's kind of like seeing each other again all new, maybe."

"Ha." Naomi tossed her head back. "Well, sometimes. More in the first five or ten years of our marriage, we were happy to see each other when he got home. I mean, we still are. But sometimes I wonder about him; it's almost like he resents coming home sometimes."

"How do ya mean?"

"He seems like he's happier when he's gone. I guess he gets more peace and quiet away from our house." She gave her father a *you know what I mean* glance. "And I wonder . . . I wonder if he ever . . . sees other women."

Joe cleared his throat and looked off in the distance. Not a subject he was happy to discuss. "Naomi, you have to understand that things are different for men than they are for women. I don't know if Frank ever sees other women, prob'ly he doesn't, but it don't mean anything if he does. He knows his wife and family are the most important in his life. And he pays for your keep. You don't want to be complaining to a man who's paying for your keep and your children's." He looked away again and saw that Charles was approaching them. Happy for the chance to change the subject, he waved. "Hey there, Charley, come on over here and have a glass of lemonade. You surely have earned it."

Charley took off his broad-brimmed hat with the colorful woven hat band and nodded to Naomi with a cautious smile. "Hey, Mrs. Wolff. You having a nice afternoon?"

Naomi smiled. "Yes, I'm enjoying my time here, such as it is," she said. "Have to go back to Ogden soon, so I'm livin' the Life of Riley for a few days."

Charley didn't recognize the expression but tried not to let on.

She seemed to notice his confusion. "Yes, sir," she added, "Like in that radio show, I'm just tryin' to learn to be lazy!"

He chuckled. "I'm sure you deserve it, Mrs. Wolff."

"Now, Charles, I told you before you can call me Naomi. I have to call you Mr. Foreland if you call me Mrs. Wolff."

"Yeah, Charley," Joe interjected. "We don't stand on ceremony around here, ya know. Well, I'm goin' to clean up. I'm done for the day. I'm about done *for*, in fact!" Joe laughed and heaved himself up from the bench.

Charley cleared his throat and took a sip of his lemonade. He felt like doing normal things might hide the slight nervousness he felt around Naomi Wolff. "What are these little ones' names?" he ventured.

"Oh, my baby girl here is Dorothy, and that rambunctious pup there is Willie," Naomi said. "He's just turned two recently, and the best place for him is right there in that playpen!"

"Hey, Willie," called Charley softly, so he wouldn't wake the baby. "You got some pretty nice toys in there, I see."

Willie picked up one of his blocks and tossed it out of the playpen. Charley picked it up, dusted it off, and tossed it back in, which elicited a big giggle out of Willie.

"How are your other children doing . . . Naomi?" Charley asked, carefully allowing himself to use her first name.

Naomi glanced down for a moment. "Well . . . I don't know if my mother told you, but I lost my little boy Grant early this year. He had the influenza, and then it went to pneumonia. His twin brother, George, was okay, though . . ." Naomi's voice trailed off as she gazed across the fields, pain apparent in her expression.

"I'm sorry," Charley said, regretting asking about her children.

"Oh, it can't be helped," Naomi said, as if the situation didn't matter. "Part of why I'm here is to take some time away from everything and everybody. The other kids are all fine. Frances is gonna be fourteen—she and her next sister, Anita, are holding down the fort while I'm gone. All my kids are good kids. My ten little Indians. You know that song? 'One little, two little, three little Indians,'" Naomi sang.

"Huh," Charley said with a chuckle. "Yeah, I've heard it, but we never sang it in our family." He thought it bad luck to talk about those who had died, so he changed the subject. "Say, when you called your boy Willie a pup, that made me think of a story. Hey, Willie, you want to hear a story?" He looked at Naomi and smiled and winked.

Willie exclaimed, "Sto-wee!" and pounded on the rungs of the playpen enthusiastically.

Charley took his response as a yes. "Okay. This is a story about a coyote. People on the reservations around here say the old Indians called them *coyotls*, but I just call them coyotes like most people do." He cleared his throat. "Coyote was hungry. Coyotes are always hungry."

Charley rubbed his belly and Willie shouted, "Hun-gee!" and pounded one of his blocks in response.

"Coyotes are also tricky. You can't always trust 'em. And when they're hungry, they're goin' around with big eyes, lookin' for somebody to eat!" Charley opened his eyes wide and stared down at Willie.

Willie opened his eyes wide too.

"Coyote was on the prowl, and he saw some possums up in a tree. 'Hey, possums, why don't you come down here and we'll talk a while?' he said, thinking the possums weren't too smart. The biggest possum said, 'Hey, Coyote, I know you want to eat me, but you can't get me!' and went out on a branch and danced, thinking he was outsmarting Coyote—and the branch broke!" Charley gasped and his eyes widened again.

Willie was mesmerized, and Naomi seemed well entertained as well. Encouraged, Charley continued.

"So Possum fell to the ground, and he and Coyote tussled." Charley picked up two of Willie's toys, a rag doll and a little stuffed animal, and pushed them together, making them have a pretend fight with quiet, guttural growls and little yips.

Willie giggled and laughed, his eyes sparkling, and Naomi chuckled.

"But Possum was stronger than Coyote expected, and he ran away, into the woods. Coyote complained, 'I'm so hungry, and I still have no dinner!'" Charley rubbed his belly and made his eyes wide again.

"Hun-gee for dinnaw!" Willie said.

"Coyote trotted off into the woods to look for someone else to be his dinner." Charley trotted around in a circle, imitating a coyote. "He came up on three turkeys at the top of a small hill. 'Hey there, turkeys, what are you up to?' he asked them. 'Oh, we're trying to get into these three burlap bags so we can roll down the hill, cuz that's a lot of fun,' one of them answered. Coyote said, 'Hmm. How's about if you all get in one bag, and I'll push you down the hill?' That sounded like a good idea to the turkeys. Excited, they all flapped their wings . . ."

Charley flapped his wings and walked like a turkey back and forth in front of Willie's playpen, glancing at Naomi to see if she was enjoying the show. Willie squealed with delight, Naomi laughed out loud at Charley's antics, and Dorothy stirred in the carriage.

"Coyote closed up the bag and said, 'Now I've got you!' But when he opened the bag to get a turkey for his dinner, they flapped and pushed with their feet and their wings so that Coyote couldn't hold on to the bag, and they all got out and flew off into the woods. Coyote moaned, 'I'm never going to get my dinner!'"

Charley made a sad face like he was going to cry and walked in a circle looking like a mopey coyote with his shoulders hunched.

"Coyote walked deeper into the forest and came on an old, old turkey standing in a clearing. He thought, *Oh, this is it, he will be a little tough, but he'll be my dinner for sure.* So he said, 'Hey there,

Turkey, I have a deal for you. I know you're old, but I won't eat you if you can fly away from me.' Coyotes are known to be liars, but Turkey didn't know this. 'I'm not sure I can fly away from you, but I'll try,' said Turkey. Coyote told him, 'Just fly over the prairie and then you'll be able to fly a long ways,' knowing that Turkey was old and would get tired. 'Okay,' said Turkey, and he flew off over the prairie, with Coyote running along underneath him."

Charley stretched his arms out and "flew" around the yard a couple of times as he told the story. Willie's eyes were wide and attentive, and Naomi was laughing and only watching Charley now.

"Sure enough, Turkey got tired and landed on the prairie. Coyote pounced on him and they wrestled, feathers flying everywhere. But Turkey was pretty big, and even though he was old, Coyote was tiring after all that running. So Turkey managed to fly away—and as he did, one of his feathers floated down and landed on Coyote's shoulder when he wasn't looking. Feeling that feather on his shoulder, Coyote got startled, and started running away. He was a-scared, and kept looking back with his big eyes to see who was after him!"

Charley ran around the yard a couple of times, looking back over his shoulder, his eyes wide. Willie stood stock-still, his mouth open, mesmerized.

"So now, when you see a coyote anywhere, you will see that they always look a little frightened with their eyes big and wide, and they always look back over their shoulders, cuz they think someone's"— Charley reached down in the playpen and gently grabbed Willie's shoulders—"*after them!*"

Willie was startled, but when Charley started to laugh, he laughed too. Now Dorothy was awake and fussing, but they were all having such a good time that Naomi just picked her up and bounced her until she cooed.

"Well, I'll say, Charles, you are quite the storyteller," she said. "Where'd you learn that story?"

"Oh, one of my uncles tells it, and everybody in the family likes to tell that one and other ones like it," he said quietly, suddenly bashful. "Lotta animal stories."

"Well I've surely had a good time listening. Thank you for making a lady forget her troubles."

"Oh, I'm happy to oblige, ma'am."

"Time to go in and change this one's diaper. Perhaps we'll see you at dinner, then."

"Yes, ma'am, I expect so."

Nancy had been glancing out the kitchen window from time to time and had begun to stare when Charley had become unusually animated.

"What the devil was Charley doing out there?" she asked her daughter when she came into the house with the two children. "I saw you and Willie laughing while he was runnin' around crazy-like!"

"Oh, he told Willie a story about a coyote and acted out part of it. Willie liked it so much, you'd think Charles was Santa Claus."

"Looks like you enjoyed yourself as well."

"Yes, I gotta say I liked havin' a good laugh. I was glad to have an easy afternoon."

Nancy arched an eyebrow. "I think Charley is a little sweet on you, though."

"Oh, baloney. He's just being nice. I told him I'd lost Grant, but I figured you'd mentioned it before. Maybe he was just tryin' to take my mind off it, and give Willie a little show too."

"Yes, you're prob'ly right. He's usually pretty quiet, but he puts in his long day's work alongside everybody else until it's time to call it quits, and doesn't complain. Good manners too. I kinda miss 'im when he goes back up to Dover to his folks' farm."

"I'm glad you've got good help, Mama. You never know with farmhands."

Chapter 17

Ogden, Utah
Summer to Winter 1923

Frank let out a hoot from his spot on the sofa as he read his paper, and called out to his wife in the bedroom.

"Would you listen to this, Naomi? You remember I told you that train in China got jumped by a bunch of bandits? Well, they took hostages, some of them Americans! They shot some of the Chinese but are holding on to the foreigners for their ransom value! Oh, boy, that would never happen here. No American train is gonna get hijacked."

The last thing Frances wanted to hear about was some train problem in China. Turning fourteen in the recent November and being a sophomore at West High School that year had been exciting—she'd even made several new friends, despite her inherent shyness. But here it was, another summer, and her parents had just made clear that they weren't going to provide her even with shoes and underwear anymore. *That* was what she wanted to talk about in her parents' bedroom.

"Oh, really?" Naomi called back to Frank.

"Mother! You and Daddy . . . you think I'm an adult like you. I'm not! I'm still in high school," Frances implored her mother as Naomi folded diapers.

"Frances, your dad and I have less schooling than you do and we've done fine. If you need to go to school part of the time and work part of the time, that's okay."

"The high school won't let you just go whenever you want!" she cried. "You have to do at least a whole semester and finish it in order to get credit. They have to take attendance daily in order to get money to run the school. Only the farm labor kids come and go like that."

"Listen, Frances, you have to think of yourself as a woman now. You got your period, after all. And you know how to manage a little money, and cook, and bake, and take care of children . . . You have to start thinking different about yourself. You're not a child anymore."

Frances blanched at the mention of her menstrual cycle. "I'll quit school then! I hated geometry anyway. Is that what you want, you want me to quit school? Lucille's parents want her to stay in school and graduate." She glared at Naomi.

"Her parents have not got ten kids at home," Naomi said gently. "And her dad has a job that pays better for a small family. Our money, your dad's paycheck, gets spread thinner. I know you want nice clothes and you want to go out with your friends for a soda or to a movie. We can't provide that for you."

"What about Sister? Does she have to work too?"

"You know she's been doing little odd jobs too. Babysitting. Sweeping out the market once a week. So, yes, she's working too."

"But not so much that she has to quit school."

"I don't know if she's going to quit or not. We haven't talked about it. But Frances, you're the oldest. You can figure it out. You can live here. We'll feed you and put a roof over your head, and that's it, now."

"Does Daddy think the same?"

"Yes, we've discussed this. Now, I don't want to hear any more about it—and I mean it. That's the end of it, no arguing."

But Frances wasn't done yet.

In the living room, Frances ventured, "Daddy, that's interesting about the train in China . . . but Mother says you guys aren't going to pay for any of my needs except food and a roof over my head from now on. Is that true? Is that what you think too? I might have to quit high school to get a job!"

Frank lowered his paper and took a deep breath. He didn't want to deal with Frances's issue. He had argued with Naomi about this—again—just last night. He knew she was right about not paying for their eldest child's expenses. It was the enforcement that he didn't want to deal with.

It seemed like he and Naomi were arguing every time he came home these days, even if they agreed on things. Just the slightest thing would set her off. What did she expect? He worked hard and he supported the family. It was normal to want to have sex with his wife, and that's when he felt close to her emotionally. If it resulted in more children, that was mostly her problem. He couldn't be home any more than he already was. Besides, a man had a right, too, to a personal life outside the home. Naomi was getting suspicious, though; one time she'd mentioned that his coat smelled like perfume, and he'd had to invent a story about a passenger on the train spilling on him.

It had only been four months since the Ogden train station burned down. It was expected to take until May '24 to rebuild. The lack of a big station had hurt commerce in Ogden badly. The city was motivated to get the job done, but it had been disorienting, to say the least, for Frank, and Frank hated feeling unsettled. In fact, he hated any kind of change. It did give him a good excuse to stay in Evanston overnight more often, though, which was the silver lining.

"Yes—that's about the size of it, Frances," he said sternly. "You older kids are going to have to start bringing in your own money for whatever you think you need. Carl's got his paper route and gets farm jobs in the summer. Sister does what she can, little odd jobs. You know, I only went through eighth grade, and that was good enough for me to work my way up to a good job with Union Pacific. You've already had more schooling than I'll ever have. I'm sure you can find some work until you find a husband and get married. Or else do without and live here as you have been."

"Daddy, it's 1923, not 1903! Things are different now. And I'm still growing out of my clothes! I'm only fourteen! I'm too young to get married."

"But you're not too young to work. Now that's it. There is no use in arguing about it."

He returned to his paper.

Her teeth clenched, Frances left the house and walked angrily over to Lucille's to tell her the bad news.

"Gosh, Frances. What are you going to do?" Lucille asked.

"Look for work. Quit school, maybe."

Lucille was quiet for a few moments, and then her face brightened. "I know someone who got a job in a boardinghouse. You've done a little of that already. Cleaning it and stuff like that. Maybe you could do that for the summer, save up enough money, and then go back to school."

"Yes, maybe." Frances was feeling resentful once again and at loose ends, and still a bit in shock at the distressing financial fate her parents had decided upon for her. But Lucille's idea was a good one.

❧

Mrs. Birch had a boardinghouse, all right, on Twenty-Fifth Street, where there were a few other rooming houses. And she was strange. She was older than Frances's mother but a lot younger than either Grandma Wolff or Grandma Sims. Maybe about the age of Naomi's half sister. She had some gray hair, was chubby, and wore house dresses—newer than most of Naomi's, but still cotton calico. She had a habit of licking her lips in between sentences, and sniffing before she spoke.

Mrs. Birch sniffed. "I take it your parents know you're lookin' to get a job like this?"

"It's their idea. We have a big family, so we older kids have to get jobs."

[*sniff*] "Yes, that's pretty common. I get a lot of roomers who stay just a month or two, doncha know? [*lick*] Drifters sometimes. Then their rooms need to be completely cleaned from top to bottom for the next person. Some of 'em's more stable and stay for months or even longer. [*lick*] But their rooms still need to get cleaned up some days and their linens washed and so on. Now, I can pay you forty cents an hour. If you live here, room and board for a month is thirty dollars, doncha know. So if you live here, I'd pay you forty dollars a month after your room and board, prob'ly. Whaddya wanna do, then?" [*lick*]

"Um . . . I guess I'll work here and live at home for now. For the summer."

[*sniff*] "So, you're gonna just quit at the end of the summer and go back to school? And then I'd have to find somebody else?"

"Well . . . if that's okay."

[*sniff*] "It's not, but I don't have anybody else right now. You can start tomorrow and we'll see how it goes. You do know how to clean a house?" [*lick*]

"Oh, I know how to clean all right." Frances nodded. Boy, did she.

She checked the impulse to roll her eyes and tell Mrs. Birch what her situation was at home.

Frances started the routine of working from eight-thirty in the morning until five every day at Mrs. Birch's, starting with doing the breakfast dishes and washing the towels and sheets in the wringer washer out behind the boardinghouse. Then she'd hang them on the clothesline to dry, and near the end of the day, iron and fold them and put them into the linen closet or make up clean beds. Then there was vacuuming, dusting, and mopping floors, and helping make lunch for the boarders, herself, and Mrs. Birch, and sometimes helping with or making the dinner. All the same things she did at home.

"How d'you like working for Mrs. Birch?" Anita asked after the first couple of days.

The rest of her siblings were all ears around the dinner table, amazed that their big sister had a job, more of a real job than babysitting or picking beans.

"It's about the same as working around here all day," Frances said. "Except no babysitting."

"Frances, maybe you can put in a little money for groceries around here too," Naomi suggested.

Frances's jaw dropped as she looked at her mother. "You said you'd provide my food and a roof over my head if I worked."

"Well, things change. I'm just suggesting that it might be the fair thing to do, to help us out a little. Then maybe some of us will be able to have some of the things you will be able to have with your pay."

Frances finished her dinner, then went to her room to rest and read the new Agatha Christie book she'd picked up at the library. Anything to stop thinking about her parents and all the darn decisions she felt faced with.

In July, Frances asked Mrs. Birch if there was a room available for her in the boardinghouse. Just the business of going back and forth every day, and then sometimes her mother expecting her to babysit the littlest ones in the evening, or help with dinner, or do the cleanup, was wearing her out. It wasn't that she couldn't do it, it was just that . . . she felt like they were pushing her out, and she was sick to death of babysitting—almost every day of her life since she was six, starting with Carl and then Hermann and Henry and then little Frank and then Marie . . . it just went on and on. First in Salina, and then here in Ogden.

[*sniff*] "Well, I always try to keep a room for a maid, doncha know? So you'd have a room, here, yes. [*lick*] Does that mean you'll stay on? What about school?"

"I'll stay on . . . and I don't know about school yet. If it's okay with you, I'll decide that in a month or two."

"Well . . . okay. [*sniff*] You just tell me as soon as you make up your mind so's I can put an ad in the paper, doncha know?"

Anita watched as Frances packed up all her summer clothes and many of her scant belongings—her good hairbrush and comb and some other things she'd need right away, plus her few favorite books, a dresser scarf she'd embroidered. Anita was a little put out that she took the dresser scarf, but the fact that she'd temporarily have the room to herself was recompense.

"You know that Mother will move Marie in here if I'm not here, don't you?" Frances reminded her sister.

"Well, yes, she will, or she'll have me do it, rather, but maybe for a week I'll have the room to myself. And then a teenager sharing a room with a six-year-old. Just great." She pursed her lips. "Will you have your own room at Mrs. Birch's?"

"Yes, of course. I'm the only housekeeper there, and the cook lives at her own home; Mrs. Birch does a lot of the cooking. She has me doing some of the cooking and baking too."

"Huh. Your own room." Anita thought about what a luxury that would be. She wasn't thinking about the fact that Frances would be working all day, every day, part-time on weekends. She was considering what this would mean in terms of her own role in the Wolff household. The babysitting and chores Frances wouldn't be doing, at least for the summer. "Are you gonna wanna move back in before school, do you think?"

"I don't know. I'm going to see how it goes. It's just easier to be there than going back and forth."

Anita crossed her fingers. Life would be a lot harder for her with Frances gone.

Frances sat down in the kitchen with her mother, eyeing Naomi's belly. She looked to be about five months along. Why did her parents keep having more children?

"When will you be coming back?" asked Naomi.

"I don't know, Mother; I'm just trying this. I can earn money, and I can have a room to myself there. It's easier to be there than to go back and forth. I'm tired when I come home, and then I have to do my share of work here too. I never have a minute to myself. I might

come back home at the end of the summer and go back to school . . .
We'll see."

Naomi bit a fingernail. Frances wouldn't miss seeing that.

"Huh," she finally said. "I guess Sis can absorb your chores and
take on more babysitting. I'll miss having you here, Frances, and
not just for the chores . . . You're my firstborn. Come back and have
Sunday dinner with us, okay?"

Frances welcomed her mother's gentle attitude and smiled. "Yes,
I'd like to do that."

The work at Mrs. Birch's was tiring, that was for sure. It was like every
day was Saturday at home. But no babysitting, she got her own clean
bathwater once or twice a week—heaven—and at least ten dollars was
going into her pocket each week.

She learned quickly that she had to keep track of her hours herself or Mrs. Birch would estimate them, invariably on the low side.

Lucille and Frances were enjoying Sunday afternoon at Lucille's
house, lying on her bed and talking lazily. Frances had gone to church
with Lucille a few times in the last month, and she liked the Mormon,
or Latter-day Saints, services. She loved to sing and there was a lot
of that—a cheerful hymn after each section of the service—and
instead of wine for the sacrament, which was passed around to all the
members, they had water, symbolic of how Jesus had turned water
into wine. She liked that the Mormons didn't drink. She had never
enjoyed being around people who drank, including her older family
members. She was also invited to Lucille's for lunch after church each
time she went. It was nice to be in a home with a smaller family where
things weren't chaotic and there were only a half dozen people at the
table.

"Frances?" Lucille asked as they lay there.

"Uh-huh?"

"Do you think you'd like to join our church?"

"I've been thinking about that. Maybe. But first I need to make up my mind if I'm going to quit school or move back home. I can't keep my job full-time and go to school."

"That's a big decision. Don't you think you should stay in school?"

"My parents don't want to support me anymore. They didn't mind a bit when I moved a lot of my things out and that I'm not there. I go by for Sunday dinner . . . but when I do there are comments about 'did I bring anything.' I'm making money now and my mother isn't. I have more money to spend on what I want or need than she does. I've made myself some really great dresses, and I can buy lipstick and hand cream . . . It's like being an adult."

"Yes, that green dress you made to go dancing in—that one with all the beading—is beautiful! You're starting to have a nicer wardrobe than I do!" Lucille caught herself. "Oh, I don't mean that like it sounded. I just mean, yes, you can afford to have things you want now."

"I just have to work my fingers to the bone to have them." Frances snickered. "But it's not just things—I can have a soda with you at Farr's! An' I don't miss the babysitting, believe you me."

At the end of August, Frances made her choice. She had come to Sunday dinner with her family, bringing with her two berry pies she'd made at the boardinghouse (she'd reimbursed Mrs. Birch for the ingredients). The pie pans were on loan; Frances was thinking she might start buying some of her own kitchen tools to keep at Mrs. Birch's house, however. She might be able to sell a pie now and then.

While everyone enjoyed the berry pie, Frances put down her fork and cleared her throat. "Mother, Daddy . . . everybody . . . I have something to tell you."

Frank looked up, looking a little annoyed that this apparent announcement was interrupting enjoyment of his pie.

Frances was a little nervous, and took a breath before speaking. "I'm going to move to Mrs. Birch's and quit school."

Everyone was silent.

Frank put his fork down too. "Well. I suppose this is the right thing to do. You'll do fine, Frances." He got up from the table and took his pie into the dining room to finish it while reading the paper.

Frances was a little surprised that was all he had to say, but her father was like that, undemonstrative.

"Wull . . . so, you're not going to live here anymore?" Carl asked tentatively.

"No . . . I'll live at Mrs. Birch's. But I'll still come by. Maybe not as much. But I'll come and bring a birthday cake for Dorothy's first birthday in a week, how's that?"

The children looked from one to each other around the table, wide-eyed. She was their big sister, and they spent almost as much time with her as they did their mother—and although she did use a paddle on the littler ones occasionally, she sometimes cried afterward, so they knew she didn't enjoy it.

Naomi brushed some crust from the table, where Willie was making his three-year-old's mess with his little wedge of berry pie, and shifted her increasing weight. "You kids . . . you all need to learn to take on a few more chores, now. Especially since we're gonna have a new baby around Christmas. Sis can't do all of what Frances has been doing. And we'll miss her, won't we? We'll miss your singing, Frances, and everything you've been doing for us."

George piped up, "I'll miss you reading me storybooks!"

Frances leaned toward George. "Oh, I'll miss that too. But I can still read to you sometimes when I come over. And Sis can read to you, or Carl . . . or Hermann or Henry."

"You used to sing to me when I was real little . . ." Marie's eyes teared up.

"Oh, Marie, I'm only moving a few blocks away, over near Twenty-Fifth Street!" Frances hadn't anticipated this conversation being so emotional.

"Will Sis get the bedroom all alone?" Marie asked.

"No, Marie," Naomi said. "You will be sharing the room with Sis now, instead of the little kids' room."

Anita looked at Frances and rolled her eyes toward the ceiling.

Frances was starting to feel moved, herself. She had felt torn for weeks. She was afraid she might cry. She wished her parents hadn't cut her off financially. She wished she could stay in school. She liked the social life; she liked becoming educated, reading, learning new things. She didn't want to be like her parents, uneducated, or to use a lot of slang like Mrs. Birch did. And she felt a little lonely at the boardinghouse. At least Mrs. Birch kept an eye on the male boarders and didn't allow any hanky-panky.

But . . . when she did have a little free time, it was hers. And she had some money. Enough to save up—she didn't know for what, but she knew it was a good idea to save. "Never a borrower or a lender be," her dad always said. She was going to open a bank account.

And that was it, as her parents had said back in June. Now she was an independent young woman, like it or not, at fourteen-going-on-fifteen.

❧

Christmas at the Wolffs' was special this year; a new son had arrived just two days before.

Frances came home to help with the Christmas preparations. She made mince and apple pies and Christmas cookies, and supervised the children's decorating them. She wrapped the few gifts for the littlest children and hung up everyone's stockings, including her own, with oranges down in the toes that she had bought with her earnings. She had to be at the boardinghouse to make cinnamon rolls for the boarders' breakfast, but then the cook would come in to provide Christmas dinner for those few who didn't have a home to go to or couldn't make it back to their families, and Frances would be free to go home.

Frances and Anita took turns cradling little Clarence in their arms that afternoon to give Naomi a break. Frances was glad to be home and realized she would miss waking up on Christmas mornings at home, with all the children excited. They had waited until late morning to open gifts with her. But, again, there were all the children, all day every day, and she preferred this new mode of coming by to visit. She felt almost like an aunt to the kids now that she wasn't there all the time.

In the evening, they sang carols, played games and laughed and had a ham for dinner, just big enough for everyone who was old enough to have a piece.

Another baby. Frances wondered how long her mother could keep this up. What could women do if they didn't want so many children but still wanted to get married and have a family?

Anita looked tired. *She's getting to see what it was like to be me in this house*, thought Frances. *I'm never going to have this many children. I don't know how you keep from it, but I'm not going to do it. Not like this.*

Chapter 18

Ogden, Utah
Autumn 1924

"Carl! Carl? Can you come hold Clarence for me and feed him while I finish frying this chicken?" Naomi called out from the kitchen.

"Jack asked me to come play ball with him for a while before dinner . . . Can't you get Hermann to do it?" Carl pleaded. "He likes doing girl things."

"Hermann? Can you get in here?"

"What?" Hermann called out from the boys' bedroom.

"Come in here and help me!"

Hermann dragged himself away from the Sears and Roebuck catalog to help his mother.

"Goodness sakes!" Naomi exclaimed. "Whaddo I have to do to get some help around here? I swear, with Frances and Sis gone this place is a madhouse."

Anita had also decided to quit school after her freshman year and get a job like Frances had. She'd moved out in June, to Naomi's dismay.

Frank Sr. appeared in the kitchen doorway, smoking his pipe. "What's the commotion?"

"I am just trying to get some help with this baby—with *our* baby—so I can finish fixing dinner. You don't know how hard it is for me now with nine kids and no older girls here anymore to help!"

Frank cleared his throat. "Well, Sis comes by to help you when she can . . . and you could probably get Frances in here from time to time. All's you'd have to do is ask."

Naomi stopped what she was doing, turning the heat to low under the chicken, and faced Frank with one hand on her hip and the other holding the long-handled fork. She pointed it at him, fire in her eyes.

"Oh, all right. Yes. Just take Clarence, Dorothy, and Willie with me, two in the baby buggy while I push it with one hand, and holding Willie's hand with the other, walk the mile down to the boarding-house, and ask Mrs. Birch to please let me talk to my daughter while she's working, and then ask Frances could she come over here and watch the little ones while I do whatever it is I have to do? Is that what you think I should do?"

Frank recoiled a little. "You don't have to get all haughty about it."

Naomi was close to seething. She turned back to the stove, then turned around again. "Frank, I've been a good wife to you. I have been a good mother to these kids. But you are almost never here. You're here for a week to enjoy your paper and go to church with us or do whatever you want to *do*." Her eyes widened at this last bit, implying that *she* was what he wanted to "do," and reminding him she had always complied with that. "You don't change diapers or do laundry or grocery shop or cook or even work in the garden much. I'm not saying you're supposed to, but it's a lot for one woman to do, *and* keep an eye on nine kids. I don't know what I'd do if Hermann didn't like to do 'girl things,' as Carl calls it. Don't you *see* all that?"

"Well, I see that Hermann needs to do more boy's activities, that's for sure," Frank said sharply. "I caught him dressing up with Marie in girls' clothes last Saturday afternoon. Marie said they were playing house and pretending they were grown-up ladies and she needed him to be her neighbor friend. How could you let the boy do that?"

Naomi darted a look at Hermann. Frank was acting as if he were not right there in the room. Luckily, Hermann didn't seem to be paying much attention.

"My job's to bring home the bacon, and I do that," Frank said. "I've done that since day one. I put a roof over your head, and for all these kids too. Your job is to take care of the children and also to do things for me when I need you to. Nothing's changed, Naomi, and I don't appreciate your attitude. It seems like every time I come home you're in a rotten mood." He turned on his heel and went out to the front porch to smoke his pipe.

"Oh, that's just grand," Naomi muttered under her breath. "Maybe I won't be as friendly the next time you feel amorous . . . coming in from the rails like I'm your floozy and should be at your beck and call. Well I'll tell you what . . ."

"What, Mama?" Hermann asked from his spot at the kitchen table, feeding Clarence his bottle.

"Oh, nothing, honey. Mama's just tired." She called out, "Marie! Come set the table! And tell your brothers to come on in for dinner."

"Daddy? Did you and Mother have a fight?" Henry asked his father on the porch.

Frank didn't answer Henry at first; he was busy staring off into the distance. Gazing at the hills on the horizon helped him calm down, and he was angry with Naomi for acting like her problems had anything to do with him.

Marie scampered out to the porch and yelled, "Ca-arl! Geo-o-orge! Fra-ank! Dinner!" and skipped back inside to set the table, oblivious to the tense atmosphere.

Frank saw Henry still standing there. "Hmm?" he said. "Oh, no, we didn't have a fight. That's none of your concern, anyway. Has she got dinner ready?"

"I think so," Henry said. "Smells good, anyway."

The eleven Wolffs made their way to the table and quietly sat. Marie pulled up the high chair next to Naomi for Dorothy. As soon as all the food was on the table, Frank said grace.

"God is great, God is good, and we thank him for our food. Amen."

"Amen," came the chorus from all but Clarence, and Dorothy said, "'Men."

"Now," said Frank, "I want us to have a nice Sunday dinner here, so let's keep it quiet. There's nothing we need to talk about; let's just eat this nice fried chicken and then enjoy the evening. No ifs, ands, or buts."

"Yes, Daddy," the older children said.

Naomi kept her own counsel and dished food onto the plates.

Frank, ignoring his wife's tight expression, helped himself to chicken legs.

Chapter 19

Evanston, Wyoming
April 1925

"You got yourself a real fine house, here, Minnie." Frank was deeply impressed. The house was huge, three stories, one of those gingerbread affairs on a big corner lot with a lot of well-cared-for trees. He gazed up the stairwell with its polished wood banister. "How many bedrooms?"

"Well, I can make it six if we wall off part of the attic room," she answered. "The kids can be up there in those, and a housekeeper in the basement. So, I can rent out at least two, if not three. And with the money from dressmaking, I can get by pretty well now."

"You're a smart woman, Minnie." Frank nodded. "I take it you used the money from the sale of the Missouri farm . . ." Then he wondered if he shouldn't be nosing into her finances.

"That, and my mother helped me get a low down payment and a good price," Minnie said with a little reservation. "She has a lot of connections here in Evanston, with her running that hotel."

"You'll be real comfortable here," Frank said.

"And I have a lot more privacy. With the back bedroom . . . and there's a back stairwell, too, going up from the kitchen."

Frank chuckled. He understood the implication. "Well, yes, there's that, I suppose. I . . . uh, I look forward to taking a look at that back bedroom."

"You'll likely see it soon enough, Mr. Wolff!" Minnie smiled and, her hand on one hip, tilted her head and looked up at him. "I'm glad you like the place. I'm real pleased too."

"Can we sit down and talk a bit before the kids come home from school?"

"Why, sure. Let me pour us some coffee and we'll settle in the parlor."

At least the furniture is familiar, thought Frank as he waited for Minnie to reappear. Mein Gott, *she must have more money than I'd realized. This place is a palace. I could never afford this, with all our kids, even though I've got a pretty good salary now. This place must have cost her $2,000. But would have cost her a lot more in Ogden.*

When Minnie came in, coffees in hand, he patted the seat next to him. "I wanted to tell you some things, Minnie," he said. "Since we might not get a chance later."

She handed him his coffee with a quizzical look. "What is it, Frank?"

"Oh . . . I probably shouldn't burden you . . . but I've got no one else to tell, except Naomi. And we've been having words, sometimes, when I'm home."

"I don't doubt. You're gone a lot, and she's got . . . how many kids at home now?"

"Well, there's nine, now that Frances and Anita moved out."

"What about your oldest boys? Are they still at home?"

"Yes, Carl is working as an apprentice carpenter and still going to high school. But Sis . . . Anita . . . she's working at a boardinghouse and moved in there, quit school."

"You don't mind that?" Minnie held his gaze. "I think it's important for girls to get an education too."

"I suppose it might be, but it was their choice," Frank said, a little defensively. "They could've kept working part-time and gone to school too, or just lived at home."

"And continued being the second mamas in the house, with part of their financial support cut off?" Minnie pursed her lips. "I can see why they chose what they did. I'm glad Edward left me enough that I can keep my kids in school, you know. My eldest is just a couple years younger than your Frances. And really, I'd like to go back to school myself someday."

"Well, I don't know why you'd want to do that. You've got this house, us boarders, and the dressmaking; you're pretty well set up. I'll tell you another thing: Frances went and joined that Mormon church! I never thought I'd see the day my children would not be Lutheran. And I think she's got Anita going over there sometimes too."

"She's grown, Frank, and living on her own. Young people make their own choices. And you haven't been there much to influence her."

"I never thought of her as a rebel . . ." Frank disliked the thought of his daughter breaking away from the faith they'd been brought up in—*his* faith.

"You know, the Mormons are good people: they spend a lot of time at church, and they take care of their own. They've got that deal where they put in a tithe to pay for the preacher and also to take care of people if they get sick or if a woman gets widowed."

"I think Frances was taken partly by all the singing," Frank mused aloud. "She used to sing some of their songs around the house. Well, I guess times change and children don't feel the need to take up their parents' ways." He paused. "I guess the only good news I have is they finished the new station in Ogden late last year . . . except then I don't have as much excuse to be here in Evanston as often. So, it's good news, bad news."

Minnie patted his knee. "We'll get by, Frank. We always have. Anyway, try and forget all that for now. Have a cookie and I'll pour you some more coffee."

"You don't happen to have a little wine hidden away, do you, Minnie? That would suit me more than coffee. But I don't want to get you in any trouble, of course."

"I do," she said. "But I don't like to let the younger kids know in case they talk. I think we should wait until everyone's in bed before we share a glass."

"Okay, you're right." Frank nodded. "I can wait."

Minnie craned her neck to look out the front window. "Oh, here comes Ellen, home from school. Good thing we waited."

The little girl climbed up the steps and opened the front door, barely able to reach the handle.

"Look, Ellen, Mr. Wolff is here."

"Hello, Mr. Wolff!"

"Hi, there, Ellen," Frank said, trying to suppress a smile. She was the only blonde in Minnie's brood. Really cute little tyke—older than Willie but younger than George.

"You go on and change your clothes if you want to play outside, Ellen, or else go in the kitchen and have a cookie and a glass of milk. There's milk in the icebox." Minnie turned back to Frank. "I'm going to look into getting myself an electric refrigerator one of these days. With all these people, having to keep food on hand for both the kids and roomers . . ."

"Oh, I don't know . . . we've got a houseful in Ogden, and Naomi gets by with an icebox."

Minnie gave Frank an exasperated look that he didn't notice; he was watching Ellen make her way down the hallway, her blonde curls bouncing.

Minnie enjoyed Frank's attention and company, but she didn't think she could ever be married to the man. Sometimes he was . . . what was the word? Obtuse. He didn't often see things from other people's point of view. But his physical affection was something she'd come to crave. He was handsome, fair in coloring, slender, and she liked having a man who took charge a bit. She had to manage too many things on her own.

She knew her mother suspected their relationship. That one time, when Irene had come by while she and Frank were in the kitchen laughing over something, her mother had said later, "This has been going on a long time, hasn't it?"

She'd replied, "What has?"

"You and 'Mr. Wolff,' Frank."

"I'm not sure what you mean, Mother."

"Oh, I think you know exactly what I mean. You are, on the one hand, lucky to have him, both for the rent and for the friendship, the *special* attention he pays you." Irene paused to give her daughter a pointed look. "I remember when he used to board at the place over in Lyman as well. But on the other hand, you better be careful. His wife's not that far away—just barely far enough. A three-hour train ride is nothing."

Minnie wasn't worried. Frank was more than a dalliance but less than a partner.

In any case, tonight they'd have time for each other, and a glass of wine.

Chapter 20

Ogden, Utah
Summer 1925

Frances had learned to appreciate living on her own at Mrs. Birch's. She would never get used to her constant "Doncha knows?"—but she now had access to a sewing machine, and the money to buy just about any kind of fabric she liked. Mrs. Birch had let the boarders know that Frances could sew, and ever since she'd been making a little extra money mending clothing and socks for the men.

Here she was, darning again, having thought that was over since she could now afford her own new socks. But at least she got paid—forty cents an hour. She now knew that her dad probably made about $1.50 an hour. Although this was four times what she made and she knew Frank worked really long hours, she realized it must have been hard for her mother to make that salary provide for a dozen or more people in the house. Well, now, eleven, with her and Sis not living at home anymore, and Grant gone. Although he'd never gotten old enough to cost much.

When the boarders gave her too much mending, she passed some of it to Sis. Frank had said much the same thing to her as to Frances: "Education is more important for the boys, since you'll just get married anyway." Frances still felt melancholy about quitting school, but

Anita hadn't minded. She now worked cleaning boardinghouses too, and in the summer she worked in the canneries.

Frances was working on a royal-blue silk dress with a drop waist. She planned to do some beading on the bodice. It would look beautiful in the lights at the White City Ballroom, where she and Lucille, Lucille's brother, and several of their friends had started going to dance now that she and Lucille were seventeen. Sis often joined them.

It was thirty-five cents a night for a ticket, except on the nights they had a drawing for big things like cars—those nights were fifty cents. But your ticket on the other nights got entered for the drawings too.

Frances was not supposed to go to the dances at the high school, since she was no longer a student there. She'd sneaked in with Lucille a couple of times, though; sometimes even kids from the Brigham City high school would drive down for the Ogden High dances. Some of the older girls dated boys from out of town, if the boy had a truck or access to his parents' car.

Since she'd joined the Mormon church, and influenced Sis to join as well, the sisters had also started attending the dances there, where the musicians were oftentimes men of the church. The church even had dance lessons, and she had learned the foxtrot, the samba, the waltz, and some other dances there. She'd met Frank Sims at one of those dances—a tall, dark, and handsome Mormon boy nearly two years older than she was. His grandfather had been one of the early Mormons prior to their pioneer trek to Utah, so that was impressive. Frances wondered what it was like to be raised in a Mormon family— if his folks were more strict than her folks had been. She couldn't imagine they could be. She thought it was both funny and a nice coincidence that he had both her father's first name and her maternal grandparents' last name. She couldn't wait to tell Grandma Sims next time she saw her.

"Say there," he'd said to her at the church dance, and put out his hand. "Would you like to dance?"

"Yes, I would," she'd said, putting her hand in his, charmed by his manner.

It turned out he was a good dancer. They really cut a rug together, and she saw him and danced with him several times after that.

Frank seemed to be quite confident for eighteen, and was the first older boy she'd gotten to know. He talked about saving money, and maybe moving out of Ogden one day, which seemed almost an exotic idea. He told her in one of their conversations that he had a young sister, Rose, and spoke of her with affection. Frances took from this that he was family oriented, like many Mormons seemed to be.

The last time she'd gone to a church dance, as they were standing on the sidelines each enjoying a glass of punch, he'd said, "You ever go to that new place, the White City Ballroom?"

"Yes, Lucille and I—you know Lucille Klumack?"

He nodded that he did.

"Lucille and I and her brother and some other kids go there sometimes. And my sister Anita."

"Maybe we could go there together," he said. "I hear Duke Ellington might play there."

"Oh, I would love to go!" Frances answered, then realized maybe she should have been a little more coy.

"I think I've seen you at the bakery where I work a couple of times, over at Twenty-Fifth and Lincoln. But I go in early and get off early, so maybe only once or twice I've seen you there," he said.

"Oh, you work at Ward's?" Frances frowned a little, trying to remember if she'd seen him in there. She was glad that he remembered her. And was also thinking that bakers made about twice as much money as she did.

"Yeah, but like I say, I get off around noon. I'm in back; I don't work at the front counter. I think I've seen you come in to buy things in the morning."

"Oh, yes, sometimes. I work in Mrs. Birch's boardinghouse, and sometimes we run out of the bread we make ourselves. And I like to get some pumpernickel for myself if there aren't any boarders who like it."

"You like that old-style bread, then?"

"Oh, yes. My father is Swiss . . . German Swiss. He loves that kind of bread. We always had it at home."

"Don't you live at your folks' place?" Frank cocked his head, looking into her eyes intently.

"No . . ." Frances didn't want to tell him everything—that she'd left her home because her parents wouldn't buy her the things she needed anymore. "No, I moved out and started working and living at the boardinghouse two years ago. So I wouldn't have to babysit all my brothers and sisters anymore!" Frances laughed.

Frank leaned toward her, smiled, and said, "Okay, well, if you'll go dancing with me at White City—my treat—maybe I'll bring you a loaf of pumpernickel, or maybe some Danish or something."

Frances's cheeks flushed pink. "Oh, that would be really nice."

"Well, when do you want to go?"

"Gosh, I don't know. We go there at least once a month, sometimes every week . . . When do *you* want to go?" She believed, as she was raised to, that you should leave important decisions to men most of the time.

"We could beat around the bush like this for weeks, goin' round like a Will Rogers rope trick!" Frank laughed.

Frances laughed in return at his humor. That was one of the traits she most enjoyed about him.

Frank suggested, "Let's go next Saturday night. Maybe they'll have somebody famous."

"Okay, you can pick me up at Mrs. Birch's at eight o'clock, and we can walk over to the ballroom. It's only a couple of blocks."

"Her place is on Adams, right?"

"Yes, that's it, the big boardinghouse."

"Okay, it's a date!"

Frances smiled to herself, feeling quietly elated.

Chapter 21

Ogden, Utah, &
Stone Township, Oklahoma
1926

Naomi was sick to death of arguing with Frank. It seemed like every time he came back from Evanston, they had an argument. She couldn't imagine why that town seemed to set him on edge.

When he had come in from his last run, she'd rushed to hug him and had detected perfume. It was that new one, "My Sin." Ha! Pretty funny. She recognized it because Frances liked it and had bought a tiny bottle of it. And she wasn't going to ignore it.

"What's that perfume I smell?" she asked as she pulled away from him.

"Perfume? Ha! You're imagining things. It's probably yours from the last time I left."

"It's definitely not mine," Naomi responded, a chill in her voice. Hers was cheap, besides.

"Well, I have no idea how it got there, if it's even there at all. Maybe one of the maids at one of the boardinghouses had a lot on and moved my jacket or something."

Naomi decided to let sleeping dogs lie—for now, in any case. She couldn't prove it, but she was suspicious and decided to be on her guard the next time he came home.

The thing was, men did this kind of thing. He may have gone to a dance with a woman or something. *But he wouldn't have worn his denim jacket to a dance*, she reasoned. *And he doesn't even like to dance!*

She had heard women at church gossiping about how railroad men had a floozy in every town where they stayed overnight. Would Frank sleep with another woman, though? Naomi just didn't have the time or energy to worry about that. But she didn't like it.

"Well, if you're out there doing things you ought not to, I will never know for sure," she said flippantly. "But that isn't my perfume. Frances wears that—but you haven't seen her today, have you?"

"Matter of fact, I was by Mrs. Birch's on my way here and we had a hug. It was on my way home, so I stopped in to say hello."

Naomi bit a fingernail and looked at the floor, then back at Frank. "Well, you're gettin' off easy this time, Mister," she said, and forced a smile. She didn't want to spend the few days he was home in a snit.

Naomi decided to take little Clarence with her to see her mother at the Oklahoma farm again in June, after school was out. She asked Sis to come and watch the family while she was gone for a week or so. Dorothy was almost four now, and Naomi thought she was old enough to stay with her big sister.

Anita was not sure she could get that much time away from the boardinghouse or the cannery, but she talked to Frances, who said she could step in once in a while. With Carl there, too, they figured it would work.

A monkey wrench in the works was that some of the boys

clamored to go to the farm. Since Naomi didn't want to spend her time with her mother tending several little ones, she finally decreed that the oldest and youngest kids, except for toddler Clarence, would all stay home and the middle boys—eight-year-old George and ten-year-old Frank—could come with her. They were old enough to entertain themselves and pretty much knew not to get into serious trouble. Six-year-old Willie was upset he didn't get to go, but Naomi told him and Marie they'd get to spend a lot of time with their neighborhood friends and their big sisters and brothers. Marie didn't really want to go to the farm anyway, and she helped calm Willie down, encouraging him with potential trips on the streetcar to get an ice cream at Sawyer Brothers', which they couldn't do out in the country. Carl, Hermann, and Henry, all teenagers now, didn't have any interest in going on the trip; they had summer jobs and looked forward to palling around with their buddies, swimming and playing baseball, or just doing nothing.

So it was settled, and Naomi, Frank Jr., George, and Clarence boarded the train to Oklahoma to visit Grandma Sims.

Once again, it was lovely to be on the farm and have some time just reading under the trees near the house and drinking lemonade. Naomi and Nancy caught up on all the news; Nancy was surprised to hear that Frances and Anita had both converted to the Mormon church.

"My land, why'd they want to do that?" she asked her daughter, as she took a puff on her pipe.

"Well, Mama, I guess it's as good as any Christian church. We all had heard the Mormons had horns on their heads when we still lived in Kansas, but that was a lot of hooey. They just think different. The main thing is they think Joseph Smith was a modern-day prophet. That's the part that makes me shake my head."

Nancy took a puff on her pipe. "I guess it makes me shake my head too. Why not just stay with a good old-fashioned church, like you were raised in? Methodist or Lutheran."

"Well, you know, there are Catholics too, Mama."

"Yes, but they worship Mother Mary. That's a different way too."

"I don't know as they worship her . . . maybe so. But all of 'em believe in God and in Jesus the Savior. I guess it's all okay if you think about it."

"Mercy. I suppose so. I suppose so."

"Mama, do you just smoke around anybody now?"

"Oh, not if there's company; I know people think it's peculiar for a woman to smoke a pipe. I still hide it under my apron if somebody comes by unexpected. But it's just family and Charley here now, and he's around so much I don't hide the pipe from him. He says his mother has been known to smoke a pipe too." Nancy chuckled.

Charles Foreland was still working for Nancy. He didn't go home up to Missouri much anymore to work, just sent money home to his folks.

The boys were having a great time running around the farm, playing cowboys and Indians. Naomi had heard Charles kindly telling them what Indians did and didn't do when he heard them pretending to be one. She still wasn't sure if Charles was really an Indian or not, but he did seem to know a bit about them.

"He sure looks like an Indian," George said at breakfast one day.

"Now, you don't go saying that to his face, George," Nancy told her grandson. "He might take offense, we don't know."

"Isn't it okay to be Indian?" George asked.

"Well, it's okay if you are Indian and spend a lot of time with other Indians, but a lot of white folks don't like Indians, or at least don't like them to spend time with white folks."

"Why?" George asked, hanging on his grandmother's words.

Nancy sighed. "Well, some folks think it's better to be white than any other color, and sometimes even we think that. But Charley has a white father, and we don't know if he just happens to have dark skin or if his mother or grandmother were Indians . . . or what. So we just have to be careful talking about it."

George knitted his brow. "I still don't understand. But if I have to keep my mouth shut about it, I prob'ly can do that."

When it came time to pack up to go, Frank and George put up quite a fuss; George actually had tears in his eyes. Naomi shook her head and looked at Nancy.

Nancy offered, "You know, they can stay a little longer if it's okay with you. Maybe I could have Charley go back on the train with 'em so they'd have someone to watch over them."

They called him in from the barn to ask him what he thought.

"Oh, I've always wanted to see Ogden," he said readily. "I'd be happy to take the boys back in another week or whenever you want."

"I don't want them in Mother's hair much longer than that," Naomi said. "Are you sure you wouldn't mind? The boys get free tickets, but I can't offer you that . . ."

"I'll pay your ticket, Charley," Nancy piped up. "It's worth it to me to get time with my grandsons. Maybe I'll even put 'em to work!" She laughed when the boys' eyes got wide. "Don't you worry," she told them, "just doing something around here that has to be done that's easy for you to do, like sweep out the shed or feed the horses."

George and Frank looked at each other and smiled.

"Can we, Mother?" Frank asked Naomi.

"Oh, sure, why not." Naomi smiled at the boys. "Listen, Charley, when you get to the station with these two little outlaws, send me a telegram, okay, that you're leaving, and let me know what day and time the train's supposed to get in? You can sleep on our couch, or maybe stay at one of the boardinghouses where my daughters work."

"All right, Naomi, I'll do that. And thanks for the invitation, but I'll stay at a boardinghouse." He turned to his boss. "And thanks for your offer, too, but I'll share the cost of the ticket with you. I'm gettin' kind of a vacation out of it."

Like that, it was all decided.

Chapter 22
Ogden, Utah
1926

About a week after Naomi came home from Oklahoma with baby Clarence, Frances came by to visit on her way back from the dentist. She'd ended up getting false upper teeth, and they looked real pretty. She wanted to see how her mother's trip had been, get the news of Grandma Sims—and show off her new teeth.

She was surprised to find Charles Foreland in her parents' house, sitting on the davenport as if he belonged there. She gave him a tepid hello, then joined her mother in the kitchen, where the familiar aroma of frying chicken and roasting potatoes filled the air.

"Mother," she said in a hushed voice, "what is *he* doing here?"

"Oh, I thought maybe Sis might have told you. Little Frank and George wanted to stay on the farm another week; your Grandma Sims said it was fine, and we agreed that Mr. Foreland would bring the boys out on the train. Besides, Mr. Foreland wanted to see Ogden. He's staying at the boardinghouse where Sis works."

"Oh . . . does Daddy know?" Frances knew he wouldn't like this one bit.

"Your dad hasn't been home since I got back," Naomi told her. "I think he's on his way home from St. Louis. I'm sure he wouldn't want the two boys traveling on their own, even though Frank's going on eleven. And Mr. Foreland is going to fix the back door for me while he's in town too. Your father . . ." Naomi started distractedly, then seemed to consider her words. "Your father is gone so much he can't always be here when I need something fixed."

Frances wondered what it was her mother had been about to say, and wasn't at all happy that she had a man in the house alone with her, even though the children were there. She'd rather her father had been the one to hire him to fix the door.

Oh well. It was her mother's house.

"Is he staying for dinner?" she asked.

"He is." Her mother shot her a look that meant, *Drop it.*

Since he was staying, Frances did as well, just to keep an eye on him. Mostly she just wanted to see what he acted like, and that he was polite and didn't expect too much of the Wolff household for himself.

And that all appeared to be the case.

A couple of days later, Charley took the train back to Oklahoma.

"Thank you so much for watching the boys," said Naomi, biting a nail, when he came by to say goodbye. "And are you sure I can't pay you for fixing the door?"

"Oh, no, no, it was no trouble, and neither were the boys. Just a couple of boys acting like boys always do. I think they had a good time on the train, and I didn't let them run too wild."

She laughed and insisted he take some applesauce she'd canned. "Yes, they can be like wild Indians, but I try to raise 'em so they only act like that outside."

"Well, I wouldn't say that, about Indians—not too many are wild anymore that I know of, heh—but yes, the two of 'em behaved pretty good. I think they had a real good time on the farm too; I let them help with the horses and kept an eye on them for your mama."

."Well, thanks again," Naomi said, regretting the Indian comment. "I hope you got to see some of the sights, such as they are, here in Ogden. Not much more to see here than in Tulsa or Kansas City, I guess."

"Oh, but at least it's a different city, and I got to see all the land between there and here." He tipped his hat. "Hope to see you again one day, Naomi."

"Yes, same here. Have a good trip! Say hi to my mama. And don't take any wooden nickels!"

On his way down the sidewalk toward the station, Charley looked back over his shoulder and smiled.

Naomi thought, *Oh, like the coyote.*

Chapter 23

Ogden, Utah
1927

Frances had been dating Frank Sims for two years now, ever since that first evening at the White City Ballroom. She was really sweet on him, and he had stopped dating other girls. He would sometimes borrow a car and take her on long rides out into the country where they'd picnic. On one excursion, they started at dawn, packed extra food and a can of gas, and drove south where he could show her the scenic, colorful desert area in Utah, of which he was fond. They sat together in church every Sunday too. He would reach over and hold her hand, right there in front of their friends and sometimes his family. It felt so romantic!

For her part, she was inspired to sew ever-lovelier flapper dresses, and she knew they pleased Frank.

She had never expected to have a boyfriend this soon, especially after quitting high school. He had graduated, and encouraged her that someday she should finish school too. She hadn't known you could still get a diploma once you quit.

One evening when Frank walked Frances back to Mrs. Birch's place, he didn't let go of her hand when they got to the front porch.

"Frances..."

"Yes?" She was a little afraid of what he was going to say; did he want to break up? She searched her mind to see if there was anything she'd done, something she shouldn't have said.

"I'm going to be moving to Los Angeles," he said. "I've been thinking about this for a long time—going out to California, where the weather is better and the pay is better and, gosh, *everything* seems like it might be better."

Frances's heart dropped into her stomach. "Oh?" she said, swallowing hard. "And when do you think you'll go?"

"Well, soon, within a couple months. But . . . I was wondering . . . I was wanting . . . I was hoping you'd go with me."

Frances was stunned. "What would I do in Los Angeles?" she asked, incredulous.

"Well, I would like . . . I mean, I wanted to ask you . . . would you marry me? We can start a new life down there—new friends, all the fun around Hollywood, and who knows what else."

He seemed nervous, but sincere. Her heart calmed and she could breathe easier, aside from the excitement she felt.

"Oh, Frank! Yes, I'll marry you. Gosh, if you think it's better for us to go to Los Angeles, I'll come with you. But is there a Mormon church down there?"

"Oh, you bet. I'm sure there is. I mean, we can check, but there are Mormon churches all over now." He pulled Frances close for a bear hug and kissed her passionately. Those kisses were another thing she loved about him! Sometimes his amorousness made her knees weak, and she'd been hoping he might be the one to someday show her what married love was all about.

Mrs. Birch flipped the porch light off and on. She didn't like public displays of affection, especially on her front porch, and had been peeking from the side of one of the front windows.

"Oh, Mrs. Birch wants me in. When do you want to talk some more? Tomorrow? Oh, you know what, we can get free tickets on the train! I think Daddy can request one for you too; our family rides free."

"Well, if not, we'll still go. I may go down there first and find us a place to live, and you can come after."

"Oh, Frank, this is so . . . I don't know, exciting." She stared up into his dark eyes. "I'll go tell Mother and Daddy tomorrow, if I can get off work. Or the next day. Are you really sure?"

"I'm sure, Frances. We've been together a while, and I want to start a family and all with you."

"But . . . what will I do down there?"

"You'll be my wife! You'll be the mother to our children. You can get some work if you want, but the job I'm getting should cover us, mostly at least. They told me I'll be manager if things work out. And you can go to school and get your high school diploma."

A way out of Ogden? This was sounding too good to be true. She wasn't as attached to this town as Frank seemed to think. She didn't want to sound too eager . . . but it was probably too late for that.

Frank Wolff was visibly disappointed that he was losing his little girl, his firstborn. He took the news solemnly.

Naomi was surprised; Los Angeles might as well be New York. When would she ever see Frances again? And who besides Sis could she call on for help with the kids?

"Well . . . that's good news, Frances," Frank told his daughter. "I'm sure you'll make Frank a good wife. And sure, I can get both of you tickets down to Los Angeles."

"Oh, thanks, Daddy! I was hoping Frank could count as family."

"I'll just tell them he's my son-in-law. Are you getting married here, before you go?" he asked.

"No, he wants us to do that in Los Angeles," Frances said. "I'm not sure exactly why; maybe it has something to do with California law. He'll go down and then I'll follow soon after."

Naomi hugged her daughter. "We should have a nice dinner for you and the family—and Frank—before you go. Since your wedding won't be here. And you could invite Lucille and her family if you like too."

She was happy that someone had chosen Frances, and her future was taken care of. Frances could be judgmental and uppity, but maybe Frank Sims liked that in her. Maybe he was the same way. Even if they were Mormons, they seemed pretty well suited. He was a nice enough fellow, judging from the few times Frances had brought him by.

So that was the first Wolff all the way out of the nest for good.

Naomi felt a little old.

Frank Sims did take the train to Los Angeles—with a free one-way ticket, compliments of Frank Wolff, who said it would be his wedding gift. (Frances thought this seemed cheap, since it wasn't costing her father anything, but was just glad her fiancé didn't have to use his savings for the ticket.) Naomi had given them a very nice dinner party—modest, but complete with a nice cake with flowers on top. She'd also given Frances an ivory comb and brush set, paid for by a little money she'd saved up by selling canned goods and doing mending for wealthier people at the Lutheran church. Frances was touched by her mother's gesture.

Frank Sims, good on his word, found a little cottage to rent for a hundred dollars a month on Denker Avenue in southwestern Los Angeles. It wasn't far from the bakery where he'd found work, so he could walk until they could buy a car. His wages would be almost double what they'd been in Ogden. He called Frances in early August at Mrs. Birch's and told her to get on the first train she could.

Frances had been embroidering pillowcases for her trousseau, such as it was, and already had a trunk packed; she could leave on short notice. In it was a simple dress she'd made for her wedding; she had been told it would be hot in Southern California in August, so a double layer of white voile with embroidery on the bodice and a little ruffle around the slightly scooped neckline had seemed like the right choice. And she'd be able to wear it for other occasions, too, since it wasn't too fancy.

Not having an actual wedding was a disappointment, but she was delighted to be marrying Frank; it was like a fairy tale that he'd asked her to follow him to California. Here she was, not quite nineteen, and about to become a wife with a home to manage. She daydreamed about what it might be like to become Frank's lover, thinking that part of marriage must be wonderful; about starting a family—a small one—and hoped she'd have a daughter she could guide to be virtuous, sing to, and teach domestic skills. She and Frank would still go dancing, and Frances would go back to school. After the baby came, he'd be such a good father, and would make all of them laugh. Her thoughts tumbled one upon another every time she had a moment to think about Frank and the future. She was staring out windows so often that Mrs. Birch reprimanded her once or twice.

With stars in her eyes, she gave Mrs. Birch a week's notice—she wasn't sorry she'd never hear her say, "Doncha know?" again—went by her parents' place to bid farewell to her family, and headed to the West Coast on the Union Pacific. "Tea for Two" kept running through her head on the way there, and she hummed it to herself as she rocked across the miles.

Denker Avenue, Gramercy Park, Los Angeles, California

The cottage was a joy to her—her very own house. Well, it wasn't *her* house, but it was her and Frank's home, at least. It would take a while to completely furnish it, but as long as they had beds and a kitchen table, she'd be happy for now. She slept in the second bedroom at first, keeping herself chaste.

They were married on August 15. Her father had finally relented and had a phone installed in the Grant Avenue house in Ogden, and she called her mother afterward to tell her that they really had tied the knot and she was now Mrs. Frank Sims, of the Gramercy Park neighborhood of Los Angeles. That sounded high-tone, but really it was an area of inexpensive small homes, which was just fine with Frances and Frank. She got a part-time job at the bakery where he worked, where they soon benefited from her superior pie-making abilities.

Life with Frank was perhaps not a fairy tale, but it was pretty darn good.

In September, she signed up for night school classes to begin the long process of getting her high school diploma.

Chapter 24

New York, New York, & Ogden, Utah
March to December 1928

Marie Emilie Palmen had sailed into Southampton, New York, on a brisk March day, having left Hamburg ten days before on the ship *Deutschland*, and was now on the ferry to Ellis Island to complete her immigration to the United States. She was thirty-two years old and excited to see her American husband, Walter, whom she'd married five years earlier in Germany, where he'd been a Mormon missionary after World War I. She had converted to that faith for him, gladly, and Walter had applied for her US visa so that she could emigrate.

Before her departure, Marie's father, Wilhelm Uhlrich, had gone to the bank and procured twenty-five dollars in US money just in case, so she wouldn't arrive empty-handed. She felt secure in her near future, with US money in her purse—which she likely wouldn't need, since Walter would be there—and a suitcase of clothing.

She recombed her curly strawberry-blonde hair and stayed out of the wind, although she would have liked to be on the exterior deck with a better view of the famous Statue of Liberty. Walter had told her that New York was warmer than Braunschweig, but she knew it would still be late winter, as it would be in Ogden. She pulled her good wool coat closer around her slim torso. Ogden was near some beautiful mountains, according to Walter, hence she'd feel almost at home.

Some of the people on the ship were Americans returning home, some were Germans seeking US citizenship, and some were Germans who were visiting the US or coming here to work temporarily—at least, that was their listed reason on the passenger manifest. Some, like Marie, were brides who'd married overseas, which was preferable to coming as a single woman. It was fortunate that this was essentially a German voyage, because Marie spoke almost no English other than *please, thank you, excuse me, good morning,* and *good evening.* Oh, and *yes* and *no,* of course, although if she nodded and said "*ja*" or shook her head and said "*nein,*" the Americans she'd encountered thus far seemed to understand what she said. Walter was fairly fluent in German, so they'd had no problem in Braunschweig, and she assumed that many Americans spoke German.

Marie stood in the long line at the port with her suitcase, occasionally straining from side to side to see if she could spot Walter waiting for her at the other end of the process, but she couldn't see past the table with all the administrative people sitting at it, only that there were doors leading outside beyond that.

The couple she'd met on the ship was ahead of her and helped translate when she arrived at the table, for which she was grateful. She would have flirted with her blue eyes if she'd needed to, but she didn't know if that would have been of much good here. She smiled when they asked her questions, then turned to Herr and Frau Schafer to hear what the questions were; once she understood, she related the answers to them, and they to the administrators. The main things they were interested in, aside from her name, date of birth, where she was from, and so on, seemed to be that someone was meeting her, that she was married to an American citizen, and that she had some money in her purse.

At last they were out of the processing room and stepping into the cool New York air. But where was Walter? The Schafers felt protective and stayed with her, the three of them moving across the ferry dock for the boat into the city. They encouraged her that perhaps he had meant he'd meet her at the dock in the city. Perhaps she'd misunderstood his letter. She told them no, he'd said *at immigration, when you get off the boat.* They wondered if he'd meant at Southampton and she'd missed him, but she insisted he'd meant at immigration. That seemed like it must mean on Ellis Island.

They made their way up the ramp to the ferry to New York City. Marie was dismayed. Had something happened to Walter? She couldn't suppress her tears, and Frau Schafer put a kind arm around her shoulder.

When they arrived at the next dock, there was still no Walter. The Schafers waited with her until the crowds had cleared.

"Mrs. Palmen, do you have a phone number for your husband? Where he'd be staying in New York? Or at his home in Ogden?"

"I have a number for him in Ogden."

"I think we'd better try calling there, and then we need to get on to our destination. We don't want to leave you here, but we may miss our train."

Herr Schafer put a washer slug—he knew it would pass for a nickel—into the phone, and contacted long distance. The operator told him the call to Ogden would be about fifteen dollars for three minutes.

Marie was aghast. "I can't pay that. I only have twenty-five dollars in my purse, and what if I need to get a hotel and a meal?" Her tears flowed again.

The Schafers looked at each other for a long moment. Finally, Frau Schafer said gently, "Mrs. Palmen, come with us. We are staying on the Lower East Side with friends, and there is a large German community around Tompkins Square. I'm sure we can find you a place to stay, and possibly someone who will make the phone call for you."

"But how will my husband know where I am if I've left the dock here?" Marie was almost frantic, in her reticent way.

"I think maybe something has happened that prevented him from meeting you," Frau Schafer suggested. "Come, please, come with us; we'll get a taxi, and you save your money in case you need it."

Marie relented, her shoulders slumped. What could have happened?

The Schafers set Marie up at a women's rooming house, where the German-speaking mistress, Mrs. Muller—her parents had emigrated from Germany—offered her a shared room for fifty cents a night, a bit more if she wanted meals. Marie calculated that with no other expenses, including bus fare or anything else, she had about enough for perhaps three weeks. This would not do. The Schafers suggested she ask the mistress if there was some work she could get in order to pay for a telegram to Walter and possibly a train ticket to Ogden, advice she followed gratefully.

Marie quietly cried herself to sleep in her shared room, skipping dinner. She took a small breakfast of toast and coffee the next day, to conserve her funds, and soon learned that meals at restaurants or even dime-store counters were going to cost more than the rooming house would charge for a lunch or dinner.

Where is Walter? she wondered despairingly. *And what am I to do until I find him?*

❧

Mrs. Muller put a hand on Marie's shoulder at lunch one day and told her, "I've found you a position. You'll be a nanny and maid for a violinist here in New York; they have steady income, and you can earn enough to set yourself up here or go on out to Utah, as you wish."

So she moved in with the Guidi family. She had wondered how these Italian people would know how to communicate with her, but it turned out they also spoke some German; the director of the New York Philharmonic was Dutch-German. She breathed a sigh of relief and began the challenging job of managing the Guidi children, who did *not* speak German and told her in no uncertain terms, "You have to learn to speak English! This is America!"

Perhaps all American children were this rude? Or maybe only the rich ones. She picked up what words she could, and with her wages bought a German–English dictionary to help her communicate. She didn't mind doing the housework; she had always liked a very orderly house. It helped ease her mind to concentrate on these tasks in the midst of her messy situation. She wished she had never left Germany but was sure that something must have happened to Walter, and her goal was to save enough to get to Utah to be with him.

She sent him a telegram telling him where she was as soon as she felt she had enough money to do so. The telegram was delivered, but there was no response. Still, she doggedly did her work and saved money each week. At least here she had her own room.

After a month or so, the Guidis let her know that they were going to be moving out to California—not right away, but soon—and that she should plan for that. It was hard for her to fully understand what they meant at first, but after a series of disjointed conversations she understood that she would need to move on in the near future. She was not daunted by this; she had learned by now how to get to Ogden.

She'd first need to take a train to Chicago—that would cost about $50, including meals—and from there it would cost $100 to get to Ogden. It was going to take days to get there, and she might need to stay in a hotel once or twice, rather than risk falling asleep in her seat or on a bench in a passenger car. But she had saved $200 over the last several months, working for the Guidis, and knew that once she got to Ogden Walter would take care of her financially—assuming he was still alive.

A few weeks before Christmas, Marie sent another telegram to Walter, which again went unanswered. She departed New York for Ogden, and arrived a few days later to see the mountains she'd expected covered in snow. It seemed like a wonderland after the streets of New York.

She made her way to Walter's address, carried her suitcase up the wooden steps of the nice little cottage that would be her home, and knocked at the door. Although she felt she should be able to just walk into her own house, she was concerned still that something had happened to Walter and it was possible his family might be staying here, or that he might be in the hospital or God knew what.

The door opened, and there stood Walter, healthy and groomed. Nothing at all seemed to be wrong with him.

"Marie!" he uttered, stunned.

"*Ja*, Walter, I am here," she said in her stilted English. At least she knew more than she had a few months ago; she thought he would be pleased about that.

He ran his hand over his hair, a worried look on his face.

"Are you not going to ask me into . . . your house?"

Chapter 25

Ogden, Utah
April 1928

Anita opened her parents' front door to hear soft sobbing coming from their bedroom.

"Mother? Mama, is that you? Are you okay?" she said as she half ran to the bedroom.

Naomi grabbed her handkerchief and wiped her eyes and her nose. "I'm okay . . . just having kind of a hard day."

"Did something happen?"

"No . . . no. I just . . . I'm just so tired. And there is always much more to do now that you and Frances are not living here. I mean, Carl helps, he does, but he's a boy, and your dad doesn't expect him to help with what he calls women's chores, so . . . well, you know. And your dad and I aren't getting along real well."

"Did you have an argument?"

Naomi half chuckled. "Huh. An argument. *Another* argument, more like. He's gone so much . . . even more than he used to be. He stays in Evanston a lot more overnight. He says now that he has more responsibility, they want him at the station in Evanston as much as in Ogden for one thing and another. At least now that we've got the telephone, he lets me know if he's coming home or not, and I don't spend days wondering unless he calls the Abbotts or sends me a telegram." She shook her head. "But I don't mean to trouble you with my problems, Sis. You're busy with working and going out with your friends, and going to your new church. I'm glad you still manage to come by and see us too."

"Oh, Mother, I'm so sorry." Anita was a little fearful about her mother's emotional and mental state. It wasn't like her to cry, especially in front of anyone. She was used to Naomi caring for everyone else, and she had no idea what she might do to ease her mother's mind and heart. This was an adult problem, a marriage problem, and she felt in over her head.

"I can't do any more than I'm already doing here at the house," she said defensively. "Unless I don't go out as much. It's not like it's all the time, just mostly on Friday or Saturday nights, when I don't have to work . . . I don't want to skip church, though."

"It's okay, I'm sorry you saw me cry." Naomi managed a reassuring smile. "I'm okay. Don't worry about it. Let's talk about something else. Was there something you wanted, or is this just a visit?"

"Oh, listen, I wanted to tell you—I was looking over the boardinghouse register and saw that Mr. Foreland is coming this weekend to stay. Did you know that?"

"Oh, really? Huh. I guess he wants to see some more of the sights of Ogden." Naomi smiled and rolled her eyes.

Anita grinned a half smile. "Well, a lot of people come to see the countryside, all the mountains and such. You know, he was here again a couple of months ago too."

"Oh, he was? I wonder what's bringing him out this way so much."

Naomi knew that Charley had been out to Ogden again previously; he had come by late one morning and had lunch when he was here the last time, and had fixed her wringer washing machine. All the kids (except for little Clarence, who didn't pay much attention to what his mother was doing or who came to visit) had been at school when he came, and she hadn't mentioned it to Anita or any of the other kids because she didn't want to start any rumors, being home alone with a man who wasn't a relative. She'd figured that if Deborah Abbott asked, she'd just tell her he'd come by to fix the washing machine, which Deborah could have seen anyway if she'd looked out her back window. And Frank Sr. hadn't known there was anything wrong with the machine, since he never used it and wasn't home when it stopped working; there had been no reason to discuss it with him.

It had been real nice to just have a little conversation with a man who wasn't mad at her or even just plain uninterested, and had offered to help her out.

"I just wondered if you knew he was coming," Anita said. "Maybe he's got work out here?"

"Well, your grandmother did tell me that he's been traveling some; he doesn't go back up to Missouri to see his folks as much these days as before. Maybe he does have some work here or something. He said he might come out to Ogden again, last time he came. Single men sometimes like to get around the country and see new places. But no, I didn't know he was coming."

"Do you want me to tell him to call you if he's going to be around for a while?" Anita asked.

"Oh, gosh, I don't know." Naomi's cheeks grew warm. "Why would he want to do that?"

"I remembered he fixed the door for you a couple years ago when he was here to bring the boys back, and maybe there's something around here you could pay him to do. Or trade him for something. It would be some extra help."

"That's an idea," Naomi said carefully. "As long as your dad's not going to be home. He wouldn't like him being around."

Charley did call, and asked if Naomi wanted to go walking in the park. She was surprised at the invitation and told him no, she couldn't do that. She thought maybe he'd meant to bring the children too, or something, but it still didn't seem proper. Maybe in his family, acquaintances of the opposite sex could socialize outside their marriages without people talking, but not in hers.

Then he asked if she had anything needing fixing, and she told him yes, the back fence was broken, and she'd pay him or give him some canned goods or homemade bread or some mending on his clothes, whatever would be fair, if he'd like to do a barter. Frank wasn't home from the rails; he was over in Evanston again, and wouldn't be back until next week. She figured it wouldn't matter if Charley was there on the Saturday.

So they agreed that he'd come by on Saturday morning, when the house was in its usual chaos of breakfast and chores and kids not being in school.

Naomi's son Carl answered the door when Charley knocked, and was clearly not expecting to see his grandmother's hired hand standing on the porch in his clean clothes.

"Hello," Charley said. "I don't know if you remember me, but I'm your grandmother's worker out in Oklahoma; I've come by to fix your back fence."

Carl stood and looked at Charley for a moment—eye to eye, Charley noted; he'd grown quite a bit since they'd last seen one another—then turned and called over his shoulder, "Mother? There's someone here to fix the fence . . . Granma Sims's hired man."

Naomi came out of the kitchen, drying her hands on a towel. "Oh, hello there, Charley. Thanks for coming by. Carl, I'm doing a barter with Mr. Foreland to fix our fence. Your dad won't have time to do it when he's here for just a few days next week. Maybe you could help Mr. Foreland if he needs it."

"Hello, Mrs. Wolff." Charley smiled carefully as he slowly stepped into the living room.

"Charley, if I've told you once, I've told you fifty times, you can call me Naomi," she said lightly. "You're part of my mother's family at this point. Carl, show Mr. Foreland where the fence is broken out there. We'll all have lunch later on when you take a break."

Not long after Charley's arrival, Hermann, Henry, and Frank appeared from their room and looked out the back kitchen window.

"Who's that man out there?" Henry asked.

"That's Mr. Foreland!" Frank said excitedly. "Charley Foreland from Granma Sims's farm. Remember?"

"Oh, yes, I remember him now," Henry answered.

"He's fixing our fence," Naomi told them.

"But why?" Frank asked. "Why's he out here in Ogden?"

"I don't know. It's none of my business, what he's doing here . . . Maybe he's got other work here or maybe he's on a vacation. I didn't ask him."

"A vacation in Ogden?" Frank asked, and let out a short laugh. (At twelve, Frank was a clever boy; nothing got past him.)

"Well, that suits some people," Naomi said. "It's pretty flat out in Oklahoma, you know, so maybe he likes seeing the mountains. And it's just a different place from Kansas City and those parts. Men like to see new places sometimes. Maybe he just likes to ride the train, like your father."

"I'm gonna go out and tell him hello and ask him why he's in Ogden," Frank announced. "George!" he called out. "Mr. Foreland's here from Granma Sims' farm!"

"Oh, you'll do no such thing, Frank!" Naomi warned. "You can go say hello, since you know him from the farm, but don't go asking any nosy questions. I mean it. If I hear you are bothering him, I'll see you regret it."

Frank and the other boys all descended on Charley Foreland at once, with a clamor of greetings and questions. Naomi shook her head, watching them out the window, but smiled at her sons' enthusiasm. There was no controlling what they asked him or didn't ask him.

Charley Foreland went back to Oklahoma the next day. They'd all had a nice lunch, with a lot of laughs and him teasing the kids. When the kids went out to play, Charley had mentioned that he thought it was too bad . . . sad, even . . . that Naomi was home alone much of the time, a nice woman like her.

Naomi appreciated the thought, she'd told him, but she wasn't alone, she was surrounded by her children.

"Well, that's not exactly what I meant," Charley had said.

Naomi had gotten his meaning. She'd looked at him long and directly, but hadn't responded to his remark. It was nice to have a friend who appreciated her—and, moreover, treated her like she was more than a helpmate.

She loved Frank. He was her husband, he had provided for her and the children for twenty years now, and she'd promised "'til death do us part." But sometimes it looked like a long, bumpy road from here to death.

Chapter 26

Ogden, Utah
May 1928

"The boys told me that man who works for your mother was here. Fixing our fence. How'd that come to be?" Frank asked Naomi in their bedroom, after she'd put the youngest children to bed.

"Oh, Charley Foreland." Naomi hoped she sounded casual. "He was staying at the boardinghouse where Sis works. She talked to him; he asked her if I could use any help around here. So he called up and I told him he could mend the fence; I mended a shirt for him and gave him canned peaches and a loaf of bread. We did a trade."

"You know I don't like strange men coming around here, especially when I'm not home," Frank said tersely.

"Oh, honey, we know him, and it's the same as if I hired someone to come and do the work. Except better, since we bartered and I didn't have to give him money. I thought you'd be glad the fence was fixed. I knew he'd do a good job, since he does that sort of thing for Mother all the time."

"Well don't let it happen again." Frank gave her a hard look. "He's an Indian, besides. He might get ideas, being here when I'm not. What would the neighbors think?"

Naomi didn't admit she'd had the same thought, except Charley had been outside working, so anyone who cared to could see him out there doing something normal.

"Well . . . he's a very nice man; who cares if he's Indian? And we don't even know that he is. He just has black hair and kinda dark skin." She shrugged. "Anyway, I doubt we'll ever see him around here again."

"Why'd he come here in the first place? Little Frank said he said 'he just likes seeing the mountains.' He doesn't have to come a thousand miles to see a dang mountain."

"I don't know! Maybe he likes seeing a different big town besides Tulsa or Kansas City. Maybe he likes the scenery. Maybe he likes the ice cream flavors at Farr Better or Sawyer Brothers." Naomi opened her eyes wide and shook her head at her husband. "Maybe he likes to ride the rails, like you do. Gosh, Frank, what do you want me to say? I hardly know the man."

Frank looked away as he unbuttoned his shirt.

"I mean, why do you like to stay in Evanston so much when you could take just a few hours to come on home? If we're asking questions here." She raised her eyebrows at him.

"You know I have to be there at the station house. They ask me to stay on extra days sometimes nowadays," he said evasively.

Yes, and that powder from time to time on your shirt collar and perfume on your coat came right from the station house; I'm sure they've got a new station master who likes to use Jergens lotion . . . like Hermann does. But Naomi didn't want to dwell on that last thought. She was worried about her son; he was very different from his twin. He was different than everybody they knew, come to that. She had hoped he'd grow out of this fascination with female things, but he still hadn't. She needed to have him talk to the pastor, before Frank laid into him again for being a sissy.

She decided to make peace. "I know . . . they keep you on there more than you want to be, dear. Let's just forget about all this." She put her arms around Frank's waist. "I know you're tired, but at least we can cuddle, huh?"

His face softened and he returned her embrace. "Okay, let's drop it for now. I just don't want to come home to any more reports of a man being here when I'm not."

"What about the iceman? Or the milkman?" Naomi teased.

"Heh!" Frank snickered. "Especially not the milkman!"

At last, she'd gotten him to lighten his mood and change the subject.

Yes, she did like Charley. And he sure didn't put her through the third degree when he came around. And yes, he happened to be handsome . . . and considerate. But there were lots of men like that in Ogden, and none of them were going to threaten her marriage. Frank had always been jealous, and she kind of liked that. At least if he did have someone on the side—or maybe even more than one someone—he still cared about her, still cared if someone else paid attention to her.

And even more importantly, he supported her and their children who still lived at home.

Chapter 27

Ogden, Utah, &
Stone Township, Oklahoma
Late Summer 1928

Naomi told her children, "Before school starts up again, I'm going out to see your Grandma Sims, and taking Dorothy and Clarence with me. The rest of you kids are old enough to stay here on your own; just you mind your p's and q's. Carl and Henry will be in charge, and Hermann and Marie can make sure there's always food on the table and the kitchen gets cleaned. Your brother Frank . . . well, he can help Carl and Henry. You all just make sure the door's locked at night and you don't stay up too late."

Naomi dished out cold roast beef left over from Sunday dinner and passed around the Best Foods mayonnaise. She was glad she no longer had to make it herself, remembering standing over a bowl whipping all those eggs and oil by hand.

The boys looked around the table, sharing the special, anticipatory look of older boys who'd be on their own for a few days. Marie, now ten, had no idea what she was in for. Naomi knew the days ahead would include a lot of dirty dishes on the counter and dirty laundry on the boys' rooms' floors, not to mention belongings all over the living room.

But apart from the expected mess, Naomi figured things would be okay. Frank Sr. had agreed to be here for a couple of days with the kids, and then Carl would take over, and Anita would come by each day to make sure they didn't burn the house down.

Clarence couldn't stop talking on the train to Oklahoma—asking what was that river called and how about that mountain and hey there were some more sheep or cows or horses. Everyone who passed by them had to comment on what a pretty little girl Dorothy was, especially the other mothers traveling east.

Charley picked them up at the station in Enid. Naomi had to admit she was happy to see him. She felt like she'd made a good friend, and she was glad he was there with her parents to help, since Joe and Nancy Sims were now in their early eighties. Joe didn't go down to California anymore, but what he could do on the farm was limited. Nancy was a bit more fit; though six months older than Joe, the years hadn't been as hard on her.

The children loved playing on the farm, and Charley played hide-and-go-seek with them, which generated a lot of giggling from both Dorothy and Clarence. Naomi could tell they appreciated having their mother to themselves on this vacation, and she was glad to be able to pay them more attention than she had time for at home, letting them climb up on her lap almost any time they wanted and singing "Yes! We Have No Bananas" or "If You Knew Susie" and dancing with them.

Nancy commented at the kitchen table, "Seems like you're feeling pretty good these days. It's good to see you happy. As much as I can see of you, anyhow, with these old eyes."

"Well, Mother, it's good to get away from taking care of nine children at once." Naomi took another sip of coffee. "The little ones are much easier; they don't get into much trouble. I do believe I don't have to switch them as much as I did the older kids. Or maybe I'm just getting tired of paddling them all. And Dorothy is such a sweetheart and Clarence is really funny, even for his age. Next month he'll start kindergarten, and all my brood will be out of the house in the daytime. So this trip is kind of the end of being a mommy to tiny kids. "

"How are you and Frank getting along? Better than two years ago?" Nancy took a puff on her pipe.

"Oh, I'd say the same. You know, ups and downs. We don't have relations as much as we used to. Which is kind of a relief, because I'd just as soon not get pregnant again, and the less we do it, the less the chance, to be frank. Ha ha . . . frank." She glanced down at her lap. "I think he's got a woman in Evanston, Mama. I'm just glad she must be clean, because I haven't had any sickness like I've heard some railroad wives get. If you get my drift."

"Oh, I was drifting on out that direction as soon as you said, 'woman in Evanston.'" Nancy sighed. "You know there's nothing we can do about that. Your father might have had other women; he was gone a lot. And who knows what he saw out there in California, women in short skirts and those halter tops."

"Mama, there are short skirts and halter tops in Ogden too; you're just a little old-fashioned. It's 1928, for heaven's sake! You should see the dresses Frances and Sis get up in. All those flapper things. Besides, Daddy is eighty-two now! I can't imagine anyone's in a hurry to jump on him."

"Ha! Including me."

The two women laughed.

"You hear from Frances?" Nancy asked.

"Yes, she writes to me and Frank every so often and says this and that . . . how they go out dancing with friends . . . She's working in the same bakery as her husband, Frank. She doesn't ever call on the telephone; she's real thrifty that way. A stamp is cheaper, and there's no emergency. And oh, she's pregnant! Finally going to have a baby, in maybe January? She tends to be so secretive, I was surprised she told us at all before the child popped out. It seems like her letters are more for Frank . . . my Frank, I mean . . ."

"Well, I agree with people who think their lives are nobody else's business. But Frances *was* always more like her daddy," Nancy mused. "Tight-lipped. She sure didn't get pregnant as fast as you did, but these kids now, they have ways so they aren't just having one baby after another. I don't even want to know how they manage that and still have relations."

"Well, it's not a big mystery. They have these rubber caps the woman puts up inside, and they use quinine with them to keep from getting pregnant. Sis told me that Frances and one of Sis's friends at work told her all about it."

"Sis isn't . . . she's not . . . well, you know, with boys, is she? Not yet?"

"I haven't the foggiest, but she goes to church so much I can't imagine she'd do anything like that before getting married. She does have a boyfriend. But you know what they say: 'People do what everybody else does, given half a chance.'"

Naomi sat in the twig chair out under the shade tree. She saw that the chair was getting pretty worn out and had one leg shorter than the others, but she propped the short leg with a flat rock, and with a couple of cushions from the house, it was comfortable enough. While the two kids napped, she read a copy of *Better Homes and Gardens* her mother had splurged on at the general store in Enid. Even Nancy liked a little culture, Naomi was happy to find.

She put her feet up on a stool, started nodding off, and laid the magazine on the little side table they'd carted out from the barn so's anyone could sit and chat and have a place to put their lemonade. Her hand rested on the magazine . . . she thought she'd just close her eyes a moment.

Just as she was drifting off, she felt a large hand laid gently on top of hers, and her eyes popped open.

She turned to see Charley sitting beside her in the other chair. She didn't pull her hand away at first, looking into his eyes with an obvious question. She thought perhaps something had happened to her mother.

Charley looked right back at her openly and didn't move his hand, and didn't say anything either.

Naomi slowly drew her hand back to her lap.

"Charley. Is everything okay?" She felt a rush of something like embarrassment, something like excitement, something like good trouble, his touch still a memory on her skin.

"Everything's fine. Just fine." He put his hand on his knee and looked off in the distance.

"Nothing's wrong with Mother or Daddy? You didn't come to tell me something happened?"

"No, nothing like. I just saw you sitting there nice and quiet and looking so . . . pretty. I just wanted to be near some of that. I'm sorry."

"It's okay. I was just . . . surprised." She looked at him, and he turned his head and gazed into her eyes again.

"Gosh, Charley, you're not . . . you don't feel . . . I don't know what to say."

"I don't know what to say either. It was easy to just show you I felt something. I do feel something."

Naomi cleared her throat. "If I wasn't married . . . if I wasn't married with nine children at home and I met you long ago . . . oh, if a lot of things . . . but here we are. Here in Oklahoma. Far away from my real life. You know, things might look different when I'm here. But they're not." She was bewildered that they were even having the conversation, but felt almost a revelation when she quickly thought back on those times . . . the coyote act, making her laugh, fixing the door, the washer, the fence . . .

"The way I feel is never different," Charley said simply. "Mostly I just feel lonely when I don't feel tired from working. Except your ma and pa—they make me feel like family, like when I lived with my folks, almost. And except when I'm around you. Then I just feel . . . glad. Glad I know a nice lady who is my good friend, even if she's married to somebody else. I feel . . . good around you, Naomi. There, I've said it all. I got nothing else to say about this, but I just wanted to tell you. I hope I didn't upset you."

"No, no, I'm not upset at all. Just maybe surprised. Gosh, thank you . . . you paid me a real nice compliment, Charley. And like I said, if things were different . . . but they're not. Things are the way they are." And now she was wishing maybe things weren't the way they were. But her life was so big, so overwhelming . . . and Frank, as distant as he was, still wanted her. Sometimes more like owned her.

She reached over and touched Charley on the arm, and he again gently laid his large brown hand atop her small but capable and tanned one, which he gave an almost imperceptible squeeze before he got up and walked to the bunkhouse.

Chapter 28

Evanston, Wyoming
Fall 1928

"Frank?" Minnie tilted her head, reminding him of Frances. "What is it? You seem like something's on your mind. I mean, you're a quiet man, but not usually like a stone."

Frank looked up from his paper, from his special spot in one of Minnie's overstuffed chairs. The woman knew how to buy comfortable furniture.

He sighed. "I don't know that I want to talk about it. I will tell you that this Indian man who works for my mother-in-law out in Oklahoma has come around Ogden a couple of times when I wasn't there. And then Naomi went out there to visit for a couple of weeks just before school started. I'm starting to wonder if something's not going on."

Minnie threw her head back and laughed. "You, of all people, don't want your wife to have somebody interested in her?"

"It's different for men than for women."

"Oh?" Minnie arched an eyebrow. "And what am I? What must you think of me, Frank Wolff?"

"It's different with you, Minnie," he said hastily. "We have an agreement, don't we? That this works well for both of us? You get to own your big house, your kids have a man around from time to time, it's a boardinghouse, so no one's the wiser if we are more than a landlady and a boarder . . . Isn't that right?"

"That's right, Frank. Yes, you're right. So right."

Minnie got up and went to the kitchen.

Frank sat there a moment and wondered if something had just gone wrong. He wasn't sure what it might be. He stood up, folded the paper and laid it on the coffee table, and slowly walked down the hall to the kitchen.

"Are you . . . mad or something?"

"No," Minnie said coolly, "I'm not mad."

"Well, now you're the one with the tight lips, are you?"

Minnie let out an exasperated sigh. "Frank, don't you see that I'm the same as Naomi? I'm just a widow, is all. She's like a railroad widow, though. What if she did have an affair? What difference would it make if you have me . . . and God knows probably somebody else east of here too?"

Frank didn't like this turn in the conversation. He looked down at the floor, at his shoes, and went to the back window to gaze out at the sycamore and elms, the leaves turning. This was such a nice corner lot Minnie had. "I don't see a reason for us to talk about this," he said. "Let's drop it."

"Well, of course," Minnie snapped. "Let's just drop it. As soon as things get a little messy, we don't talk about it. The kids will be home from school any minute anyhow."

Why can't things be simple? Frank thought. *I have a wife. Wives are supposed to be loyal to their husbands. I have paid for everything she and the children have for the last twenty-odd years. And Minnie . . . Minnie has everything she needs or wants, and no strings attached. I pay her to stay here, and she doesn't have to go without physical affection. Why can't we just go on without doing all this talking about who does what? Why should she care what I think about what my wife does? "Railroad widow"? She likes me being here as much as I like being here. Oh, man, oh man. I really don't want to think about any of this.*

He was glad to be off the hook. "Yes. There's no time to talk about all this right now anyway. I'll wash up for dinner and maybe take a nap."

"Yes, Frank, you do that," Minnie said, not looking at him. She went on about getting the pork chops ready for dinner.

Halfway down the hallway, Frank heard the unusually hard slam of the refrigerator door. Huh. Maybe she *was* mad. He just did not understand where women got some of their ideas.

He climbed the stairs to his room. And it was pretty much *his* room now; he had a cupboard in there where he could lock away an extra change of clothes and a second shaving kit when he was away, in case she needed to rent the room out. He fell back on the bed and stared at the ceiling until his eyelids became heavy and he dozed off.

Chapter 29

Ogden, Utah
January 1929

Marie Palmen had no qualms about refusing to have marital relations with her husband. After the way he'd left her in the lurch in New York, this seemed to her to be completely appropriate. Especially now that she knew why he hadn't shown up.

Her arrival a month prior had not been the cheery *Tannenbaum* gift she had anticipated. Within a day, they had the comeuppance conversation about what had transpired.

"Why did you not meet me in New York as we agreed?" she asked in German, knowing Walter was fluent enough that no aspect of her meaning would be lost on him.

He cleared his throat and looked away, then at the floor as he spoke, stealing quick glances at her blue eyes, which were riveted on him.

"Marie . . . I don't know how to say this. I guess the best way is to just blurt it out. My parents were angry with me for marrying in Germany, to someone they hadn't met, to a woman who didn't speak English . . . It didn't matter how much I loved you. They told me to just drop it, and it was not likely you'd ever come and find me. I didn't want to lose my family."

The blood rose in her cheeks. "Walter. I am your *wife.* Your WIFE. I am Frau Palmen. This is legal. This is a fact. Did they think I would just stay married to you in Germany? You knew I had booked passage to New York."

"I know, I know . . . I felt bad about it." He hung his head while he spoke. "But my parents convinced me you would just give up and stay in New York or go back to Germany. I am sorry. I really am."

"I came here with twenty-five US dollars! Did you think I had some fortune I brought with me to make a life for myself? You know my family is not wealthy and things are not so good in Germany right now. Just a loaf of bread costs too much. You know this. And did you think this was a good Mormon thing to do? To just leave your wife stranded in New York City, not knowing even how to speak English? Just saying please and thank you? No one I met at immigration knew 'Bitte' or 'Danke,' or even 'Guten Morgen'! I was lucky there was a home for women immigrants, and that a German couple at immigration translated for me. Can you imagine how afraid I was? I cried bitter tears!"

"I'm sorry, Marie. I said that. But can't you see?" he pleaded. "I didn't want to displease my parents . . . and I didn't want to lose my family over one person. I was too young to make this romantic decision that far from home. Can't you see?"

"I see that I am married to you. I see that your parents are more important to you than I am. The woman you said you loved. Do you still love me?"

"I . . . I'm not sure. It's been a long time apart, and I see things a little differently now."

"You're not sure. I am sitting here next to you, and you're not sure."

"Yes. I'm not sure. And . . . there's something else."

"What more?! *Ach!*" Marie shook her head and looked away, tears beginning to fill her eyes. *I should never have believed this fickle American boy.*

"Before I went to Germany, there was a girl. A girl I had wanted to marry. She broke up with me and met someone else, so I thought when I met you that it was meant to be. But then I came home . . . and time had passed . . . and she was single again . . . and . . . I've been seeing her. My parents encouraged me. I told them I was married and this wouldn't be fair to . . . to Rhoda . . . but they said, 'Your marriage can be annulled.'"

"And what is 'annulled'?"

"It's when the marriage is not . . . complete. Not consummated. And you can just file papers saying it was never a real marriage."

"Oh, I think when you and I were sleeping in the same bed in Germany it was pretty 'consummated'! Quite a bit of *consummated*." Marie stood up and went to the window, wiping her face with a lace-trimmed hankie her mother had given her. She gazed out on the snowy streets of Ogden, and at the majestic mountains not far from the edge of town. It reminded her a little of parts of Germany. She had thought she would be happy here, and now she was so angry she couldn't express it fully.

"So what about this Rhoda?" she asked woodenly.

"What do you mean, what about her?" Walter had one of those "poor me" looks.

"What are you going to tell her now? To go away, your wife is here?"

"I don't know. I don't know what to say to her or to you."

"Well I can tell you what to say. You tell her you are married and that married men don't see other women!"

"Marie, I don't know what to do."

"Okay, I can tell you one thing *I* can do! I can not sleep in the same bed with you! I can not cook for you! I can not clean for you or do the things a proper wife should do! Why do I want to serve a man who isn't sure he loves me? Who leaves me at the dock thousands of miles away? You tell me that! You can sleep on this settee here."

And that's how they'd lived for the last month, with Marie in the bedroom, Walter on the sofa, and each of them making separate meals and doing their separate laundry. (Well, Walter took his to his mother's house.)

The one thing Marie did with Walter was go to church. Though there were almost no members there who spoke German, one woman, Sarah Gerhardt, befriended her. Through Sarah she learned there was a German community in Ogden, and that the German Lutheran church in particular had many people who spoke German. In confiding her situation to a woman at the Lutheran church, Mrs. Schneider, she was told there was an attorney who would help her file for divorce if that was what she wanted to do.

Although this didn't appeal to Marie, she saw no other choice, and decided to file the papers at the end of January.

Marie was happy to have Mrs. Schneider there with her to translate in court. Her new friend stood and addressed the judge when they called the case of Marie Palmen.

"Your honor, I am speaking for Mrs. Palmen, who has almost no English. She is asking for a divorce from Walter Palmen, who she married in Germany, and then he never came to get her in New York, leaving her stranded with twenty-five dollars, no English, and having to find her own way. She found work, then traveled out here to Ogden alone. Mr. Palmen says his parents did not want him to marry a German girl who doesn't speak English and he is sorry he married her now."

Judge Roberts looked at the paperwork. He looked at Marie. "Do you understand all this, Mrs. Palmen?"

Mrs. Schneider told Marie all of what she'd told the judge, and asked her if she understood.

"*Ja*," Marie answered, nodding. "Yes. I know dis."

Judge Roberts looked through the paperwork again. "Okay. This is an unusual case, but I find for the plaintiff. I am granting twenty-three dollars a month in temporary alimony until this can be further settled." He banged his gavel, giving Marie a start.

Back at home, Marie showed Walter the papers.

He blanched. "What?! I have to pay you that much? Well then you can find another place to live, since you have all that money to live on! Or get yourself a damn job! You should pack your things and go!"

Mrs. Schneider had told her that if she found she needed a temporary place, she could stay at their home. Once again, Marie Palmen was taking up residence in an unfamiliar place.

At church, her friend Sarah confided that Walter had told Rhoda not to worry—that they'd be together one day, if she could just wait.

A fine kettle of fish, thought Marie.

Chapter 30

Ogden, Utah
March 1929

Frank was home from the rails. While he read his paper on the davenport in the living room, Naomi fixed her hair in the bedroom, thinking if she looked nice, maybe Frank would be amenable to a request. She turned her head from side to side, decided she looked as good as she was going to get, and tried a smile. *Looks put-on*, she thought.

She took a deep breath and tried to walk into the living room as casually as possible. Nothing up her sleeve.

She stood in the doorway. He didn't look up.

"Frank?"

"Hmmp . . . what?"

"You know, I'd really like to go down to Los Angeles to see Frances. To see the new baby girl—LaVon. She's six weeks or more now. What do you think? I could take the train."

Frank slowly put down his paper and repositioned his glasses on his nose. He sighed, then said, "I don't think so," and started to lift his paper back up to reading level.

"But why? Clarence and Dorothy will be in school, and Marie and the boys can watch them after school. Just a quick trip to see my first grandchild—*our* first grandchild."

"Naomi, you'd be gone too long. I don't want these kids left without their mother when I have to be away."

"Well, how far is it?" she asked, biting a fingernail. This wasn't going well, but the prospect still seemed possible.

"It's too far. Taking the train down there, it'd take more than a day. Two days, maybe three. Where would you sleep if you had to stop for a few hours? It goes to San Francisco first, and then you catch another train to Los Angeles. It's well over seven hundred miles."

Frank sounded a little hesitant about this information, and Naomi wondered if his distance estimates were true—but she had to accept what he said.

"Okay, maybe three days of travel and I'd stay down there maybe four days; I'd only be gone a week. That's only five school days and a weekend. Please, Frank, let me get a ticket. Maybe just this once I could get a sleeping berth since it's only me, one person."

"No. We're not talking about this. It's too far, you'd be gone too long, you'd get down there and be calling me wanting to stay a few more days with the baby and Frances."

"Frank, I'm only going to have one first grandchild. Please." She worked to keep her voice level, trying to match his firmness.

"And that baby is my grandchild too. Do you see me wanting to run off to California? Huh?"

"Frank. The only place I ever go is to visit my mother. On a farm out in the middle of nowhere in Oklahoma. Before that, Kansas. It's not like I take some big ol' vacation every now and then. I'd like to see another place sometime . . . like you do."

"Like I do!" He slapped his folded paper on the side table. "Oh, yes, like I do! I'm gone because I have to be. You think I like working on those trains all the time? I used to shovel coal into that damn engine. Now at least I don't have to do that much as an engineer; I get to call the shots. But it's still tiring, dirty work. You think I like that? Being gone all the time? No, I don't!"

Naomi saw that nothing she said was going to change his mind now. Feeling powerless, she held her tongue, but she wanted to say, *Oh, I think you and I both know you like to be out there. Free, riding the rails, sleeping God knows where or with who. And you've got me here to take care of all your kids and our home. What happened to us? I was so happy the day we married, that you wanted to take care of me and give me a home and children. What have I ever done that you don't think I deserve this little trip?*

A few days later, the phone rang. Naomi answered, and Myrtle down at the telephone switchboard said, "Naomi?"

"Yes," she answered. "Hi, Myrtle." She still wasn't used to having a phone, and was never sure if she was answering right or talking so people could hear her.

"Hold on, got a call for you."

A woman's voice came on. It wasn't Nancy, and it wasn't Frank's mother, and it wasn't Frances either.

"Hello? Is this the Wolff residence?"

"Yes, it is." Naomi wondered what in the world this call was about.

"May I speak to Mr. Frank Wolff?"

"Yes, I'll get him." She didn't know if she should ask who the caller was or what. Should she have asked what the woman wanted?

Puzzled, she went to the kitchen and told Frank he had a phone call. Frank looked up from his paper and cup of coffee and looked at Naomi for a moment. "Who is it?"

"It's a woman. She didn't say who she was, and I didn't ask. I didn't know if it was polite to ask her."

Frank set his lips firmly together.

Oh, so that was another mistake. Just great, Naomi thought. *Maybe somebody should have explained to me how these things are done.*

Didn't the woman have the sense to ask who it was? Frank shook his head. Well, she hadn't been around telephones all that much. He walked into the living room and picked up the phone.

"Hello? This is Frank Wolff."

On the other end, Minnie's voice said, "Hello, Frank!"

"Oh, hello." *Why is she calling here?* He was glad to hear her voice, but this was a first and he wasn't sure it was a good idea.

"I just wanted an excuse to talk to you. Are you still coming next week?"

"Oh. Yes, yes, I am. I'll be in Evanston on the Wednesday. You can reserve me a room," he added, thinking quickly.

"Ha ha . . ." Minnie chuckled. "Okay, I'll do that. I wanted to plan the shopping, and this way I can be sure and have pork chops and applesauce for you."

"Okay then." He smiled. She remembered what he loved to eat.

"Well, bye for now."

"Yes. Goodbye. Thank you for your call."

He thought he'd better wipe the smile off his face before he went back to the kitchen.

"Well, who was the mysterious caller?" Naomi was so intrigued she could hardly contain herself.

"Oh, that? It was just the boardinghouse where I stay in Evanston. Wanted to know if I wanted a room next week because they've got someone else wants a room too. I didn't book it in advance, but since I stay there sometimes, they called me."

"Oh. Okay." This seemed odd to Naomi. "No one's ever called here before. Don't they have more than one boardinghouse in Evanston, anyway?"

"Well, yes, of course, but I like this one the best, and I usually stay there. So they were being considerate to check with me." He sat down and picked up his paper. He gestured toward his coffee cup, now cold. "Could you heat that coffeepot up for me?"

"Sure," she said. "I'll have some too."

She looked at Frank for a moment, but he didn't look up. She sensed something funny but couldn't put her finger on it. *Was that woman the one with the powder, the lotion, the perfume I smell on him sometimes? If it was, if I knew that for sure, what would I do, anyway?*

She felt trapped, like a bird in a nice cage. *Well, not always all that nice.*

Chapter 31

Ogden, Utah, &
Stone Township, Oklahoma
Late March 1929

Naomi approached Frank again not long after the conversation about Los Angeles and the strange phone call.

"Frank, my dad is sick. I'm going to Oklahoma during the kids' Easter vacation. I want to see him in case he's dying, and I can help Mama taking care of him. I'll take Clarence, and Carl can take care of Dorothy and the other kids if you won't be here. I have to do this."

Frank thought a moment, this time from his overstuffed chair. He put his pipe in its holder. "Okay. I guess you'd better go. I won't be here part of the time, but will you be back for Easter, to take the children to church?"

Naomi hadn't thought that far ahead. "Yes, of course. I'll be back on the Saturday. We'll leave the Saturday before, and I'll leave Enid early on Good Friday and come back home. Do the trains run on Good Friday?"

"Yes, they run on Good Friday. They run seven days a week. I've never known of a train that didn't run on some holiday," he said, not without a smidgen of impatience. "And I hope you're gonna do something about the kids' Easter. Coloring eggs or getting them some candy or something." He didn't look up from his paper.

"I'll make sure Marie does that in case the train is late on Saturday. I can't color Easter eggs a week in advance." She wondered if this man ever noticed anything that went on around their house. She was so tired of his comings and goings and acting like the children were only her responsibility.

Well, she reminded herself, he took the boys fishing sometimes, and he often came home with candy for all of them. And he made sure they went to church. That counted for something.

She just wished he were home more.

Naomi went to Western Union and sent a telegram to her mother and arranged for her and Clarence to be picked up in Enid on the Sunday before Easter.

Joe Sims was sick in bed. Naomi was worried about him, but Nancy said he'd pulled through things like this before.

"But Mama, not when he was eighty-two. He's worked awful hard all his life. All that farming and traveling to other farms."

"Well, maybe that's what has kept him alive," Nancy said. "He'll pull through, don't you worry. I appreciate you bein' here to help me out. But I don't think this is the end."

Naomi took a deep breath and tried to just let God take care of this. She'd prayed pretty hard for her dad these last weeks. Maybe he was another one of those men who had other women in his past, but when he was here, he was kind, and she knew he loved her and her brothers and sisters. Especially the ones that were his blood kin, although he had always been good to his stepchildren, Alice and Fred, as well.

Her sisters, Julia and Jessie, had come when they could, and her half sister, Alice, too, and she was happy to see all of them in passing when she'd first arrived on the Sunday. Having some of her family together was comforting. In this group, she felt like the baby and they still treated her like a little sister, even at thirty-nine, in both the good and the teasing or annoying ways.

She'd noticed Charley smiling, seeing this family dynamic, at the dinner table. He was always included now; after all, he was a distant cousin to the half-siblings, the Chalmerses, and no one thought of him as just a field hand. He was indispensable on the farm.

On Tuesday, Joe was asleep, Nancy was trying to sleep, and Clarence had lain down for his nap. Naomi put on a sweater, grabbed an afghan, and headed out to her favorite spot in the back of the house. It was nippy out, and the early spring sun was thin, the sky having that pale blue color, almost white. But it was better than sitting in the house for yet another hour, wondering and waiting.

Charley had just finished fixing something in the barn. He waved to her, paused a moment, and then walked on over to sit next to her.

"How you doin'?" he said kindly. He knew she was worried about her dad.

"Oh, okay, I guess." She looked down to her lap. She was afraid if he was too nice to her, she might cry.

"We haven't talked much this time."

"I know. You know, I think about you and that last time I was here."

"Oh, good. I mean, I am glad to hear that. That you think of me. I know there's nothing can be done . . . but I . . . just am glad."

She took his hand—dusty, strong, and cool. "Charley. Frank is . . . he's just . . . he's just not as nice to me as he used to be."

"Oh. I don't know if I feel sorry about that or . . . or what."

"Well, I've been thinking sometimes . . . and maybe I shouldn't . . . but I've been thinking sometimes, if only things were different. Like if for instance I stayed here in Oklahoma part of the time, more often, and then stayed in Ogden and . . . and I don't know what else. That's as far as I ever get in my thinking about it. About you."

"Well, I get a lot farther than that."

Naomi laughed and then Charley did as well. They had a long look at each other. He had such nice blue eyes—but not ice blue, like Frank's. Warmer, somehow. And that high forehead and that thick, dark hair, even for a man who was probably . . . probably how old? Hard to tell. Older than her, she thought. He didn't take his hand away. *And he doesn't even know everybody is asleep.*

He cleared his throat. "I'm gonna go clean up at the pump by my place. You want to take a walk with me after I wash up?"

She nodded. He walked, standing tall, toward the barn.

She got up and wrapped the afghan around herself. This time, she followed him to the bunkhouse.

Clarence woke up and rolled himself out of the trundle bed Nancy kept for visiting grandchildren. He went to the room where his mother slept, but she wasn't there. He peeked into his grandparents' room, where both were sleeping. He knew to be quiet.

He went downstairs to the kitchen, and his mother wasn't there either. She must be outside. He went out the back door and let the door slam behind him. He walked all around the house, looking out toward the barn, the pasture, and the fallow wheat fields. His mother was nowhere to be seen.

What if she left without me? What if she left me here? Mama wouldn't do that . . . Maybe she went to town. But the truck's parked there.

Clarence went back in the house. He climbed the stairs and checked in the extra room; maybe she was in there. No, she wasn't.

"Mama?" he called out. "Mama!"

Nancy had been roused by the slam of the back door but figured it was Naomi. Now, hearing Clarence calling for his mother, she dragged herself up from the bed and stepped to the doorway.

"Clarence? What's the matter?"

"Oh, Granma Sims, I can't find Mama."

"Oh, I'm sure she's somewhere. Where could she go? She's probably outside." Nancy knew it was a bit cold to be outside for long. She glanced at the bedside clock. She'd dozed off earlier in the afternoon and slept for over an hour.

"No, she's not outside. She's not in the house and she's not outside!" Clarence tried to choke back his tears.

"Oh, here, Carey, don't cry," Nancy said soothingly. "Let's find something to do. I'll bet she's just gone for a walk and will be right back." *A walk in this cold? Well, maybe.* "Let's bake some cookies! Would you like that? And you can draw me a picture. Before you know it, your mama will be back."

"Okay. Yes, I'd like to bake cookies. Can I lick the bowl?" That was a delight that had to be shared with the other kids at home.

Nancy busied Clarence with baking oatmeal cookies and glanced out the back window frequently. Finally, she saw Naomi emerge from the bunkhouse, Charley beside her. *Uh-oh,* she thought. *Well, I was afraid this might happen one day, and here's the day.*

She didn't tell Clarence she saw them coming, hand in hand.

But when he saw her staring out the window, he rushed to the door, opened it, and looked out toward the barn.

Naomi and Charley saw the door open and dropped their hands—not quickly enough that Clarence couldn't have seen, but he ran out so gleefully that it didn't seem to matter. Naomi and Charley glanced at each other, the knowing look of lovers almost caught.

"Mama! I woke up and you weren't there! Where were you?"

"Oh, honey, I went for a walk," Naomi said, thinking fast. "And on the way back I saw Mr. Foreland. And he said he'd walk me back to the house so's I wouldn't turn my ankle on rough ground. That's all."

"Me an' Granma Sims's baking oatmeal cookies!"

"Oh, did you help?"

"I did, Mama, and she let me lick the bowl."

Naomi and Charley glanced at each other again, and she was sure he was wondering the same thing as her: Had they gotten away with this . . . or not?

That evening, when Clarence was in bed and Joe was resting upstairs, feeling good enough to sit up and read, Nancy and Naomi were alone together.

They sat in the living room and spoke with hushed voices, but Nancy still conveyed her acute concern.

"What the Sam Hill were you doing?" she admonished. "No, don't tell me. I'm pretty sure I know. You'd better watch it. That was taking a big damn chance."

Her mother didn't usually swear.

"Mother . . . I just couldn't help it. Here I am, far away . . . every-one was asleep . . . Charley is *so* nice to me . . . and Frank just isn't anymore. He just isn't. I feel like Charley . . . like he *likes* me. Not just in that man and woman way, but he *likes* me, for myself, as a friend."

"Well that's just ducky. May I remind you that you are *married*?"

"That doesn't seem to stop Frank, or even Daddy, from what you and he have told me." Naomi was a little miffed at being judged.

"What has your dad told you?" Nancy was now on high alert.

"Just that I shouldn't expect Frank to be faithful when he's gone all the time . . . and that it doesn't mean anything. That it's different for men. So I figured, you know, since Daddy's gone a lot too, or used to be . . ."

"Well, you probably figured right. But it *is* different for men. For one thing, they can't get pregnant!" Nancy whispered as emphatically as she could. She really didn't want Joe to hear all this.

"We were careful."

"Oh, so you *were* doing what I thought you might be doing."

Naomi turned her face away from her mother. "I think that's all I want to say."

"You just be careful. *Real* careful. I'd leave this right here, go home Friday, and not give poor Charley any more encouragement. It's plain to see the man's like a sick cow around you."

Naomi hadn't thought it was that obvious. He didn't jump up and do things for her or anything like that . . . Well, sometimes he did. Gosh, maybe people could see it. And she knew for sure now that she cared for him too. She knew for sure.

Chapter 32

Ogden, Utah
April 1929

Walter Palmen was furious about the temporary alimony. He went to court and filed papers for a countersuit, claiming Marie had been cruel to him.

What's cruel if refusing a husband his right to sex isn't cruel? What's cruel if not a woman being bitter toward you every day, in your own house? And what about refusing to let your own parents in the house to visit?

When the judge reviewed the paperwork in court on April 4, he said, "Your wife, Mrs. Palmen, claims you failed to provide for her."

"I was married in Germany, your honor," Walter said. "And then I was unable to bring my bride to the United States, and needed to come home in 1925. My parents had asked me to come home. I hadn't heard from her after 1927, and then she showed up last December, out of the blue, at my house. You'd think a wife could write to her husband for the two years he was away."

"What kind of funds did she have when she arrived in New York?" Judge Roberts asked.

"I'm not sure, sir."

"You're not sure."

"No, sir. Like I said, she hadn't written to me in two years."

"And you had made no arrangements to bring your wife here in that two years?"

"Well, I was thinking about it, of course, and I . . . well, I had to earn her passage and all, and then she didn't write, so . . ."

"Did you provide for her here in Ogden?"

"I put a roof over her head, and there's always groceries in the cupboard."

"And what about yourself? Do you need nothing but a roof over your head and groceries in the cupboard? I find it strange, Mr. Palmen, that you didn't send for your wife, pay her passage, pay her train fare, and do all that you could to ensure that your wife would feel like you were her husband. This case needs further review."

The judge banged the gavel, and Walter turned and made his way out the door.

Marie Palmen was finding her way around town and trying to learn some damnable English. She didn't think she'd ever really be able to get it right. At least there was the Mormon church, one thing that had been the same for her in Germany. Except she'd see Walter there. She noticed he didn't come every time now. Well, she wasn't going to give up her religion just because he belonged to it too.

One day during social hour after Sunday school, a young woman she'd never met before approached her.

"Hello, I'm Anita Wolff," she said, offering her hand over the table laden with cookies in the recreation hall.

Marie extended her hand as well, and they had a cordial, ladylike shake. "Hello." She smiled tenuously. "I am Marie Palmen."

"I heard you've moved here from Germany?"

"Yes," answered Marie, not entirely sure about the phrase "moved here" but gathering that the young woman was asking if she came from Germany.

"My father is German Swiss. He speaks German, but I haven't learned much. '*Eins, zwei, drei*'—one, two, three! That's about it. And '*Gesundheit*'!" She laughed. "His mother and father came over; he was born here, in Missouri. And I have a sister named Marie."

This was a lot for Marie to process, and she only really understood "father is German Swiss; he speaks German," and "mother and father" and "sister named Marie," and her bungled pronunciation of four German words. But she knew the young lady was trying to be friendly, so she nodded and smiled.

"I'm sorry, I'm talking too much," Anita said. "Do you speak English?"

Marie finally was sure she understood, and answered, "Only a little."

"Oh, well, I hope we'll see each other again here. I've got to get going; this is my only day off from work."

Marie thought the girl probably wasn't working on the Sabbath but knew she'd said something about work, so she smiled and nodded. And they did see each other again, occasionally. It was nice to finally be making some friends besides Sarah and Mrs. Schneider.

Work. I'm going to need to get some kind of work too. Well, she'd managed in New York City, and she would manage here.

Naomi found herself distracted in a way she'd never been before. She'd stare out the kitchen window with a dish in her hand, lost in thought, until one of the kids would say, "Mother?" bringing her back to the moment. Then later, even the same day, she'd forget what she'd gone into the bedroom to get and have to stand there for a minute to remember that it was a handkerchief. She felt like she was acting the way her mother said the change had made her feel, but Naomi wasn't going through the change. She'd heard from the women at the church that the more children a woman had, the later her change came. It wasn't that.

She knew exactly what this was, and no matter how many times she told herself, *Leave it in Oklahoma; forget it ever happened*, she couldn't control the mishmash of unsettling thoughts that kept tumbling through her head.

Now I'm a fallen woman. But shouldn't I be sorry? I feel guilty, but I don't feel sorry. At least for once at my age someone was tender to me. More than Frank was, truth be told. More than he ever is now. But when I see Charley again—and I will have to see him again; he's practically family now—I will be firm. I will make it clear to him we can only be friends. I will not be alone with him, ever. Oh, Lord. Please, God, if you can forgive me and not damn me to hell, let my mind be at peace. No wonder they tell women they can't do these things like men can.

Then came that afternoon when things got tricky.

Frank was home and they were all at the kitchen table, finishing up lunch on a Saturday. There was lively talk, all the kids talking at once, which of course annoyed Frank. Carl and Henry were talking about having seen their friend Paul at the high school holding hands with his new girlfriend, Mildred.

Frank Jr., who was now in junior high, said, "Oh, I'll bet it wasn't Paul; I bet it was Carl holding hands with Mildred! Carl and Mildred, sittin' in a tree, k-i-s-s-i-n-g!"

"I'm not sweet on Mildred!" Carl protested. "I'm not sweet on anybody!"

This brought laughter from the five oldest children, and just as Frank Jr. was about to give his brother another verbal jab, Clarence piped up, "Mama held hands with Mr. Foreland!"

There was dead silence in the kitchen, and Frank dropped his fork on his plate, no longer interested in his last bite of berry cobbler.

Naomi felt a tingling all over, and not in a good way. The hair on her arms stood on end, like when you hear a gunshot you aren't expecting and get the pie scared out of you. She got up from the table, feeling like her knees might give way, and started moving dishes to the sink.

"Carey!" she said. "You're mistaken. That never happened."

"But I saw! When you came back from over by the barn with Mr. Foreland. After I took my nap and me and Granma Sims made cookies."

Naomi had thought the boy had missed that. *Damn.*

"No, sweetheart," she said calmly, "I think you saw Mr. Foreland hand me his shirt to bring in to mend."

"Oh. Maybe that was it." He looked around the table. "Why's everybody so quiet?"

Frank cast a searing look at Naomi's back, got up, and said, "That's enough of that talk. Clarence made a mistake. He didn't see what he thought he saw." And with that, he went to the living room to get his pipe.

On Frank's way through the kitchen to smoke his pipe outside, he said, "Naomi, when you finish those dishes, I'd like you to join me in the backyard. In fact, Marie, you do the dishes for your mother."

Naomi tensed, not looking forward to the conversation at all. She could feel her older children's eyes on her; they knew this was unusual, for him to invite her to the porch, even on a Saturday. He went out there to smoke sometimes, but he didn't usually ask her to join him.

"But Daddy," Marie complained, "I'm going over to my friend Ruth's to study—"

"You can do that after you do the dishes," he snapped. "No buts." Without looking at Naomi, he made his way to the back porch.

Naomi dried her hands and, looking down at them, removed her apron carefully, stalling for time. She slowly walked out to the porch, where Frank stood puffing his pipe and looking out at the backyard as if it were fascinating.

"Yes?" she asked him.

"What's this about?"

"What's what about?"

"What Clarence said. You know what I mean."

"There's no 'about.' I had been for a walk while Mother, Daddy, and Carey were asleep, and I had a little free time. Charles was just finishing up some work, out by the barn. I walked by and he asked me if I could take his shirt in the house so one of us could fix it for him when we had time. He went to his bunkhouse and got the shirt, I waited, we walked back toward the house as it was getting near to supper, and he handed me the shirt while we were walking," she lied. *Oh dear God, forgive me. Now here I am lying, and I've never lied in my life. I haven't always told everything there is to tell, but I've never lied.* She felt like she was falling down a well.

"You were out by the bunkhouse?" That was the main thing Frank had heard.

"Well, near there. I didn't think I had to back the heck off while he was in there." Now she was feeling a little angry at getting the third degree, even though she knew she was guilty. Well, she'd asked him about the powder, the perfume . . . the phone call. *So now two can play the same game—the liar's game—huh, Frank?*

"So you never touched him?"

"Frank, why in heaven's name would I be touching the man?" *Why indeed? And what do I have to do to get out of this conversation as quick as I can?*

"Listen, I've seen the way he looks at you. And he's been here a couple of times, with no business being here. You think I'm a fool? Are you trying to make a fool outta me?!"

"First time he came here, he brought our boys back on the train. Remember? Other time, he was staying at the boardinghouse where Sis lives. He asked her did I have anything needed fixing—I did, and you were out of town, so he came over and fixed the fence. I did a trade with him. That saved us having to hire somebody, right?"

"I coulda fixed the fence. And I don't like you offering to mend some other man's clothes either. He can pay somebody. Or learn to do it himself."

"But you didn't fix the fence." She decided not to take up the matter of mending Charley's clothes. "Besides, he's a carpenter; he's had to learn that, working on the farm."

"And you think I couldn't do it."

Now she was getting really frustrated with her husband, but she knew she had to try and keep cool. "I never said that! I know you could fix the dang fence, but this way you didn't have to do it on your time off. Right?" Frank was terrible with a hammer and nails. She was glad Charley had been the one to get to the fence.

Frank was silent for a full minute.

Finally, he said, "I'm on to you, Naomi." Then he walked down the back porch steps, turned around the house, and went for a long walk.

3051 Grant Avenue
Ogden, UT
May 3, 1929

Dear Charles,

 If you can help it, don't let my mother see this. I didn't put my address on the outside of the envelope and I hope you get to the mail before she does, because she'll probably know my handwriting.

 Clarence blurted out something about you and me holding hands about a week back. I said he was mistaken and you were just handing me a shirt to mend, but Frank about blew a gasket. He asked me a lot of questions. I never told a lie before, but I learned real fast.

 Things aren't too great around here. I hope you are well and that Daddy is feeling better.

 Please don't tell them I wrote to you.

 I just thought you should know.

Your friend,
Naomi Wolff

She hadn't known how to sign it. *Your friend? Ha! What if somebody sees this? Now they'll know we held hands. Oh my land.*

 PS Please burn this.
 NW

Chapter 33

Ogden, Utah, &
Stone Township, Oklahoma
June 1929

Marie Palmen realized that the twenty-three dollars a month was only temporary, and she didn't know how long Walter was going to give her this money. He could just stop, and then what? She didn't know if American law would go and get him and make him pay. Besides, she had been here long enough to know that the money was only enough for some expenses. Mrs. Schneider had not asked her to pay any rent or board yet, but she knew this couldn't go on forever. She decided to start going to boardinghouses to look for a job.

She knew by now that Anita Wolff worked in a boardinghouse, and she asked her at church one day if there was work there for her. Anita said she didn't know, but wrote down the name and address of the woman who owned the place. Marie checked there, and there wasn't any work available. But the matron gave her the names and addresses of some other boardinghouses in town near the station, and told her a lot of other things besides, most of which Marie didn't understand. She did hear "railroad men" and "station," however, and thought she knew what the woman was probably trying to tell her.

On her third try at the houses that catered to railroad men on

Twenty-Fifth Street, the woman in charge nodded and asked her a question in response to her work inquiry.

Marie hesitated a moment, but the last two words of the woman's question were "clean rooms," and she knew what that meant. Besides her work in New York, she'd also done her best to keep things up around Mrs. Schneider's house, too, to the point that Mrs. Schneider had said, "Marie, my gosh, I barely put down my coffee cup before you've picked it up to wash. Leave it be, I'll have a second cup!" and shook her head at Marie with a smile.

So Marie nodded vigorously at the matron and said, "Yes, I can clean!"

Now she had a job. Walter had told her in Germany she'd automatically be a citizen in the US because they were married, but she'd learned he was wrong about that when she was in New York. The law had been changed three years before their marriage, and now she'd have to do something, she wasn't sure what, to be a US citizen. And what if they were divorced? What then?

She couldn't think about that now. She just took the job and was glad of it.

One afternoon, a gentleman she'd seen around the boardinghouse a few times, who never seemed to spend the night, laughed and said, "*Ach, du lieber!*" at something one of the men he was sitting with had said.

Marie turned to look at him directly.

He looked at her at the same time and said, "Here, girl, can you refill our coffee?"

She approached and, with her best smile, said, "*Sprechen sie Deutsch?*"

"*Ja!*" he replied with a quizzical look.

They exchanged a few words, and she was glad to have yet another person with whom she could speak her native tongue.

In the later conversations they had from time to time, he mentioned to her that if she ever thought of moving to Evanston, Wyoming, there was a Mrs. Woods there who owned a very nice boardinghouse that also catered to railroad men, over on Main Street. Not far from the station.

She didn't plan to move to Evanston; she was only just getting to know people here in this town, plus there was the divorce and all of what she needed to learn to survive . . . none of which she told Mr. Wolff. She thanked him and had him write down the particulars, then tucked the note into her pocketbook to later put away with the rest of her scant belongings.

Naomi took Clarence, Dorothy, and Willie to the Oklahoma farm when school let out, with Carl and his safeguard, Anita, watching the other kids while they were away. Anita told her mother that it wasn't going to work out as well now that she lived in North Ogden, but she'd come by one day on the weekends to give Carl, Hermann, and Henry a break. Frank Jr. wasn't really old enough yet at thirteen to be fully responsible for other children, especially since he was the one who always seemed to have a wild hair, although he could play with the younger ones and knew how to make sandwiches.

Frank Sr. didn't like Naomi's going out there one bit.

"I'll be going through Jackson on my next run, I think, so I'll take a train down to Enid and come by there if I can," he said. And aside to her when the kids weren't in the room, he added, "And if you think I'm coming down there to check on you, you're right. I may show up at any time."

Naomi didn't care. She just couldn't be bothered with what men, including her husband, thought or wanted; she still had nine children to raise and was rarely without at least a couple of them hanging on her dress or needing a swat for talking back or wanting something to eat or coming in crying with a skinned knee. She told herself she was going to be firm when she saw Charley. She just didn't need this trouble.

Joe Sims was feeling considerably better, and picked Naomi and the kids up at the station in Enid. He lifted the suitcases into the truck, Naomi saying, "Oh, no, Daddy, I can do that," and Joe insisting that he wasn't frail.

"I kind of thought Charley would drive over to get us, to save you the trouble," Naomi ventured. "But I'm glad to see you, Daddy."

"Charley has gone up to Jackson, Missouri," Joe said. "His mother died, ya see. He seemed to take it pretty hard. You know she was a Chalmers too? Like your half sister and half brother . . ."

"I heard that. Mother told me." Naomi wasn't sure if she was deeply disappointed or relieved that Charley wouldn't be at the farm. A little of both. But she soon realized she was hoping he'd get back before she had to go back to Ogden . . . and nervous he would, and that Frank would be there.

If he was going to show up, she was hoping he'd do it before Frank did. If Frank came down to Oklahoma at all. Maybe he was just trying to keep her on tenterhooks by saying he'd come to Stone Township. That'd be just like him, trying to have some sway over her even when he wasn't around.

Nearly all her nails were bitten to the quick while she cooked, helped clean the house, worked in the garden, made sure her mother and father were okay, fed the new help while they tended the wheat, sometimes got a moment to read, tried to play with the kids and not think about things, and waited.

How do people live with these nerves? Don't men get anxious about this kind of thing too? I wasn't made for this much drama.

Chapter 34

Stone Township, Oklahoma
Late June 1929

Charley returned from Missouri. Naomi could see he was drained emotionally, and was not surprised that he threw himself into checking and maintaining the wheat, supervising the small crew, making sure the families had food to eat. Food was becoming expensive these days, and they were lucky they raised and grew much of it themselves—ham, chicken, corn, fruit, and some vegetables. Naomi took on hand-watering the salad patch and tomatoes, carrying a watering can back and forth, and teaching Willie, Dorothy, and even Clarence how to pick bugs off the plants and water them at the base rather than overhead.

Charley and Naomi still found time to put their heads together, and sometimes more than that. Although she'd promised herself the affair two months ago was the last of it, Charley was in fact encouraged that she'd written to him. He hadn't replied, as she'd requested, though he told her he might not have been able to keep from writing back had it not been for his mother taking deathly ill.

After a few sessions of all-too-brief kisses behind the barn, and a few times when they were actually able to talk alone, one Wednesday there was a surprise opportunity.

While Nancy and Naomi were washing the breakfast dishes, Nancy said, "Your dad and I are going into Enid to the feed store and maybe picking up a few groceries. Is there anything you've noticed we need around here?"

"Oh, if you can get more sugar, I'll make a cobbler this Saturday," Naomi said. "We've got berries. But we need more flour. And lard, and maybe some Crisco oil, if they've got it. And baking soda. Gosh, I'll write you out a list."

"I knew about most of that but wouldn'a thought of the baking soda. Okay, if they've got everything and the prices aren't too dear, I'll bring all that home."

The children were out of earshot, so Naomi asked, "Mother, do you think you could take the kids in too, maybe get them an ice cream soda or just a soda? Let them see something besides wheat fields and their mama for a while?"

Nancy looked at Naomi hard and long, took a puff on her pipe, and sighed. "I suppose. I know what you've got in mind. And you know I think it's a bad idea, even though I can't say I blame you. Charley is a real nice fellow, and it's plain for anyone to see he loves you in a way I haven't seen in Frank in some years. But that's not all there is to life, Naomi, getting what you want. Frank supports you, and that gives him some rights."

"Oh, Mama, I'm sure Charley will be working all afternoon." Naomi maintained a poker face. "Don't worry. Should I tell the kids to clean up?"

Nancy gave Naomi a look of resignation. "Okay. Tell 'em to be ready in twenty minutes."

Naomi's heart was beating a little faster, and she hoped she was keeping her composure. While the kids were washing up, she walked deliberately, without hurrying, out to the chicken coop with an egg basket. Never mind they'd collected most of the eggs yesterday and there were unlikely to be a lot of them this morning.

Charley spied her from the barn, as she'd intended, and ambled over equally slowly.

Charley knew after the truck left the dusty drive out to the main road that they had at least two hours. Even with an unlikely flat tire and the family turning back, they had that much time.

Afterward, they lay in Charley's bed—his arm around her, her head on his strong shoulder.

Naomi murmured, "I had a dream the other night."

"Yeah?" *I hope it was about me, and I hope it was good.*

"Yeah . . . I dreamed Frank took the kids someplace."

Huh. Well, not what I hoped, but she is still married to the man. "Where was he taking them?"

"Oh, I dunno, someplace . . . like taking the boys fishing or something. You know how dreams are, they don't always make sense or go someplace that ends like a regular story." Naomi shifted on his arm. "Charley . . ."

"Uh-huh?"

"Um . . . what are we gonna do? Just keep on like this, me going back to Ogden, seeing each other every few months . . . until you finally meet a woman you can marry?"

Charley chuckled. "Oh, Naomi . . . Listen, I know a fella would say somethin' like this, especially with what we're doin' here right now—but there isn't gonna be anybody else. I mean, if I never saw you again, maybe. But here I am, gonna be fifty years old next year, and a farmhand. I don't see a line of pretty girls waiting to be the one to dance with me."

He looked down at her face with its dainty features, lovely to him, looking much younger than her almost-forty years, despite the many births and hard work she'd seen. He hoped she understood what she meant to him.

"You know, I'm inheriting my folks' farm now that they're both gone. My sister and brother live there, but I don't think they want to keep the place. I don't know how much we can get for it, being how's the price of goods are up and the price of land is down, and not too many people buyin' farms now. But I should end up with a little money. And . . ." He felt Naomi's body shift slightly away from his, and he hoped what he said next was received well. "If you ever think you could leave your husband . . ." He just couldn't say Frank's name, that made the man too real . . . "If you ever thought that, I could take care of you."

"Charley," she said, her voice regretful. "That's such a sweet idea. And it's romantic. But I have nine children at home! Carl is almost old enough to move out . . . well, he and Henry and Hermann I s'pose all could; Frances left at fourteen, but she's a girl and didn't need to finish high school . . . but still, that'd be six kids I got to take care of, and Frank Jr., boy, he's a handful. I wouldn't leave him in charge of the little kids for more than three hours. You ready to be a father to seven, eight, nine kids? Hmmm?" She chuckled. "No, my dear man, I think we best leave things like they are."

Charley's heart sank. He had hoped. *I see her point. But I'd do my best. They could all come live here and I'd build another house . . . or I'd move to Ogden and we'd get a place and Frank and her could share the children.* He closed his eyes. *What am I thinking? We'll just have to live with this the way it is.*

"I can hear you thinking." Naomi gave his ribs a gentle poke.

"Yeah, I am, and trying to find a way that what you say isn't the truth."

❧

Joe Sims was pretty sure he knew what was what. He'd had a couple of affairs before he was married and when he was off working out of state, and he could see the look on Charley's face—and, worse, the look on Naomi's—when they were in the same room together, or even within twenty feet of each other outside. The way they avoided looking at each other, except when they thought no one would see. *Oh, my darling daughter. This is okay for a man, but not for a woman with all those kids and a husband who's a provider.* He understood—Charley appeared to be a sweeter man, and he sure was around more than Frank—but Frank made a good living and always came home. Eventually. He'd heard how railroad men had a woman in every town they stayed in. The boardinghouses across the US attracted young and middle-aged women who either hadn't married, were from poor families, or were widowed. And there they found work and the attention of men, however fleeting it might be. But Naomi? She didn't need this.

Frank Wolff sent no letter, no telegram before showing up on a Tuesday in a hired car. He stepped out of the car, trainman's duffel in hand, and walked up to the house like a man with a mission. He had changed from his overalls into proper pants and coat—not quite fancy enough for town but a little dressed up for the farm.

Nancy saw all this from the front window; she'd been sitting in the parlor darning socks.

"Naomi?! Frank's almost at the door!"

She hoped she was in the house and not out by the barn, where everyone knew they could usually find her if she wasn't in the garden or the house. To her relief, Naomi appeared and met her husband at the door.

"Frank! You did come! Come on in and I'll fix you some coffee; you must be tired! I think there's some leftover cobbler in the icebox too!"

She put her hands on Frank's arms and stood on tiptoe to kiss him on the cheek he offered her. He did not return the kiss.

"Yes, I come down from Kansas City to Enid on the train and then got a driver out here. I'm tired from the trip. Been on the rail run for a couple weeks this time, from Chicago through St. Louis and all that."

Naomi exchanged a glance with her mother and hurried to serve her husband refreshment.

Frank took every opportunity to get each of the kids alone and grill them. He started with Clarence, the most likely to blurt out something he wouldn't know he was supposed to keep secret. All he could get out of the boy, when he asked him if he saw his mother with Mr. Foreland sometimes, was "I don' know"—and then, when he pressed him, "Well, yes, Daddy, we're all around here together all the time. What do you mean?"

Questioning Dorothy was not much more fruitful, although she did say that her mother spent time, yes, out at the barn, and the chicken coop. But also out in the garden, and in the house. Sometimes Mr. Foreland was out there, but not always. "Why, Daddy? Did you want to know when you can go out to the barn with Mama? I think you can go anytime you want," she answered him with a perplexed look.

But when he asked Willie, who was almost nine, he wrangled more specifics out of him.

"Well, yes, sometimes she goes for a walk around the farm with

Mr. Foreland. They look at the horses and the wheat . . . and the chickens . . . and the pigs . . ."

"Does he ever touch her?"

This alarmed Willie. "No! Why would he touch her?" he answered, his eyes wide and a furrow in his brow, searching his father's face.

"I just wanted to be sure he was a polite man, since you kids and your mother are here," Frank said. "You go play, now."

Frank could see it. He could see what his father-in-law saw, the two of them avoiding looking at each other. It was unnatural. If there was nothing between them, they'd be indifferent and as friendly as you might be to the foreman of your mother's farm. He just knew it. He knew it—and yet he couldn't prove it.

Finally, he confronted his wife, when they got a moment alone.

"Okay, I can see it. I can see that you have an interest in Foreland, because you and him both won't look at each other. That's just not normal. You used to be friendly with him. Now it's as if you are thieves who have to keep something out of sight. What the Dickens are you up to?!"

"Frank . . . I don't know what to say. We've been married for over twenty years. I think you and I both know you probably have other women out on the rails. I've heard the stories about railroad men from other wives. But it's different for women, right? That's what everybody says. We can't get away with that kind of behavior. And do I like Charles? Yes, I do. He's a kind man and takes care of the farm, and my parents, too, come down to it, and makes sure the children have a good time when they're here. He is cousin to my half brother and half sister. And he is a hard worker and dependable. It would be hard not to like him. But I have nine children. And you. And here we are, married twenty years. So . . . maybe I have some feelings for him, but there's nothing I can do about that, no matter what."

Frank could hear what she wasn't saying in there with what she was.

"You come home. Your dad's not sick right now. You pack up tomorrow and we're all going home. That's it. No buts."

Naomi knew Frank meant it. And she knew with him watching like a hawk she couldn't sneak any kind of goodbye with Charley—so she settled for asking her mother to tell him Frank had insisted he saw they had feelings for each other, and that she was to come back to Ogden immediately.

Nancy drove them to the train station; when they started up the truck, Charley stood back by the corral, pretending to fix the fence, his eyes steady on the Dodge.

"Wave goodbye to Mr. Foreland, kids," Naomi told them, and gave a wave herself—a noncommittal, wave-to-the-farm-foreman wave, veiling her eyes as best she could.

Chapter 35

Ogden, Utah, & Stone Township, Oklahoma
July 1929

Naomi and Frank barely spoke. What was there to talk about? Once, he took her too forcefully when they were in bed, making sure she knew she had no say. She gave in—better that way. He wasn't usually a rough man, aside from occasionally hitting the boys to keep them in line. But she didn't want to tempt fate.

Naomi wrote to Charley when no one was home, and walked the letter down to the post office.

3051 Grant Ave.
Ogden, UT
July 10, 1929

Dear Charley,

You know I care for you. I do very much. I wish there was a way for us to be together, but it just can't be. You know what all I have in my life. And Frank is suspicious and sometimes furious. We will just have to leave this be and see what Providence brings in the future. You know that saying, "God moves in mysterious ways, his wondrous works to perform"? Well this has sure been a mysterious thing, no two ways about it.

Please know that no matter what, I will always think of you.

I don't think it matters if Mama and Daddy see this, but it's probably better if they don't.

Don't write back, please.

Your friend forever,

Naomi Wolff

As if he didn't know I was married, she thought when she underlined her last name. But she just felt she needed to emphasize the—What would they call it? *Futility*, that was the word—of the situation.

Charley had convinced Nancy and Joe to get a phone installed; they didn't cost as much anymore, and you only got charged for the service of paying the operator in Enid if you made a call. Since they were both in their eighties, it just made sense, in case anything should happen to them and they needed to call a doctor out to the farm. And they could make orders at the feed store and sometimes have them delivered instead of having to go into town. He even offered to help put up the poles and the wires to save on the cost, if the phone company would let him.

As soon as the phone was installed, Charley suggested Nancy call Naomi and let her know they had the phone, so she'd know she could call and check on them, and she'd know they'd call her if anything happened to either of them.

Nancy did call her daughter. When she learned Frank was not there, she asked Charley to get on the line and tell Naomi how they had come to install it, insisting that her eyesight had gotten so poor that she really didn't know the details.

Charley was grateful to Nancy, who clearly knew what she was doing. *And now Naomi knows she can call me, too, or I can call her,* he thought, his heart swelling with the possibility.

Which, of course, was what he'd had in mind all along.

They were really careful. She didn't call him often; it would cost too much. Once a week, at most, and never when Frank was in town. She decided it would be better if she went downtown to the public phone booth. She tried to call around mealtimes, when she knew he'd be likely to jump up from the table to answer the phone, seemingly to save Nancy and Joe the trouble.

In late July, Charley's heart overruled his head and he took the train to Ogden, leaving Buck Rhodes, his lead man on the crew, in charge. Charley made him and his wife swear to look after Nancy and Joe, and Buck's wife nodded, saying she understood; she had older parents back home. He gave Buck the name of the boardinghouse where he'd be staying—the one where Anita worked—in case he needed to call.

When Charley arrived in Ogden, he strode quickly to the boarding-house. He was relieved to see that they had a room available, and that Anita was working that day.

"Oh, hello, Miss Wolff," he ventured, nervous and trying not to show it. "I'll be here in town a few days. You well? Your mother okay?"

Anita was surprised to see him; she always checked the registers to see which rooms needed to be set up or cleaned, and his name hadn't been there when she looked.

"Oh, Mr. Foreland, hello. I'm just fine, working hard. My mother is well too. I'll let her know I ran into you if I see her."

"Oh, you don't see her every day?"

"Well, no, I don't have time to go by there every day with my work an' all; I live a little ways north now. Did you have a message for her?"

"Oh, no, no . . . just tell her I said hello. And if there's anything I can do for her. And her mother sends her regards."

"Oh, how is Grandma Sims?"

"Oh, okay I guess . . . You know your grandparents are getting on. Things change from day to day."

"Gosh. Maybe I'll have Mother come by and you can tell her how they are. I'll give her a call."

"Oh, that'd be nice, Miss Wolff."

"Mr. Foreland, call me Anita, okay? We don't need to be so formal."

"Oh, all right, you're all right, then. Well, thanks."

Naomi came by the boardinghouse a few hours later. They sat in the parlor—near, but not too near, so they could speak quietly.

"Charley, what are you doing here? My gosh. Is something wrong with Mother or Daddy? Why didn't you just call me?"

"Nothing's wrong with your folks, Naomi." He ran a hand through his hair. "It's me. I hate to be away from you. We gotta figure out a way to change things."

"Charley, we've been over this. There's nothing to be done. Now, if you want to come by the house, in the daytime, Frank's out of town for at least a week. He's been sent off to St. Louis. You might've even passed him in a train station along the way, for all I know."

"No, I'd've seen 'im, I'm sure, and stayed outta his way."

Naomi hmphed and shook her head. "Well thank God for small favors. Just don't be expecting anything, you know what I mean?"

"That's not what I'm here for. I just had to see you. And if this is how it's gotta be, it's okay."

"Charley, it's only been a month since we left Oklahoma. My goodness. I'm sorry I wrote. I have encouraged you and I didn't mean to." She gave him an exasperated look, then smiled. "You come on by. All the kids are home; I'll find something for you to fix or somethin'."

Charley went by Grant Avenue the next day, and the day after that. Naomi had him mend the screen doors; everybody in the house knew the summer flies were getting in, so that was a good excuse. He went to the hardware store and bought new screens, even, and did a real nice job. Once, when all the kids were out of the house, they stole a quick kiss in the hallway where there weren't any windows.

On the third day, they were all having lunch in the kitchen, except for Carl, who'd gone to play ball with his friends over at the high school. The front door opened and closed, and Naomi called out, "Carl, that you?"

"No, it's not Carl," came Frank's voice. "I'm home; they canceled the last leg of my run because another guy needed one. They've been doing that since shipping has slowed down."

Frank walked into the kitchen and stopped in his tracks.

"What is he doing here?!" he shouted.

The children gaped; Frank wasn't prone to shouting, especially when there was a guest in the house. Naomi's heart beat a mile a minute. She looked up at Frank, trying to breathe steadily. Charley looked down at the egg sandwich crumbs on his plate and wiped his mouth with the cloth napkin Naomi had provided. Naomi felt like they were all suspended in time as they waited for Frank's next words.

"Get out! Get out of my house!"

The children looked from their father to their mother and then to Mr. Foreland, who rose slowly from the table.

He started to speak, "Mr. Wolff, I was fixing—"

"Just get out!"

"Frank," Naomi started, "the screen door had a big hole and Charles was here in Ogden . . ."

Frank set his jaw and took two steps closer to Charley. Through clenched teeth, he said, "Get. Out. Of my. House. Anything in this house needs fixing, I'll be the one to take care of it. You get out before I call the police. You have no business here."

Charley glanced at Naomi before sidestepping Frank out to the living room, where he picked up his coat. He quietly shut the front door on his way out.

The children didn't know what to make of the scene. Nothing like this had ever happened in their home, or anyplace else they'd been. They sat frozen at the table.

"You kids, go on," Frank commanded. "You go on outside."

"Daddy," Marie said, "we have to clear the table . . ."

"You leave it. Your mother can do that. Go on outside, all of you."

When the children were gone, Naomi sat looking down at her plate, thinking how that was what Charley had done too.

"You're a *whore*. And in front of the children. My children."

Naomi was stunned. "Frank, what do you think was happening here? The man's in Ogden, he came by, he asked if I needed any help, he told me how my folks are doing . . . Same as it's been before." She wished her heart would slow down.

"Oh, I am pretty sure I know how it's been before."

"Frank, nothing has happened here."

"I told you before I did not want any men in the house when I was gone. And I sure as hell did not want that Indian here. What do you think the children think? What have they seen?"

"They have seen nothing but all of us having lunch together, and they think Charles Foreland is a nice man who works for their grandparents and once in a while comes by here to help us out."

"STOP!" Frank shouted. "Just stop. You are worthless. You are a worthless mother. You run off to Oklahoma and leave most of your children here to fend for themselves, gallivanting all over the country."

Naomi rushed to defend herself. "I went to visit my *mother*. You see your mother every time you go through Kansas City, Frank! Carl and the twins are here. They are young men, old enough to be in charge here. Young Frank is not little anymore, thirteen . . . and Marie is twelve and a half, she knows how to cook . . ."

"That's enough out of you," Frank spat. "Don't you talk back to me. You don't deserve the food I put on your plate. You should get down on your knees right now and ask God for forgiveness. Matter of fact, you should beg *me* for forgiveness."

He stood over her, his words like nails hitting her bent head and the back of her neck.

Naomi started to sob and couldn't stop. She shook with her tears and her regret and her wishing things were different and her love for Charley and her spurned, bruised, used-up, meager scraps of love for her husband and how it had started twenty years ago and how different it was now. She sobbed for being a woman. She cried for being home alone all those times when she was sure Frank was with some-one else. She cried for the unfairness of it all. She cried because she felt like a caged animal being readied for slaughter. For her confusion about whether Frank was right. Because she didn't know what God wanted from her. She wept from far deep in her being, remembering when Grant had died. She had tried. Was she to blame for his death? She had done all the doctor had said to do . . . Frank hadn't wanted to pay for the hospital . . . *Oh, Lord, take this cup from me.*

Finally, she steadied herself. "Yes," she whispered.

"What? Yes, what? Yes, you are a whore?"

"No, Frank," she said, her voice barely audible. "I am no whore. But yes. The question you want to know, the question you aren't asking me . . . Do I love him? Yes, I do. I can't help it."

Frank realized he hadn't expected this. He hadn't thought she'd admit to anything. For her to say she loved another man . . . he was tongue-tied for a minute, until his ire at what he saw as his being cuckolded revived him.

"I will make you sorry you ever met that man. You hear me?" He made his voice low now, and menacing. "I will make you *sorry.*"

He went out the back door and slammed it. Clarence, Willie, and Dorothy were there; the others had gone off down the street, to the park, to their friends, wherever it was the kids went when they weren't home. He looked around for them, but he had no idea where they might be, or if any of them had heard what had gone on inside. How his wife had shamed him in his own house.

"You kids go back inside now. Go on back inside."

"But Daddy," Willie said, "you told us to go outside, and we're playing a game . . ."

"Go on back inside," he said. "Right now."

They did as they were told.

Frank walked to the far edge of the backyard and began to weep, alone.

Chapter 36

Ogden, Utah
August 1929

Frank Wolff went to the German branch of the Lutheran church and talked to Pastor Elmquist, telling him he feared his wife was a sinner and needed to get her away from the children.

Pastor Elmquist answered, "Herr Wolff, this is a grave thing, and I have known Frau Wolff to be a good and God-fearing mother. What could lead you to these thoughts?"

"I think my wife has been unfaithful. I know she has."

"Did you see this?"

"I did." He was lying, sort of, but he knew he was doing the right thing. "She had the man in our house when I was away at work."

"In your bed?"

"I did not see that, thank God, but I suspect. And with the children in the house."

"*Mein Gott. Ja*, I see you must do something. If she will not repent, you can divorce her."

"I do not want to do that." He had his own thoughts on why, which he chose not to share with the pastor.

"Well, I'm not sure what you can do . . . other than have her declared an unfit mother. That is usually reserved for the insane . . ."

"How do I go about that?"

"Inquire at the courthouse. Or see Herr Wagner, he's an attorney."

Frank wasn't going to pay somebody if he didn't have to, so he went down to the courthouse that afternoon to inquire what paperwork to fill out to have Naomi declared an unfit mother. He filled it out on the spot, but was a little exasperated by the need to provide so much information, especially the names and ages of all his children.

Naomi Nellie Wolff, formerly Sims, age 39, did commit adultery within our marriage.

He paused. *Will they ask me to prove this? Ach. I'll wait and see.*

Names and ages of children in her care:

Uh-oh. I know all their middle names, but their ages? And the birth order? Why do they need this? Why can't I just put down their damn names?

I know for sure Carl, the twins, Frank Jr., and Marie, because she just told me . . . and Sis is a little more than a year younger than Frances, and Frances was born I think the year we got married, 1908, so . . . Oh, I'm just going to guess. They aren't asking for birth certificates.

After more deliberating, Frank wrote out the list as best as he could manage. He finished with:

I apply for sole custody of the above named children.

Signed, Frank Joseph Wolff, age 41, August 13, 1929

He gave the paper to the woman clerk behind the desk, thinking she was attractive, and noticing she was not wearing a wedding ring. She looked too old to not be married, maybe in her late twenties. *Maybe another fallen woman. But who would hire her? Maybe she came from out of the area. Or maybe she's just one of those women who wants a career more than a husband.*

He realized his thoughts were getting away from him, and that the woman had said something to him.

"Sir?"

"Oh, yes. What was that?"

"Can you appear this Friday at 9:00 a.m.?"

"I can. If the railroad doesn't call me in."

"Okay, well, if something changes you must let us know. If you don't show up, your paperwork will be voided and that could mean your case will be dismissed."

Frank was at the court at 8:45 a.m. that Friday. He prided himself on always being on time, even if the trains weren't.

His case was not called right away, and he was annoyed with the delay. He had thought being there at nine meant that was his appointment, but he had to wait through two divorces and a person suing for back wages.

Finally, the bailiff called out, "Frank Wolff."

Frank stood and came forward.

The judge glanced at Frank and spoke. "I have reviewed this paperwork requesting that Naomi Nellie Wolff, née Sims, age thirty-nine, be declared an unfit mother and that you, Frank Joseph Wolff, be given sole custody of your . . . let's see, one, two, three, four . . . my goodness, ten children. Even your oldest daughter, Anita, who is grown?"

"Well, sir, she's not my oldest daughter; my oldest daughter is almost twenty."

"She is also not of age yet, then."

"But she's married and lives in Los Angeles."

"Oh. Then her husband is responsible for her. Okay. Does the next-oldest daughter live at home?"

"No, sir, but she is not of age or married, and I will take responsibility for her."

He knew Anita was not going to like this, but she didn't have a choice.

"Is Mrs. Frank Wolff here in the court?"

"You mean, my mother?"

"No, I mean your wife, Mrs. Naomi Wolff."

"No, sir, she is not." He hadn't told Naomi he was doing this. He had hoped the court would not summon her, and evidently they had not.

"And you are not asking for a divorce at this time?"

"No, sir, I am not." *I'm not giving her the freedom to marry that bastard. Let her live alone or live in sin. She can have that on her conscience for the rest of her life. I told her she'd be sorry.*

"And do you have the means to support these children alone?"

"I do; I work for the railroad and have since I was a boy. I have been the one supporting them their whole lives."

"In that case, as in any case of adultery with no apology, contrition, or reconciliation, and with the parent having demonstrated ability to support, I grant custody of these ten children to the father, Frank Joseph Wolff, this day, August 16, 1929."

Naomi was finishing up canning some tomatoes in the kitchen. Doing normal things was helping her cope with the thick hostility in the house. She had been sleeping on the extra cot, which she'd moved into Marie and Dorothy's room. The kids knew things were not good between their parents, but they were hoping it would blow over; Naomi and Frank had had arguments before, after all.

Naomi had called Anita after that terrible day, and they had met up at the boardinghouse to talk. Now Anita knew everything, except the fact that Naomi had actually had relations with Charley. No one really knew that for sure but Naomi and Charley, although she'd as much as told her mother.

Naomi heard the door slam and recognized Frank's determined footsteps, only like that when he was angry or had something to prove.

He entered the kitchen and flung the papers he held down on the table.

"There. Read that."

She looked at him, trying to keep her composure, sure that this must be divorce proceedings. She washed and dried her shaking hands, sat down at the table, and picked up the papers, which looked like legal things. The only legal papers she'd ever seen were her marriage license, the deeds to their two houses, the kids' birth certificates, and the death certificates of the three children she'd lost.

At the top of the first sheet, in fancy script, it said, *Declaration.*

And then the words jumped out at her: *That Naomi Nellie Wolff is an unfit mother, due to her having committed adultery, and this court grants sole custody of the following children . . .* [*Where did they get all their ages?* she wondered. *Frank couldn't have known them all.*] *. . . is hereby granted to Frank Joseph Wolff, who has testified that he is able to support his offspring.*

She let go of the papers and looked up at Frank, her heart in her throat. "You are doing this? I have never said I had relations with Charles. You cannot prove this."

"They didn't ask me to prove it."

"So, what about divorce and sharing the children?"

"I am not giving you the satisfaction of divorce. You will never be able to marry that man. You will live in sin or live alone," he said, smug and vindictive satisfaction dripping from his words. "And now you pack your things and get out."

"What?!" Naomi's eyes widened.

"You heard me. These kids are no longer your children. You get out of here and make your own sorry way."

Naomi was again stunned. She had thought, she had hoped, that this would, in time, just blow over—an outcome it had seemed the children awaited as well. She had decided she could live with Frank if she just kept doing normal things, at least until the children were grown. She could tolerate the sexual relations; he had a right. When she would visit her folks, maybe she'd be with Charley and maybe she wouldn't. She had children to care for, and Frank probably wouldn't let her use her rail pass to go down there anyways.

She knew now she'd been foolish . . . but *this*?

Naomi did as she was told, and numbly packed as many suitcases as she could manage. Where would she go? She had about five dollars of her own. She'd go to Anita's boardinghouse first, and just hope there was a room . . . or something. She couldn't just be out on the street.

"Kids?" she called out. "All of you! Please come to the living room."

She went to the back door and called for Willie and Clarence.

Carl and Henry were over at the park with their friends. She'd try to find them later. Hermann was making himself a shirt. The family had pretty much given up on his learning the things other boys liked to do, but she appreciated that he was different and had taken it upon himself to learn to sew. Too different, but still her son.

The seven of them that were home came to the living room while Frank sat in the kitchen. He'd asked Marie to make him a cup of coffee and a sandwich.

"Kids, I'm sorry. Your father thinks I cannot be a decent mother. I have tried to be a good mother. I know I haven't always been." Tears filled her eyes and dropped to her bodice; she wiped them from her face. "But now I'm being sent away. I can't live here with you anymore."

"Mama! No!" cried Dorothy and Clarence at once.

She knelt on the floor, drew Dorothy and Clarence close, and held them tight, her tears continuing to flow.

"Mama, you're getting my neck wet," Clarence said gently.

"I'm sorry, son." She looked around at the other five; every one of them was wide-eyed with shock. "I'm sorry. All of you, I'm so sorry. I never meant this to happen. I love all of you so much. I know I'm not always as kind to you as I'd like to be. I hope you can forgive me."

She hugged each one and kissed even her sons on the cheek.

"Mother, where will you go?" asked Hermann.

"I don't know yet. I'm going to go see Anita right now. I maybe will go down to your Grandma Sims's. I don't know. This is all new to me too. You kids tell Carl and Henry when they get home. They can come to the boardinghouse later to say goodbye."

Frank Jr. was angry. "Why are you doing this? Was this your idea or Daddy's?"

"Frank, it's hard to put a finger on that exactly. Your dad didn't like it that I was friends with Mr. Foreland and had him here while your dad wasn't home. And it's mostly his idea that I have to leave."

"So it's partly your idea too?"

"That's not . . . that's not exactly how I'd put it. But I coulda not been friends with Mr. Foreland . . . I coulda not let him come here." *Is this another lie? Am I lying? I just want to protect them from thinking their mother is . . . what Frank thinks I am.*

"I don't understand."

"I'm sorry, son. There's really not much more to explain." The tears started coming again.

"Your mother is unfit to be your mother anymore!" came Frank's booming voice from the kitchen. "You've said your goodbyes, now *go!*"

Chapter 37

Ogden, Utah, Stone Township, Oklahoma, & Los Angeles, California
August 1929

Naomi had spent a night at the boardinghouse where Anita worked. Carl and Henry had come by after dinner to say good-bye, and were unsure who to side with. They were as stunned as the rest of the children. Anita gave her a little money she had saved up—enough for the train fare to Enid, food on the trip, and ten dollars extra just in case. Naomi told her she'd pay her back, but Anita shook her head no.

"Mother," she said, "you have taken care of all us kids for twenty years. This is the least I can do. Don't worry about it. I have enough for the things I need."

"I'm sure your father is expecting you to come by to watch the kids, especially Clarence, Dorothy, and even Willie."

Anita gave her a look of vexation. "What was he thinking, declaring you unfit? I can't believe this is happening."

Naomi called her mother to tell her what had happened, and that she was leaving on Sunday to come down to the farm and should be in Enid by Tuesday night, maybe sooner. She'd sleep on a bench in a station if she had to. Nancy asked her if she wanted her to wire a little money. Naomi knew that would be a hardship for them, so she told her no. She had enough with what Anita had given her.

Charley picked her up at the station when she arrived that Tuesday, and she fell into his arms and wept. She told him she couldn't tell him everything yet, but Frank had the children and she wasn't allowed to see them. Charley didn't seem to know what to say, but his expression told her how concerned he was.

For the first week, Naomi just slept, barely ate, stared out the windows, and sometimes sat outside.

Nancy and Joe had more than one long talk while Naomi slept.

"Land sakes, what has that girl done," Joe said, not really a question.

"We just got to let her be. There's nothing can be done. They shoulda known better, the two of them, but they just gave in, not thinking about what would happen. I shoulda tried harder to put a stop to it." Nancy paused. "Although I understand why. Charley is a considerate man, maybe more simple than Frank, but a kind man. And when your husband is gone all the time and you're home alone with ten or however many children? And another man comes around not caring about how many kids there are, liking them, being there when your husband's not? And you know what they say about railroad men . . . I can't say I blame her, other than how foolish it was. What a mess. But now, Joe, she's here, and he's here, and I don't guess they will suddenly fall out of love and Frank will forgive Naomi and everybody will live happily ever after. This is no fairy tale."

"No. No, it ain't. And she's still our daughter, and he's the best foreman we'll ever have, plus he's practically kin. They made their bed, so to speak, and we are lyin' right next door to it." Joe snorted.

"Already hard times in the last few years, though, since the government stopped those subsidies. Hard to find anybody wants to pay a
good price for the wheat and the corn. She'll need to find work . . . but
I hate to ask her right off, so I'll wait on that. And you and me got to
accept things as they are and go on livin'."

"That's all we can do," Nancy agreed. "Just let those two know
they're welcome here and leave the judging to God. And I think they
do love each other. At least there's that. May come out okay in the
end. And Naomi's a hard worker. She'll pull her weight around here."

Charley didn't know what to do to help Naomi feel better, so he asked
Nancy.

"I think you just gotta wait for her to come around," she said. "I
think the two of you love each other. Maybe that's gonna be enough to
make things all right in the long run. We'll have to see. Meantime, you
know, bring her some flowers, maybe, I don't know. It's a pretty big scab
she's gonna have to grow. There's really nothing but time going to help.
You just be yourself. I'm not sayin' none of this is your fault. The two
of you got into this and now here we are, all of us livin' with it. But me
and Joe talked about it; we are willing to have you both here, however
the two of you want to set things up. It's not for us to judge. We think
we can all come to some peace—maybe not this week, but eventually."

Charley did find some coneflowers and phlox to pick in Nancy's
garden, and he asked Nancy if she thought they looked nice enough.

She smiled. "That's real thoughtful, Charley. Here, let me help."

She put them in a vase and cut the stems a bit; they made a nice
arrangement.

"There you go. You take those on up to your . . . girlfriend, knock
on her door, and I'll bet she'll let you in."

He hoped so. They'd all been having dinner together each night, at least when Naomi came down to eat, but those had been quiet meals, as if someone had died. He desperately wanted her to talk to him.

He knocked quietly three times and heard Naomi answer, "Yes?"

"It's me. Charley. Can I give you somethin'?"

Her curiosity up, Naomi opened the door to the man she knew she loved with his offering of beauty and kindness. Those flowers. When was the last time Frank had done that?

"Oh, gosh, Charley, you didn't have to do that. Nobody died or anything. But come in and sit with me. I owe it to you to tell you everything that happened. The whole sorry mess."

She left the door open; she still didn't know exactly how this was all going to go, living with her parents and all. She felt almost like a teenager, when she would never have been allowed to have a boy in her room alone.

She told him everything. She couldn't help but cry again, and when she did Charley got a guilt-ridden look in his eyes. He got up from the chair, sat next to her on the bed, and held her, with the door open. Naomi could see his remorse all over his dark, handsome face. He was given to holding his expression so that you couldn't exactly tell what was going on in his head, but it was all out in the open now.

He blurted out, "I've been a selfish son of a gun!"

"Charley, don't you blame yourself. I had as much a hand in this as you, maybe more; I coulda said no. I coulda said once and that's it. I coulda treated you only as a friend. Although I think Frank would have always been jealous and suspicious, even if we'd done nothing. And I never told him we'd really been together. He just assumed. But I did tell him . . . I did tell him that I loved you."

"Do you think you could tell me?"

"I just did; I told you I told him I loved you."

"No, I mean, could you say it *to* me. Only if you want to," he added shyly. "I'll say it first, though I think I said it before: I love you, Naomi."

"Oh, Charley. Charles Foreland. Of course. Yes. I love you. I do love you. Would I be here otherwise?" She laughed a little bit then.

"Wull . . . where else would you go?"

"You got a good point there. I guess here is where I'm gonna be for a long while." She gave him a long look. "My sadness, Charley, it's not about you. It's about my kids. That's the thing that's killin' part of me inside. That Frank drove a wedge between me and my children. That he took them away. I mean, I wasn't always the best mother. I hit 'em when they wouldn't behave. I didn't always have time for them when they needed me; I was so busy just doin' all the damn chores and almost like bein' two parents in one person. But I love them all. I just hope someday they'll want to see me. I'm afraid now Frank will poison their thoughts about me."

He looked at the floor. "Naomi, I'm so sorry. This is my fault. It is."

"Charley, we both got to stop sayin' that. We just have to live with how it is now, and try and make a good life somehow. I can't marry you because I'm not divorced. Not that you've asked me." Her cheeks flushed. "Thing is, if we live here together, we're gonna be livin' in sin. And that's just what Mr. Frank Wolff wanted."

"I don't care. I'd sure marry you if we could, tomorrow. You're the only woman I've ever felt this way for, Naomi. So I don't care. We don't have to call it living in sin either. Let's just call it . . . I don't know. We got to be together. Nobody around here has to know what the deal is."

❧

They kept things cooled off a bit for a while, until they felt like Joe and Nancy were comfortable with their relationship. Naomi went out to the bunkhouse one day, looked around, and decided the place could use some sprucing up, a woman's touch. She started taking things out and bringing things in, and sewed new curtains the next day.

Charley was elated. He looked at the sky in a new way and felt like the buttons were going to pop off his shirt. Maybe she really was his. Not that he would ever own her, but that she wanted to be his . . . partner. This was more joy than he'd ever known, even though he knew it had that sadness that might always be there about losing her children.

If he had his way, they'd be welcome here and he'd treat them as he always had: as the children of the woman he cared more for than any other person on this earth. He knew her pain was part of why she was busying herself with the cabin, and only asked her to not put his things where he couldn't find them, not wanting to put a damper on the only cheery moments she'd had since she got to Oklahoma.

Anita called Frances in Los Angeles and told her all that had happened—that Daddy was living with the kids in Ogden, and Mother had gone to Grandma Sims's farm and probably was going to be living with Charles Foreland there, she wasn't sure.

"That *Indian*?" Frances gasped.

"Well, you know, we don't know that he's an Indian. But yes, Charley, from the farm. He's the foreman there now . . . and you remember he's some kind of cousin to the Chalmerses, by marriage or something."

Frances was silent for a long moment. *I wish I didn't know things*

ahead of time sometimes. Mother has that too . . . I guess it's intuition.
"Sis, I dreamt she was holding hands with that man," she confided
in a hushed tone. "We can't tell anyone about this. I don't even want
Frank to know . . . I mean, my husband. This is horrible."

"Frances, it's awful what Daddy did, to take custody away from
Mother. But . . . I think Mother is really in love with Charley. I'm
not saying it's right, what she did . . . but I do understand. You probably can too. I have a boyfriend now, Caleb, and when you really
love somebody . . . *you* know . . . it's not easy to keep your distance.
Especially with Daddy being gone all the time and treating Mother
like she's his servant when he comes home. Did I already tell you this?
I went over to the house one day and she was crying; she told me it
just got to be too much sometimes, being the adult home taking care
of all those kids. Daddy was sure willing to make a lot of babies that
he wasn't home to help care for."

Frances countered her sister, "But he is the one who worked and
made the money. That's her job, the kids and the house. And they
promised to be faithful when they got married." *I used to cry, too,
sometimes, when all the kids were too much for me.*

"Frances, I don't think Daddy has kept up his part of the bargain
in that. I've smelled perfume on him before that didn't smell anything like Mother's. Railroad men have a reputation for having other
women. And he told Carl that men sometimes have other women
when they're away from home."

Frances recoiled from this thought. "I don't believe that about
Daddy, though. I don't think Daddy would do that. Besides, even if
men do that, women shouldn't."

"Who do you think men 'do that' with if not women, Frances?"
Anita pressed. "It has to be somebody. Somebody's wife, somebody's
mother, somebody's daughter. Anybody can fall in love or even just

get lonely. Anyways, I believe Daddy would. And it looks like Mother did, and now she's paying a big price."

"And that's what she gets for what she did," Frances snapped. "She'll have God to answer for this."

"Well, we'll see. You always liked Daddy more than Mother, and I'm the other way. Anyway, here we are and I just wanted you to know. I gotta go—this is a long phone call and I know you don't like to call much, so I had to call you. It's not a pretty picture, but we all have to live with it."

Frances hung up the phone and felt her face and arms flush with the shame of her mother's transgression. If she could help it, no one was ever going to know about this scandal in her family.

Chapter 38

Ogden, Utah
September 1929

It came to Frank pretty soon after he kicked Naomi out that he was going to need to find somebody to watch Clarence, Dorothy, and Willie some of the time, especially when he was away on the rails. He went over to the church and asked one of the women there about childcare. He didn't tell them exactly why he was inquiring, but they didn't ask either. He found a young woman, Betty Hoffman, who could come by and even spend the night sometimes. But darned if she didn't charge fifty cents an hour. Adding it up in his head, he saw that even if he only needed her about twenty hours a week, that would be ten dollars a week. He figured he could keep that to a minimum by having Anita come by as much as possible, but he saw there was going to be a problem once school started because the older kids wouldn't be home when the little kids arrived there.

Anita was angry with her father. She did her best to contain it when he called her to come to the house yet again.

"Daddy, I'm workin' full-time now. How do you think I'm gonna come and take care of the kids? I can't just drop everything . . . It's a job; you know how important a job is."

"Well, I need you to help me with this."

"I know you do. I know you're not used to takin' care of kids." *And now maybe you see how it was for Mother, and for Frances, and for me, all these years.* "Listen, I'll take Clarence and Dorothy over to the boardinghouse some days after school. But I can't promise to do it every day, or even all the times when you're gone."

"Okay. We'll see how it goes. Maybe you will be able to take them every day once you get started with it."

Anita burned inside but held her tongue. What had his plan been? It was clear he didn't have one.

She asked Mrs. Hancock to let her go get her little brother and sister at the school several times a week and bring them to the board-inghouse, where they could stay in an empty room and read. They were usually quiet kids.

Mrs. Hancock gave her a look that said, *You've got to be kidding,* but said yes—with the condition that it could only be until her family worked out something else.

"What about your mother?" she asked. "Is she ill?"

"My mother is in Oklahoma right now . . . with her mother, who's getting on and isn't always well. And my father, as you know, works the railroad, so he's gone a lot. The older kids don't get home from school until after the little ones. Daddy's arranged for a sitter, but it gets real expensive . . ."

"Uh-huh. Well. I understand, but you got to tell your daddy that his problems are not my problems. If the kids cause any fuss, that's the end of it."

Things went well for about a week, and then one day Clarence couldn't contain himself and chased Dorothy through the dining room, giggling and sliding along the floor, stumbling once and almost knocking over a vase.

Mrs. Hancock heard the ruckus but didn't see how close the kids had come to causing a disaster. "Hey, now, you kids, you belong in the extra room," she chided them. "You go on up there and be quiet."

Anita was using the carpet sweeper in the parlor and thought she'd had an eye on the two rascals. She thanked her lucky stars that the kids hadn't broken anything.

"Mrs. Hancock, I'm sorry; I'll keep a closer eye on them."

And then came the wail. She and Mrs. Hancock exchanged a look, Anita's saying, *Oh, no . . .* and Mrs. Hancock's saying, *That's two times . . .*

Anita ran up the stairs to find Dorothy face down on the floor, sobbing. She shut the door, sat down on the carpet, and gathered the little girl into her arms. Clarence watched with wide eyes, not knowing where this was going; they were already in trouble.

"Honey, what is it? You two weren't hitting each other, were you?"

"Nooooo!" Dorothy wailed. Her sobs were not subsiding a bit.

"Honey, you've got to calm down and tell me what's the matter."

"I want Mama! I just want Mama to come home!"

With this admission her crying only increased in intensity and volume, and she was soon hiccupping to catch her breath.

Clarence got caught up in the emotion, tears forming in his eyes, and soon he was crying too, though more quietly. "I want Mama too," he said plaintively. "When is she coming home?"

Anita reached out her arm to invite Clarence to her other side, and he fell to his knees and leaned against her.

"Listen. Mama is gonna be gone a while. You kids have to be good. I can't have you here if you're gonna be cryin'. I could get in trouble and lose my job, and I need this job. I don't live at the house anymore, remember? That's because now I am grown-up and I have to work. So can you please be good? I know it's hard. I miss Mama too."

"Where is she?"

"I think I told you before, she's down at Grandma Sims's farm."

"Can we go on the train to see her?" Dorothy asked.

"No, you can't, you're in school."

"Well when is she coming home?" Clarence asked again.

"I don't know. We just have to try to get along without her for now."

Anita called her father the first chance she got.

"Daddy, this is not working out well. I think you've gotta make different arrangements. The kids . . . they really want their mother, and it causes trouble here when they're upset. Plus, they can't go runnin' around the boardinghouse, and I can't send 'em to the park while I work—they're too little."

Frank was silent.

"Daddy?"

"I'll think of something. Just keep picking them up, and I'll keep paying Betty for the times you and the other kids can't do it."

Anita was once again clear on one thing: her father didn't have a plan.

Frank had already told his mother about Naomi having the affair—or at least that he thought she had had an affair—and that he'd gotten custody of the children and sent Naomi away, likely to live in Oklahoma.

Upon hearing all this, Caroline Wolff had thought her son should have had his head examined. He could have just beat his wife and told her he'd divorce her if she didn't straighten up. But he didn't hit women, she knew that. This was a time it might have been a good idea.

When he called her again, she tried to be tactful with her son.

"Frank, I don't know what you were thinking. What do you plan to do?"

"Well . . . *Mutter*, can you take the children?"

Caroline Laschevski Wolff was not surprised by much anymore, at seventy, but she was completely taken aback by her son's request.

"What?! *Mein Gott*. No, for heaven's sake, I can't take your nine children, Frank!"

"Well, can you take some of them, then?"

Caroline paused and thought.

"*Mutter?*"

"Yes, son. I'm thinking. You know I'm here alone except for if one of your sisters or brothers come by. With your *Vater* gone, I could use some help. Maybe I could take the three older boys—Carl, Henry, and Hermann. They're old enough to work around here, and when they get out of school they can all get summer jobs."

"What about Frank Jr.?"

"Oh, son, you know he's too much of a handful for me. He can help you at home, there. So just the three oldest boys."

"Well, that would help, I suppose, even though the oldest ones don't need a sitter. Carl will graduate in June, so he could even get a permanent job, if he can find one. Okay, can I send them out there to you?"

"I guess so, Frank . . . but what about the other kids? What will you do?"

"Well, Anita takes the littlest ones some days, and I hire a sitter if I need one. Marie can watch the kids when she's not in school. And Frank Jr. is thirteen and a half."

Little help, but something, she thought. "Frank, isn't Anita working full-time now? And how old is Marie?"

"Marie's twelve. And a half. Old enough to babysit. And yes, Anita works over at a boardinghouse."

"Well, I would think she can't be with the kids much while she's working. And twelve and a half . . . that's pretty young to run a household, cook for the family and all . . ."

"Well, it can't be helped, *Mutter!*" he almost shouted. "There's no other solution."

I beg to differ, as the Americans say, Caroline thought, and sighed audibly.

"Okay, send the three boys out. They should get started in school before it gets too far into the school year anyways. You call and let me know when they're coming."

"*Danke, Mutter.*"

Caroline hung up the phone. *What have I agreed to?* She shook her head. *Well, the boys will get some work done around here for me.*

Frank sat the three older boys down in the living room in the late-afternoon light after talking to his mother, making sure the other kids were all outside. Frank Jr. wanted to know why he wasn't included, and Frank told him he'd tell him later—to just go on and visit a friend or something. Frank Jr. gave him a suspicious look but did as he was told.

"You boys know that I can't be here all the time, and I have been thinking where we will all live now that your mother is gone."

He didn't miss the dark looks that passed among all three boys at the mention of their mother's absence.

"I've called your Grandmother Wolff, and she's agreed that you can all come live with her in Missouri—in Prairie, near Kansas City. It will be a lot like being in Ogden, as far as school and friends and all."

Carl asked, "You mean, *all* us kids . . . except Anita . . . are going to Missouri?!"

"Oh, no, no . . . your Grandmother Wolff is seventy. She can't take you all. But she said she'd take the three of you, and you could help her out at the house and then get summer jobs to help pay for room and board."

Carl looked disheartened. "So, she's not really taking care of us; we're taking care of her. And what about leaving our friends, and the teams at school? What about transferring?"

"No, she'll cook and clean and wash and all those things. You'll run errands and do yard work and odd jobs for her, wash dishes maybe, and just behave yourselves, because she's getting old. Plus, she's got no one living there with her. It will be safer for her too."

"I don't want to leave Ogden," Henry piped up. "I've lived here as long as I can remember. Like Carl said, our friends, and our teams . . . Do we have to go?"

"You do have to go," Frank said decisively. "That's how it's going to be. You'll leave as soon as you can get packed up, before I take my next run."

"I'm not going to Missouri," Hermann said emphatically.

"What? What do you think you're going to do? Do you want to be the one doing all the babysitting here? Because that's the alternative," Frank said just as emphatically.

"I'll . . . I'll go live with Frances, in Los Angeles."

All three of them looked at Hermann like he'd suddenly grown an appendage.

Frank hadn't expected this. He cleared his throat and ran his hand through his pomaded blond hair, now interspersed with the very beginnings of gray. "Well . . . okay, if you want to call Frances and ask her, maybe you can do that."

That'd be one more out of the way.

"And what about Frank Jr.?" Henry asked.

"Grandma Wolff can only take you older boys. You know Frank is . . . well, a handful, as she put it."

Henry smiled and glanced at Carl, who looked down and hid a smirk.

"Okay, it's settled," Frank said. "You boys start packing."

"Frances?" a young man's voice said at the Ogden end.

"Yes? Who is this?"

"It's your brother, Hermann."

"Oh?"

"Yes. It's me. I wonder if I can come live with you."

Frances was stunned. "Come live with me?"

"Yes. You and your husband."

"Do you know Daddy's brother, your uncle Otto, is already living here with us? He's been here a month or so."

"Oh, I forgot that." He paused. "Well, could we share a room, him and me?"

"I don't know, I'll have to ask him." Frances pondered the idea. "You know, he's ten years older than you; I don't know if he'll want to do that. Why do you want to come live with me?"

"Well, Carl and Henry are going to live with Grandma Wolff, and I don't want to move to Prairie. I think I'd like it better in California."

I'll bet you would. "I'll have to ask my husband and Uncle Otto. I'll call you back tomorrow. Is Daddy there? Can I talk to him?"

Hermann put Frank Wolff on the line.

"Hello, Frances. This is your father."

"Yes, Daddy, I recognize your voice. What is this all about?"

"Well, two of your brothers are going to live with your Grandma Wolff, and Hermann doesn't want to go."

"That's what Hermann said. What about Frank Jr.?"

"Grandma Wolff said he's too much for her to handle."

That sounds about right. Too much for me too—don't you send him here.

"You know Uncle Otto is still living here, right?"

"Oh, I forgot, of course. Well, ask him if he wants a roommate." Frank chuckled.

Oh, that'll go over real big. "Yes, I told Hermann I'd ask him. But I have to ask Frank too."

"You mean your husband."

"Yes." Frances felt like they were starting to talk in circles. "How are you . . . doing?" She meant without her mother there.

"Oh, it's okay. Sis takes Clarence and Dorothy some of the time, and I hire a babysitter, and Marie takes care of the cooking."

Poor Marie. I know what that's like, right when you are in junior high and starting to have more grown-up friends. At least she's a really good seamstress and a pretty good cook.

"Well, I'll call you back tomorrow and let you know. I love you, Daddy."

"I love you too, Frances."

Frank Sims agreed that Hermann could come stay with them too, although he was feeling like their house was turning into the Wolff Hotel.

But he had something he wanted to discuss with Frances first.

"Umm . . . there's one thing, though . . . I always thought your brother Hermann was . . . you know, different."

"What do you mean?" She glanced out the window.

"You know . . . it always seemed to me that he might be . . . well, queer."

"I don't know that!" she said defensively. "I mean, yes, he seems like he is more feminine than other boys. But he goes to church!"

"Frances, going to church doesn't keep you from wanting what you want or even doing what you want to do, if you've a mind to."

"Hermann would never do anything that was against God's will."

I wouldn't be too sure, Frank thought. *And who's to say what God's will is?* He'd been feeling much less committed to the Mormon Church lately, though Frances was still a devoted member.

He cleared his throat, choosing his words carefully. "I'm just thinking that . . . well, I don't want the neighbors or our friends starting to talk if there's anything . . ."

Frances challenged him. "Anything *what*?"

"Well, if he acts that way, you know. But it's okay with me if he lives here, as long as everything is . . . normal."

Frances called her father back the next day and gave him her assent. Otto, she said, didn't plan to live there much longer anyway; he had a good job now and would be getting his own place, maybe elsewhere in California.

Carl and Henry were packed up and put on the train for the

two-day trip to Prairie, Missouri, where they enrolled in high school, and Hermann took his suitcase to Los Angeles and moved in with Frances and Frank Sims.

And Frank Wolff Sr. still had a problem regarding how to care for all his children.

Chapter 39

Ogden, Utah, & Evanston, Wyoming
Late September 1929

Frank had a good idea. *This will solve everything.* Why hadn't he thought of this before? It was so simple.

"Kids, pack up your things by next weekend. Frank, you and Marie help the other kids pack."

"*All* our stuff? Or just some of it? Are we going to see Mother?" Marie asked.

"No, I'm taking you someplace as a surprise. A short train trip. But pack up everything you can."

They actually didn't have eight suitcases left in the house, since Naomi had taken two with her and the older boys had taken a couple as well. They bought some suitcases at a church jumble sale and used flour sacks and shopping bags for their toys and other odds and ends.

Frank went first to South Junior High, where he signed Frank Jr. out and got the paperwork to transfer him, as he'd done for Carl, Henry, and Hermann previously. Then he went to the grammar school and signed the other five children out and got their paperwork.

He next went by the Nelson Real Estate Office on Twenty-Fifth Street to list the house on Grant. He didn't let Naomi know he was doing this; there didn't seem to be any need.

The agent told him he ought to be able to get a pretty good price for the four-bedroom house, even though it was small and the two upstairs dormer bedrooms were tight spaces. He said that although the economy was lagging, people were still moving to Ogden and prices were pretty stable on residences. He thought it would go for around $6,000.

That sounded optimistic to Frank, but at least he'd be likely to get back what he paid for it. What they paid for it. Naomi's name was also on the deed. When the time came, he'd just say she was in an asylum or something, pull out the unfit mother document and that would be that. Or so he hoped.

Frank called Anita and shared the plan he'd come up with.

She sounded incredulous but didn't say much. He gave her the number where she'd be able to reach him, and they hung up.

Frank locked up the house and took the kids to the station about a week later, boarding with them and claiming the shrunken family's seven seats. They were headed for Evanston, Wyoming. The ride was only a few hours, so they brought lunches packed by Frank Jr. (under duress) and Marie.

The younger kids were excited. "Where are we going, Daddy?" was their frequent question on the journey.

"Oh, just you wait. Someplace really nice."

Frank Jr. and Marie didn't pester him; they just stared out the windows most of the time. That was a relief to Frank Sr.

When they arrived in Evanston, the family paraded the twelve blocks to Minnie Woods's rooming house. Frank Sr. helped Clarence with his bag, and Frank Jr. carried Dorothy's along with his own.

When they arrived in front of the three-story house the children's faces were awestruck, as if they had gone to some glamorous place from a fantasy. The curlicues, the scalloped shingles, the fancy windows, the big front porch, and a large yard with a white picket fence and mature shade trees . . .

"Whose house is this?" Dorothy asked, her eyes like saucers.

Ignoring the question, Frank Sr. told the kids to stand on the steps and not clamor around him on the porch. Then he rang the bell.

Minnie was home; the kids were in school. She opened the door, expecting perhaps the postman or a neighbor, and was shocked beyond measure to see Frank Wolff and six children.

"Frank! Mr. Wolff!" she was finally able to say after regaining her composure.

"Hello, Mrs. Woods! We've come to stay, and we're hoping you've got rooms for the lot of us!" Frank beamed, clearly expecting an equally exuberant greeting from Minnie.

"My goodness. Uh . . . come in, come in."

The family trooped into the house, the children marveling at the polished banister on the staircase, the bay windows, the fancy furniture in the parlor.

"Mrs. Woods, these are my children. Line up, kids. Here's Frank Jr., Marie, George, Willie, Dorothy, and Clarence. Say hello to Mrs. Woods, kids. Mrs. Woods's house here is where I stay when I have to be in Evanston overnight for my work."

Minnie attempted a polite but tepid smile. The children all murmured their hellos.

"Well, whaddya think?" Frank grinned at her. "Got room for all of us?"

"I think we can put you all up for a bit . . . I don't have any other roomers right now, and my children can double up if needs be. Come on upstairs and let's get you settled." She gave Frank a *What the devil?* look, not caring if the children saw it.

She put the boys in one of the attic rooms and the girls in the other, then decided Clarence would have to sleep in the same room as Marie and Dorothy. That would be three and three, and Clarence could sleep on the floor if necessary.

The two littlest kids were clearly tired.

"Why don't we all go downstairs for some milk and a cookie, and then Clarence and Dorothy can take a nap?" Minnie suggested.

And then you and I can have a talk, she thought, darting a look at Frank.

Once the little ones were sleeping and the other kids were shooed outside, Frank and Minnie sat down to talk.

"All right, Frank, what is this all about?" she demanded. "Is this because you banished your wife to Oklahoma?"

"Well, more or less. I just thought . . . you know, rather than keeping up two households, we can put our resources together. I can pay more for rent and groceries, and when I'm out on a run this will be a stable place for the children. We can make a life here. No one needs to know about you and me; we'll all just be boarders, like I've always been." He winked at her.

"Now, just wait a minute. You're proposing that I am going to take care of all your kids, and mine too?"

Frank didn't see what the problem was. "Well, Naomi took care of this many and more."

"Huh!" she tutted. "I am not Naomi. If I wanted eleven children, I would have had them myself. And I'll tell you what, I don't need another teenage boy in this house either. You're going to have to send him to your mother's or something."

Frank wasn't happy to hear this, but he knew better than to push Minnie on this one.

A couple of days later, Frank Sr. sent Frank Jr. off on the train to Prairie with a big lunch, five dollars, and a slip of paper with Minnie's number on it, though he knew his mother would likely give him an earful for this.

Caroline called him when all three boys were out at the park, playing ball.

"Frank, what in the Sam Hill are you doing?" she demanded. "I told you I cannot take Frank Jr. too!"

"*Mutter*, I've got the rest of the kids here with me . . . and Hermann went down to Los Angeles with Frances. . . so it's the same number of boys you agreed to. Surely you can handle that."

"No, no, I cannot. He will have to go someplace else. We will see if we can find him a rooming house here in Prairie, or maybe Kansas City."

"*Mutter*, the boy . . . I don't think he's ready to be on his own."

"Well as I said to you before, you should have thought this through. I think you could have told Naomi if she didn't straighten up, you'd divorce her."

Yes, and if I actually divorced her, she'd be able to marry that Don Juan.

Frank sighed. "Okay, well let me know where he is, then. When you find him a place."

"And you will send money for his rent and support?"

"Oh . . . yes, of course, of course." Frank hadn't anticipated this.

He hoped that Frank Jr. could get a job. *I started working when I was under fourteen; it won't hurt him any. Not all the boys need to finish high school.*

The Wolff children were all introduced to the Woods children, and they began to adapt to being a houseful over the next few days. The Woods brood was stunned at this new development, and Lawrence, Beatrice, Martin, Nina, and Ellen all came to their mother one by one and asked what the heck was going on. Minnie had to smile at how they'd all come up with the same expression. She told them this was just something they were trying out and it was not going to be permanent. Although she hadn't told Frank this.

Marie soon became a little moony-eyed over Lawrence and Martin, finding the novelty of living with boys that were not her brothers intriguing. Willie and Frank Jr. thought Ellen was pretty special. But sixteen-year-old Beatrice was not happy about sharing the bathroom with all these kids. She hoped her mother was telling the truth, and this was temporary.

Frank went off on a rail trip, but not before sneaking one late night with Minnie, sweetening her up since she was going to be like a stepmother to his children, and he appreciated that. He began to think this might all work out like . . . what did the kids say? The cat's pajamas.

Frank arrived back in Evanston to a house in turmoil. It seemed pretty normal and lively to him, same number of kids he was used to living with anyhow, but he could see that Minnie was fraught. Frazzled. The kids seemed to get along well enough, although the oldest girl, Beatrice, seemed sullen and he hadn't recalled her being like that in the past. He must not have noticed.

After dinner, when the kids had dragged themselves up to bed, he could see Minnie was going to pin him down for "a talk." He was tired but he didn't have rights on Minnie, so he knew he'd have to comply. When she beckoned him to the parlor, he came and sat with her.

"Okay, Frank. You can stay, but this—the kids all being here—is not working out," she said. "We are too crowded. Since we've got the kids into the school here and I understand how hard it is for children to go through the change of losing a parent, they can stay through Christmas. At least they'll have a good holiday. But first of the year, in January, you've got to find a different place for them. And that's final."

"But . . . where do you expect me to take them?"

"That's your problem, Frank. Take them home to Ogden and live there; take them to your mother's in Missouri. Take them to live with your brothers or sisters out there. I don't mean to be stinko about it—you know I care for you—but I didn't ask for this, and you never asked. I'm not raising ten children. Period."

Frank stared into his coffee cup. How could she do this to him?

Well, she was saying that he could stay, so there was that.

He nodded. "Okay. I will figure something out. In January."

Chapter 40

Stone Township, Oklahoma, &
Evanston, Wyoming
December 1929

Anita had called her mother, back in October, and told Naomi that Daddy had taken some of the kids to Evanston to live in that boardinghouse where he stayed, with a Mrs. Woods. And that Henry and Carl were with Grandma Wolff in Prairie, and Hermann had gone to Los Angeles to live with Frances. Frank Jr. had got sent to Prairie, too, but Grandma Wolff had said she couldn't handle him (Naomi understood why), so Frank was going to have to live in a rooming house, and nobody knew exactly how that would work out.

Poor little Frank, thought Naomi. *He's almost a man, but not quite, and not ready to be on his own, that's for sure.*

Frank Jr. had called Anita, angry about being shuttled around, and threatened to go down to the farm in Oklahoma, but Anita had told him she thought that would be illegal. That Naomi might get in trouble.

Which is prob'ly true, Naomi thought. She and Joe and Nancy had discussed that if the kids came down there, there might be trouble. They weren't sure if Utah could enforce its laws in Oklahoma, but they feared Frank Wolff might do his own enforcing, and nobody wanted to see him.

Naomi strongly suspected that this Mrs. Woods was Frank's lover, and felt the cruelty in what he'd done. Her children would have Christmas in their dad's lover's home. It broke her heart, and the hypocrisy was hard to take. But she was glad that Hermann had gone to Los Angeles. *Maybe people out there will be more kind about his being different.*

She started getting mopey again. Christmas was coming, and she wouldn't get to see her kids, wouldn't get to make them presents, buy them new shoes, stuff stockings with an orange and candy and little toys. No Christmas morning with the tree and all the excitement. She missed them more than ever now, especially knowing where they were.

She had busied herself in November with making fruitcake. They hadn't been able to get the candied fruit in town, so she'd just used raisins and currants this year. It was hard to get anything right now. So strange that the stock market crash had affected even folks out here in the middle of nowhere. At this point they were happy just to get flour and sugar for a few cookies. And they'd have ham, at least.

"The government was paying us to grow wheat and other grains, corn for the cows, and hogs, especially, in order to provide food for the troops in Europe in the World War," her father told her. "But when it was over, almost ten years ago, they cut back on the subsidies. So everybody out here had bought a lot of equipment and such to produce more, and now there's not as much use for it, but you still got to pay the loans—and then the price of grain and hogs and all goes down, because there's more than is needed. I didn't get much schooling, but I know about that. When the market crashed, the folks who were spending lots of money didn't have it anymore, and the ones who make stuff or grow stuff cut back too. We're all in this together, seems like."

Naomi sighed. She felt the weight of being another mouth to feed on the farm. Maybe she could get some sewing work in Enid.

Charley wanted to give Naomi as nice a Christmas as he could. He had not had much to spend his wages on in recent years, except those few trips to Ogden, and he had a little money stashed. He asked Nancy what he should get Naomi; he'd never bought a present for a woman before, except his mother and sisters. He guessed Naomi might like the same kinds of things but wanted to be sure.

Nancy told him Naomi wouldn't expect him to spend much, but if he wanted to go into Enid, that Jewish store, Kaufman's, had nice women's things. Harry Woolf's place too.

"They're real nice folks," she told him. "Lotta Jewish people came out to Enid from New York City before we moved here. You tell 'em you're the foreman at Nancy and Joe Sims's farm. They might give you a better price; they know farmers are fallin' on hard times."

He took the truck and shopped in Enid. He got Naomi a winter dress, warm and pretty, although they didn't have as much to choose from as he expected. While looking around, he impulsively bought her a pretty hankie with lace on the edges as well, and decided to get one for Nancy too. He shyly told them he worked at the Sims's farm; he didn't want to brag about being the foreman, nor did he ask for a price break. But they must have noticed how his shirt was worn at the cuffs, because they did give him a good price on the gifts.

At the dry goods, he got Joe some tobacco . . . which he knew Nancy was going to smoke too. He smiled to himself about how she tried to hide her pipe. Everybody knew she smoked.

At the pawn shop, he found one last gift for Naomi: a little locket.

He hoped his gifts would lighten her spirit, and help her not think about where her kids were spending their Christmas.

Minnie Woods knew how to put Christmas together. Over the last couple of months, she'd stored away all the ingredients she needed for cookies and cakes and such. Frank took some pride in this—that he'd brought his children to a place where they'd have a nice Christmas, maybe even more generous than they'd had at home.

After the stock market fell, Minnie had become more frugal. She was getting no money from roomers these days, but now Frank was giving her much of his paycheck to support the house, and with that, her sewing, and her savings, they were actually doing all right. About the same as before the market fell.

For gifts, Frank bought all the kids new shoes, and sent a little money to Caroline to buy shoes for Carl, Henry, and Frank Jr. (if she knew where he was). He gave Minnie some money to buy some extra gifts for his children and for her own kids too. He anticipated a cheery Christmas and hoped that if it was enjoyable, Minnie would change her mind about sending the kids off someplace.

Chapter 41

Evanston, Wyoming, Prairie, Missouri, & Winfield, Kansas
January 1930

Minnie didn't change her mind. On the third of January, she reminded Frank that he had to pack the kids up before he went on another run. He tried to reason with her—said he thought the kids were all having a good time together, hers and his—but she was firm. She said it again: "I'm not raising ten children."

He called his mother, out of the kids' earshot, who said, "Frank, they cannot stay here. They cannot. I'll ask around and see what I can find out."

Resignedly, he told the kids to pack their suitcases again.

The children were bewildered.

"I thought we were gonna live here, Daddy," Dorothy said, those big blue eyes questioning him with alarm.

"No, we're not. Or you kids aren't, anyhow. This was just a place to stay for a while."

Maybe his siblings might each take a couple of the children.

The wheels were turning in Frank's head, but they felt like they were grinding up whatever gears he had left in his brain.

The long train trip to Kansas City and then the ride to Prairie, not far from the station, was tiring for everybody. Carl drove his grandmother's car and Frank's sister Louise came to the station too, since there were six people needing a ride to the house.

When the gang of them trudged into Caroline's home, she gave Frank a disapproving look.

After they'd had dinner, they found places for all the kids to sleep, all the boys except Carl and Henry, who had beds, on the floors here and there, and the two girls in another extra bed.

In the kitchen, Frank and Caroline sat at the large maple table that had seen so many Wolff family meals.

"Frank," Caroline started quietly in German. "I know you're between a rock and a hard place. But some tough decisions have got to be made. I went to the church and told a friend that my son had lost his wife and had some financial difficulty, and needed a place for his children. She told me about the Lutheran Children's Home in Winfield, Kansas. It's apparently near Arkansas City, south of Wichita, and they take children, no questions asked. You could take Frank Jr. too. He's in that rooming house we found not far from here. I don't know if you were going to pay his rent or not, but I'd say take him along if you decide to do this. Otherwise, take them home to Ogden and you'll make out somehow."

Frank looked at his mother. He had actually looked into the Lutheran Children's Home after Minnie had told him in the fall that the kids couldn't live there permanently. He'd heard some men at the church in Ogden talking about how humiliating it was that the Volker family had to send their two children there, and he had casually asked where it was. He didn't want people in Ogden thinking he also was hard up financially, because he wasn't, and they certainly didn't need to know that he was thinking of . . . placing, they called it . . . his children elsewhere. He had thought at the time, *That's a last resort; surely we can live at Minnie's.* But now here he was.

He decided this was the only solution. Especially since he wanted to live at Minnie's. He couldn't imagine not having a woman in his life to take care of all his domestic needs. He was damned if he was going to start learning all those things now, and he had a ready setup with a woman who was, well, affectionate toward him.

All of this went through his mind within a minute.

"There's nothing else left to be done," he told his mother. "I'll have to take them down there. At least they'll probably have a good place to live. Somebody to see they eat right and go to school, and there will always be somebody there when they get home. Right?"

"All of that, yes, it's probably true." His mother turned her palms upward. "I mean, we can't know if they are nice people, but at least we know they're Lutheran and the kids will go to church."

He called the home the next morning and told them his version of his tale of woe. Some of it was true, in his estimation—at least the fact that he couldn't keep his kids—and they heard that a lot. So, no questions asked.

Hanging up the phone, Frank breathed easier.

They were on another train, headed south, the following day, Thursday, January 9.

"Daddy, *now* where are we goin'?" Dorothy asked in her very tired little girl voice.

"Arkansas City!" Frank answered. "This train is headed for Wichita, Kansas, and then we're going to a nice little town called Winfield, near Arkansas City. But this won't be a long train ride.

Only about four hours." He tried to make it sound like this was an adventure.

"But where are we going when we get there?" Marie posed, her face solemn.

"You'll see!" Frank answered with feigned enthusiasm. He wasn't about to field any upsets on the train. He'd just drop them off and be done with it, and the orphanage would handle it however they handled upset children left by their parents. He couldn't call it "abandoned."

Once they arrived in Wichita, they rented a car to take them the forty miles east and south to little Winfield. When they pulled up to the house on Park Place, everyone, including Frank, was awestruck by the mansion's size and elegance. Two stories on top of a basement with below-ground rooms as well, a huge front porch, and a front balcony on the upper story. A sunroom jutted out of the left side, and it looked like the house might even be bigger toward the back. Frank thought it looked like a damn fancy hotel.

"Who lives *here*?" George asked in wonder.

"You're about to find out," answered Frank.

"I think I know," muttered Frank Jr.

They carried their gear up the ten broad steps, noting the engraved sign above the door, *1921*, and deposited the bags and themselves in the front hallway, where Frank Sr. approached a woman behind a desk.

"Hello," said the round-faced, bespectacled older woman. She held out her hand to Frank. "I'm Susanna Weinrich, the matron here. Welcome." She waited a moment and then said, "And you are?"

"Oh . . . Frank Wolff. I called a couple days ago, and these are my children."

"Oh, yes, Mr. Wolff. We have some paperwork for you to fill out. And may I ask, how old is your oldest boy, here?"

"Oh, Frank Jr.'s just turned fourteen yesterday."

"I see. May I talk to you in the parlor for a moment?"

Frank was wary. "Of course. Kids, you wait here and be quiet."

Mrs. Weinrich took Frank to the other side of the parlor, as far from the front hall as was possible, and said in a whisper, "Mr. Wolff, we don't take boys over thirteen. They're hard to place. We've been at this for twenty-three years, and we've had to make some hard-and-fast rules. Boys that age are closer to young men than they are children, and sometimes children are here for a couple of years before we can place them with adopting parents. Few parents, especially childless ones, want to adopt a young man. And your oldest girl?"

Frank was a little jarred by the realization that the home was going to make an effort to find new parents for the children. He had assumed they'd just live here.

"Mr. Wolff?"

"Marie's . . . she's . . ." He had to think. Oh, right, somebody had mentioned she had a birthday coming. "I think she'll be thirteen at the end of January."

"That shouldn't be a problem. Girls are easier to place than boys, and often someone will want an older girl to help out in the home."

Like an indentured servant, thought Frank. *Well, Frances left home at fourteen; it won't hurt Marie to earn her keep. Especially with her being good at sewing. She'll be okay.*

"So you're saying I can't leave the oldest boy here?"

"No, I'm sorry, you can't."

"Huh. Well, okay, if that's the deal." *Another problem.*

Frank and Mrs. Weinrich returned to the desk, where she offered him a chair so he could fill out the full names and birth dates of the children. He had to ask Marie, who knew them all, for some of the exact dates.

Dorothy approached Mrs. Weinrich and asked, "Who lives here?"

She answered, "I live here, and my husband, Mr. Weinrich, and several children live here with us."

"You must have a lot of children—this is a big house!" exclaimed Dorothy.

Mrs. Weinrich smiled kindly at the pretty little girl. "No, they aren't my children; they are children of other people. We find homes for them, and they live here until someone comes to give them a new home."

"It's an orphanage," said Frank Jr. "Daddy's putting us in an orphanage," he explained to his siblings with contempt.

"Well, son," Mrs. Weinrich said, "your dad will be taking you back with him, as it happens, because you are too old. Unfortunately, that is our policy."

"Oh, that's just the bee's knees, Dad," he said, his voice dripping with sarcasm. He walked out the door to the front porch and sat on the railing, looking out at the town.

"Daddy, is that right? Are you putting us in an orphanage?" George asked.

Frank cleared his throat and said, "Don't bother me, son, I'm filling out this paperwork."

"To give us away. To other people. Why?"

"I can't keep you kids," he answered. "Now just let me finish here."

The five children exchanged glances. Clarence and Dorothy were not at all sure what this was going to mean, but Marie, George, and Willie had all heard of orphanages. Their mood changed from awed to dismal.

"Thank you, Mr. Wolff," Mrs. Weinrich said when Frank was finished with the application. "If you could please send us photos of their birth certificates when you get back home, that would be help-ful. Otherwise, we'll go with what you've given us."

Frank wasn't sure he even knew where their birth certificates might be; Naomi had taken care of things like that. He guessed if he could find them he'd go downtown in Ogden to the photo shop and they'd take pictures of them there. He took one of the home's brochures with their information on it, thinking he'd be less likely to throw it away than the slip of paper in his wallet with the address and phone number on it.

"Children, say your goodbyes to your father and I'll show you to the rooms you'll share with the other children and introduce you to some of them . . . unless you'd like us to show you around, Mr. Wolff? You are of course welcome to visit at any time you're in the area."

Unlikely, thought Frank. *Highly unlikely I'm going to come 1,200 miles to see them. Nor will anybody else. A clean break will be better for everybody.*

"No," he said, "I need to get back to Wichita to catch the evening train back to Kansas City and then on back to Ogden tomorrow for work."

"Daddy!" Dorothy cried out. "Noooo! Don't leave us here! It's so far away! We don't know anybody!" She started to sob and clung to his leg. Clarence followed suit, hugging his father's other leg and tears beginning to fill his eyes now that he had some understanding of what was about to happen.

"Now, you kids. You be good here. I can't take care of you."

Willie approached his father. "Daddy? Are you really gonna go?"

"Yes, son, I have to. You kids will have each other here."

Mrs. Weinrich said in her kind, grandmotherly way, "We try to keep children together in their families. This is a big group, but we'll do our best to make sure they are all in the same town and can see each other as often as they like."

Frank appreciated that, though he could see it was small comfort to the children. He gave them a nod and walked out on the porch. Frank Jr. sullenly accompanied him to the rented car.

As soon as her father passed through the front door, Dorothy began screaming—"Daddy! Daddy! Don't leave us! *Daddy-y!*"

Mrs. Weinrich knelt down and tried to put her arms around the little girl, having been present to many wretched scenes like this one, but Dorothy shook her off and fell to the floor sobbing.

Clarence cried with a little less volume, tears streaming down his cheeks and his nose beginning to run, looking down at his hands. Marie took her hankie and wiped his nose and put her arm around him. Mrs. Weinrich was pleased to see her maternal instincts, anticipating that she'd be a help with the little ones.

The two older boys, George and Willie, stood there with downcast faces.

This was the most difficult part of Mrs. Weinrich's job.

Lutheran Children's Home, Winfield, Kansas

Chapter 42

Prairie, Missouri, Ogden, Utah, &
Evanston, Wyoming
January 1930

Caroline once more told her son that Frank Jr. couldn't stay there. He heard the discussion and shouted from the living room, "I don't want to stay here! Nobody wants me! I'm going to become a hobo! You'll never see me again, and that's just what you want, isn't it?"

Carl and Henry were surprised at this turn of events. They could stay, but their brother couldn't? They feared the worst for him. And now their youngest sisters and brothers were in an orphanage hundreds of miles away, up for adoption, and Hermann, with his leanings, was in Los Angeles with Frances.

They looked at each other and Henry whispered, "I never thought Dad would be this mean."

But they didn't approve of what their mother had done either. They realized they were the lucky ones of the bunch, to be in a quiet household with a grandmother who cared for them, and they'd get to finish school.

Probably, anyway. Nothing seemed certain anymore. Their family had been decimated within a few short months, and not due to the financial hardships they were hearing others faced. Although they had heard their father complaining about how much a babysitter cost.

They'd also heard their aunts, talking with their grandmother, say more than once, "What was Frank *thinking* when he had Naomi declared unfit?"

If only Mother hadn't liked Charley so much.

Ultimately, Frank Jr. went back to the rooming house; his father gave him twenty dollars and told him to try to stay in school and get himself a part-time job, and go to dinner at his Grandma Wolff's on Sunday nights. She'd surely allow him that. If he even stuck around.

The arrangement completed, Frank Sr. went back to Ogden and organized the rest of his things to be hauled up to Evanston. He wished he didn't have to pack all this stuff, but he just left what he couldn't use, including what Naomi had not been able to carry with her, the rest of the children's toys, clothing, and mementos, and a lot of household things. He took some of the furniture, figuring worst case, they could put it in Minnie's basement, sell it or give it away. These days people wanted used furniture, if they could buy anything at all.

He had Anita come and clean the house out when he was done. He'd already told her that he'd taken the kids to an orphanage in Kansas. He knew she was furious with him, but she did as he asked. She did insist that he give her the name and address of the orphanage, however, even though he told her he thought it better and easier for the children if there were no contact. She retorted that they should know someone in their family still thought of them, and she would at least write to them.

The Federal Reserve Bank had raised interest rates, and wages had dropped too, so it would be more difficult to find a buyer for the Ogden house—but the stock market had been high the previous August. Frank hoped some lucky people might have sold stock and kept their proceeds.

The agent at Nelson Real Estate now told him that he'd be lucky to get $4,000, but that he had an interested buyer. That was disappointing news, about the price falling, but even at this lower price he'd be able to pay off the mortgage and put a little in his pocket, likely enough to pay for the move to Evanston.

He was disconcerted that he was feeling glum about the children, and the loss of his marriage. A few times, he thought, *I'm not sure I made all the best choices, but what else could I have done? My wife became a whore. None of this was my fault. I don't owe any apologies.*

Anita called her mother late in the month to tell her where the children were—only about a hundred miles away from the farm. Naomi knew approximately where Arkansas City and Winfield were. Anita had learned that it was the kind of orphanage that would put kids out for adoption as soon as they could.

Naomi cried over the phone and said, "Oh, Sis. Well, that's the nail in the coffin, isn't it? I dreamed he took them somewhere . . . I never thought he'd go this far."

"I remember, Mother, that Grandma Sims said you had 'the sight.' Frances has it too. She had a dream about you and Charles—that you were holding hands—before any of this happened."

Naomi was not surprised; she knew this about Frances and thought it must be something handed down through mothers somehow.

Anita also let her know that Frank Jr. was more or less on his own, and they both knew what a poor idea that was. Naomi's thoughts tore her in several directions: wanting to go up and see the kids, not knowing if she'd be sent to jail if she did, not knowing if the orphanage knew she was deemed "unfit," and thinking maybe she *was* an unfit mother if the law was more important to her than going up there to see her youngest children.

But wouldn't she just upset the children if she went, since she couldn't bring them all to the farm? And who would she bring, anyway? Just Clarence? Draw straws?

Then there was that court document, which implied she didn't have a right to them anyways. Things had gone from bad to worse.

"Mother, don't cry," Anita consoled her as Naomi tried to compose herself. "This isn't your fault, this part. Daddy is just . . . he's out of his head. He's spiteful. And that's a sin too."

Anita called Frances right after hanging up with her mother and gave her the news as well. Frances knew her father got back at people if he felt slighted, usually by just not talking to them for weeks, but never in a million years would she have thought he'd do this.

At least he didn't ask me to take the kids—thank heavens.

But an orphanage 1,200 miles away from everyone they knew? He was banishing his own children from their family—awful. Another scandal to keep under her hat forever.

She was glad she had a life away from all of this so that her new friends wouldn't know these things. And she would make sure her little daughter never found out either.

Frank arrived in Evanston by train, and the truck arrived the next day. Minnie was tickled by some of the furniture; she didn't need much, but there were a couple of pieces she could put out. They'd put the rest in the basement, as Frank suggested. She did have a twinge of guilt about these being Naomi's things—because what was she but a wanton woman, herself, sleeping with a married man?

She was glad she'd never met Naomi, and would likely never see her face-to-face.

The Evanston household settled into a regular domestic life. He had his room and she had hers, and when it was prudent—when the kids were either asleep or not home and there wasn't another boarder in the house—they'd have relations. They had a couple of close calls, but the back stairs were a godsend. She rented out a room or two sometimes; she still was doing sewing, if not quite as regularly. They had Frank's income, and he wasn't always around. Things were better financially for her and the children—and Frank too—than they'd been before the market crashed, other than the scarcity of goods that seemed to be worsening. But they could even afford to go out to dinner now and again.

Frank seemed to like the kids; it certainly had to be easier for him than it had been living with twice as many. He even played with them in the snow when he was in town. She wondered how he felt about giving his children away, especially when he'd occasionally stare out the window. But she didn't press him for his thoughts. Better to let bygones be bygones.

Chapter 43

Lutheran Children's Home, Winfield, Kansas
Winter 1930

M r. and Mrs. Weinrich were quite genial. There was no question about that. Firm, but gentle, and sometimes the kids thought, well, they were more merciful in some ways than their parents. No beatings, for instance. But they weren't their parents, and they were told on the first day to call them "Mama" and "Papa."

That just didn't feel right, but they did as they were told.

Initially, the Wolff kids didn't fully believe that they were going to stay here and never see their parents again. But as the months wore on, especially with the snow and cold outside and no one they knew coming to see them, reality slowly set in.

They hated that they all had to get up at the same time, real early, wash their faces and hands, get dressed, comb their hair, and be down in the kitchen by seven. Sometimes they'd sing a worship song, and there was always grace, which was said either by the Weinrichs or one of the children. When it came Marie's turn, she said the one her family had been taught: "God is great, God is good, and we thank him for our food. Amen." After grace, one of the Weinrichs or Margaret read to them from the Bible.

Breakfast was often oatmeal, or toast and jam, and sometimes eggs. So that was all right. Some days they even got juice.

There were twenty-three other kids also living in the home, mostly boys, each of them in various states of sadness or thankful gratitude. Some had come from homes where they were beaten worse than the Wolffs had been; the Wolffs understood that their own infractions were things their parents had wanted to train out of them, but here they learned that sometimes parents beat their children just because. Some of the children arrived very sick or with long-standing medical conditions that were addressed by a volunteer doctor. Marie and George heard the Weinrichs talking about how much they appreciated the contributions made by Lutherans from all around Kansas. They didn't fully understand what a contribution was, but they'd heard their dad say he didn't have more money to contribute to the church one time.

Some of the parents lived in the same town or Arkansas City. The ones still living in Winfield came by sometimes, and told the children things would be okay and gave them hugs. Those kids would tell the others, "My mom and pop are going to come get me someday," even though it seemed like someday got farther away. Some of the ones in Arkansas City or around Wichita would come once a month. A couple of times a dad came from Kansas City, and Marie and George thought, *Why don't Grandma Wolff or Carl or Henry come down to see us, then?*

Marie heard Mrs. Weinrich say to a new couple who brought in a little girl, "We don't encourage visits so that the child's expectations don't get up, but we don't discourage them either. The purpose here is to find *new, stable* homes for the children. We like to have them concentrate on their futures, not their pasts."

That made Marie's arm hairs stand on end. She had been thinking this might be just temporary, but to never see her mother again, and maybe not her other brothers and sisters . . . well, it was hard not to cry when she thought about it.

Marie decided to pretend that their father had brought them here because he couldn't afford to keep them. This was bending the truth, but it was easier than accepting that he just didn't want them. She assumed he'd gone back to that house in Evanston; she had seen that he already had a room there. It had sure looked permanent. So he was going to live with those other kids. But this was too confusing to consider, and she would rather pretend.

George was more realistic, but as boys sometimes don't pay close attention to the details, he wasn't sure if this was about money, a lack of love, his mother's mistake, or what. Willie was in between being a big boy and a little boy, so how he felt day to day varied—glad to have other boys to play with, three meals a day prepared by the same people, and a warm bed where he slept by himself instead of sometimes two or three to a bed . . . but missing his mama.

Dorothy and Clarence were still reeling from not being with their mother. They loved their daddy, but sometimes it was because they were supposed to, not because they felt it like they did in the arms of Mother. And they missed Anita a lot, who had always cared for them up until a few months ago. The other kids missed Frances, too, their second mother for most of their lives, but Dorothy and Clarence barely knew her.

Anita wrote to her siblings and told them how much she loved them and she wished she could come see them, but she had to work and it was winter, too, making it harder to take a train trip. Maybe in the summer she could come for a visit. Marie and George read the letter to the other kids over and over. It made them feel less forgotten. They wrote back to Anita in North Ogden, now that they had an address for a family member. One of the questions the younger children had, which Marie wrote out for them, was why didn't their mother write to them?

When Anita got that letter, with every child writing a little bit—even Clarence and Dorothy, though all they could do was sign their names as best they could—it made her cry. She composed a letter telling them that their mother wasn't allowed to write to them because of what the court said. She decided to keep it simple and not put all the blame on either of her parents. She wasn't sure if it was legal for Naomi to write to them.

The children were enrolled in school in Winfield, and the local kids didn't seem to discriminate against them for being orphan kids. There were some mean kids, but there were mean kids everywhere; they knew their bullying had nothing to do with Winfield or the children's home. Besides, it seemed like there were a lot of poor kids at the school, and they didn't look much happier than the children in the orphanage who missed their parents. At least they had a comfortable home, Marie and George would say to their siblings. And at least they got to be together. For now.

On Sundays, they all went to the Lutheran church. Marie had been thinking about becoming a Mormon, like her two older sisters, but realized she'd have to put that off. She did check to see if there was a Mormon church in Winfield, or even Arkansas City, since people went down there quite a bit, and there was not. But the Weinrichs considered a big part of their mission to bring all children to Jesus, so church was not the only place they studied the Bible; they read it at all mealtimes, and sometimes in the evenings. And of course, they were all expected to say their prayers before bed—but that was nothing new to the Wolffs.

If children at the home needed more clothing, local people either donated it or made it for them. They didn't all wear uniforms, but the clothes did tend to be similar, and the girls all had white, bleachable pinafores.

Everyone had chores. The older you were, the more chores. Making beds, changing beds, sweeping, dusting, ironing, mending, bringing in firewood, doing yard work if there was no snow on the ground, or digging out the snow from the walkway if there was. That was George's job sometimes, and Willie would help him.

It wasn't all bad. It just wasn't home.

Chapter 44

Winfield, Kansas, Stone Township, Oklahoma, & Evanston, Wyoming
April 1930

Marie and the rest of the Wolff children had grudgingly accepted that their family wasn't coming to get them. They had seen people come and look at the children, kind of like they were picking out a new puppy, except orphans could talk. On the days when a couple was coming to browse for children, everyone was inspected twice to make sure they were clean behind the ears and wore clean clothing. There was also encouragement that if children wanted a new home of their own, it would be wise to be polite and not rambunctious. George said to Willie and Marie, "Well, they better get used to how boys behave if they never had a kid before," but he didn't say it to the Weinrichs, and certainly not to any of the prospective parents.

Marie noticed that every once in a while, someone would have their eye on Dorothy, who was cute and little, like a storybook doll, and looked younger than she was. The women especially would say, "Aww . . . and what's *your* name, dear?" and lean down to get a good close look at her face. But she was shy and was not exactly flirting with the parents. She might have acted differently if someone had

said, "Oh, this is a family of five children? Let's meet all of them!"
But of course no one did that. And when they found out that Dorothy
wasn't four but actually seven, they would say, "Oh, well, it was nice
meeting you, honey," smile, and move on to another little girl.

Sometimes people did want boys, and sometimes they'd take the
older ones, the ones who had lived there awhile and become teenagers in the home. Marie had an inkling that the parents took those
boys because they needed help on their farms; one of the boys in the
house said his older brother had been adopted, and he'd told him he
did a lot of hay hauling and wheat sheaving and it was harder work
than living in the orphanage, but that the people were kind enough.
Sometimes two or three children in a family got taken home all at
once. But Mrs. Weinrich tried to make sure that if someone took only
part of a family, the other siblings went to the same town, or stayed at
the Winfield home until they grew up.

Marie saw some of the young men and women who used to live
there come back and say hello to the Weinrichs. Some of them lived
in Winfield and would come around to help. Some became teachers,
and some even went to college. She was glad to see that it seemed
none of these former orphans were unhappy, and it was clear they'd
never say they hated living there. Marie didn't hate living there either.
It just . . . wasn't home.

The census taker came on April 10. Marie, George, and Willie were
in the parlor, reading, when the man, Mr. Farvot, showed up with his
briefcase and papers. Marie exchanged looks with her siblings, wondering what was up; he didn't seem like he was selling anything. They hoped
he wasn't some kind of man from a court, with all those papers. She and
the others were leery of anything with the word "court" involved.

He asked to speak with Mr. or Mrs. Weinrich, and said he was
from the federal census bureau. That sounded pretty important.

Ruth, the Weinrichs' daughter, was at the front desk that day and knew where to find the records of all the children, plus knew the ages and birthplaces of the Weinrichs and Margaret, who lived there. She pulled out the papers she had on each child, and started with older girls Edith, Lila, and Dora. The Wolff children heard Ruth read off their names, ages, and what state they were born in, and then the state in which each of their parents were born, whether they were citizens of the United States, and occupation, "none."

Willie looked at Marie and whispered, "Do they know where we were born, and where Mother and Daddy were born?"

"Maybe," she said. "I don't know if Daddy gave them that when he was here."

"Are we citizens of the United States?"

"Of course," she whispered loudly, and shook her head at him.

"I just thought maybe not because Grandma and Grandpa Wolff were born in Prussia and Switzerland, right?"

"That doesn't count for us. We were born here."

"They're going by who got here last," George said. "Edith was the last one to come here, and Lila and Dora before that. And then it was us."

Then, sure enough, the Wolff children. They listened carefully as their statistics were entered into Mr. Farvot's sheet.

Willie asked Marie, "Did they have it all right?"

"It sounded to me like they did mostly, us born in either Kansas or Utah. But they had both Mother and Daddy in Missouri, and that's wrong. Mother was born in Kansas. And they had my age down as twelve; I'm thirteen now."

Marie didn't jump up to correct the errors—she didn't see the point—but she did wonder what they did with the information. Who was going to look at this? Who knew what adults did with all the things they wrote down?

In Evanston, the census taker was a woman, Mrs. Agnes Edwards. Minnie thought Mrs. Edwards was rather fortunate to get this job and be paid by the government. Minnie gave her all the information she asked for, including about the current roomer, Mr. Strabinger, another man of German ancestry who worked for the railroad. Since Frank was there, she had him come in and give the woman his own information: Frank J. Wolff, "Roomer" (*Ha*, thought Minnie), male, white, 42, D (for divorced; Minnie thought this wasn't accurate but didn't say anything), not in school, could read and write, birthplaces Missouri for Frank, Switzerland for his father, and Germany for his mother. And occupation, railroad engineer, currently employed.

Minnie felt no rush about marrying Frank. Things were working out just fine: they had more money than most folks, and she owned her house. She wasn't in a hurry to put him on the deed as her husband, anyway. But they'd just see how it went . . . and whether Frank would ever really divorce Naomi.

Charley proposed to Naomi at the farm. He tried to make it real special by waiting until Nancy and Joe had gone to town to shop, then making Naomi a nice lunch and putting on his best clean shirt.

"Naomi, I think we both know we're gonna be able to get along real good," he began, his stomach swirling with jitters. "And we love each other. I want it to be like this for us forever. And if someday we can have any of your kids here with us, that would be fine with me too. I mean, if it's legal and all and we've got the money here . . .

which I know maybe will be a long time. Gosh, I never tried to do this before . . . What I'm trying to say is, I'd be real proud if you would marry me."

"Oh, Charley." Naomi cast her eyes down. "I wish I could say yes. But you know, I don't think Frank has got us divorced yet. I have no way of knowing. So that would be polygamy . . . and I'm not a Mormon. It's not even legal in Utah anymore!" She laughed.

"I heard about something," Charley said. "A different law here in Oklahoma. I'm going to find out, and we'll talk about this again . . . alright?"

Naomi looked uncertain, but she smiled and nodded. "alright."

Charley asked Nancy if she knew any lawyers, and she chuckled.

"Now, just what is it you are fixing to do?" she asked.

"I want to find out if there's different laws about marriage in Oklahoma than there is in Utah. In case Frank hasn't divorced Naomi yet."

Nancy didn't pursue the implied topic, but Charley thought she looked happy—probably glad that he had good intentions for her daughter. "We don't know him personally, but there's a fellow, brother of Kaufman who owns the clothing store, and I think he's a lawyer. Seems like he knows a lot about the law. But you'd probably have to pay him. Maybe go to the library to ask first and look things up."

This felt daunting to Charley; using a library was not something he'd ever done. He'd been to school as much as he could until he was ten and needed on his family's farm, so he knew how to read and write, even being a farmworker all his life. His help had made it possible for his father to buy a place of his own. But a library? Where would he even begin in a place like that?

He sighed. "Okay . . . well, maybe I'll go to the library and maybe I'll go see Mr. Kaufman. I got to find some things out."

He did go to the library, a big important building right downtown on Main Avenue, and he talked to a real nice lady there who did the looking up for him. She seemed to know something about marriage in Oklahoma already.

"See here in this book?" She pointed to a paragraph. "It says that Oklahoma has common-law marriage. If a couple can't afford a wedding or can't get to a justice of the peace or whatever reason they might have, if they just declare that they are married and live together, they are married in the eyes of the law in Oklahoma. That's the common law, or the law everybody can take for granted without having to prove it. More or less."

This was good news, and Charley hurried back to the farm to let Naomi know this.

She still looked doubtful about a second marriage, and Charley understood why, but she also looked hopeful.

After all, Charley thought, how long could a person go thinking they were "living in sin" if they wanted to be married and the local law said it was legal and okay?

"Okay," Naomi said after a long pause. "We can say we're married, then, I guess. I mean, who's to know? People around here aren't going to go looking for Frank, that's for sure. And Lord knows I feel like we have a marriage here, Charley. Yes. I will be your wife."

Charley thought his heart would burst. He grabbed her and hugged her so hard she thought a rib might crack. Then they went to tell Nancy about their plan, to declare themselves married . . . if anybody needed to know.

"Well, now," Nancy said. "I suppose I might've been able to tell you that if I'd known that's what you were after. I've heard about that for people living way out in the country who have a hard time getting to town. But I didn't know much about it. If this is what you both want, I'll say the same thing, anybody asks." She smiled, turned her palms up, and shrugged. "How about we have a little party? Just to make it like we had a wedding. I can make a cake, and some punch. Then at least you can have a day to mark it. I got sugar and flour, and juice canned up. Yes, we can have a nice little . . . reception. That sound good?"

It sounded like about the best thing in the world to Charley.

Joe had gone up to Kansas City to stay with his and Nancy's other kids through the winter, where he'd be nearer a doctor if he caught the pneumonia, so it was an intimate celebration. But it was good to have a little merriment in their life, especially with the sad news about Frank putting the kids in the orphanage and then also having to be real careful about what they used or bought all the time. The plowing had been done, and they were about ready to plant—no drought yet this year, and everyone was feeling optimistic despite the shortages they'd endured.

The census taker, Mr. Arnold Spencer, came out to the farm on April 8. They sat in the kitchen and gave him all their information.

Because he was the man and Nancy was old, Mr. Spencer listed Charley as the head of the household, Naomi as his wife, though they spelled her name wrong (Naomi didn't want to make him change it after he wrote it down), and Nancy as Charley's mother-in-law.

Nancy smiled at this, not letting on anything. Charley puffed up a little. It felt good being called the head of the household.

When Naomi and Charley were in bed that evening, she said to him, "When he asked for race, you said white. I noticed he asked instead of assuming you were Indian, like a lot of folks think you are. So can I ask you something real personal?"

"Sure."

"Are you part Indian? I see when we go to town, sometimes the Indians nod to you like you are one of them, but you say you're white. It doesn't matter to me either way, but I just wondered."

"The Indians nod at me because they think they see one of their own, sometimes, but a lot of the Indians sneer at me on account of they think I'm part Indian but living with white people, like a white person," Charley said. "The whole truth is, on my mother's side, her dad, he had Indian blood. They think Cherokee. A lot of the Chalmerses—that was my mother's kin—used to live out in Tennessee near the Cherokees, and one of them, somebody way back there early, went to live with the Cherokees and left the white community. I'm proud about that, but I don't like to talk about it because a lotta people think the Indians are not as good as the whites. So what we tell anybody, if we ever have to, is we're white."

"So that's why you knew that coyote story. I love that story. And so did my kids."

"Yes, my mother and grandfather would tell that story and others. And that's another thing I don't usually talk about, except with people I trust. I knew you and your kids needed some cheering up after your little boy died . . ." He held her closer. "I'm sorry to bring it up; I don't usually ever talk about the dead."

"It's okay," Naomi said. "Not like I don't think about him all the time."

"Anyway, I got more stories like that; I just don't tell 'em unless it seems right."

"Maybe if we have a child someday, it'll have some Indian blood too," she said. "I'd like that."

Charley looked at her with surprise. "Well, yes, if we ever did that . . . that would be true."

He hadn't dared to think he'd ever have a child. And he knew Naomi was forty; that seemed old to be thinking of children, for a woman. But here she was talking about it, even after having all those kids. *She must really miss being a mother.*

Chapter 45

Ogden, Utah, Evanston, Wyoming, & Prairie, Missouri
June 1930

Marie Palmen was elated to receive the final divorce decree. It had taken a year and a half, but the judge had ruled in her favor, against Walter, for "lack of support." *Ha!* she thought. They awarded her $700, to be paid at $25 a month over about two years. It wasn't enough to live on, but it would help. She had had so much expense supporting herself and getting out here to Ogden to find the man.

With an eye to a new start, she decided to contact the rooming house in Evanston that Mr. Wolff had told her about. She called the week after the divorce was final.

A woman's voice answered, "Minnie Woods speaking."

Marie paused; she had expected a hello, but maybe this was how businesswomen answered the phone.

"Hello?"

"Yes, hello, who is calling?"

"This is Marie Palmen. A Mr. Wolff told me about your rooming house. I work as a maid in Ogden and want to move to Evanston. Do you have any work for me?" she said in her stilted English.

"Do you have experience in rooming or boardinghouses?"

"Yes, I do."

"I do need someone to clean and keep up with the wash and all. But I also need someone to look after my children some, make them meals and such. None of 'em are little, so no diapers or anything like that. Is that okay? What are you expecting to be paid?"

Marie wasn't sure how to answer this, and that was a lot of information this woman was giving her, but with her guaranteed income, she thought she could probably take whatever the woman offered. She just didn't want to run into Walter anymore.

"Well, I'm sure you will pay me the right price. And I can cook for children. Would I live in your house there?"

"Hmm . . . I can pay you $125 a month, plus you'll have your room and board. How does that sound?"

Marie knew she could make more in Ogden, but this seemed a fair enough amount. "That's good. When can I come?"

"Come on up as soon as you can. The address is 571 Main Street. We are about ten or twelve blocks from the station, so if you have more than one bag, you probably want to take a cab here. Or the bus, if it's running."

Marie figured the journey would not cost her that much: train fare maybe a dollar or two, maybe twenty cents for a taxi, and she'd bring her lunch from home. "I will be there next week," she said.

When Marie arrived at the house in Evanston, Minnie was surprised to learn that this little strawberry-blonde woman was apparently in her mid-thirties. She wondered what her background was, and why she needed work and wasn't married.

Anyway, she looked agile enough to perform the tasks at hand.

It became apparent in the first two days that Marie Palmen was more meticulous than Minnie herself—maybe a little too much so, Minnie thought, but better too picky than incompetent. She was satisfied that this was going to work out well.

Carl graduated from high school in Prairie, Jackson County, Missouri. He found work helping to fit parts and do repairs for railroad cars in Kansas City, following his dad's suggestion. Frank had told him to say that he was the son of a railroad engineer and that might pave his way, even though jobs were starting to become hard to get. Carl felt like he'd done all right, given all that had happened to his family in the last ten months. He hadn't missed any school, he'd got a job, he did right by his grandmother and helped her out.

Carl and Henry did all of Caroline's yard work and fixed things for her when they broke, which wasn't too often, and took out the trash, and went to the general store and to the pharmacy. Whatever she needed. She still cleaned the house, but they washed the dishes. Carl knew Henry was going to have to take on his tasks now that he was working; he'd be taking the bus from Prairie to Kansas City every day except Sunday and some Saturdays, forty-five minutes each way. But Henry was an easygoing boy; he didn't seem to mind.

They both missed their brothers and sisters. But Carl had to admit it was easier living in a house with fewer people and nobody mad at anybody else.

Frank Jr. sometimes came around for Sunday dinners, and they saw him at the high school. But he wasn't always there, and they weren't sure what he did with his time; he implied that he got odd jobs but was vague about that. He had a chip on his shoulder, and Carl couldn't blame him.

He suspected his younger brother might really be going on the trains like a hobo sometimes. At least he kept in touch.

Chapter 46

Evanston, Wyoming, Winfield, Kansas, & Stone Township, Oklahoma
Autumn 1930

The Woods boardinghouse on Main Street was always bustling. Minnie took in a roomer or two every week, always railroad men, and continued to work as a seamstress; sometimes there was no extra work, but that was okay. They now had Marie Palmen there to make sure the five children's few needs were taken care of when Minnie worked downtown at the dressmaker's. Lawrence was old enough to work, but Minnie was hoping he would go down to Weber College in Ogden first, even if only for a year or two, since they were not desperate for him to contribute to the household. Frank was still sharing his salary from Union Pacific with Minnie, giving her a generous share of his paycheck to cover the expenses of the big house and its family.

Marie got a mysterious letter in the mail every month, but no one had the temerity to ask her what it was, although Minnie's curiosity was about killing her. Marie always went downtown the day after the letter came, so Minnie suspected it was some kind of check, or maybe something that she had to take care of at Western Union afterward. Something she had to wire to Germany, maybe. Frank told her she was nosy for bringing it up to him; it was none of their business.

He liked Marie; he got to practice his German with her when he was home from the rails. Minnie knew it had been risky to speak German during and for a few years after the World War—the United States had required Germans to register as enemy aliens, for gosh sake—so she understood Frank's excitement about being able to converse in it more freely now. He and Marie had lively conversations, which they both seemed to enjoy immensely. Minnie often wondered what all they found to talk about, since Frank had never been to Germany and all they had in common was Ogden, the language, and Wiener schnitzel. When she asked Frank about it, he teased her and accused her of being a little bit jealous, which tickled him. She denied it, but he wasn't entirely wrong.

In Winfield, Marie Wolff was resigned that her family had abandoned her and her siblings. When parents came to review the children, she and the other Wolffs usually found a subtle way to be sullen or project some other mood that would deter people from wanting to take them home. Sometimes Marie thought it might be better if they did find a home, but she didn't want to be separated from her siblings, and it had become apparent that prospective parents didn't want five children.

Sometimes a parent would think about taking both Dorothy and Clarence, but at some point Clarence would usually start dancing around acting goofy or poking at his other brothers and sisters to make them laugh, and parents would shy away from his clowning. It was cute, but they weren't sure they wanted a boy who was that active and silly. People wanted perfect children.

And then one day in December, a woman looked at Dorothy as if she were an angel come down from heaven. She talked with her for twenty minutes, misinterpreting Dorothy's hesitancy and distrust as timidness. When she learned her name, she exclaimed, "Oh, just like in *The Wizard of Oz*! Have you read that book, dear?"

Dorothy politely shook her curls no. She was eight now, and knew about the book—they had it in the orphanage—but it was too big a book for her to read alone. Marie had read parts of it to her, but the woman had not asked her if someone else had read it to her.

The pretty woman in a blue suit turned to her husband, her face beaming. "Oh, Thomas, I just love her. Isn't she . . . just the sweetest? She even looks a little like your sister."

Thomas and Edna Miller came back several times to visit Dorothy and finally decided she was the one who would make their lives complete. Dorothy did not want to be rude, and she eventually warmed a little to Mrs. Miller. She had only in the last several months gotten used to calling Mr. and Mrs. Weinrich "Mama" and "Papa," and now here she was looking at a woman who lived in another town who wanted to be her new mama. She already had a mama. But she never came from the farm to see her, wherever that was. So maybe not just her daddy but her mama, too, didn't want her anymore.

Mrs. Weinrich questioned the Millers at length about their intention to keep their residence in Arkansas City. She made it clear to them that this would mean that the orphanage would be limited to placing the three boys and their older sister only in Arkansas City, and then the siblings could grow up near each other. She added that the Wolff children had been here for almost a year. And there would be a surcharge for taking just the one Wolff child.

Yes, they understood, and they agreed to actively look among their friends for prospective parents for the other children.

"We'd love to take her home and have her with us for Christmas," Mrs. Miller said, darting a look in Dorothy's direction, "but we really can't do that. We'll be traveling over the Christmas holidays, and although we want her to meet our families, we think it would be too much for her. We'd rather have her home for a good amount of time before we take her traveling."

Susanna Weinrich agreed. "We'll get all the paperwork started and complete it, and you can come back in January to pick up little Dorothy."

Before they left that day, Mrs. Miller bent down and gave Dorothy a hug and a kiss on the cheek. "Oh, Dorothy, we're going to be your parents. We have a lovely home for you in Arkansas City. And if ever there's a way, your brothers and sister will be welcome to come visit. Okay?"

Dorothy nodded, although she was uneasy. She didn't want to think about what was going to happen. She'd been moved around and seen too much and was used to being here in the orphanage, where people were kind and mostly everybody got along . . . and where she was with her brothers and Marie, who watched over her.

Marie told her later, "Don't worry, Dorothy. We will know where you are, and Mrs. Weinrich . . . I mean, *Mama* . . . will try and get us homes near you."

Naomi was seven-and-a-half months pregnant. She thought to herself more than once, *Frank probably was worried I was already pregnant with Charley's dark-haired child . . . and people would know it wasn't his. Well, I am now.*

Anita had come down once in the summer, and that had been a boon. But she could only stay just a few days on account of her work.

I wish to God I could see my other children, Naomi thought. *God, grant me that someday.*

Charley thought Naomi looked beautiful pregnant, and he couldn't wait to see if she had a boy or a girl, and what the child would look like. He hoped it would have his dark hair. Were you supposed to call an unborn baby "it"? There was so much he didn't know about being a father. But he liked Naomi's kids, so he expected he'd like this one, their own child.

He counted up that he'd be fifty-one when the child was born, sixty-one when it was ten . . . He knew he was old for a new father, but he guessed other men had done this and he was going to do his best.

Joe's health had continued to be poor, so he was still staying up near Kansas City with his other children, where they could take turns caring for him, but Nancy seemed a little excited about her soon-to-be grandchild.

Everybody was happy that a new baby was coming, in fact. Despite the farm's diminished production and their meager food supplies, the birth was something to look forward to in the new year.

Chapter 47

Ogden, Utah, Evanston, Wyoming, & Arkansas City, Kansas
January 1931

O n January 2, after celebrating the new year with her beau, Caleb, Anita turned twenty-one.

Anita and Caleb had become close and now knew each other well enough to have personal conversations about family. Anita was not a secretive young woman, and that day, when they were sitting in the parlor when all the visiting residents were either in their rooms or out on the town, she opened up about her family's situation.

Caleb was dumbfounded.

"So, he got custody of the kids, and then he gives them away? Because he wanted to live at this place in Wyoming and the matron there didn't want the kids around?"

"Well, I think there's a little more to it than that," Anita said. "I am pretty sure this matron, I think her name is Woods, is my father's girlfriend. I mean, this must have been going on before my mother . . . made her mistake." *If it really was a mistake. Maybe it wasn't.* "And the woman has children of her own. Having a houseful of children, half of them not your own, when you have a boardinghouse to run—well, I can see why she wouldn't want all my brothers and sisters living there. But—"

Caleb interrupted, "Yeah, but why didn't your dad just bring them back to Ogden, then?"

"I think mostly because the little kids needed someone there all the time, not just my twelve-year-old sister and my teenage brothers. And my dad was gone a lot. He has always been gone a lot, often for weeks at a time."

"He was between a rock and a hard spot," Caleb conceded. "But to give your kids away like that? Man, oh man."

"Yes." Anita felt a familiar anger toward her father. "I know he didn't think about how it all was going to work out and just wanted to get back at my mother."

"While he was probably doing the same thing she'd done. But it *is* different for women."

"That's the thing that is true . . . but it's also . . . I don't know." She shook her head. "Unfair."

"I wonder if it is actually legal, what he did," Caleb said. "I mean, he gets custody, then he gives them away, and they could have just figured something else out so the kids could be with your mother. Or he could have just hired somebody to take care of them. Didn't he support the family all those years? And how many kids were there?"

"Ten of us kids—for a while there, anyway. And with my mother gone, that was one less mouth to feed. So yes, he probably could have had some gal move in to be the nanny and the housekeeper and paid her. That was what I thought too."

Caleb leaned forward. "I think maybe you should look into this and see if he did something that was not only unkind but also not what the judge expected when he gave your dad custody. My parents have a friend who works for a lawyer. Let me ask him. Is that okay with you? I won't give him your name or anything."

Was it really possible that something could be done? "Yes," she said eagerly, "I'd appreciate that!"

And so it was that Anita Wolff showed up at the courthouse in Ogden three days after her birthday, on a cold January morning, in her best dress and her wool coat, with papers in hand.

The judge's bailiff called out, "Anita Wolff in the case of Frank Wolff custody case," and Anita stepped to the front of the courthouse, nervously clenching the papers they'd told her to fill out. The judge had the original, and she had a carbon copy.

"Miss Wolff, am I given to understand that you are challenging Mr. Frank Wolff's custody of your siblings . . . Mr. Wolff being your father? Did you think the children should not have been put solely in the custody of your father, or that your mother should not have been declared unfit?"

Anita was a little taken aback and unprepared to answer those particular questions.

She stuttered, "N-no, no, Your Honor . . . not exactly?"

"Well, what exactly is it that has brought you here today? Take your time. No need to be nervous, I don't bite." He smiled.

"Your Honor, after my father got custody of the children in the fall of 1929, he took them to a boardinghouse in Evanston, where he stays all the time because he's a railroad engineer. The matron there didn't want to have his five children in the house while he was gone so much because she has her own children. It was a lot of kids. So my father took them to the Lutheran Children's Home in Kansas and gave them away. The five youngest ones. And they were left there to be adopted. They are still there; they have been there for a year, and so far no one has adopted them. And now my father is helping raise the children of the boardinghouse matron."

The judge took off his glasses, rubbed his nose, and then put the spectacles back on and looked at the paperwork before him for a few moments.

"You mentioned only five children, and there are ten listed here. Where are the others? And why did you wait so long to bring this before the court?"

"Your Honor"—Caleb had coached her to always address the judge as "Your Honor"; he said she'd look more savvy—"I am one of the ten, and I couldn't file anything until I reached the age of . . . majority." Anita hadn't known before that this was what it was called, but she had known that being twenty-one meant the world considered you a legal adult. "As for my other brothers—two of them went to live with my grandmother near Kansas City, in Missouri, one of them went to live in Los Angeles with my older sister, and the other brother . . . well, he was too old for the orphanage and my grandmother didn't want to take three boys, so he's been kind of a leaf on the wind. He stays in touch with my two older brothers. He goes to school or gets jobs so he can stay in rooming houses."

The judge appeared partly moved and partly annoyed by this story. "Miss Wolff, this is an unusual case. It's not unusual for parents to give their children to an orphanage at this time, with the financial ruin many people have faced. But I take it your father has been gainfully employed this entire time?"

"Yes, sir. Your Honor. He has always worked, since before I was born. I don't know that he's ever had more than a week or two off at a time. He started working when he was fourteen. So . . . gosh, that's . . . maybe thirty years. Steady."

The judge cleared his throat and looked at the papers again. "You are not asking for something specific?"

"Well, Your Honor, it seems to me my father should probably have my brothers and sisters with him, so they can remain a family and not get adopted by someone." Anita's voice cracked, and it was hard for her to keep her composure. She had to stop. She looked down, hoping the tears that began sliding down her face would just wait until she got outside. "I just . . . My brothers and sisters don't want to be adopted. I am afraid we might all never see each other again." She choked back a sob and looked down again, then made an effort to hold her head up and look directly at the judge. "Your Honor."

"Miss Wolff, I can see how much you love your younger brothers and sisters, and I am not generally moved by a plaintiff's emotions. But the facts in this case definitely speak for themselves. Are you able to take your siblings in yourself?"

This surprised Anita, and it took her a moment to gather her thoughts. "Oh, no, Your Honor. I wish I could. I work full-time at a boardinghouse and . . . you would probably know I don't make enough to support children with that work. And I'm not married either. Yet."

"Miss Wolff, with a heart as big as yours, I'll bet someone's going to want to marry you sooner rather than later—but that's neither here nor there." Looking a bit flustered, the judge said, "Reporter, please strike my last comment from the record." He cleared his throat. "I rule in the case of Anita Wolff vs. Frank J. Wolff that Frank J. Wolff is required to collect, provide residence for in his own domicile, and support the children for whom he was given custody in 1929—save for Anita Wolff, who has come of age. If any of these children are in stable domiciles agreed upon with other relatives, they are allowed to remain so as long as there is an adult fully supporting them with food and shelter and the other basic needs of a child who has not reached majority or is not working of his or her own free will. The children in the Lutheran Children's Home must be reunited with their father at the earliest possible date, and no later than . . . January 22, 1931. A copy of this declaration is to be delivered immediately both to Frank J. Wolff in Evanston, Wyoming, at 571 Main Street, and also to the Lutheran Children's Home in"—he looked at the paperwork again—"Winfield, Kansas. So ruled on this day, January 5, 1931."

His gavel's strike echoed through the courtroom, and Anita felt chills up her back and along her arms. The good kind.

"Miss Wolff, I am sorry, but you will need to hire someone to serve your father with the papers the clerk will provide, and of course that is going to involve probably a train trip," the judge said kindly. "Are you able to pay for these expenses?"

"Yes, Your Honor," Anita answered. She had wiped the tears from her cheeks and could barely keep from smiling. She knew this was a solemn occasion, but her joy was bubbling up inside. She'd get an advance on wages, or borrow it from Caleb if she had to. She had a little money in the bank. It was only paying some man and a round-trip train ticket.

Whatever she needed to do, she would figure it out.

Frank Wolff was home when the process server came to Minnie's door two days later, looking like some kind of salesman in a suit. Her daughter Nina answered the door that Wednesday, January 7, and then stepped back into the house and called out for Frank, who came to the door, bewildered; no caller had ever come there for him except when Anita had visited once.

The man in the suit asked, "Are you Frank Joseph Wolff, who used to live in Ogden, Utah?"

"Yes," Frank said, his brow furrowed.

He handed Frank the thick envelope, Frank accepted it, and the process server said, "Sir, you have been served."

Frank looked at the man, and at the envelope in his hand. He couldn't imagine what it contained.

He took the envelope up to his room; he didn't want Minnie or anyone else asking him what was going on, especially since he didn't yet know what that might be. He opened the envelope, unfolded the papers, and read through the brief statement and the background complaint Anita had filed. Then he read them again.

Alarmed that his life was now taking another turn, Frank took off his glasses, rubbed the bridge of his nose, and shook his head. How could this be happening to him? *Damn. There is no way to get out of this.*

He had to think of a way to break the news to Minnie that he was bringing his kids back to her house. This wasn't going to be pleasant.

Edna Miller was thrilled. After she and Thomas had come home from visiting their two respective families over the holidays, she'd set about furnishing their extra bedroom for Dorothy. She bought curtains she'd seen at the dry goods store on impulse, and they'd gone up to Wichita to buy a child-size bed. None of the furniture stores had one, so they'd gone to a couple of secondhand stores and found a maple twin-sized that was in excellent condition. Edna knew that because the bed had only been brought in recently, that probably meant that a family in financial difficulty, like so many were in Kansas, had been forced to sell it and put several children in one bed.

Or they may have had to move out of Kansas altogether. This made her sad, but she thought, *One child lost a bed, and another who needs it, our little Dorothy, will soon put it to good use. There's some kind of poetic justice in that.*

She had purchased clothing and dolls too—some also used; it had become hard to find just about anything since October '29—but everything she'd found was in excellent condition.

She wanted to get everything just right before they went to Winfield to pick Dorothy up.

Chapter 48

Evanston, Wyoming, Prairie, Missouri, Winfield, Kansas, & Fair Play, Missouri
Late January 1931

Minnie was fit to be tied when Frank told her he had to go get the kids and bring them back to Evanston. He showed her the court order and said there was just no dang thing he could do about it but go get them before Thursday, January 22.

Minnie set her jaw and wouldn't even consider any canoodling for the rest of the time before he left.

I guess that's no surprise, he thought.

On top of that he had to get a week off work, which was damned inconvenient. No pay. When he'd taken a vacation before, it was always when they didn't have him scheduled for a run.

Frank was irritated, but he also didn't want to get into any legal trouble. He didn't know if anybody was keeping tabs on him, but with Minnie being angry, and the kids . . . well, Marie was, what, fourteen maybe? Old enough to know the calendar and when things did or didn't happen, if asked. So he felt trapped into picking the kids up as soon as possible. He thought this probably meant Frank Jr. too, but since he didn't know for sure where he was . . . he'd just leave that for now. If he found out, he could send for him, and Frank could come out on the train.

Resigned to his fate, he took the trip, stopping at his mother's place in Prairie to say hello to Carl and Henry. They were a little cool toward him. And his mother, though she didn't say, "I told you so," gave him a look that only a mother could give, even to a forty-three-year-old son.

On Tuesday, January 20, Frank took the early train to Wichita and rented a large Chevrolet to go down to Winfield. It was about forty degrees outside; at least it wasn't as cold as Evanston, and he was thankful it wasn't raining. He arrived in front of the Lutheran Children's Home feeling like the many steps up to the big porch were going to be even harder to climb this time.

He stood at the door a moment, composing his thoughts and assuming a neutral facial expression, before entering.

"Oh, Mr. Wolff. We've been expecting you," said Margaret, the orphanage assistant. "Let me go fetch Susanna."

Who the devil is Susanna? Frank wondered, knitting his brows.

"Mrs. Weinrich," Margaret said, when she saw he was perplexed.

Mrs. Weinrich soon stepped into the front hall from the kitchen, and she was immediately all business.

"Mr. Wolff," she greeted him. "We got the papers from the court almost a week ago and were hoping to hear from you. I must tell you . . . we are in the process of placing Dorothy. A couple in Arkansas City has adopted her; they have paid her fee, and they were coming up this week to get her until I called them and told them that there was . . . a delay. They were a bit upset and I told them not to worry, that we just had to work a few things out with records from the father. I didn't want to tell her the adoption wasn't going through until I spoke with you. I had hoped you'd call."

Frank had not thought of calling. He'd just gotten down there lickety-split so he could get it over with. Now he was even more irritated with the whole situation. "Listen here, I did bring my children here hoping they might have a better life than I could provide them. But now I'm legally required to take them back, and that's what I'm here to do."

"Mr. Wolff, you led me to believe you were unable to support your children financially. From these papers, it appears that was not the case." She gave him a look more searing than the one he'd endured from his mother.

"I never said I couldn't support them financially; I said I wasn't able to keep them." He couldn't remember exactly what he'd said, but he'd be damned if this woman he didn't know was going to put him on the spot.

Mrs. Weinrich simply stood there holding his gaze.

Damn the woman. "I'm here to pick up my children! All of them!" Frank tried to keep his voice low but firm.

"*Daddy?*"

Frank turned to see a wide-eyed Willie peeking at him through the kitchen door. He turned toward his son and said, "Yes, Will, it's me." Then he turned back to Mrs. Weinrich.

"Mr. Wolff, this is going to be very inconvenient for the Millers. They have gone to considerable expense; they came to see Dorothy several times before they made their decision, and have purchased furniture and other things for the girl. Are you sure you want to take your little girl with you, and that she'll have a better home with you than with a couple who are sure they want her? I realize you are under a legal obligation, but we have one here too."

"That's not my problem," Frank said. "And you just said it. She's *my* little girl. She belongs with her brothers and sister. I'd say that my court order is more . . . *lawful* . . . than your adoption papers." He wasn't really sure if this was true, but he thought probably his did take precedence since it came from a court. "It's too bad for that couple, but they can find another girl. There are lots of children need homes these days. And that's final. So, do I go get my kids or are you going to?"

He might have been more polite if he weren't so frustrated with the whole situation, but he felt that taking a strong stance was the only way this woman was going to give in.

"All right, Mr. Wolff. I need for you to sign some papers showing that you picked up the children, with full knowledge that Dorothy was in the process of being adopted by a couple who had already paid the adoption fee. We will require you to reimburse us for that, because we have to repay Mr. and Mrs. Miller."

Will this never end? he thought. "Okay, gimme the papers; where do I sign? And I only have about twenty dollars on me. I'll have to make payments for that fee. You can bill me. 571 Main Street, Evanston, Wyoming."

All three of his younger boys now stood to the side of the reception desk, waiting for an acknowledgment from their father.

Frank glanced at them. "George. You go tell Marie and Dorothy we're going back to Evanston. And to start packing their things."

"Daddy? Marie's not home from school yet," George informed his father.

Frank didn't think he could get much more irritated. He ran his hand through his pomaded hair—and was immediately sorry, since now he had to deal with the papers with Brylcreem on his hand.

"Okay, well go tell Dorothy. What time does Marie get home?"

"If she doesn't have choir practice, she gets home around now," George offered. "If she does, it'll be another hour."

"Okay, go up to your rooms and tell Dorothy and start packing your things. If Marie's not here soon, George, you can go to the church and get her."

Frank had hoped to have Marie supervise the packing. It seemed like nothing ever went smoothly when it involved women or children.

By the time Marie was home and packed it was six, time for dinner, and they all remained there for the meal. Afterward, the children said their goodbyes to the friends they'd made. Mrs. Weinrich hugged all of them and gave them each a gift—books for the older kids, a doll for Dorothy, and a toy car for Clarence.

Frank was just this side of fuming that it had gotten so late; now he'd have to drive in the dark to Wichita. Fortunately, there was a late train to Kansas City. He called Caroline's house from a pay phone in Wichita and told the boys to be prepared to come pick them up, somehow, even if they had to call a taxi.

They spent the night in Prairie, and the next day Frank Sr. and the children caught the train back to Evanston—without Frank Jr. His father hadn't managed to locate him before leaving town.

Charley, Naomi, and Nancy decided to get away from the farm while they could in mid-January, given it was winter and there was little to be done with the fields, and left their young farmworker—sixteen-year-old Harold—in charge.

They took the truck and drove up to visit Joe where he was staying with Julia in Dallas, Missouri. They had a laugh around the kitchen table about how people always confused Dallas, Texas, with this little spot of a town three hours away from Kansas City.

On the way back home, Naomi went into labor in the truck. They stopped at a farmhouse in the area of Fair Play, Missouri, five hours from home, and that was where their daughter, Connie, was born. The farmer's wife had birthed more than one baby, and Naomi was an old hand at this, of course. Everything went smoothly enough, considering, and the farmer and his family were delighted and amused by this unusual event in their quiet home.

They put Naomi and Charley up for a couple of days in the currently empty bunkhouse, a place that felt almost like home, and Nancy stayed in their older daughter's bedroom. The farmer's wife gave Naomi a worn baby blanket in which to wrap little Connie.

Charley was "over the moon," as Naomi would later describe it. His first, and possibly his only child. His darling daughter. Her shock of dark hair pleased him further still.

Naomi wished she could do something to compensate their hosts for their trouble, having saved the cost of a doctor, but the generous couple refused, despite it being clear that like other plains farmers, they were having a hard time of it.

Naomi resolved to knit them an afghan and mail it to them when she felt up to it and could obtain the yarn, and that's just what she did.

Chapter 49

Evanston, Wyoming
April 1931

Minnie Woods was at her wit's end. Ten children in the house, from age eight to nineteen. The regular roomers could not stay there anymore, so there went at least twenty dollars a month. Frank's income was now spread much thinner. And just having thirteen people living in her house, even though it was large, was more than a bother—it was a downright disturbance.

Finally, one night when Frank was home for more than a night and at last all the children were asleep, most of them sleeping two to a bed, she said, "Please come talk in the parlor with me."

Frank didn't like the sound of this, but he knew Minnie was managing a lot and had repeatedly said that the living arrangement was unsustainable. He had hoped she'd just settle down and get used to it, like Naomi had—although of course all the kids were hers, not half-and-half.

Frank sat down on the davenport, lightly slapped his hands upon his thighs, and looked at Minnie expectantly, acting as if he didn't know what this was about.

"Frank, you know I care for you. But we had this discussion over a year ago, and I have been telling you over and over that this is *not* working out. It is an unlivable situation. So, I am telling you again: I am *not* raising ten children. I am not. You must find a different place to live and take your children. You *must*. I need you to be gone with them by the end of the month."

Frank swallowed. This sounded too much like an ultimatum; he thought he'd see if there was room to negotiate.

"Minnie, I know it's been hard, but it's only been a couple of months. And if we go, there goes my income, which you have enjoyed. And we wouldn't see each other much, besides."

"Frank, you're paying me at the room-per-night rent, and part of your income is going to support your five children. And what if your other sons come back here? That would be sixteen people living here! For goodness' sake. I am not prepared to live like this, and what's more, I don't *want* to. You have to go."

"I don't know," he said. "I think you haven't given it enough time."

"You don't seem to understand. You have to go. There's no back and forth, maybe this and maybe that. I can't do this. And this is *my* house. It was fine, of course, when it was just you. That was working out well for everyone . . . except your children. So you start looking for a place tomorrow. *Tomorrow*, Frank."

It seemed like she was not going to give in on this. Still, he'd wait and see how she felt in the morning. *Maybe she just had a tough day.*

In the morning, Minnie handed him a cup of coffee—and the newspaper, turned to the ads for places to rent. He saw she wasn't kidding and was just trying to be as nice as she could.

"So, I guess you mean it." He exhaled in resignation.

"Yes, I do. I should never have allowed you to bring them here the second time, but it was an emergency. I didn't want to be nasty about it, and I thought you'd start looking for your own place. But you seemed to think somehow it was all going to work out hearts and flowers. But then of course you weren't here when Marie and Nina were mad at each other because they had to sleep in the same bed and one of them took too much room, or when Martin and George both wanted to use the football to practice with their friends and I had to be the referee, or when Clarence cried because the last of the cookies were gone. Sharing is good, Frank, but not when there's not enough to go around. So yes, I'm sorry, but I mean it."

The kids were a little surprised that they were moving yet again, but given how unstable their lives had been for the last two years, no one but Clarence was really upset.

"We're moving *again*?" he groused. "Is Mother coming with us this time?"

Marie hastily explained that she couldn't, she was living with Grandma Sims now, in Oklahoma. Clarence didn't really understand why but accepted the answer.

Dorothy still very much missed her mother and had also hoped her mama was coming to the next house. People would comment, when they saw her, "Such a pretty little girl, but she looks so sad. You should be happy, dear, that you have a family! Let's see you smile!"

Willie, as the middle child, felt like it didn't matter much what he thought; the older kids had more say, and the younger ones got more attention. But he tried to remain optimistic.

As a group, they were not going to complain, because at least they were together, and with their real parent, whatever his shortcomings, and soon they were settled in a calmer home—in a five-bedroom (one in the basement) house their father had rented on Eighth Street, across town from Minnie's place. Besides, Marie and George hadn't liked living with a woman who was clearly too important to their father but wasn't their mother, or even their stepmother. Marie had become a Mormon, and her values didn't include relations outside marriage, including what her mother had done. The Mormon church was just up the street from their house, making it easy to attend Sunday school. The other children attended whatever Protestant church they cared to on any given Sunday; there wasn't a Lutheran church in Evanston.

Northern Evanston, Wyoming, neighborhood

Frank paid a nanny to come stay with the kids, just in the day-time after school for two weeks, when he went on his first run after their move. Then he got what he felt was a brilliant idea.

He took the bus down to Minnie's the second day after he came home from that run, at the time of day he knew Minnie was usually at her seamstress job. He hadn't spoken to her since moving out but assumed she was still keeping the same schedule.

It felt strange to knock, but this was what would be expected.

He was pleased when Marie Palmen answered the door.

"Oh, hello, Marie," he said in German. "You're actually the one I wanted to speak to."

"Oh, really?" This brought a smile to her face. "Come in, I'll pour you a cup of coffee."

Marie had only an inkling of what had led the Wolffs to move out and had noticed the tension, but she assumed it was due to so many people in the house. It seemed perfectly normal to her that Mr. Wolff would come by to visit; it was only unusual that he specifically wanted to speak to her. Maybe he wanted to talk about what was going on in Germany, and didn't have anyone else with whom to discuss it.

When they were settled in the parlor, Mr. Wolff asked, continuing in German, "Are you the only one home?"

"Yes," she said. "Well, the second boy, Martin, is doing his home-work in his room."

Mr. Wolff gave her a half smile. "Marie, what is Mrs. Woods paying you? If it's okay for me to ask."

"Oh, she pays me pretty good, and I don't pay for rent or food."

"I wondered because . . . I need a nanny and a housekeeper myself. And there's a basement bedroom at my house in the north part of town where you could live if you wanted to come work for me. I'm already paying someone to be a nanny, but she's not there all the time, and I'm gone a great deal."

Marie was both surprised and almost delighted. She liked Mr. Wolff, and it wouldn't be a bad thing to live in a smaller house with less work. And with so many people out of work, she thought Mrs. Woods wouldn't have much trouble finding another housekeeper.

"*Ach, du Lieber!* What a nice offer! I think I might like to do that. Let me talk to Mrs. Woods. But you'd have to pay me the same as she does."

"And how much is that?"

She realized she could tell him anything but also that he could ask around, since he was already paying a nanny. She told him the truth.

Mr. Wolff's mouth pursed at the number, but he nodded. "Okay, then, it's settled. When can you come and start, and move in?"

Marie laughed. "I told you, I have to talk to Mrs. Woods first." She was hoping maybe Mrs. Woods would offer to give her a raise to keep her there. "But I'm interested. You have a phone in your house? I can call you when I know."

Mr. Wolff didn't seem pleased that she hadn't given an outright yes, but he didn't argue. "Yes, we have a phone."

A few days later, Marie called Frank and told him she accepted his offer and would move over in a week.

And this will also show Minnie maybe she should have thought longer about making us leave, thought Frank. *Now I have taken something you needed, Minnie Woods.*

Chapter 50

Prairie and Kansas City, Missouri, & Los Angeles, California
June 1931

Henry Wolff graduated high school and was glad that part of his life was done. He had excelled in auto shop, so he got an apprentice position at a garage in Kansas City. Even though folks didn't have much money these days, they needed to get their cars fixed. One fellow who came in said he and his family were living in the car, but probably going west to get out of the prairie life.

Seemed like everybody was talking about what they were going to do or what they couldn't do anymore these days. Henry and Carl, who rode the bus to work together—Carl to the railway station and Henry to the garage—were both thankful to have the work, and to be able to pay somebody to do their grandmother's house repairs if it wasn't something they could fix. Like their father, they were both better at machinery than at carpentry.

Hermann graduated high school in Los Angeles, and Frances begrudgingly attended his graduation in the hot Southern California sun. She was four months pregnant. And nobody in her family had celebrated much when somebody graduated high school, since some finished school and some didn't; she felt like it made the graduates special (and ignored the girls who had worked at home and couldn't finish school, like her).

She'd just gotten her high school diploma too, though, after four years of night school. Nobody threw a party, but they did all go out to dinner. Frank borrowed a car from a friend, and the four of them—including little LaVon, who was barely old enough to behave in a restaurant—drove over to West Hollywood to the Formosa Café.

"This isn't just for Hermann," Frank told Frances. "We're celebrating you getting your diploma too—first girl in your family!"

This pleased Frances quite a lot, partly because she'd developed a taste for Chinese food. She'd also grown partial to Mexican . . . but she thought with her pregnant tummy, she'd do better with Chinese.

Later in June, sad news descended upon both the Wolff and the Sims families.

First Frank Wolff's sister Louise died on June 25; then, just a day later, Joe Sims passed. Both of them expired in the white section of General Hospital in Kansas City.

Joe's death had been partially expected; after all, he was eighty-five and had worked hard all his life. Everyone was thankful he was no longer suffering, and Naomi, Charley, Nancy, and the baby were able to drive up from Oklahoma for his funeral service.

Louise, on the other hand, was only thirty-five, and it came as a shock to Frank to lose his little sister. He knew his mother would be distraught. Frank's father had been gone for twenty years, but this was their youngest, and that just felt out of the natural order. When his mother called, Frank got leave and traveled out to Kansas City right away, sleeping on the train and transferring as quickly as he could to the next train east at a few stops.

Coming out of the Passantino Brothers' Funeral Home on Independence Avenue in Kansas City, Naomi was stunned to see Frank Wolff Sr. walking up the street. *What in heaven's name is he doing here?*

Frank spied her too—she was coming out of the door he was clearly fixing to step into. They both stopped for a moment, thirty feet apart, and looked at each other in disbelief, but didn't speak.

Naomi was the first to break eye contact. Charley and Nancy were with her, and when they saw Frank they guided her in the opposite direction, up to the corner and across the street.

There's the man who took away my children, Naomi thought as she walked away, her jaw set. *The man I gave my life to for over twenty years. But I guess I made my choice.* She glanced down at Connie, in her arms. *And now he can see I have a different family. Oh, heavens, my gosh. I hope he won't report to somebody that Charley and I had a baby; he may think we got married, and he hasn't given me that divorce. Well, I just hope Oklahoma law will hold if anybody comes all the way the heck out to the farm to ask. And I hope he sees that this child is too young to have been conceived two years ago.*

She felt unsettled for several days. Charley soothed her as best he could. Naomi wanted to see her sons but didn't try, fearing Frank would do something, anything—she couldn't imagine what.

Chapter 51

Los Angeles, California, Evanston, Wyoming, & Prairie, Missouri
Late Autumn to Early Winter 1931

Frances gave birth to a baby boy, Gene Sims, on November 14. She called each of her parents with the happy news; now she had a little girl, who'd be three in January, and a boy—and that was all she hoped to have.

Anita had let her know in January that their father had been required to take the children out of the orphanage and bring them back to Evanston. And that it was because she had gone to court and told the judge that Frank Wolff was raising someone else's five children and had put his own in an orphanage.

Frances had felt humiliated when her dad had taken the children to the orphanage; now, although she was glad the kids were back with their father and would remain part of the Wolff family, she was further chagrined that he had a court order against him. How could her sister do that to her father, even if it was the legal thing to do?

This family, she thought. *This is why I am glad I am in Los Angeles, far away from all of that. Except Hermann and his strange leanings, anyway. Now the whole orphanage story is over, and we never have to tell anyone.*

❧

The Wolff children living with Frank had settled into a routine again and were glad they were at least together with one of their parents. It looked like a nice Thanksgiving and Christmas would be theirs. Their father, as far as they knew, had the same work and pay he'd always had, unlike many other families' providers.

They did have to adapt to Marie Palmen, who was nice enough but extremely tidy. They felt like they could never leave a toy out on the floor or spill a crumb in the kitchen without her immediately picking it up, and that was nerve-racking.

Willie mentioned this to his father, but Frank replied, "That's her job. I like that she keeps things neat. We didn't have it like that when . . . when we lived in Ogden."

Frank tried never to mention Naomi and their former life. He certainly hadn't mentioned to any of the children, or his mother, that he'd seen her in Kansas City.

He also didn't go by Minnie's, having poached her maid and feeling self-satisfied about that. If he wanted to have sex, he could do that when he was out in St. Louis or Chicago with one of those other willing gals on the railroad line. He missed Minnie, but he hoped she missed him more.

Minnie did miss Frank, not to mention his income, but he'd been difficult sometimes, and it was easy to get another maid these days. In fact, she was paying the new girl less. When Marie had announced her resignation and that she was going to work for Frank, Minnie knew he'd taken Marie to spite her, but she didn't care; she just smirked and shook her head.

Six months after the June deaths—on December 29, just short of her seventy-second birthday—Caroline Wolff died in Prairie Township.

Carl called to tell his father.

What a sad start to the new year, thought Frank.

"Daddy, what are we supposed to do now that Grandma is gone?" Carl asked. "What will happen to her house?"

"I'll have to handle all that, since your Aunt Louise isn't there anymore." Frank paused and thought. Carl and Henry were still not of age, which meant he was still responsible for them. "I'll bring you boys back here with me. Have you seen your brother Frank?"

Another child he was responsible for, wherever he was.

"I don't see him regularly; usually he comes for Sunday dinner, though. I'll see if I can find him."

Frank let the rail dispatcher know he'd had another death in the family, this time his mother, and had to go out and settle her affairs. *And bring my boys home,* he thought, but didn't relay that part. The less others knew about their spread-out family, the better, even though many people were putting their children in relatives' homes these days.

And so it was that Carl and Henry came to live with their father and siblings in Evanston. Now there were nine people in the house, and beds were shared—Marie and Dorothy in one room, and the five boys sharing two bedrooms. Carl found work at the railroad—as a carman helper, doing the same parts work he'd done in Kansas City—and Henry got work as a mechanic, though only part-time, as there was not as much work in the smaller town.

Frank Jr. had said he wasn't sure if he would come out to Evanston. He might take his chances with finding work in Kansas City and the surrounding area and continue to stay in rooming houses. If he had to, though, he'd come out, he told his brothers.

Frank Sr. crossed his fingers mentally that the court in Ogden wouldn't find out.

Chapter 52

Bountiful, Utah, & Evanston, Wyoming
1933

Anita married Caleb in a Mormon ceremony in Bountiful, Utah, about forty miles south of where she'd been living in North Ogden. Bountiful was where Caleb's parents lived, and it was not far from Salt Lake City, so the young couple settled there. This meant she was farther away from Frank and the kids, but not so far that the family couldn't visit each other by train.

At Frank Wolff's house, Marie Palmen was dating quite a bit, and bringing men to the house when Frank wasn't home—which was often. She would draw the shades so the neighbors couldn't see, and she and whichever fellow she'd taken a liking to would sit on the couch and neck.

Clarence, now nine, took to hiding behind the couch when Marie brought men around. He'd jump up when they were in the thick of things and shout, "HEYYYY!" waving his arms around and laughing. He managed to keep this game irregular enough that Marie didn't expect it, until she finally told him enough was enough.

Clarence decided that if he couldn't participate as he'd been doing, he was going to take a different tack.

One Saturday when Marie was out shopping and Frank was home, he said to his father, "I know something."

Frank looked up from his newspaper, looking slightly annoyed, and said to his son, "*What* do you know?"

Clarence smiled. "What will you give me if I tell you?"

"A swift kick if you *don't* tell me!" Frank smiled too, letting his son know he was kidding.

Clarence paused, to create suspense, then told him: "Mrs. Palmen brings men over and they kiss and hug on the couch."

"How do you know this?" Frank frowned, but Clarence could tell he was intrigued.

"I see them all the time! I hide behind the couch and jump out and scare them! It's really funny to see them flinch and stop kissing."

Frank pretended to cough, but Clarence saw his smile.

"Well, I'll talk to her about that," his father said. "You don't go hiding behind the couch, though. If she knows you're in the house, she might not do it."

Clarence already knew he couldn't get away with it anymore and felt smug about telling on her. He wondered if his father would fire her and get another cook and housekeeper who wouldn't be so picky. He hoped so.

Frank was having coffee in the kitchen with Marie Palmen.

"I hear you've been bringing men here."

Marie was on alert; she hadn't thought Frank would ever find out. "*Ja*, if I am dating someone, this is the place I can bring them.

Here is my home too," she said, smiling, thinking she could cajole him, as she'd been able to do in the past. *He clearly likes me, and if I am smiling, he usually lets me have my way.*

"I don't want you necking in front of my children." Frank looked at her with a half smile, and she wondered if he meant it or not.

"I am a mature woman, and if I want to kiss someone in my home, I think that is okay," she said, with confidence. "It is kissing and hugging. Nothing more. But I won't do it in front of the children."

"What if I told you I would like you to kiss and hug me?" Frank said, now teasing her.

Marie gasped and then giggled, happy for the compliment. "Oh, well, I don't know about that! We live in the same house, and I am your servant here."

"What if we got married?"

Marie's eyes widened. "Are you serious?"

"I am. We cannot have a relationship unless we get married, and I would prefer that you not kiss and hug other men in my house. You have been a good housekeeper, and we like each other pretty good. What do you say?"

This was likely the best offer Marie was going to get. She knew this would also be a good deal for Frank. She pretended to think about it so that he would not think she was too eager. But the alimony payments from Walter had run out, so being married to a man—one she liked, and who would provide for her—was probably a good idea. Some security. And he spoke German.

"Let me think about it, but I think *maybe* yes," she said coyly.

Her future husband smiled back at her.

Chapter 53

Ogden, Utah
Autumn 1933

Frank asked to be put on the Ogden run. He took the train down there and went to the court, and filed for divorce from Naomi. He said she had not only had an affair but had moved to Oklahoma to live with an Indian seducer and had been declared an unfit mother four years before. He was asked by the judge, who had done his research, if he had taken his children back into his household, and Frank was glad that he could answer that he had. He didn't mention that Frank Jr. had only moved back in recently. (Now they had ten in the household; it was feeling a lot like the old Ogden days.)

He wasn't going to let Naomi know he'd gotten the divorce. *Let her live in sin*, he thought again.

Frank went back to Evanston and collected Marie Palmen, whom he'd given some money a couple of weeks prior to buy a nice suit for the wedding. They got married in Ogden in late October, since they could get an expedited license there, had a brief honeymoon, and then returned to Evanston.

❧

Now the children had a stepmother—one whose primary language was German. She and their father engaged in even more conversations the children could not understand, laughing and talking everywhere in the house. The younger Marie thought it was nice to have their father in a good mood—and after having heard about sex from Anita and her girlfriends, she could guess where his cheer came from—but it was a little strange to have their housekeeper become their mother.

"What are we supposed to call her, Daddy?" she asked him. "Do we have to call her 'Mother'?" This just didn't feel right to her, or to any of her siblings; she had discussed it with them, and they'd agreed that it felt just as strange as when they'd had to call Mr. and Mrs. Weinrich "Papa" and "Mama."

Frank took a minute to think about this. Finally, he said, "Why don't you call her 'Mother Wolff'?"

Marie found this a little peculiar but decided it was better than Mrs. Wolff or Marie or just Mother. "Well, okay . . . should I tell the other children, then?"

"Yes, and I'll tell Marie. Your stepmother. That that is what you'll be calling her."

What an odd family this is, thought the younger Marie.

Chapter 54

Evanston, Wyoming, Ogden, Utah, & Los Angeles, California
1933–1936

Adolf Hitler came to power in 1933, and spent years after that spreading the Nazi doctrine and implementing genocide—mostly for those of Jewish ancestry, but also those who were not "Aryan" or who had physical disabilities—and invading neighboring countries, striking terror throughout Europe. As a dual citizen, Marie (Mother Wolff) was following the war news on the radio.

One evening at their Evanston home, she was reading the paper and said to Frank, "I agree with Hitler. I would be glad if all those people were gone."

Distracted, Frank barely looked up at first. "What people?"

"The Jews, the Negroes, all of them," Marie said.

Frank put down his section of the paper. "You'd better keep that to yourself. Don't go telling people that."

"Why not?" Marie countered. "It's what I think."

"Because that war is . . . Hitler is anti-democracy. I mean, yes, maybe we don't associate with people who are not . . . white . . . but a lot of people here in the States won't like to hear you say things like that. There are a lot of Indians, Negroes, and Jews in this part of the country, and they aren't causing any trouble . . . They're like a lot of people, just looking for work these days."

"Well, I wouldn't hire them. Let them stay in their own places."

Frank chuckled. "The thing with the Indians is, this was their place. And they weren't making it into a great country, so the whites took it from them."

Marie tossed her head. "Well, that is what Hitler is doing, making Europe better."

"Marie, don't say that to anyone else outside this house." Frank pointed a finger at her. "Ever. I'm telling you. Especially because you're German, and I speak German, and my mother was German . . . That war is not popular over here. My mother just missed having to register as an enemy alien when we had the First World War. You can tell *me* these things; you're my wife, and I know how you feel. But don't go saying that at the church or anyplace else."

Marie had continued to be devoted to the Mormon church, even though she liked to drink alcohol, which was absolutely against their doctrine, the Word of Wisdom, which also forbade tobacco, caffeine, and too much meat. At least she didn't smoke tobacco, and she thought that was good enough regarding giving anything up.

Prohibition was repealed, at least in several states, in December 1933. Frank and Marie were excited about this; they both loved beer and wine, and though they had obtained it from time to time during the last decade, getting alcohol now would be easier and, thankfully, legal.

They toasted their recent marriage first. Now they could have a beer with egg in it, something Marie said was popular in Europe. That was Sunday breakfast for them sometimes, and they liked a glass of wine in the afternoon when Frank didn't have to work.

❧

The same year in Los Angeles, Frank Sims had started smoking. This good Mormon boy whose family dated back to the days of Joseph Smith, their prophet, had also started drinking. Frances didn't drink, but she very much enjoyed going out dancing, as they had back in Ogden. She felt carried away when she was in Frank's arms doing a waltz or the rhumba, and they went out with friends whenever they could afford it. Pretty much everyone they socialized with drank, except her Mormon girlfriends.

One evening when they were at a dance club, and all the men were drinking and smoking, Frank said to Frances, "I dare you to smoke a cigarette. I bet you won't."

Frances had never been one to pass on a dare, back to the days when she got her tongue stuck on the backyard water pump. She was twenty-five, and she'd be darned if Frank was going to hold cigarettes above her head as if she were a child.

"Okay, I'll try one." She coughed and could barely stop that first time. But she kept trying.

Soon she was addicted to nicotine. She started using Sen-Sens, the licorice bits that people used to mask bad breath, before she went to church.

1935 rolled around.

At one point, Frank Jr. approached his father in the backyard on a Saturday afternoon.

"Dad, I've met the girl I want to marry."

"Oh?" Frank chuckled. "I think you're a bit young for that, son, at nineteen."

"Well, I know we can't do it right away; she's younger than I am, sixteen."

"Who is this lucky girl?" Frank Sr. asked, amused that his son was interested in settling down.

"Her name is Ellen Woods. You know, she's the youngest daughter of that woman who had that boardinghouse."

"You can't marry that girl," Frank Sr. said urgently. "She's your sister."

"What d'ya mean? She's not my sister . . . She wasn't even a stepsister."

"No, son. She is your blood sister."

Frank Jr. looked flabbergasted. "Wait a minute—wait," he fumbled. "She's sixteen. So she was born in . . . 1918 or 1919 or something."

"1918. Mrs. Woods's husband died just before she was born."

"So . . . that means that you and Mrs. Woods . . ."

"Yes." Frank saw no reason to mince words. "They had a boardinghouse in Lyman before Evanston, and I stopped there with the railroad sometimes. Mrs. Woods and I . . . we liked each other."

Frank Jr. shook his head. "Dad, this is . . . I don't know what to say."

"Well. If you've been seeing that girl a lot, you have to break it off."

Frank Jr. wanted to talk to Anita about this. He waited until no one was home and made the phone call.

"Anita, Dad told me last week that . . . that I shouldn't date Ellen Woods anymore, because she's his blood daughter. We were talking about getting married, when she's old enough. Is she really our sister?"

"Mmm . . . I don't know, Frank, I don't think that's true," Anita said slowly. "It's not impossible . . . but it's very unlikely. How old is Ellen?"

"Sixteen. She was born in 1918."

"I don't think he knew Mrs. Woods until he was at the boardinghouse in Evanston. Maybe 1920 or 1921?"

"He says he stayed at the Woodses' boardinghouse in Lyman."

"I don't know. Maybe it's true. Or maybe he just wants you to think that, because he doesn't want our family tied to the Woods family." Anita had a note of disgust in her voice. "I imagine that after her husband died they were . . . you know, intimate. But whether one of her children is his . . . that's kinda far-fetched."

"Well, Ellen *is* blonde, like Dad. She's the only one in the family that is."

He heard Anita sigh over the phone. "I guess the best thing is to not have a relationship with her," she said. "We don't know, and there's no way to find out."

Frank was silent, disappointed at his big sister's assessment.

"You'll meet someone else, Frank. Maybe you should go down to Los Angeles and stay with Frances and try to forget about her."

Frank felt like this was yet another pounding his father had given to him, to his heart. From now on, he'd be tough. Tougher than before.

It was 1936, and Frank and Marie Wolff decided to move back to Ogden. Some of the children considered other options. Henry (now twenty-two), Marie (now eighteen), and Dorothy (now fourteen) decided they wanted to go down to Los Angeles to see what life offered in sunny California. They called Frances and told her they were taking the train down. She told them there was not a lot of room for three people, but they did have two extra beds, and Henry could sleep on the couch until he found a job and a place of his own.

Carl, the oldest son, had met a nice girl, Anne, and when they decided to marry, the wedding was near Ogden in a little Utah town. Carl was still a carman's helper for Union Pacific, and this didn't require him to go out on the rails as his father had. He'd seen enough of how that affected a family.

Frances had now had one sibling after another come and stay with her until they got on their feet. But she particularly loved Marie, and it was nice to have her there; fortunately, she enjoyed Dorothy's company as well, since the girl was now enrolled in high school and would clearly be around for a while. Frances encouraged her to stay in school and not quit and get a job as she had done; her prospects would be better with a high school diploma. Still, she felt like she was thirteen all over again, taking care of the younger kids, and she complained to her husband and even her little daughter about her role.

Frank took her to a new restaurant, The Chili Bowl, one night to get her mind off the subject. She added additional hot sauce to the chili there, and people stared. She was loving this spicy food they hadn't had in Ogden. Or maybe smoking had just deadened her taste buds.

Henry got a job as a mechanic and moved into a hotel catering to men, and Marie got work in a dress factory, became a member of the garment workers' union, and soon could also afford her own apartment.

The family was growing up.

Chapter 55

Ogden, Utah, Bernice, Oklahoma, & Southern California
1938–1940

In February 1938, Richard Wolff was born to Marie Wolff in Ogden. She was forty-three and the pregnancy had come as a surprise to everyone, given it was her first. But she treated the little guy as if he walked on water, even though it would be a while before he would take his first steps. Between having husband Frank to serve and flirt with and Richard to coo over, her new life was nothing like her old life with Walter, and she didn't even care if she ran into him at church, with his wife. She took Richard along with her, even if he fussed. He looked exactly like Frank, and she wanted to show him off.

She was a very happy wife, and kept her mouth shut about sympathizing with the Nazis. That was a secret except to some members of the family, who didn't tell their friends.

George, who had graduated high school in Evanston in 1936, found a job as a clerk, and Willie, who was still in high school and would graduate in 1939, both lived with their father and stepmother, plus their two younger brothers, at the house in Ogden. It looked like all the boys, at least, were going to have high school diplomas. Mother Wolff was happy to be surrounded by all these males.

Later that year, it was decided that the Sims farm in Oklahoma was too much for everyone to manage any longer. Too many lean years in what folks now called "the Depression." President Roosevelt's policies with the New Deal had helped a lot, but they were all getting older (Nancy was now ninety-two), so they decided to move over to where Naomi's sister Julia lived—Bernice, on the eastern side of Oklahoma, where Charley had lived as a young man. Nancy sold the Stone Township farm, and she, Naomi, Charley, and Connie hauled all their belongings in the truck.

In Bernice, Nancy moved in with her daughter Julia and sister-in-law, Lucy, and Naomi and Charley rented a home just five doors away, a lucky find. Charley's brother Bill also lived in Bernice. They were glad to be settled amongst their families, and it was a pretty spot—plus, the fishing on the Neosho River was good, and that was an easier way to provide protein for the family than animal farming or buying meat.

Nancy gave part of the farm proceeds to Charley and Naomi, since they had helped her with the place for so many years, and along with Charley's savings from the sale of his folks' farm, they were no longer desperate for income. It was a comfortable, if thrifty, life for them in Bernice.

By this point, news of Frank's remarriage had long since reached Naomi and Charley, via the Wolff children.

In January 1939, the two were lying in bed, and Charley turned to Naomi. He felt a little nervous but was pretty sure of what he wanted to say.

"Let's really do it," he told her.

"Do what?" she asked.

"Let's get married."

She arched an eyebrow. "What brought this on? I thought we decided common-law marriage was fine."

"I just think about it from time to time. I know we're legally married here in Oklahoma, but . . . I don't know, I'd just like it to be . . . in the eyes of everybody. Your family, for one. Everybody over in Stone and Enid knew us as married. Bernice is a darn small town, only about one hundred people who all know each other. And talk. What if somebody asks Connie? Your mother and aunts would prob'ly like us to have a piece of paper. Plus, Connie. I'd like her to have somethin' that says her dad and mom were married."

Naomi laughed. This was about as long-winded as Charley ever got. "Well, okay then. Let's do it."

They decided to drive over to the nearest town of any size, little Vinita, Oklahoma, where there was a justice of the peace. Naomi wore her best wool dress, and Charley wore his jacket and a clean shirt. There weren't flowers available at that time of year, but that was okay. They tied the knot on January 9, simple as you please. Almost eight years exactly from when Connie was born.

When they got back to Bernice, Julia made a cake and they had their second marriage celebration. Naomi called both Frances and Anita to tell them, knowing they'd let the rest of the family know.

That same year, Dorothy, at seventeen, announced to Frances that she was marrying her boyfriend, Bob, who was nineteen. Frances sighed, but thought that at least Dorothy had gotten one more year of schooling than she originally had. (Bob would eventually become a famous stuntman in Hollywood, allowing Dorothy to live a fairly easy life after all.)

❧

In early 1940, Frank Wolff's youngest brother, Otto, was to be married in Madera, California, two hours north of Los Angeles. Frank was in an ebullient mood and decided that he, Marie, and his youngest sons, Clarence and Richard, would all pile on the train and go down to see the family, and attend his little brother's wedding. Willie couldn't go because he was working as a pinboy at a bowling alley in Ogden.

Frances attended the wedding as well; it was the first time Frank had seen his eldest daughter in a dozen years. At the small reception, she approached her dad and gave him an awkward hug and a kiss on the cheek, which he received warmly.

"Frances," he said with pride, "this is Mother Wolff, your stepmother!"

Frances nodded her head and gave a wan smile, and Marie extended her hand, smiled, nodded, and said, "How do you do?"

Frank was pleased at her manners.

"How is Willie doing?" Frances asked.

Frank thought he remembered that Willie hadn't even been in school yet when Frances moved out, and it was nice of her to ask. He'd been surprised at how gleeful Clarence had been to see his big sister, who had only come to the house occasionally when he was little.

"Oh, he's got himself a job as a pinboy at the bowling alley!" Frank laughed. He knew this wasn't a career but was just glad the boy had found work. "His boss wouldn't let him get time off."

"Well, at least he's got a job," Frances said, giving her dad a look that seemed to say, *Thank heavens.*

Frances leaned down to Richard, the toddler of the family, and said, "Hi there! I'm your big sister, Frances!"

The shy boy held on to his mother's skirt and hid behind her. Everyone chuckled at this.

Marie took Richard to get a cookie, and Frances and Frank had a moment together.

Frances quietly confided to her father, "I don't know what you've heard, but you know, Mother got married to Charles Foreland, and they have a daughter, Connie."

"Yes, I heard it from Carl, who heard it from Anita," Frank answered curtly, looking away. "Maybe we'll all come out to California more often," he offered, changing the subject.

"Well, that would be nice, Daddy. I'd like LaVon and Gene to know their grandparents."

Frank nodded, looking to see where Marie had gone. "Yes, yes . . ." But he didn't pursue the topic any further. He had enough children in his life already.

The afternoon passed pleasantly, with everyone catching up on the superficial aspects of their lives, without ever speaking of deeper issues in the family.

Chapter 56

Southern California, Ogden, Utah, & Bernice, Oklahoma
Spring and Summer 1940

Henry joined the army and was stationed in Riverside County in Southern California. He was a thoughtful young man, at twenty-seven, and didn't share his stepmother's pro-German political sentiments.

His twin, Hermann, did not fare as well at this time in the lives of the Wolff children. Although he had a good job in insurance, he was caught kissing a man one evening, and was advised to go in the next day for psychological evaluation. (Frances had callously told him previously that he needed to have his head examined.) He was of course upset by the examination, broke down, and cried. The next obvious step, according to medical professionals, was for him to enter a mental hospital in Southern California. Men didn't cry over personality traits, everyone knew that. The idea was that this proclivity to want to be physically close to men and being sensitive could be therapized out of him, and he was having a crisis of consciousness about whether this was true. He knew what he wanted and how he felt, but everyone around him was telling him this was wrong, so he acquiesced.

It was yet another thing Frances tried to keep under wraps; only the family would know, and possibly not even some of them.

Hermann began to feel isolated from his family, several of whom were ashamed of him.

The Porter Street house in Ogden was a little bigger than the Evanston house, necessary because there were so many living there: Frank Sr., Mother Wolff, little Richard, Carl and Anne, Frank Jr., now twenty-four, George, twenty-two, who worked as a clerk, Willie, twenty, and Clarence, seventeen, who would graduate from high school in June. There were a lot of bunk beds in the house.

Porter Street neighborhood, Ogden

On August 7, Nancy Sims died in Bernice. She was ninety-four.

Naomi grieved, as did Charley, Connie, Julia, and Lucy. Naomi thought, *Well, all in all, she had a good life. God will have nothing to punish her for, if there is such a thing in the afterlife.*

Aloud, at the funeral, she softly said, "My mama was a good woman. She didn't judge, and she gave you whatever she had. She took care of my daddy and didn't ask questions when he was gone and come back over and over. He took care of her, and she took care of him. God will be happy to see her walk into heaven."

Charley was a little choked up, and he squeezed Naomi's hand when she sat back down.

Chapter 57

Southern California
1941

Frank Jr. was twenty-five and decided to move to Los Angeles. He of course stayed with Frances and got lucky; he got a job as a house painter. And luckier still, he met Flora, and they married. He never stopped being a tease, or having a chip on his shoulder.

Then George and Willie moved to Los Angeles, and they, too, stayed with Frances and Frank Sims.

Frances confided to Frank one evening in a whisper, "I'm sick of this! I took care of them all during my own childhood, and now I'm taking care of them again!"

Frank spoke in a low voice as well: "Well, at least this time you know there will be an end to it. You're damned if you do and damned if you don't."

"I don't want to be stinko. I just . . . probably won't go see them all much when they move out."

Naomi, Charley, and Connie, who was ten, now had a car that could manage a longer trip than the old truck, and about a year after Nancy Sims died, the three of them drove out to Los Angeles. They stayed with Frances first, and then with all the other children who were able to take them in.

This was the first time LaVon and her brother, Gene, had gotten the chance to get to know their real grandmother a little. They'd met Grandma Wolff, the German woman—Mother Wolff, as the aunts and uncles called her—and LaVon thought she was a nice enough lady, though very different from anyone else they knew.

Grandma Foreland, the original Grandma Wolff, was more casual and spoke with a country accent. She would say things like, "We come out the back door to see if we could find 'em," when telling a story. Twelve-year-old LaVon was a bit surprised to learn this. Her mother had such careful diction, as did her aunt Marie.

After the Forelands left, LaVon said to her mother with mild disdain, "Mother, they're just Okies!"

Frances looked out the window and took a long draw on her cigarette, then sat with her elbow on the table and her wrist bent, the Chesterfield burning between her first and second fingers. "Don't call them that," she said. "They didn't have much education. He went through maybe fourth grade, and my mother got only through sixth before she had to stay home and help on the farm. They're not Okies just because they're from Oklahoma. That's something people started calling people from Oklahoma because they came out here looking for work during the Depression. There's no shame in being from Oklahoma."

But LaVon knew that Frances didn't want to be like her mother, and that she was still ashamed that her parents had split up. She didn't know the details, but she could tell Frances felt cool toward her mother.

❧

When they were alone, staying with the next of Frances's siblings, Charley asked Naomi, "Seems like Frances isn't real warm toward you. Is that right? Does she hold us against you?"

"I can't blame her," Naomi said, slowly shaking her head. "And she was always her father's girl, so I'm guessin' she sided with him about those days. Seems so long ago now . . . but only twelve years! You know what they say, 'Forgiveness is the sweetest revenge.' For my former husband, and for all of them. I'm just glad to get to see as many of 'em as I can now that it's long past and I'm not worried Frank Wolff is gonna try anything on me. I spent years feelin' bad about them bein' in that orphanage and missin' 'em all so much I thought it would kill me. Now that's all past us. And they get to meet their little sister. It's a whole lot easier to raise one little girl than ten or twelve kids. Everybody can see that. Frances most of all."

Chapter 58

Utah, Los Angeles, San Francisco, and Overseas
1942

Clarence, who had turned eighteen the previous December—not long after Pearl Harbor—enlisted in the US Army Air Force in early 1942.

Henry left Los Angeles when the army stationed him in Illinois, and there he married Barbara, a lovely, kind woman who was as nonjudgmental as his grandmother, Nancy Sims. They were content to settle near Barbara's family. Henry had always been a peaceful, easygoing boy, and he didn't miss the Wolff family drama.

Willie enlisted in the US Army Infantry in the later part of the year, in San Francisco.

All three brothers were proud to serve their country and assist in defeating the Nazis. And all of them survived.

Chapter 59

Eastern Oklahoma
1943

Naomi, Charley, and Connie had moved over to Sapulpa, on the other side of Tulsa, ninety miles from their home in Bernice. Sapulpa was bigger than Bernice but a lot smaller than Tulsa.

Naomi was beside herself when Charley dropped to the floor the morning of July 29, clutching his chest, but his cousin was there and said they'd take him to the hospital in the Waggoner Building, just downtown, and he'd probably be all right. One of the reasons they'd moved was to be closer to services like that. They carried him to the car and called ahead to the hospital, so they'd be ready to admit him.

But the doctor couldn't save him.

Naomi could not be comforted. They'd had only fourteen years together. It was true that he was sixty-three, ten years older than she was, but so many in her family had lived into their eighties that nothing in her had been prepared to lose the man who had been devoted to her in this later time of her life.

Connie, only twelve, was shocked to lose her daddy. Naomi held her, and together they cried copious tears at home. At least they had each other.

Naomi wondered if he hadn't known in some way that he was not going to live a long life, and that's why he had asked her to marry him legally four years before . . . so Connie would have a record of that, and there wouldn't be any doubt that she was legitimate. And also if anything happened to him, Naomi could prove she was his wife. She wondered. And she was grateful for the years they'd had, that she had been able to be his wife and give him a daughter. But none of these ponderings took away her grief.

The Wolff children didn't attend his funeral. Naomi didn't really expect they would, although she called Anita and Frances to let them know and ask them to tell their siblings—if it was even possible to contact everyone. Her children were scattered all over the United States, and some were at war.

Charley was buried ninety miles from Sapulpa, in the McLaughlin Cemetery at Cleora, just a few miles south of Bernice, also not too far from the Neosho River and the Grand Lake O' the Cherokees, where he'd loved to fish. The cemetery resembled a farm, bordered by its white plank fence, and Naomi thought he'd rest in peace there. He'd been on farms all his life; he ought to be there for eternity too.

Chapter 60

California, Oklahoma, and Kansas
1945–1949

Frances had learned from her parents the practice of beating children, and in order to mold her daughter and son into whom she thought they should be, they were hit regularly—with her hand, a yardstick, a paddle (the toy Hi-Li paddles with an elastic and a ball on the end were perfect when the elastic broke and the ball was lost, she said—"They cover a lot of territory, and then I don't have to hurt my hand"), and eventually, in Gene's case, with a wooden coat hanger, until it broke. Sometimes she would go into the bedroom later, close the door, and cry, but she didn't stop hitting them until they were strong enough to resist. And so, the degradation of corporal punishment was carried into the next generation, Frank and Naomi's first grandchildren.

Frank Sims had started drinking quite a lot and going out to bars and clubs frequently in the evenings. The good Mormon boy had become an alcoholic. Frances became spiteful as a result, having learned this from her father. And Sims eventually met another woman (at a bar) with whom he found more peace, having become increasingly uncomfortable with Frances's disciplinary measures with the children and her complaining about his drinking. Of course,

Frances had not in any way expected to be entering a marriage with a drinker. The two of them had become incompatible. Frances wanted to stay married and Frank wanted to leave, so he filed for divorce and married his girlfriend. He moved on to another bakery, and Frances found work in a bakery with a cottage apartment across the way on Seventy-Seventh Street, where she lived with her two teenagers while they finished high school. She got additional work selling Avon cosmetics from door to door, walking multiple blocks in the attractive but heavy high heels that were popular at the time, and wearing the glamorous makeup she was successful in selling.

Clarence married Iris when he was twenty-three. Willie married a lovely girl named Rose, and George married Julie. Hermann decided he needed a fresh start when he left the mental hospital in California, and left the state. He ended up in Tampa, Florida, where he found a community of people who accepted him as he was.

In 1946, Frances was fortunate to meet Robert Allen. He happened to be her milkman and happened to be cute. He had an honorable discharge from the navy, having been on a battleship in World War II, and he was searching for a wife and family and stability, as was true of many men in that year.

She told her bakery boss she wanted to meet Bob Allen and didn't know how to accomplish this. She always gravitated toward the advice of men.

He answered, as if it were obvious, "Bake a couple pies and put 'em on the windowsill when he brings the milk. Invite him in for a piece of pie."

"What kind should I bake?" she asked.

"Cherry!" he said without hesitation.

Frances got up two hours early one morning, pitted cherries, made two pies with lattice tops, opened the window, and put them there to cool.

Right on time, Bob came by and said, "Boy, Mrs. Sims, those pies sure do smell good."

"Oh!" she answered. "Would you like to come in for a piece of pie and a cup of coffee?"

A marriage made in heaven: a milkman and a baker. They tied the knot on January 1, 1947, and moved into their own rental home in the same Gramercy Park neighborhood she'd lived in with Frank. LaVon was almost eighteen by then; she moved out and went to work for the phone company. Gene lived with Frances and Bob, and resented Bob's not allowing him to take the milk trucks out alone to pal around in.

Although Frances was now in her late thirties and had back problems, she wanted to have a child for Bob, and she did: Francine was born in December 1947.

In October 1949, Naomi died at home in Sapulpa, Oklahoma, of unknown natural causes, at a somewhat young fifty-nine. Connie was eighteen.

Bob drove Frances out from Los Angeles for the funeral, and they brought along little Francine, a toddler who had never met her grandmother. As many of Naomi's children as were able also drove out and gathered at the McLaughlin Cemetery at Cleora, where Naomi was buried near Charley.

All of her children knew the challenges she had faced, both raising them and having them taken away from her. Naomi had not had many opportunities to make choices in her lifetime. Her major decisions had been to marry Frank Wolff, to stay married to Frank Wolff, and to become Charley Foreland's lover and eventual wife. Almost everything else in her life had been dictated by others or by the needs placed upon her by her husband, children, parents, other family members or society.

Though some of them had felt betrayed by her, and some had felt abandoned, all of her children had loved her, each in their own way.

Chapter 61

Yuba City, California
1951–1955

In 1951, Francine contracted polio and was hospitalized for six and a half months. During that time Bob decided they needed to get out of Los Angeles; the polio epidemic was still going strong, and there was not a vaccine for it yet. So he found a milk route for sale up in little Yuba City, California, north of Sacramento, and the three of them moved north (Gene no longer lived with them).

In 1953, Frank Wolff, his wife, Marie, and their son, Richard, also moved to Yuba City. They bought a home less than two blocks away from the Allens, with the expectation that Frances would be available to care for Frank in his later years. She had mixed feelings about this.

In September of 1954, Frank Wolff Sr. took the train with Bob and one of the milk route drivers, Van, to St. Louis, Missouri, where Bob had purchased two new International Harvester milk trucks. He was excited to acquire them and get them back to Yuba City. The plan was for the two younger men to trade off driving with Frank.

On Monday, September 27, Bob called from Topeka, Kansas, to tell Frances they were leaving at five the next morning.

When she hung up the phone, she said to Francine, "Your Grandpa Wolff is going to drive, and they are leaving at five in the morning. I feel like I should call them and tell them to wait and leave later. I have a bad feeling about Grandpa driving. He's sixty-seven."

Francine knew her mother was right; everyone who knew Frank Wolff had seen him fall asleep in front of the television after a few minutes.

But Frances didn't call Bob back.

The next morning, a sheriff arrived at Frances's door in Yuba City to tell her that Frank had fallen asleep at the wheel of the new truck, which had plunged over a ravine into an embankment. Bob had gone through the windshield and been killed—instantly, or so it was hoped.

Frank sustained a broken knee and a punctured lung, and recuperated in a Topeka hospital until he was well enough to take the train home.

Frances's attorney, Mr. Hadley, suggested she sue her father for wrongful death. Shocked by this, she refused and found a different attorney. She grieved Bob's death for thirty years, however, and forever blamed herself for the accident—for having not followed up on her intuition, "the sight," that she and her mother had been blessed (or afflicted) with.

Francine endured Frances's paddlings until she was eight, without the comfort of her affectionate father.

All of the Wolff sons and daughters married, and all except for Hermann had children. There were eventually more than twenty-five first cousins, some of them beaten into shape and some trusted to turn out well without that practice—all of them living into the next century, and most having a passel of grandchildren.

Some of the Wolff children's marriages were lifelong and happy, and some were not. Some divorced and remarried. All of them attended various Christian churches. All the siblings except for Hermann (and little Grant) lived into their eighties or nineties.

None of them had more than four children.

Epilogue

Yuba City, California
1957–1958

Almost three years after her father died, Francine came home from her first ever week of Camp Fire Girls' summer camp in the Sierra Nevada Mountains. She'd returned through the winding roads lined with tall pines and cedars the same way she'd gone up to the mountains: with a friend's mother, because Frances didn't like to drive except around town. It had bothered her a great deal to drive any distance since Bob died. She said she sometimes felt like she had a rope around her neck if she drove over a bridge.

When Francine walked into the house, tired from four hours in a car, she plopped her suitcase and sleeping bag on the living room floor and called out, "I'm home!"

She found her mother sitting in the kitchen with a glass of iced RC Cola, smoking a cigarette. Francine took the ice cube tray out of the freezer, ran water over it, pulled up the release handle, and picked out three rectangles of ice, which she clunked into a glass and filled it with cola. Perfect for the Central Valley hundred-degree heat.

"So, how did you like the camp?" asked Frances.

"I liked it," Francine said. "I couldn't go on all the hikes, we found out, because they were too far, but I learned to swim!" Her right leg had been paralyzed from polio.

"Oh! You learned to swim. I never learned to swim." Frances bobbled her head side to side, then gave her daughter a smug look. "Your Grandpa Wolff won't speak to me. He hasn't spoken to me since the day after you left."

"Why?! What happened?"

Frances blew smoke into the room and sighed. "I mentioned that I wanted to have some cupboards built in the garage, for storage of canned goods. The church recommends that you have at least six months' supply, in case Russia ever attacks. While I was at work one day, Daddy got into our garage and built a cupboard with scrap wood. It's awful. When I saw it, I said, 'Daddy, that's not what I wanted . . . at all!' He looked at me, turned on his heel, walked home, and I haven't heard a word from him since."

Francine didn't exactly know what to say. She was nine and a half. But she knew her grandfather could get into a snit sometimes, and she never knew what about. As long as it wasn't with her, she didn't care much. He hardly spoke to her anyway; it was as if she didn't really exist.

"I'm just letting him stew in his own juices—he'll get over it," Frances went on. "Daddy gets mad like that sometimes. I guess I hurt his feelings. He thought he was doing me a favor. But you should see it."

They went out to the garage.

Francine knitted her brows. "It's behind the car? But you can't get to it unless you back the car out!"

"Yes," Frances said. "But open the garage door and go around and look at it."

Francine released the lever on the big, heavy door and pushed it up until it rose on its springs. She peeked around the side of the car. There was the cupboard against the wall on the passenger side, and she could see she would no longer be able to get into the car unless her mother backed the DeSoto at least halfway out of the garage. What was he thinking?

Only of Frances getting in the car to drive, clearly. Maybe he thought Francine sat in the back seat because she was the child.

But that wasn't the half of it. The cupboard was like something some old hobo would make at his campsite—"ramshackle" was the word that came to mind. It stood about four feet tall, eighteen inches deep, the bottom of it two feet off the floor. The boards he'd used were all different, some painted ivory or pale green, some not painted at all, some rough with splinters. The doors were hung at slight angles; when closed, they didn't quite meet in the middle. The closure was a hook-and-eye latch that had been screwed in by hand.

Francine looked at her mother. "Why did he do it like this—and over here, where you can't get to the food? What are you going to do?"

"I'm going to pay a carpenter and have the ones I wanted built— over here, by the back door, floor to ceiling, made of nice plywood and stained. And with a padlock, so people can't come in the garage and steal the food."

Frances had learned woodworking and electrical repairs during the war, like many women had, and had often taken night school classes throughout the time she'd been in California. She knew how to draw too. If the cupboards hadn't needed to be tall and the parts so heavy, she could probably have built them herself.

"Are you just going to leave that one there?" Francine asked, nodding her head toward the abomination, incredulous at the lack of craftsmanship.

"Yes. It's too much trouble to take it out, and it'll just make Daddy madder. I can use it as a tool chest."

"And a black widow spider nest," Francine said wryly.

Frances tutted a laugh.

After another full week of giving his daughter the silent treatment, Frank relented, and they went back to seeing each other regularly. After Frances had the new cupboards built, she showed him and said, "See, Daddy, this is what I meant."

"A lot of money," he said. "You didn't need something that fancy."

When Francine and Frances visited Frank, Marie, and Richard up the street, Frank and Marie were often a little drunk, even on Sundays. The Wolffs still liked beer with egg in it for breakfast and wine in the afternoon. Marie often tottered sideways on her high heels at sixty-two, when she'd been drinking. But they were at least cheerful when they'd been imbibing. Francine dreaded going there because there was nothing to do but sit and be good. Frances would say, "Yes, Grandma Wolff follows people around with a dustpan picking up their lint." It wasn't true, but you could see her watching that you didn't move the doily off the couch arm an inch. The most entertaining thing that might happen would be if Richard played the piano; he was practically a maestro.

In June 1958, Frank Sr. had a heart attack and was taken to the hospital in Yuba City. He would be seventy-one in less than a week.

Frances insisted that Francine go see him, knowing that his days might be numbered. Francine was uncomfortable in hospitals, having spent six months enclosed in them when she was a small child. But she went, and was doubly uncomfortable seeing her irascible, staid old grandpa lying in bed—half asleep, and hardly aware of her presence. She'd seen her father in his casket at his funeral, and didn't really want to watch someone die, if that's what Grandpa Wolff was going to do. He wasn't a man you'd go up to and hug and kiss, and she didn't really know what to do except say, "Hi, Grandpa."

He tried, almost imperceptibly, to turn his head, but quickly gave up.

The next morning, a Wednesday, Frances looked particularly tired as she sat smoking her second or third Salem and drinking her Yuban instant coffee. Francine sat down opposite Frances in her pajamas, ready to have orange juice before readying herself for school and its last days before summer break.

"Grandpa Wolff died last night," Frances told her.

"Oh?" Francine replied, her eyes wide. She hadn't really expected him to die so soon. What did she know? How did they predict these things? He had just looked tired when she saw him, like he usually did.

"I had a feeling I should go to the hospital last night, around midnight, after you went to bed. I couldn't go to sleep. So I got up and drove down there. They let me go into his room, and when I walked through the door, he took his last breath."

Frances held Francine's gaze for several seconds, a look that said, *I knew.*

"I felt like he was waiting for me."

Brown Avenue house, Yuba City, California, Frank's last home

Author's Notes

Nothing in my childhood prepared me for the disclosure by one of my aunts that my staid and quiet grandfather had some loudly rattling skeletons in his closet.

A small group of us were sitting and talking at a long folding table during lunch in a church reception hall in Southern California. We were at yet another memorial service, this time for an uncle, attended by what was left of the original twelve (or more) of my mother's siblings. "When we were in the orphanage . . ." was just a casual comment made by my aunt Dorothy within a story that was about another subject. She continued as if this bombshell were common knowledge.

"Wait a minute," I interjected. "Wait a minute. In the *orphanage*? When was this?"

Her answer and additional details merely solicited more questions from me and the other cousins at the table; as she told part of the story, we sat wide-eyed, our mouths agape in shock.

The narrative I pieced together from these fragments from my aunt, the vaguely related stories I was told by my mother, Frances, and various facts or opinions supplied by several family members has only served to make me wonder what other secrets my mother took to her grave. All of this was kept from my sister and me so success-fully, even though I used to see my grandfather several times weekly, that I have since thought my mother missed her calling; she should have worked for the CIA.

I knew that my grandfather had eventually married my German step-grandmother, the only woman I ever personally knew as Grandma. I had, as a child, wanted to know why Mother had no trace of a German accent, unlike her youngest brother—her half brother, actually. Subsequent to my asking if "Grandma" was really Mother's mother, I learned that my maternal grandmother (the real "Naomi" in this story) had died before I was old enough to remember her. My mother always met these questions from her curious child with suc-cinct, and often vague and dismissive, answers.

The story I've told here is made up of my fictional suppositions based on a compilation of the facts I was given by relatives. Some of the story is denied by family members who offered alternative stories. I of course created many of the scenarios, the possibilities, the con-versations, the personalities, the attitudes, the details. Much of that aspect is fiction. But I researched extensively places and dates where the main characters were and events that occurred at many times in the story's sequence. I pored over census, birth, marriage, and death documents. I found the Lutheran Children's Home's written history and a photo of the place, and a photo of that significant boarding-house in Wyoming that is still standing. I looked up train schedules for the 1920s and 1930s, and stations.

If anyone wants to know, "Did this [enter specific event] really happen?" contact me at francinefalkallen@gmail.com. I'll do my best to answer honestly.

Names have been changed, at the least, all the surnames, except those of people such as an actual doctor who signed a death certificate, some other characters including neighbors and orphan-age personnel, plus my father's last name, and some of the first names of aunts and uncles. Snippets of stories my relatives remembered are slipped in wherever possible. The vignettes about my mother in her childhood and teen years were mostly things she related to me. Relationship dynamics are assumed, partly based on having known my grandfather, my mother, and her siblings (a bare minimum), and partly based on what was told to me by some of the characters.

But the bones? The skeleton of this story is real.

Discussion Guide for Book Clubs and Other Readers

1. Frank Wolff Sr. views himself as a man of principle. He has been shaped by the era in which he lives, and by his European parents. Do you see him as a person driven by his morals? What do you think his motivations are—and do you have sympathy for those motivations? What do you think of his capacity to love, and how did you see him expressing it?

2. What are Frank Wolff's overarching personality traits? Which are beneficial to him or his family, and which are not? Do you see them as a product of his time, or unique to him? Do you think he sees himself the same way you do?

3. The Wolff family is raised with the dictums "Children should be seen and not heard" and "Spare the rod, spoil the child." How has correcting children's undesirable behavior changed in the last one hundred years? Are children's interests more respected today than they were then—and should they be?

4. Naomi seems to have a narrow range of choices with regard to larger decisions about the direction of her life. Do you agree with the lines, "Almost everything . . . in her life had been dictated by others or by the needs placed upon her by . . . family members or society"? Below is a photo of the real "Naomi" and "Charley," taken in the early 1940s. How would you compare her friendship with Charley vs. her marriage with Frank? Today, having five

children is considered to be a large family. Do you think Naomi expected to bear so many children? What would you guess about her attitude toward sex? Do you think she has relations with Frank out of obligation, joy, or passion, or all three? What do you think leads her to make the choices she does, and do you think she may have regretted any of them? What would you have done in her circumstances?

"Naomi" and "Charley," Los Angeles, early 1940s

5. The railroad united the US both horizontally and vertically and created opportunities for people to move to more affluent economic centers if they wanted to, but it also allowed them to travel more easily for recreation and to stay in touch with family. Frank Wolff is gone on the railroad for his work much of the time. How do families today cope with long separations due to work, in ways unavailable to families a century ago? The Wolff family can travel

anywhere in the US by train for free because of Frank's job, but they mostly only use the train to see their families. Do you think this would be true today for a family that had access to unlimited free transportation within the US?

6. Railroad men in the 1800's and early 1900's had a reputation for having girlfriends in many towns, especially since they were absent from their wives much of the time. Do you think some of them may have chosen this line of work with this in mind? Discuss how attitudes about men or women having affairs have changed or remained the same over one hundred years and why you think this is so.

7. Minnie Woods has fewer children and more financial resources available than does Naomi, which makes her life much different from Naomi's. What do you think of Frank's attraction to both of these women? At one point, Minnie asks Frank, "What must you think of me?" What would you imagine Frank does think of Minnie and the choices she makes, especially with regard to him? Do you think he thinks of his relationship with her as being dissimilar or unrelated to his relationship with Naomi? Does he see it as necessary, convenient, his good fortune, or something else? What reasons can you see for his wanting to stay in Minnie's boardinghouse? (A drawing of the real house, which still exists, is included at the top of Chapter 19.) Is Frank "taking advantage" of Minnie? And for Minnie's part, do you think she ever thinks of Frank as a potential long-term partner? Why or why not?

8. What did you think of the life Frances leads as a child? How does this affect her relationships with her siblings, and how does it influence her attitude toward life and toward men? What do

you think her idea of a "good time" is, both as a child and as an adult? Do you find it surprising that she leaves the religion she was brought up with? Do you think that a century ago it was more unusual for a person to do this? How do you think this departure was seen then, and how would it be considered today?

9. Marie Palmen, arriving on her own from Germany, appears as a sympathetic character starting in Chapter 24. What do you think of her husband, Walter? Do you have empathy for his point of view? What do you imagine it would be like to arrive alone in the US, with little English, and find yourself in an unexpected situation? What do Marie's subsequent decisions imply about her personality? Did you still find her to be a sympathetic character by the end of the book?

10. At one point Anita says to Frances, "Well, we're not exactly poor, but we're not exactly rich either." Do you think this is said defensively, since Frances is complaining about her lack of new clothing, or just as a statement of fact? Do you think Naomi or Frank think of themselves as impoverished? How about the children? How would you describe the family's financial condition?

11. What are Charley's overarching personality traits? Do you think his being drawn to a friendship with Naomi is shaped by their both being "farm people?" Do you think it at least partly grows out of his never having been married? Does Naomi encourage the friendship? If you think she does, what actions or attitudes does she take that make you think this?

12. Racism is touched upon as a theme throughout the story, and discrimination against people referred to as "Okies" later in the saga. Charley is described as an American Indian, or a man who looks

like he might be one. What is your experience, if any, regarding racism, or discrimination against lower economic status? Do you think attitudes are better or worse today than they were one hundred years ago? What personal experiences have led you to form that opinion? Below are photos of the real "Connie Foreland," who was raised on a farm. How would you describe her looks? What would you imagine her personality to be?

"Connie Foreland," Oklahoma, mid-1933 and c. early 1940's

13. It was common during the late 1800s and early 1900s for children to be put in orphanages. This was primarily an economic necessity, and often caused by the death or illness of one or both parents. How do you think the orphans in this story are affected by their time in the Lutheran Children's Home? How do you think the experience influences their emotional ties to their parents? Which children do you think side with their father and which with their mother? Do you think Frank actually believes the children are going to be better off without him or their mother when he leaves

them at the home? (The drawing at the end of Chapter 41 is taken from an actual photo of the Lutheran Children's Home during its best days. It has since been torn down.)

14. Below is a portrait photo of the real "Wolff" orphans, including "Frank Jr.," taken in Winfield, Kansas, immediately prior to their being taken to the orphanage there. From the way they are clothed and groomed, what would you imagine their family's financial status to be? Who would you guess suggested that the photo be taken, and why?

The "Wolff" Orphans, Winfield, KS, c. 1929

15. When Anita learns the truth about what her father has done, she takes what might be considered a brave and bold step. What do you think about her in light of those actions? What kinds of attributes do you imagine she has? Do you think she fears retribution from her father? What does her decision and its follow-through tell you about her relationship with her siblings?

16. Everyone in this story faces daunting hardships, some born of the times and some of their personalities. In Naomi's case, losing just one child would have been enough tragedy for one lifetime. What assumptions can you make about her character and qualities, especially after seeing the photo of her in the 1940s? Do you think Frances has these same qualities? Why do you think Frances keeps her parents' actions a secret for her entire life, even from her children?

"Naomi" and "Connie," 1933

Acknowledgments

I would love to be able to thank my aunt Dorothy in person for setting this novel in motion. May she rest in peace. I especially hope I represented her mama respectfully and truly. Knowing my own mother was ashamed of "Naomi," I wanted to vindicate her behavior as best I could.

I feel I should thank my cousins for their potential tolerance, if they read this book, because some of them may feel the story I've created is dreadful or untrue. I apologize if so. I took the facts, elaborated, and created a fictional story. (For instance, I don't know which of my uncles fell in love with "Ellen"; I used "Frank Jr." because he was the most likely, given the time frame.) I believe that many of my cousins, like me, had not even heard the facts of the story I've told here, let alone some of the conjectures.

Thanks to my cousin Jim for sending me the 1930 census page from the orphanage in Winfield, Kansas, which led me to the correct state to which my aunts and uncles had been sent. Dorothy had said, "It was Arkansas, or some state." (Winfield was very close to Arkansas City, Kansas.) She'd been too young to remember the geography; she just knew it was far away.

I am grateful to my beta readers: Marcia Naomi Berger, Katy

Caselli, Ilze Duarte, Karen Holloman, Jerry Mikorenda, and Marlene Tobias. You caught lots of potential snafus (several of you the same name goofs), assisted me in clarifying a few passages, and assured me of the parts of the writing and story that worked well. Thanks especially to Katy for helping me discover the title.

Always, my thanks to my writing group, Just Write Marin County. In addition to Marcia and Katy above, Maryan Karwan, Aline O'Brien, Denise Renye, Briony Everoad, and Jaylee Nash listened to me talk about this story for a few years—the discoveries of additional facts and the challenge of creating personalities.

Thanks to one of my meditation guides, Alison Shapiro, who suggested something really helpful when I said that I had trouble creating my grandfather's personality because I was posthumously rather angry with him. She said, "Try this practice I learned: 'My grandfather had feelings, just like me. My grandfather loved his family, just like me,' and so on." I did this and was ultimately able to create his personality as a human being who may have been conflicted about the decisions he made regarding his marriage and family.

Thanks to Danny Baugh at the Winfield Public Library and the kind people at the Winfield Historical Society, especially Lou Tharp, who gave me a bit more info than I found online about the Lutheran Children's Home.

I'm grateful to have been able to utilize the following sites as well: Ancestry, FamilySearch, Archives, Zillow, Shutterstock, and the Ogden and Evanston newspaper sites. US census records were invaluable in establishing where everyone was through each decade, and Union Pacific Railroad historical sites with maps and schedules helped me lend realism to the "Wolff" family's travels. I slogged through Wallace Stegner's *The Big Rock Candy Mountain*, another early-twentieth-century family history novel set in Western states with a bad daddy, to get a sense of the era, the locale, and in some instances, the diction. A whole 639 pages of detail. Whew. And Jeannette Walls's *Half Broke Horses*, which I listened to a while back, helped me decide that I had a story people might want to read.

I am ever grateful to my editor, Krissa Lagos, for her kindness and perceptiveness in surgically improving my work, and also for being fun to work with. She worked on this manuscript in between getting married and going on her honeymoon, and made it all work for our publishing deadline! And this time around, she also did her best to explain the elusive concept of characters' point of view, since this was my first work of fiction. As with most systems created by other people (in this case, probably creative writing professors), I had to get in there and do the "lab" work before I understood and could see it. Whew. You *can* teach a seventy-five-year-old gal new tricks.

Thanks to Brooke Warner of She Writes Press for saying, "We welcome you back with open arms," when I told her I had a third book, and to Lauren Wise, my project manager for the third time at SWP, for accepting my idiosyncrasies and saying yes when I needed "a few more days," as usual. Thanks to Katherine Caruana for her eagle-eye proofreading. The crew at She Writes makes it possible for women to publish their work without going up against the machine of the traditional publishing industry. Not to mention that SWP lets us have more control over what we get to say and how we say it. Thanks to Julie Metz for her collaboration and patience on our intriguing cover creation, with the wedding picture of the real "Naomi" and "Frank."

Thanks to Hannah Orth for her charming line drawing interpretations from the photos I provided of some of the real homes and some of the types of homes inhabited by the "Wolff," "Sims," and "Woods" families.

And, of course, last but never least, thanks to my husband, who supports me generously, which allows me to indulge in my creative endeavors. If I were not married to him, I believe I would still be slaving away full-time doing blankety-blank taxes, and would not have been able to publish three books. Thank you, Richard Falk; I love you always and look forward to our second three decades.

About the Author

photo credit: Patty Spinks

Francine Falk-Allen has published many essays and articles in national journals. She is the author of *Not a Poster Child*, which has won gold and silver literary awards, and of *No Spring Chicken*, which was named to *Kirkus Reviews'* Best Books of August 2021 and was a finalist in *Foreword Reviews'* Indie Awards. Francine has facilitated a writing group for ten years. She loves the outdoors, swimming, gardening, movies, literature, ancestral and historical research, British tea, and a little champagne. She resides in San Rafael, California, with her husband, Richard Falk.

https://FrancineFalk-Allen.com
www.Facebook.com/francinefalkallenauthor
francinefalkallen@gmail.com

Looking for your next great read?

We can help!

Visit www.shewritespress.com/next-read
or scan the QR code below for a list
of our recommended titles.

She Writes Press is an award-winning
independent publishing company founded to
serve women writers everywhere.